WORLDS COLLIDE

Max Salt

First published by the Zelkova Press in 2008.

ISBN 978-0-6151-9527-8

For Lisa,
who loves books more
than anyone else I know.

With memory set smarting like a reopened wound, a man's past is not simply a dead history, an outworn preparation of the present: it is not a repented error shaken loose from the life: it is a still quivering part of himself, bringing shudders and bitter flavours and the tinglings of a merited shame.
George Eliot, *Middlemarch*

WORLDS
COLLIDE

Prologue

Everything below her waist was agony. Even though he was across the room, she could still feel him in her, tearing her apart from the inside. She lay on her side, curled up to try to minimize the pain, and felt something warm and wet trickle down across the top of her leg just below her butt. She suppressed the urge to vomit, and instead lay very quietly, listening to him move around her bedroom, violating her in a new way as he examined and commented on everything he saw. She lifted her head slightly and chanced a look.

He was focused on one of the posters, paying no attention to her. *God, I need you now—please help me get out of here...* He took another step away from the room's door and her path to it, not looking back at all. *Please, if he can just move a little further away.* The monster took another step; he was standing by the desk now, looking at the pictures of her high school field hockey team. *Please, God, please...* Slowly she extended her legs, gritting her teeth against the pain inside her. *Please...*

* * *

"I can't wait!" Shailene said excitedly, grabbing the light blanket on her bed in both fists, which she bounced off her concealed legs.

"Well, you're going to have to, because school doesn't start until tomorrow morning. And if you don't settle down and get some rest you'll be too tired tomorrow to want to be at school. Now—"

"Is the real school far from here? Farther than the kindergarten school?"

"Um," her mother paused, thinking. "Um, no, they're—they're about the same distance away. What difference does it make?" She asked, her tone changing from thoughtful to a mix of amusement and exasperation. "Now come on, settle down and say your prayers, and then it's lights out."

"Can I have another story first?"

"No, one story per night—that's the rule."

* * *

In some stories I've read, usually the ones about magic, knowing the true name of someone or something gives you power over it.

* * *

"Now say your prayers so you can get to sleep."

"OK," she said, finally giving up her attempts at procrastination. She clasped her hands, closed her eyes, and bowed her head. "Our father, who art in heaven, Harold be thy name. Thy kingdom come, thy will be done, on earth as it is in heaven. Give us this day our daily bread, and forgive us our trespasseses," (she always had trouble with that word), "as we forgive those who trespass against us. And lead us not into temptation, but deliver us from evil. Amen."

Shailene opened her eyes and looked up at her mother.

"Did you—did you say '*Harold* be thy name'?"

Confused, Shailene looked back. "Um...yeah?"

"'Harold be thy name'?"

Shailene felt her brow crunch up. "Yes!"

Her mother smiled. "That is so cute! But honey, it's '*hallowed* be thy name'."

"'Hallowed'? What kind of name is that?"

Her mother continued to smile. "It's not a name; it means 'holy'."

"Oh," Shailene said, suddenly feeling dumb, but still not sure how that made more sense.

"It's OK, baby," her mother said, putting her arms around Shailene and squeezing. "It makes perfect sense the way you said it. And I'm sure God doesn't mind you calling him Harold."

* * *

I wonder if that's true, if I'd remembered his name when I needed him, things would have turned out differently.

* * *

He shouted and it was like a starter's pistol going off; she launched herself off her bed; her feet hit the floor. She jumped over her mother's body and was through the door, but he was already close behind her.

Please God please God please…

The impact from behind sent her flying over her legs, past the top of the stairs, and down hard on the polished wooden floor, her chest and arms absorbing the impact of both bodies as he tackled her.

"You *gash!*" he hissed in her ear. "You're *mine* now! Can't you get that through your fucking head?"

But Shailene was still running, her knees knocking against the floor helplessly, going nowhere. *Please God please!*

Everything went black.

Part One

Shailene

One

I run down the dark hallway, get tackled from behind, but continue running, my legs flailing uselessly against the hardwood floor.

Now I'm on my back, pinned down. The knife stabs me: hot, hard pain penetrating my upper abdomen, just below my breast bone, driving for my heart, but stopping short.

The knife slides out, scorching me again. The blade makes a soft metallic clank as it hits the floor.

He straddles me, his weight pressing down, squeezing the air out of my lungs as he violates the new opening he's created, the deep, sharp ache making me want to throw up, but I don't. I'm too busy synchronizing my breathing with his movements: I take air when the weight lessens, and he forces it out of me again.

I feel the tip of the blade prick the thin skin on the inside of my forearm. My fingers find the handle; it's still warm from his grip. I pull it into my palm, and poise it, blade up, my thumb down, under my chin. In my head, everything stops for a long second or two and I see his neck, stretched and white, his head thrown back above me, oblivious to what is about to happen, focused on what he is doing.

The stabbing is wild, frantic, and desperate, but somehow, by chance, at least one of the blows finds its mark. Hot liquid sprays down on me, stinging the inside of my nose and forcing me to close my eyes.

I keep stabbing until his bulk presses down, trapping my right arm and the knife, suffocating me. I pound his back with my left fist, the only part of me still free to move.

He can't feel my punches, or anything else.

Rather than elation, I feel panic at being trapped beneath the corpse, soaked with its blood, unable to move.

* * *

My whole body jumps awake. I look around quickly, and in the pale glow from the security lighting outside I can make out reassuring details: the door to my left, closed with the wooden chair wedged under the knob, the tall shrub just outside the window, the couch against the opposite wall, and the hanging shelves which, together with the island below them, separate the kitchen/dining part of my apartment from the rest, which serves as both living room and bedroom. I repeatedly touch each of these anchors with my eyes, reminding myself where and when I am. My heart rate returns to normal, and my body feels like it sinks a little as I consciously relax the muscles up and down the five feet and four inches of my frame. *At least I don't scream anymore.* At least I hope I didn't. In the beginning, my screams were what woke me up. Woke up my father's parents too. But the screaming had mostly stopped, and the nightmares had become less frequent, by the time I was attending college at West Point, where I almost never woke up my roommate.

I reach for the watch in its night time station next to my pillow and look at it while activating its light. It's about three-thirty, an hour earlier than I planned to get up. I know from long experience it will take at least an hour of mental reassurances and redirected thoughts before I can approach sleep again, so I give up that idea. I tell myself I should just get up and get started on my day, but it's Saturday and the whole weekend stretches before me with not much to fill it. There's really no incentive to get out of bed, especially an hour early. Instead, I lie staring out the window at the outline of the tall shrub that occupies most of the tiny patch of landscaping in front of my apartment, and escape to my life before the Bad.

Reminiscing can be risky for me. I almost never think about my parents for this reason, but friends and experiences from school are usually OK, though this time I do something I rarely allow myself.

* * *

Byfield, Massachusetts
September 1985

Though Derek's brown hair wasn't long, it was long and straight enough that his bangs hung a little over the front of the microscope as he peered through it at Shailene's cheek cells. She had donated them a couple minutes earlier, scraping them from inside her mouth with the handle end of a matchstick, then prodding them off the wood and onto a glass slide. Derek had then applied a dye and the cover slide, and slid the assembly on to the viewing platform of the microscope.

Shailene had met him a little over a year earlier, when they'd both started at Byfield Academy as freshmen. As with most of the students at the boarding school, it'd been their first time living away from their parents. Shailene had been feeling homesick, but fortunately the school's administration had organized a bunch of activities during the first weekend to keep the new kids too busy to miss home, and to get the returning student body together again after three months apart. The students had been organized into teams of five sophomores and five freshmen each for a campus-wide scavenger hunt. Shailene, despite missing her parents very much, had noticed Derek silent and alone on the margin of the group, and instinctively reached out to him. Eventually she'd drawn him in to a conversation as they followed the group around the campus. They'd been friends ever since, and in that year she'd quickly stopped pitying him and began liking him for his intelligent, curious mind, and his unapologetic individuality.

Over the summer, though, she'd found herself thinking more about him than any of her other friends at school. This was new, and it had worried her. She'd wondered if this meant she was starting to like guys—*like* guys, in *that* way. Here were these thoughts, barging into her brain uninvited from who knows where, making her feel like she didn't even know who she was. The changes to her body over the past few years were awkward enough, but she dreaded becoming guy-crazy like some of her classmates had.

"So? What do you see?" she asked him impatiently.

"I don't think I have it in focus yet," he said, turning the fine adjustment knob on the microscope back and forth. "Or maybe I do. I guess that's it."

"You sound disappointed."

"Well, it definitely doesn't look like the picture in the book. I don't know what I was expecting—obviously the different parts of the cell aren't in reality huge and color-coded in bright, primary colors."

"Let me see," she said.

"Make me," he said, looking up at her and smiling.

What? "C'mon, stop screwing around." She grasped his shoulder and applied pressure to nudge him aside. He resisted at first, but was smiling as he did. She dropped her hand. "Derek, quit it—let's just get this done."

His smile faded and he stepped aside, allowing her access to the microscope.

As he'd implied, the view was monochrome and the cells tiny—little more than gray circles with dark dots in their centers. She was also unimpressed, until the significance of what she was seeing dawned on her. "Wow."

"Wow?"

"Well, it just occurred to me that the entire blueprints for me are in each of those little dark dots. Right? Every nucleus contains a complete set of DNA."

Derek tipped his head to the side, considering, then slowly nodded. "When you put it that way...that is pretty impressive." His eyes shifted and the expression on his face changed abruptly to one of mild anxiety. "We'd better get going on our sketches—there's only fifteen minutes left."

They took turns peering at the cells and transferring the image to paper, and with a little imagination they were able to convince themselves they could make out more details than just the nuclei.

After class they stepped out of the science building and into a dazzlingly bright, warm late summer day.

"Wow—it's amazing out here!" she said. "Days like this, or seeing things like those cells today, with all their tiny, intricate machinery and DNA, make me wonder how anyone could doubt the existence of God."

"Hey Shailene, what's shakin'?"

She turned her head to see an eleventh grader, Fred something, pulling even and smiling down at her while completely ignoring Derek. "Hi Fred, what's up?" she said politely, but with no added enthusiasm. Fred, who was sought after by most of the girls she knew, including her best girl friend Becky, had tried to start conversations with her before, so his approach now was no surprise. Without looking back, she sensed Derek had begun to slow down and drop behind. Before he could get far, and without looking at him, Shailene reached back and caught the sleeve of his jacket in her grip, preventing him from straying any further.

"Does anything have to be 'up'? It's a beautiful day, I see you, and I want to say 'hi'. How've you been?"

Fred was tall with black hair, dark eyes, and clear, olive-toned skin. Shailene wasn't sure she saw it, but all the girls she knew considered him a hottie. Even if she *had* been interested in flirting, the fact that he seemed to know he was hot stuff ruined any chance he would've had with Shailene. Instead, his attention just made her feel uncomfortable and a little resentful. "Oh, pretty good," she said, and left it at that, not wanting to give him any material to build a conversation out of. They were fast approaching her dorm, which gave her an idea. "Well, here I am—see you later Fred." She slowed abruptly, dropping back and cutting behind him, heading toward Boynton House and pulling Derek along with her.

"Yeah, uh, see ya," Fred said, looking around in surprise, still registering what happened.

"So Derek," she said in a voice loud enough for Fred to hear, "I want to show you where we think that ghost comes from."

"You know, Shailene," Derek said quietly, "if you wanted to talk with him, I would've been OK with that. I mean, I know he's supposed to be this hot guy, and he's obviously interested—"

"Derek," she said, stopping suddenly and turning toward him. She still gripped his sleeve tightly, so he was more or less yanked to a halt as well. "Give me some credit, will you? Sure, he's good-looking, but honestly, what an ego! And what would I talk to him about anyway? I don't want to be *anyone's* girlfriend, and even if I did, I wouldn't be *Fred's*."

He stood staring at her for a couple long moments. "So, you wouldn't be Fred's girlfriend? If you wanted to have a boyfriend, I mean?"

"Nooo!," she said emphatically and shaking her head, exasperated that he even needed to ask. She looked away from Derek and furrowed her brow. "So what was I saying? Before he showed up?"

"Um, I think you were trying to prove the existence of God."

She smiled brightly and looked back at him. "Oh yeah! You know, people talk about miracles—I don't know that I believe in stuff like that, but who needs them when there are real miracles all over the place?"

He smiled back at her, and held her eyes with his for a moment before looking away. "The universe is pretty amazing, but, like you just said, it doesn't need anything supernatural to be that way."

"But look at—look at that DNA! Microscopic, seemingly complicated but actually an entire language written with just four letters, all twisted up in the center of every cell, and somehow it dictates our shape, size, appearance—it's amazing! How could that happen randomly?"

Derek shrugged. "I don't know—billions of years of nothing but trial and error?"

"Really? You think that?"

He shrugged again. "Until I see evidence to the contrary. Anything else is just guessing. It's like that ghost you supposedly have in here—I'll believe it when I see evidence."

"What if you *did* see proof?"

"Then I'd have to change what I know about the world. But I'd still believe in science, still be using scientific method—that wouldn't change. That's what makes science better than religion—it's more honest; it's only loyalty is to the truth, and to evidence, not to what some person tells me to believe."

"And you don't think DNA or our bodies or photosynthesis—you don't think any of that is evidence of God?"

"Not as long as there's a simpler, natural explanation for those things. I mean," he added hastily, "that's what *I* think. I'm not saying you're wrong to think differently."

She smiled. "Actually, you kind of are, but that's OK—part of what I like about you is your honesty. And that we can talk about stuff like this; it makes my brain feel...happy, I guess."

They stood looking at each other for a couple seconds.

"Um, I was wondering…"

There was a sudden nervousness in his voice and his face, and it immediately made Shailene feel uneasy.

He continued: "You want to go out sometime, like, I dunno, to Newburyport? I mean, you know, with me?"

Shailene tried to keep her face neutral, but inside she wanted to scream and run, except for a tiny dissident part of her, which was happy and excited, but also completely overruled. *He's asking me on a date, isn't he? I don't believe this is happening! Oh* crap! She wondered what part of "I don't want to be anyone's girlfriend" he didn't understand. *Guys! But Derek too?* She reminded herself that Derek actually *was* a guy, but also that he was her friend, so she decided to tone down the voice in her head. "Um, I, uh, you know—this kind of sounds like you're asking me out—I mean, you know: *asking me out.*" She raised her eyebrows to further emphasize the phrase and convey its significance. "And you know I don't want to get into all that now, Derek. Like the whole dating, emotional thing with the crazy dramas. I like what we have now. I mean, you're my best friend, and I don't want to ruin that. And besides, there's too much other stuff I want to do now—I don't have time for dating and all that stuff. OK?"

He looked away, past Shailene toward his dorm. "Sure, OK," he nodded, a studied, faltering casualness in his voice. "S'no big deal—I was just wondering. I should get going now." He started to walk away without looking back at Shailene's face, but he didn't get far because she still held his sleeve in her fist.

Her hold on him surprised her, but she maintained it, forcing him to stay and listen. "Hey! What are you *doing*, Derek? Don't act weird like this. This is what I was just saying—why I *don't* want to date. Will you look at me?"

He slowly turned his head and eyes toward her, but said nothing.

"I'm just not ready for that stuff yet, OK?" she said more softly. "Can we just pretend this didn't happen, and get back to being you and me?"

He dropped his eyes and nodded glumly.

"I mean *without* acting all poopy?"

A tiny smile appeared on his face.

"Friends to the end, right?" she pressed.

His eyes met hers and he smiled and nodded. "Friends to the end."

"OK, you can have your sleeve back," she said, releasing her grip and brushing it quickly to smooth out the wrinkle she'd left.

"So I thought you were going to show me something to do with the ghost."

"Huh? Oh," she waved dismissively, "I just made that up to get rid of Fred—I figured he wouldn't be interested in something like that. I don't really believe in the ghost either. So, maybe I'll see you at dinner?"

"OK," he said. "See ya later."

"Not if I see you first!" She smiled. "Just kidding!"

He smiled, gave a little wave, and continued on toward his own dormitory, which was a little further out toward the edge of campus.

Two

"*Friends to the end...*" I frown at the sad irony that I was the one to break the promise. I sit up in bed and pivot on my butt so I can drop my feet over the side. I sit there, feeling the fuzziness of the carpet on my soles, elbows on knees and head in hands, staring into the darkness which obscures the floor.

I can't think of Derek without remembering the last time I saw him, in the hospital after the Bad, and the way I treated him. I hate myself for that, but even so, if I had it to do over again, I don't think I *could* handle the situation any differently, no matter how much I might want to, no matter how much I regret my coldness toward him when he visited me.

I never saw or spoke to him again after that, so I never apologized for my rudeness or thanked him for trying to be there for me. I regret that too, but it's too late now.

What I *would* do differently is not pose for any pictures the day *he*—the monster—photographed the field hockey team.

* * *

Byfield, Massachusetts
September 1985

"I still can't believe Fred Venter went out of his way to chat you up and you just totally walked away from him!"

Shailene could see Becky really was having a hard time with this. "*I* can't believe anyone bothered to notice; I mean, what's the big deal?" Shailene replied.

"Oh, it's a big deal," Erin, an eleventh grader, said from Shailene's other side. The varsity field hockey team was lined up in three rows, each on a different level of an old set of bleachers. "He's *only* one of the top ten hottest guys around here, not that that's saying *so* much, but he is. Probably the hottest guy in my class."

"'Hot' is completely a matter of opinion," Shailene countered, turning to look at Erin as she did.

"Actually, it's a fact: Fred Venter is really hot."

This came from the row behind and above Shailene. She turned and looked at Angie. "Well, even if he is, so what? There's more to life than hot guys."

"Look—you can't even say that with a straight face!"

"I'm just amused by all of you! 'Oh, Fred is so hot! Fred is dreamy! Oh *Fred*, take me now! Let me have your *baby*!'"

Some of the girls laughed, and Becky, nodding enthusiastically while maintaining an approximation of deadpan, said "Yeah, pretty much."

"You are so lying!" she said to Becky.

"No...no I'm serious. I'd have his baby," she said, then broke into a smile.

"You're all so messed up!" Alison, one of the team captains, said, turning around to look at them.

"All right, do we have everybody? Quiet down, people, and listen to me so we can get this done and go to practice and the photographer can move on to the other teams."

Shailene sort of heard her coach's words, but was too intent on what she was saying to do anything with the information. "Not *me*," Shailene protested. "I'm not the one swooning over Fred, or any other guy!"

"Shailene!"

This time her coach's voice got through, and Shailene looked up at her. "Sorry Ms. Rasmussen!" She stopped talking and got her face into "snapshot mode": her features composed, her smile soft. Using her fingers, she brushed her hair back from her face. The sound of the other girls' voices died away, and it was quiet enough to hear coaches' whistles and distant shouts from the other athletic fields where practices were ongoing. Across about twenty feet of grass she could see the photographer, his assistant, and Ms. R. all gathered around a camera mounted on a tripod. The photographer turned to say something to Ms. R., and she looked surprised and amused at the same time and immediately jogged over to join the team on the bleachers.

"I forgot I need to be in the picture too," she said, laughter in her voice, as she took her place on one end of the first row.

Shailene could feel the warmth of the sun on her face, but fortunately it was at an angle that didn't make her squint. The clarity and brilliance of the air and light made the grass greener, the sky more piercingly blue. She could see clearly the photographer's face, under a mass of dark, slightly messy hair. Beyond him, across the fields, she could see a line of trees glowing bright green in the afternoon sunlight.

"OK, all eyes on me," the photographer called out from his position behind the camera.

Shailene kept still, her smile steady, and watched him. He held a cord in his hand, and she could hear faintly the clicking and whirring of the camera several times.

"OK, that's it. Please form a line in front of my assistant and we'll do the individual and small group photos next."

Becky and Shailene turned and looked at each other. "Let's get Donna and Jenny too?" Shailene asked.

Becky nodded. "Sure."

"Donna!   Jenny!" Shailene called as she and Becky stepped over the first row bench seat. Donna and Jenny had been standing in the first row, and were already walking across the grass. They both turned toward her.

"Be in a picture with us?"

They smiled and nodded. "Sure!"

Alison and Tara, the team co-captains, were photographed first, while Shailene, Becky, Donna, and Jenny got in line and gave their names to the photographer's assistant. After the co-captains were done, Shailene and her friends walked past the photographer and stood in a row on the same patch of ground.

The photographer looked at them for a couple seconds. "OK, you two—blonde girl and you," he said, indicating Shailene and Becky, "each of you take a knee in front, facing each other, and then you two stand behind them—no, other knee, both of you." Shailene and Becky giggled and changed their position so in both cases the knee away from the photographer was up, and the knees closer to the photographer were on the grass. "OK, both of you rest your hands on top of the leg further from me—that's it. Back row, turn slightly toward each other…little more—good!" He bent slightly and looked through the camera, then straightened up, paused, then walked around the tripod and up to Shailene, squatting low next to her, making her feel a little nervous.

"Turn your shoulders just a little," he said, applying slight pressure on her right shoulder, "this way. Good! Now hold it."

Shailene felt a little embarrassed for needing to be corrected, but put on her snapshot face as the photographer returned to his station. He picked up the cord with the shutter button on it and she heard three clicks and whirs. "OK, thanks a lot!" He turned back to his assistant and asked for the next group while Shailene and her friends walked away.

"Shailene!" She turned to see Jess, Amy, and Katie, who were next to have their picture taken, motioning to her. "Be in our picture too!"

"What?" Shailene had heard them, but was startled. They were sort of friends, but only saw each other at field hockey practices and games. And they were juniors; Shailene was surprised they would want a sophomore in their picture.

"Be in our picture?"

"OK." She smiled, but also felt a little embarrassed at being singled out. She walked back to where she had just been standing.

"Shailene," the photographer called out. Obviously he'd heard Jess use her name. "Stand in front and turn a little to your left. That's it. Miss, in front," he said, referring to Amy, who was also in front with Shailene, both of them being somewhat shorter than Jess and Katie, "you turn a little toward Shailene. Great—OK, hold it..." He took three pictures again.

Shailene rejoined Becky. They stood together, each pulling her hair back into a ponytail and securing it with a small scrunchy, waiting for all the pictures to get done so practice could start.

"Let's stretch," Becky said.

Each one extended her right arm and grasped the other's right shoulder while, each with her left hand, she pulled her left foot up to the back of her left thigh. They wobbled a little, but stabilized each other while they held the stretch for about half a minute. Shailene dropped her foot and Becky did the same, and they turned and repeated the maneuver with the other side. Shailene closed her eyes and relaxed into the stretch, trusting in her friend's stability.

"Hey Shailene!"

She opened her eyes and turned her head to see Liz, a freshman with short, bright red hair run up.

"Be in our picture?"

Again Shailene was surprised and confused, this time because, since Liz was new to the school, she didn't think they'd gotten to know each other very well. "Um, OK."

"Cool! We're up next," she said, glancing over her shoulder. "I mean, we're up now!" She looked back anxiously at Shailene.

Shailene in turn looked at Becky. They'd both dropped their legs but their arms were still entwined. She smiled and shook her head.

"Miss Popular," Becky said.

"No—I dunno," she shrugged before dropping her arm and jogging after Liz.

"Shailene—back a third time?" the photographer asked, a teasing note in his voice.

She stopped and put her hands out at her sides, palms up. "It was their idea!"

"Yeah, sure!" he said, smiling. "Considering a modeling career?"

Shailene tried to think of a reply that shrugged it off while being humorous, but before she could, Amanda, another freshman, said "Hey, cool! Let's, like, pretend to be models!"

"What?" said Shailene.

Liz liked the idea. "Yeah, let's vamp it up!"

"What do you mean?"

"You know, pouty lips, cocked hips—that kind of thing," said Liz demonstrating for the others.

"Is that OK?" Shailene asked, turning to the man with the camera.

"Sure, it's your picture," he said. "Go for it."

They all struck poses. Shailene felt awkward and didn't really know what to do, but she pushed her ponytail up on top of her head with both hands and puckered her lips.

Three

Remembering the day of the team pictures, the day he photographed me, makes me want to vomit, scream, and cry all at once, even though it's been something like nine and a half years since. To help stop the thoughts, I get out of bed and walk to the bathroom. I sit down, blank my mind, and listen to the trickling sound the piss makes as it hits the water in the bowl.

Bladder emptied, I wash my hands and face. I look in the mirror and run my fingers through the hair on top of my head, arranging it a little more neatly and clearing out the part on the left side. The hair on the sides and back of my head is cut too short to get mussed; it actually would meet the men's Army grooming standards since it tapers to stubble around the edges and doesn't come anywhere near to touching my ears or the collar of the olive green flight suit I wear to work. The hair on top is a lighter yellow than the dark amber color of the shorter hair. I guess this is because the hair on top has had time to bleach in the sun. I've worn my hair this way since my first day at West Point almost seven years ago. Before that, in high school after the Bad, my hair was a little longer, but not much.

* * *

Cambridge, Massachusetts
November 1985

The day before was Thanksgiving, but they'd skipped it. None of them felt very thankful. Grandma Campbell had wanted to persevere with the big turkey dinner, to try to get back to normal life, but Shailene and her grandfather, in an odd moment of unity, both made it clear they had no interest.

It was during this conversation that Shailene realized just how rotten holidays would be now. They'd been transformed, like so much in her life, from opportunities for celebration to reminders of loss, from occasions for joy to catalysts for despair. She'd spent most of yesterday reading in the room they'd cleared out for her, trying not to think about it being Thanksgiving. For dinner they had leftovers; Shailene ate a cold slice of pizza in her room. She regretted eating even that, although the only other food she'd had was a bowl of cereal that morning. The pizza went down in big, hard lumps and sat heavily in her stomach, resisting digestion.

It had been a week and a half since Shailene had been released from the hospital and come to live with her father's parents. They were really her only option. A heart attack had killed her mom's father, Grandpa Holmes, two years before, and Grandma Holmes, who'd already been showing signs of Alzheimer's disease when he died, deteriorated more quickly after losing him, and was living in a nursing home. She'd been flown in for her daughter's and son-in-law's funeral, but it was clear she was only somewhat aware of what was happening around her. Which was for the best, considering.

At first Grandma and Grandpa Campbell had been really supportive of Shailene, and even praised her as a hero; that is, until the police investigation revealed the details of who the monster was. Shailene had already realized who he was as he roamed her bedroom and commented on the team photos he found there, the ones he'd taken of her and her friends about a month before. Neither of her father's parents came out and said anything, but they, especially her grandfather, had clearly come up with an explanation as to why the monster had selected Shailene as his victim. Visits to her hospital room became rare, encouraging smiles rarer still. She didn't blame them; she blamed herself.

Since getting out of the hospital, she'd spent most of her time doing the schoolwork her teachers mailed to her grandparents' house. She couldn't face going back to school, not with everyone knowing what had happened. The murders had, of course, been thoroughly covered in the newspapers and local TV news, and while her name had been withheld, the names of her parents had not. Anyone who knew her would easily make the connection, especially since she was in the hospital and not at school afterwards. She'd wanted to hide herself under the sheets when Derek visited the hospital. She felt bad about being so mean to him, but she just wanted to be alone, and was grateful no one else made the trip. She didn't need anyone else looking at her and drawing conclusions.

So she'd been doing lots of reading, and working on the lengthy writing assignments each of her teachers required in lieu of a final exam. This took up a lot of time, which was good, because when she was working it was easier to avoid bad thoughts. Now, however, after spending about six hours straight analyzing the causes of the Civil War, she was mentally exhausted. She lay down on the old, narrow bed in her room, previously her grandparents' guest room, and stared at the ceiling. At first it was good just to not think, to rest, but inevitably her mind fell into the well-worn track it had created for itself while she was in the hospital.

Why?

Over the past two and a half weeks the question had become obsessive, as if the answer would change if she asked enough times. *Why me?* She tried to block it out, but still heard his voice. *"Because you're hot."* *The pictures, the way I posed that day.* The thoughts made her want to dig her fingernails into the skin under her eyes and rip her face off, to grab fistfuls of her long hair and tear it out.

"It's not your fault." She remembered this was one of the first things Sarah, Shailene's psychologist, had said to her. *But she doesn't know.* Sarah didn't know about the team pictures, the way they'd posed for that last set of photos. She'd been over what little she could remember of those few

minutes so many times: if only Liz hadn't asked her to be in their picture, if only Amanda and Liz hadn't come up with the idea of pretending to be models. But if it was the posing that had caught his attention, why didn't he go after Amanda or Liz? They were both from Massachusetts too; in fact, Liz didn't even board at the school—she was from Newbury and her mom dropped her off every morning and picked her up after practice every evening. Shailene realized she herself must have done something no one else did. After all, if it wasn't her fault, then why did he go after her and not any of the other girls? He must have photographed dozens of girls just that one day, and who knows how many during the course of the fall season, yet it was her photos he kept. It was her he came after. *"Because you're hot."*

Grandpa knew it was her fault. She could tell by the way he wouldn't look at her, didn't talk to her anymore. She would do the same if she were him.

She wished she could cry, but nothing happened. Instead she just lay there on the old guest bed, feeling like she would burst, wishing it would happen. Impulsively, she plunged her hands into her hair, tangling her fingers in it. She pulled on it, felt sections of her scalp extend out in response, then resist. She pulled harder and her scalp began to hurt a little, but she had too much hair in her hands for any of it to pull out. She considered relieving the tension on the hair and then really yanking on it, but an image of bloody hunks of scalp peeling off her skull deterred her from this, making her feel, incredibly, worse. Then she had an idea. She sat up and swung her feet off the side of the bed. She opened the bedside table's drawer, which her grandmother had overlooked when she was preparing the room for Shailene. Shailene didn't really care, so she'd never mentioned this to Grandma, and the drawer was still crammed with old sewing patterns. She pulled some of the patterns out, rummaged around, pulled some more patterns out, and found what she was looking for.

The scissors were long enough, and appeared to be in fairly good shape even though they were old. She considered, just for a moment, doing something more extreme with them, but that seemed like handing *him* a victory, finishing his work for him. Instead, she took the scissors down the hall to the bathroom and locked herself in. She forced herself to look at her reflection even though she hated seeing herself. She looked at the bruises on her face, now turned yellow and green. She looked at the hair people had always complimented her on.

There was a lot of it, the thick, wavy blonde cascade easily reaching midway down her back. She started cutting on the left side of her head, but after the first bunch came loose it was obvious doing it this way would create a big mess in the bathroom they all shared. So, ignoring the pain in her abdomen, she bent deeply at the waist, flipping her hair forward over her head, causing the mass of it to hang down in front of her, over the bathroom's small wastebasket. She hesitated only a moment before plunging the shears in from the right side, working them shut and open and shut, and listening to the freed locks sliding into the plastic bag liner and landing softly on top of the used tissues, discarded soap wrapper, and empty toothpaste tube.

At first it seemed easy. The pieces she cut were long and relatively heavy, so they dropped neatly into the wastebasket. She realized too late, though, that she should have braided all of it first, and then cut one thick rope of hair, which would have saved her from having to chase down with her fingers all the stray strands she missed the first time through. It ended up taking much longer than she thought, and her back began to ache from being bent over for so long. Finally she straightened up and realized her method had resulted in the shortest hair being on top of her head, and the longest being around the sides and in the back. Her intent had been to make herself less attractive, but now she looked ridiculous.

Panicking, she attacked the longest hair with the scissors while making a half-hearted attempt to get the hair to fall in the sink.

She jumped at the sound of light knocking on the door. "Shailene?"

"Um, just a minute, Grandma!"

"Are you all right?"

"Yeah! Yeah, I'll be out in a minute!" she called as she frantically tried to at least get it all more or less the same length.

She heard her grandmother's light footsteps receding down the hall.

After a few more minutes she could see it was no use. Obviously there was more to cutting hair than just making the long pieces shorter. Her hair was ragged hunks of random length, like strips of cloth attached to the head of a badly-made puppet. "Shit." *I've really done it now.*

She heard footsteps in the hallway again. "Shailene?" her grandmother said quietly.

She looked at her reflection, and an undersized, skinny-looking head with the world's worst haircut looked back hopelessly. She turned to the door and opened it.

Grandma gasped, her hand automatically rising to cover her open mouth. For a few seconds they stared at each other, her grandmother apparently trying to figure out what happened, and Shailene wanting her mother, wanting her mother to hug her and tell her everything would work out all right.

"What—? Why—why did you do this?"

Shailene looked to the side, then down at the floor. She didn't want to try to explain, so she shrugged. "I wanted short hair."

"Oh, Shailene honey…"

Shailene looked up at the pause, and saw Grandma move her hand from her mouth toward Shailene. For a moment Shailene thought she might get a hug after all, but Grandma's hand merely grazed her shoulder lightly, then dropped away. "It's too late now, but tomorrow morning first thing we'll go to my hairdresser's. Janice will fix you up. You should have told me you wanted to change your hair."

Shailene looked down and shrugged again. "I know. I guess...I dunno, I guess I wasn't thinking. Sorry. I'll clean up in here."

Four

I'd actually like to buy a set of clippers and take all my hair off, but the Army frowns on crew cuts for women—it's considered a "bizarre" haircut and therefore violates Army grooming standards. The double standard is annoying, but not worth fighting about.

I turn from the mirror and face my gym clothes, which are suspended from wire hangers on the shower curtain rod. I pull off the T-shirt I'm wearing and drop it on the floor, then take the sports bra down from its hanger. I don't really need a bra for support since my breasts don't even fill out an A-cup; I wear it to avoid giving anyone a show, or ideas about me. I remember, before the Bad, hoping my breasts would grow. I didn't want big breasts, but something closer to average size for someone with my small frame—maybe a B-cup. Now I'm glad they stayed small. They're invisible under the loose clothes I wear, and, like with the short hair, there's the added bonus that they don't get in my way when I'm working out, or doing anything really. I adjust the bottom hem of the bra, my fingers passing over the vertical pink, wrinkled line nestled in the angle of my rib cage, just below my sternum. I take the faded light blue T-shirt off its hanger and pull that on over the sports bra. Like all my T-shirts, this one is bigger than I need, but I've cut some of the excess length off the sleeves so they don't stick to my arms when I'm training. Then I slip off my panties and pull on lined, baggy black running shorts and a pair of athletic socks.

Back out in the one main room of the apartment, I straighten the sheets and blanket somewhat, tucking the pillow under the blanket before folding the whole bed up into the wall. The floor space cleared, I take a black, buckwheat husk-filled cushion from the corner and place it in the center of the floor. The cushion is like a big beanbag about a foot in diameter and maybe six inches high. I sit on it and arrange my legs in a full lotus position before starting the countdown timer on my watch and layering my hands left over right, palms up, thumb tips touching, the edges of my hands resting against my lower abdomen.

I sit this way every morning for thirty minutes, struggling to keep my mind blank except for following my breathing. This never works for long. My record is probably something like ten minutes. Eleven tops. Even so, doing this helps me manage my emotions, so I almost never skip.

I guess I've been doing some kind of meditation since I was fifteen. Sarah, the therapist who helped me after the Bad, taught me a method of calming and relaxing myself by focusing on each part of my body and consciously willing the tension out of it, while keeping my mind as quiet as possible. I used this technique to get back to sleep after being awakened by nightmares. It was something like meditation, but mostly it was just a practical expedient that helped me get by.

* * *

Cambridge, Massachusetts
December 1985

"OK, and now your shoulders: let them rest; relax the muscles and let gravity have them."

Shailene, sitting in the big beige leather armchair with her eyes closed, focused on the muscles connecting her neck to her shoulders and released them. She thought she felt the ends of her collarbones droop as she did, and exhaled, letting some more tension leave with her breath.

"Aaaaand open your eyes," Dr. Krupnick—Sarah—said softly.

The room was not excessively bright, but Shailene still blinked a couple times as her eyes adjusted. She looked around the cheerful office with its deep golden yellow walls and light wood furniture, touching on the familiar points. One wall was dominated by a large painting of an old barn bathed in the warm light of sunset. Or, it occurred to her, it could be sun*rise*. She wondered if maybe that was some kind of psychological test. The wall opposite the painting was mostly taken up with a built-in bookcase, which contained not only books, but also framed diplomas and a couple running trophies. She looked to her front again, and her eyes settled on a small table a couple feet away, on top of which was a framed photograph of Sarah hugging a big yellow dog. For some reason Shailene had never thought to ask about this before.

"Is that your dog?" Shailene asked, her eyes lingering on the picture before shifting to look at Sarah sitting in a matching armchair placed a few feet away and at an angle to the one Shailene was sitting in. Sarah smiled, her teeth very white by comparison to her light brown skin. She had her long, curly brown hair, which was actually pretty big because it was *so* curly, pulled back today. When she did that, her cheekbones really stood out, emphasizing the slenderness of her face and her strong, elegant features.

"Yep, that's Carl. He's a really good friend," Sarah said, smiling and gazing at the picture before looking back at Shailene. "Would you like a glass of water?"

"No thanks."

"How are you doing, Shailene?"

"Pretty good."

"Do you have anything you want to discuss, any questions on your mind?"

Shailene looked at the painting of the barn, before shaking her head. "No, I don't think so. I guess things are going along OK."

"I like the short hair; it really works for you."

Shailene looked down, unsure how to feel about the compliment. At least she didn't say it looked pretty or attractive. "It was time for a change," she replied, shrugging.

"How's life at home with your grandparents working out?"

Shailene looked at Sarah and nodded, glad for the shift in focus. "Oh, fine, I guess. I know you thought I should try to go back to school, my old school, but I just...you know...didn't want people looking at me, knowing."

"Shailene, you don't have anything—"

"I know, I know; it's not that I'm ashamed; I just don't want people to know."

Sarah nodded. "I understand that, and respect your decision." She paused before changing topics again. "Are you sleeping all right?"

She canted her head to the side. "Pretty well. The relaxation stuff definitely helps me fall asleep, and I only had the bad dreams three times this week. Even then, I was usually able to calm myself down and eventually get back to sleep."

"Excellent! That's really great. So what's been most on your mind since you saw me last week? Any thoughts that seemed to come up a lot, or maybe that you kept coming back to when you laid down to go to sleep at night?"

Shailene looked at the picture of Carl and Sarah. The room became quiet, but she and Sarah were comfortable with these silences. "Well, the trust thing, I guess." She looked at Sarah. "You know how we were talking about how most people are safe? I mean, that I need to not be afraid of everyone, and the difference between caution and fear, and about learning to trust again?"

"Sure, I remember."

"Well...I guess I was thinking about how I know when I can trust someone, how I know when someone is safe. So I started thinking about people I already trust, and why I trust them." Shailene smiled. "The first person I thought of was you."

Sarah smiled back. "Thanks—I'm flattered. And did you think about why you trust me?"

She nodded. "Um-hmm. Part of it is because you understand—you were..." She was finding it hard to say the word, to acknowledge, with horror, that it now applied, and would always apply, to herself. She allows herself to avoid it this time. "...you were hurt too. And you're a doctor. But then I thought, anyone can say anything. Anyone could tell me they're a doctor—or even *be* a doctor, but that wouldn't mean they could be trusted. But I still trust you, and I thought about why. It seemed like the real way to tell is by what a person does. With you, you don't seem to want anything from me—you want to help me, but you don't want anything *from* me. You don't tell me what to think or do, it's more like you show me things—different ways of looking at things, but you always leave it up to me to choose, instead of telling me what to do. To me, that means you're not trying to take anything from me, you're just trying to help."

"That's very insightful."

"Thanks, but it's really just common sense. My parents were—" She stopped speaking suddenly, before her voice cracked, and she looked down at her hands clenched in her lap. Without looking up she reached for the box of tissues on the small table next to the chair and pulled one free, pressing it against her eyes. She mastered the emotion, consciously relaxed the muscles in her face, and took a deep breath. She exhaled, a little shakily, before looking at Sarah. "They were good to me too," she said quietly, then swallowed.

"But something bothered me—something my parents taught me. We weren't super-religious, but I went to Sunday school, and, you know, we talked about God. They told me— everyone told me God loves me, that God is good, and God is, you know, *God*—powerful, able to do anything. What's the—'omnipotent,' right? I mean, that's the idea, right?"

Sarah nodded. "Go on."

"But if God were a person, I don't think I would trust him. I mean, if God made the world and everything in it, and really is omnipotent, then…"

Sarah remained quiet for several seconds before responding. "Shailene, one of the requirements of a professional is to know the limits of her expertise. Do you have a clergyman or religious teacher you would be comfortable bringing your questions to?"

"I thought about that, but there's no one like that I'm really close to and, besides, I've already heard what they have to say in Sunday school. I know we're given free choice, and I know this life is supposed to be a test of our faith. I guess I'm being tested now." She swallowed hard again, and her head swam a little. "But at the same time something doesn't make sense. I mean, like I was saying, actions tell the truth." Her voice cracked and tears came to her eyes again, but she raised her voice and persisted. "What kind of love is it to allow that—that—that *fucking bastard* to do what he did to my parents and me?! How could God," she paused, almost choking on the word, "if he loved me and my parents, how could he allow that? And I'm not just talking about me. I thought about all the stuff that's happened, that does happen—things we learned in school. Like the holocaust—six million innocent people killed by the Nazis. What kind of a God allows that? Is that love? Is that someone I can trust? How could they all be so stupid, so *fucking* stupid to think God *loves* us?!"

She realized she was shouting. She stopped and closed her eyes very tightly, squeezing the tears out and feeling them run down her hot cheeks, and hating all of it. Before she knew what she was doing, she was slamming her white-knuckled fists down onto her legs, enjoying the pain blossoming in her thighs.

"OK, *OK* Shailene!"

She felt Sarah's hands on top of her fists, pressing down, preventing them from rising for another blow. She struggled against the restraining hands for a few seconds, then slumped back in the chair, her whole body limp and suddenly exhausted. The hands on top of her fists stopped pressing down, then she felt fingers prying her fists open. She yielded to them, and allowed Sarah to hold her hands. They sat in silence for a while, Shailene in her chair and Sarah kneeling on the carpet in front of her. Finally, in a hoarse, unnatural sounding voice, Shailene said "I can see as well as anyone—I don't need someone to explain it to me. Actions are truth. They've either been lying to me or to themselves. And God either doesn't exist, or we're really wrong about what he's like." She gave a quick, mirthless snort of laughter. "I'm not sure which would be worse."

Five

I refocus on my breathing. Inhale, pause and hold the air, feel the fullness of my lungs, exhale, feel the emptiness.

I began practicing Zen meditation while stationed in Korea for a year-long tour of duty—my first assignment after flight school. While I was there I read some books about Far Eastern religion and philosophy, just because I was curious and, hey—there I was. I found the Zen outlook appealed to me. It's so peaceful, and at the same time seems so strong and impervious to the world. And it doesn't have much to do with God—for or against—so it's compatible with my atheism.

Breathe in, hold, breathe out, pause.

But after about a year and a half, I still don't seem to be getting any better at this. It's odd how difficult something so simple can be. Sometimes I try to watch for the moment when my mind strays, that first random thought that creeps in, striving to actually witness the birth of that thought, which makes me wonder how my brain works. Where do these thoughts come from? What makes them happen? They seem so spontaneous, without cause.

After a while the carpet looks like it's flowing. I watch for a few seconds, then shift my eyes slightly, destroying the illusion like I'm supposed to. My stomach growls. I think about breakfast, then about breathing.

I see again my bloody handprint on the beige switchplate across the room, feel again the phone's handset sticking to my ear, my palm. I acknowledge the memory, then concentrate on my breathing.

The electronic chime on my watch sounds. I take a couple seconds to focus my eyes, then break my body's enforced stillness and grasp the watch, pressing a button to stop the sound. My legs are numb as I disentangle them. I stand on deadened feet, bend and pick up the cushion, and walk stiffly to the corner, where I drop the cushion before heading to the kitchen part of the room.

Although I'm not very good at the sitting, I have found it calms me, makes me more patient. The emotions from the nightmare and memories have subsided, and now I'm content to mix quick oats, vitamin-fortified cold cereal, and wheat germ in a bowl with water, stir the slurry, and microwave it for a few minutes. This is my breakfast every day. It's not exciting, but it works for me. The consistent dependability of it is comforting, centering.

While I eat breakfast, I read: Albert Camus' *The Stranger*. I've read this one before, as well as some of his other books, and Jean Paul Sartre's *Nausea*. I find the writings of the these men, paradoxically, both reassuring and disturbing. It's consoling to know I'm not the only one to feel so alone and uncertain about my life, but troubling to find they don't seem to have any better answers than I do. To be fair, I usually feel like I'm not getting everything they're saying, which is why I re-read their stories.

After breakfast I rinse out my bowl and put it on an extra wire shelf I pulled out of the tiny refrigerator and now use as a drying rack. Then I drop onto the couch and resume reading.

After about an hour I put the book aside and work my way through various stretches, mostly for my legs and lower back. This takes about twenty minutes, and then I shrug into the little backpack I keep my gym stuff in, pull on my running shoes, and head out, locking the deadbolt behind me.

The air outside is still fairly cool—probably in the upper seventies, but I can feel the promise of heat to come. It is April in Alabama after all, so it already feels like the height of summer back home in Massachusetts. I walk along the narrow concrete path which connects the doors of the various apartments to the parking area. As I round the corner I see

Stacey, my little aquamarine Geo Metro hatchback, sitting close to the end of the path. As I walk between her and the pickup truck that usually parks next to her, I run my fingertips along her passenger-side edge, which is still silky smooth thanks to my washing and waxing her last weekend. My fingertips glide over the metal, enjoying the lack of friction. "Mornin' Stace," I say quietly. After I clear the line of cars I lean forward and transition into an easy run, turning up the driveway. The stuff in my backpack jostles around a little, but it's packed in pretty well, so it doesn't hurt my back or make much noise.

The main gym on the post at Fort Rucker is a little more than two miles from my apartment in the little town of Daleville, so it takes me less than twenty minutes to jog there. Low, flat storefronts, boxy apartment buildings, and trailer parks bounce through my field of vision. The sunlight feels warm on me, and my scalp and armpits prickle as I start to sweat. I pass through Fort Rucker's southern gate and take a right on to Third Avenue. This is a broad, usually quiet street lined with big oak trees, broad expanses of grass, and the occasional grouping of uniformly long and white military buildings which, while well-maintained, look like they were probably built in the forties or fifties.

I started running regularly after the Bad. Like the relaxation technique Sarah taught me, it was a good way to deal with the fear, anger, self-loathing, and sadness. Some early mornings, instead of trying to go back to sleep after being awakened by a nightmare, I'd pull on running shoes and go out for a run. I realized I like to run; I almost always feel better mentally after a few miles, thanks in large part to the mild, natural versions of drugs the body produces in response to physical stress. Besides dulling physical pain, these compounds induce a feeling of calm well-being without impairing judgment or awareness, so they're my drug of choice. I don't do real drugs or alcohol because they compromise self-control and alertness, and would make me more vulnerable—something I promised myself I would never be again.

All the running I did enabled me to make the cross country running team in the fall of my junior year at the public high school I transferred to after the Bad. I wasn't one of the best runners on the team, but I did OK, and doing sports helped me get accepted to West Point.

* * *

Cambridge, Massachusetts
October 1986

"Before I start talking, Shailene, I'd first like to hear what *you're* thinking about college. I figure you must have given it some thought if you made an appointment to meet with me."

Mr. Sperry, who was Shailene's American history teacher, also served as the school's guidance counselor. He leaned back in his chair, folded his hands across the gentle bulge of his stomach, and regarded her through his wire-framed glasses. He was one of her favorite teachers—she'd also had him for ancient history when she transferred to the school for the second half of the previous year—so that made this a little easier, but not much.

"I don't know. Ms. Harrington said I should start thinking about it, and I know she's right. I mean, I know I'll be better off with a college education, but nothing is really appealing to me. I'm really not even sure what I want to study or do, so I guess I'm here to see what's out there."

Mr. Sperry nodded, looking at her and smiling slightly, and seemed to be drawing some conclusion about her. She didn't like it when people did that, wanted to ask them what they were looking at, tell them they didn't know so much, but at the same time worried that they did. He looked down at the folder in front of him—more information about her, she guessed, probably her grades and who knows what else.

"Well, she's right," he said. "You *should* think about college. Frankly, Shailene, I think it would be a shame for you to not pursue higher education."

She knew he was paying her a compliment, but something about his word choice bothered her.

"Your grades were outstanding at Byfield Academy, and that's no mean feat. You continued to do well here last year, even in spite of everything else that was going on in your life."

Don't talk about that! That's none of your business! She didn't say it, but her heart screamed it.

"Is there anything that interests you particularly? What's your favorite subject?"

She looked down, noticed the fists in her lap and consciously relaxed them the way Sarah had coached her. Otherwise her mind was blank. "I really don't know. I guess I..." She realized she had no idea what to say next. "Look, I just don't know." She met his eyes. "I'm not so sure I would fit in with the whole college thing—that whole spring break, *Animal House* thing."

"Believe it or not, some kids actually do go to college to study."

Shailene nodded, cast her eyes down again. "Yeah, I guess I'm also concerned about paying for it. I mean I have some savings; my paren—I have some savings, but I don't think it's all *that* much, and I really don't want to impose on my grandparents any more than I already am. So I guess I'm looking for a scholarship or someplace where I can work and go to school part time." She looked up at Mr. Sperry. "I want to pay my own way, take care of myself, you know?"

He looked back and nodded, but this time it didn't bother her like it did a minute ago. Then he looked down and to the side, as if he had just heard something. "You know, what you just said made me think of something. Might be not at all what you're interested in, and you might think I'm nuts, but..." He wheeled his chair back a little and pivoted so he could open a drawer in the file cabinet behind him. He paused as he thumbed through the drawer's contents before pulling out a glossy booklet about the size of a weekly magazine and handing it across his desk to her. "Take a look at this."

She looked at the front cover, which was dominated by a photo of hundreds of people in what looked like marching band uniforms throwing white hats in the air. Across the top of the cover were two words: WEST POINT. She looked up at Mr. Sperry, wondering what he was showing her.

"Have you heard of it? It's the Military Academy."

It did sound vaguely familiar to her, but she'd never paid much attention to anything military-related. "I guess..." She looked down at the large brochure again, and opened the cover. The next two pages were completely taken up with another photo of a massive granite building that looked medieval. There was sort of a castle keep structure in the middle, with long stone wings stretching off to either side. "Is this what it looks like?" she asked, studying the photo.

Sperry half stood to see what she was looking at. "That's their dining hall, and those buildings on either side are dormitories—well, they call them 'barracks'. I thought of this because you said you weren't interested in the party aspect of college, and you were looking for a means to pay your way. At the service academies, you don't pay them—they pay *you*."

Shailene looked up to see if he was kidding. "What?"

Sperry nodded. "If you go to West Point, you're in the Army. You get a paycheck every month, and the education is free. After you graduate, though, you owe the government five years in return."

"Like an indentured servant?"

Sperry laughed. "Some might see it that way, but after you graduate you're an officer—that's your job, and they pay you, like any other job. You just can't quit until you've served at least five years."

Shailene looked hard at him, thinking, then looked back down at the glossy pages in her lap. She turned the page: another photo of a massive stone fortress-like building. It looked strong, impregnable, solid. She studied the photo for several long seconds before shifting her gaze to the facing page. Three photos there, all of young men and women. They looked strange because in each picture they were all dressed exactly alike, though the attire varied among the photos. In one they were wearing helmets and green clothes and boots, like soldiers in war movies, and they seemed to be trying to help each other climb over a high wall. The next photo showed two in dark gray shirts and chemistry goggles leaning over a beaker being heated by a gas burner. The third photo showed a whole group in white T-shirts and black shorts running down a road.

"It might sound like a good deal, and it is, but they do make you earn that education. They push their students—they call them cadets—hard, but if that's the kind of education you're looking for then it might be right for you. It can be a transforming experience. There are other service academies— maybe one of them would be better suited to you. West Point is for the Army, but the Navy has one, and so does the Air Force and the Coast Guard—that one's just down in Connecticut. Of course, there are other options. With your grades I'm sure you could get a scholarship at…"

Shailene could hear him speaking, and was getting his words at some level, but she'd already turned the page and was looking at a photo of a young woman wearing a helmet and holding a rifle, her face painted two shades of green to match her clothing. She was looking directly out of the photo at Shailene, and seemed to be ready for anything.

The sound of something dropping on the front of Sperry's desk snapped her out of her reverie, and she looked up.

"MIT is another very serious school," he said, gesturing toward a more weighty catalog than the one she had in her hands. "From looking at your math and science grades, you seem to have a knack for that stuff. Of course, they're just down the street from here; you've probably already walked or driven through their campus dozens of times. And like I was saying, I'm sure there's more than one scholarship you could snag, given your academics and your," he hesitated a moment, "circumstances."

She ignored that last reference, which she knew was to her lack of parents. To think of it at all would invite more guilt feelings at the prospect of being rewarded with college money for getting her parents killed. "You know, this looks really interesting to me," she said, holding up the open West Point catalog. "Can I borrow this?"

Sperry smiled. "Sure. Think about it seriously, though. It's not a free ride—I don't want you to get that impression. I mean, it doesn't cost any money, but like I said, it can be challenging."

Shailene smiled back. "I think I like that."

Six

I slow to a trot as I approach the gym's entrance, eventually stopping outside the doors. I swing the small backpack off my shoulders and get my military ID card from the outside zippered pocket. Inside the building, I show the card to Lester, a short man with a bright red fringe of hair and matching moustache, who is behind the front desk.

"Hey Shailene," he says, giving the card a perfunctory glance too brief to really see it at all.

"Hi Lester, how's it goin'?" I say, zipping the ID card back in its pouch.

"Well, it's about 8 a.m. on a Saturday morning and I'm at work. Other than that, great."

"Don't you get tomorrow and Monday off?"

He drops his eyes but not his smile, and shrugs his shoulders a little. "Well, yeah…"

"So you have nothing to complain about—*this* is your Friday. And on Monday, when the rest of us have to go back to work, *you'll* be sleeping in, you slacker."

He looks up at me again. "See—that's what I like about you, Shailene—you can always cheer me up."

I smile back a little. "I think you just like to complain."

"Hey, *I* was in the Army—it's a soldier's right to bitch."

"Yeah, I've heard that one before. So did that cable crossover come in yet?"

There's a handful of us that are in here most weekday mornings, and the gym staff came to us for input on equipment purchases. At the top of our list was this contraption, which is basically a steel frame with pulleys, cables, and stacks of iron weights that is most often used for chest work, and is good for a lot of other kinds of training too.

Unfortunately, while the other stuff we'd requested arrived weeks ago, the cable crossover still had not as of yesterday, and we're beginning to suspect it was never actually ordered.

"Mr. Templeton says any day now."

"Um-hmm, sure."

"Hey, I don't know—I just work here," he said, smiling again.

"Well, I need to train, so I'll see ya later." I walk down the corridor to the women's locker room.

Most of my contact with other people is like this exchange with Lester. I have plenty of what I call friendly acquaintances—people I know enough to call by first name and exchange a few sentences with, but that's as far as it goes. The exception to this was Miranda. I keep to myself, and I avoid physical contact as much as possible, but that changed for her. It's been more than two months since I last saw her, but I still miss her a lot. Weekends and evenings have gotten a lot longer since she checked herself out of my world. But no matter how much I'd like to be, I'm not a lesbian, and that made holding up my side of the relationship pretty much impossible.

The locker room is long and narrow, dimly-lit, and smells a little moldy. There's no air conditioning at this gym, so things stay pretty humid in here, especially in the hot half of the year. I don't like to do weight training with bare legs, so I pull on, over my running shoes and shorts, a pair of lightweight, very baggy cotton pants, which are a darker blue than my T-shirt, but also showing signs of wear. I take my lifting gear out and lock the backpack in a locker. Back down the hall I push through a set of doors into the weight room.

Unlike the locker room, the weight room is large and brightly-lit. It's two-stories high and the floor is covered with hard rubber tiles. The gym is well-stocked, with the full line of Nautilus machines, three Universal sets, and assorted other equipment. Against one wall there is a Smith machine (which we morning regulars requested), and two old, somewhat rusty squat racks. Most of the equipment has chipped paint, cracked vinyl, and rust in places, but still works fine. Besides the barbells and plates for the squat racks and Smith machine, the free weights are all located in a couple alcoves off the main floor. This layout is another thing we're trying to get changed—move the free weights out on to the main floor and put the Nautilus machines in the more confined space with the low ceilings. We even volunteered to move the equipment ourselves, but Templeton, the small, high-strung civilian manager of the facility, is dragging his feet.

I go to my usual corner just outside the free weight area and sit on the floor. I flip open my notebook to the first page with space to write on and figure out what exercises I'll do today, how much weight to start with, and what goals to aim for. As I do this, I wipe the sweat from my eyebrows with the back of my left hand, which I then wipe on my pants. I've never really understood it, but my body seems to sweat even more for a while after I *stop* running. Maybe it's because I lose the breeze created by my motion.

I decide to lead off with upright rows for my traps. Upright rows isn't one of my favorite exercises, but it's OK. Like all the movements I do, I try to control the speed and keep my body, especially my spine, in a stable position all the time. I pause the movement both at the top and the bottom, which means I can't do as much weight, but training this way seems to be more effective and safer. As a woman, I have an advantage over most of the guys I see in the gym, who feel compelled to move as much weight as possible—often more than they can handle—to impress anyone who might be looking. Ironically, this does the opposite of impressing me, not that I care about them anyway. Relatively speaking, I think I actually build more strength than they do by training my way, with the focus on stressing the muscle rather than on how much weight I use.

At least, that's how I was taught to lift. At West Point we had to take a sports or fitness-related class every semester. For the first couple years the curriculum is pretty set, but after that we had some choice. I took all the self-defense and close-quarter combat classes I could, then decided to take a class in strength training, and have been hooked ever since. I prefer lifting over running now because being strong feels better than being able to run away. I like it better than training to fight too, because I can work alone.

* * *

West Point, New York
March 1990

Boxing Room A was brightly-lit and almost too warm, in contrast to the cold early morning winter darkness outside. Shailene's knuckles felt hot and stung a little as she punched the sand-filled heavy bag, an accurately-named canvas cylinder suspended by chains from an I-beam overhead. Her classmate Rich, who was one of the best boxers in the intramural league and her boxing tutor, had wanted to wrap her hands with cloth strips first. Figuring anything that'd make her tougher was a good thing, Shailene had insisted on training with bare knuckles. Like she would have time to wrap her hands if it were for real—not freakin' likely. A quick sidelong glance at the big clock on the wall told her she'd been throwing punches continuously for about five minutes, though it seemed a lot longer. It was tiring work, but mostly it was starting to feel pointless. She continued for what she guessed was another thirty seconds, but was probably half that, before stepping lightly backward and dropping her fists.

Rich, dressed almost identically to Shailene in the regulation black running shorts and white T-shirt with the academy's crest over the upper left chest, was still leaning into the heavy bag. "Bet you wish now you'd let me wrap your hands, don't you?"

Shailene took one last deep inhalation to get her breathing under control again. "No, my hands are fine," she said, ignoring the light throbbing sensation. "But this is getting boring. C'mon, let's spar now," Shailene cajoled Rich.

Although his brown hair was cut short, per regulation, it still always seemed mussed because it was so thick and wavy. He looked at her, as if sizing her up, his face on the verge of smiling.

Keeping her expression neutral, she met his gaze, challenging him, willing him to see her not as a female, but just as a fellow cadet. She sensed it wasn't working.

His expression softened slightly before his eyebrows came together and he shook his head. "No way—absolutely not. I told you, I'll coach you, I'll hold the bag for you, but we are *not* sparring." He dropped his eyes and shook his head some more.

"Why not?" she demanded.

He looked back up at her with an expression of disbelief. "Why not? Do you even need to ask that?"

Now he was starting to piss her off. "What's this, some 'I can't hit a girl' thing?"

Rich let go of the heavy bag to gesture at her. "Look at you—you're like half my size!"

"Don't underestimate me," she said, anger starting to come through in her voice. "Besides, you're not that big— what are you, five-seven?"

"Five-eight. And even if I *am* short, that makes you even smaller since I'm still a lot bigger than you."

"You've got four inches on me—big deal." She wondered if keeping this up might actually prod him into sparring with her.

"And at least sixty pounds. Shailene, forget it. I said I'd teach you to punch, but that's it." Now *he* was starting to sound pissed off.

She realized she was coming across like some of the women around there who were always going out of their way to prove something to the guys, as if they needed to impress them to justify their presence at the Military Academy. Shailene didn't feel that way, and she wasn't trying to prove anything. She just wanted to learn to defend herself. She changed tactics and, in the most reasonable, low-key voice she could produce, she tried again. "Look, I haven't learned anything until I get to use it on a living, moving person. If you're so good then don't punch back—just evade and block me, and let me see what I can do—how 'bout that? I really just want to add to what I learned in the close quarter combat classes—some different ways of fighting, that's all. I'm not trying to, I dunno, embarrass you or anything. Just let me practice on you, and you can critique me, OK?"

She saw the resistance leave his face first. Then he tipped his head to the side, looked down, then back up at her out of the corners of his eyes, gauging her sincerity before saying, "All right, I guess that'd be OK. Let's get some gloves."

"So you *are* worried about how hard I can punch," she said, smiling just a little.

"No, I just don't want to hurt your fists when I block them with mine," he said, not smiling at all.

After putting on the large, well-padded gloves the guys used in the freshman boxing class (female cadets took two terms of close quarter combat while the males took boxing and wrestling), they climbed through the ropes and stepped onto the canvas floor of the boxing ring.

Shailene noticed a couple of old, brown blood stains as she ducked under the ropes. She assumed the boxing stance Rich had shown her: feet about a foot and a half apart, left shoulder forward, fists up. Her gloves looked ridiculously large on the ends of her slender forearms.

Rich brought his fists up and assumed a slight boxer's crouch. "Remember your stance—left foot in front, no more than eighteen inches from the right. Keep your fists higher and closer to your face—better protection."

"Isn't the best defense an aggressive offense?"

"Not—" he broke off as she moved in quickly, leading with a left jab, which he blocked and slipped away from. What he didn't see was the right hook coming just behind the jab. He moved into it as he avoided the first punch, and actually looked surprised.

Training like it was real, Shailene continued her attack, sending her left fist out again and connecting with his solar plexus. Rich grunted and back-pedaled, trying to regroup, but she stayed on him, throwing a straight right, which he blocked, and a left uppercut immediately after that, which caught him hard on the bottom of his chin, clacking his teeth together. So intent was she on her attack, though, that she left herself completely open to a quick jab to her nose. She stumbled backward as blood flowed freely over her upper lip and dripped down the front of her white cadet-issue T-shirt. *Damn.* She regained her footing and returned to the attack.

Rich put up both gloves in a "stop!" gesture and turned away, heading for the ropes.

"What?" she asked incredulously, her fists still up.

"No! No way! Look at you!"

This would have been almost amusing to her if he weren't already stepping through the ropes. "What? This is nothing! C'mon, it looks worse than it is!" She dropped her fists as he jumped down from the canvas-covered platform. "It doesn't even hurt!" she shouted.

Rich pulled his gloves off as he walked quickly across the large room. "Forget it! We're done."

Crap. "Then hold the bag for me again?" she called after him as he pushed through the boxing room door and departed.

* * *

I don't do martial arts anymore, though I keep promising myself to take it up again.

By the time I finish my six sets of upright rows, my shoulders are burning and I can see droplets of sweat standing out on my forehead where it's not obscured by the fall of my hair. After that, I do five sets of bench press. My goal is to eventually bench my body weight, which used to be 105, but after four and a half years of this I'm closer to 120. Fortunately, I'm gaining strength faster than I'm gaining muscle weight.

I train for a couple hours. Because it's the weekend, I don't see any of the morning regulars; they usually don't train Saturday and Sunday mornings. That's fine with me— sometimes conversation at the gym is distracting. Today I find myself focusing more and more on the function of my body: the burning in my muscles, the positions of my limbs and spine, and the will in my mind to push through pain and fatigue. It all feels good, and I'm glad to be alone in this mental place. I like the smell of damp iron, the feel of the diamond grips on the bars pushing into the calluses on my hands, the sight of the veins standing out on my arms and neck as I slowly lower the dumbbells, maximizing the strain.

I finish up, then go to the locker room to take off my gym pants and pack up my gear.

Seven

Outside, I feel the heat of the sun on my face. Since it's morning, and April, the warmth still feels good, and I tilt my face up to it for a few seconds before setting off at a trot for home. I go about a block before I decide the clanking in back isn't going to sort itself out. I leave the pavement for a lush lawn by some administrative buildings, and take off the backpack to reconfigure the stuff inside. Squatting in the shady, still-wet grass, I open the zipper and peer in. The spring collars—chrome-coated springs that slide over the ends of barbells to hold the plates on—are the only things that could be making the noise I heard. I wrap one of them in my gym pants, and separate the other from it with my notebook.

Miranda gave me the spring collars last October for my birthday. I wonder, as I separate them from each other, if she'd thought about the symbolism of this gift of paired objects, neither of which is much good without the other. That kind of heavy poetry wasn't really her style, but still… The night she gave these to me was when I found out how she felt about me, and the first time I'd kissed anyone romantically.

I zip up the luggage again and, with it on my back, bounce up and down in place a few times to verify the silencing. Doing this reminds me of silencing my gear when I was learning to conduct infantry patrols at the Military Academy. Like lifting weights, boxing, and self-defense classes, learning soldier skills was about being stronger too.

* * *

West Point Military Reservation
March 1991

It had taken some convincing to secure herself a spot in the cadet Ranger Orientation Program, or ROP. Since this was preparation for the Army's Ranger School, which is open only to males, Sergeant Pike, who was in charge of the program, had been reluctant to allow Shailene to participate. It helped, though, that he and Shailene had become friends over the past two and a half years while she participated in Tactics Club, the ongoing, lower-key version of the ROP, which Pike was also in charge of. She had been one of the most active members of the Tactics Club, participating as part of the opposing "enemy" forces, or "OPFOR," for the ROP the past two years, and had done the paperwork to reserve the training areas for both Tactics Club and ROP for the past year and a half. Pike had finally relented and allowed her in on the condition she participate in every aspect of ROP: carrying the same weight backpack, running the same miles, and attending the same early morning classes during the school week. "But you fall out once, Cadet Campbell, or even *mention* quitting, and you're out of the program, got it? You understand, by signing on for this, you're putting yourself under a spotlight, so you'd better be ready for it, and make sure you really want to do this."

So here she was, lying belly-down on a thin layer of old, granular snow next to Chris Opitz, sometime around midnight in the forest near West Point. She was serving as the radio operator to his patrol leader for this mission. Sergeant Pike had made the assignments, and she could tell Chris was pissed off that she was assigned as his radio man, obviously doubting she would be able to shoulder the extra 22 pounds of backpack radio and still keep up with him over the steep, boulder-strewn, tree and brush-covered Hudson Highlands in upstate New York. So far she'd managed to be there by his side every minute, ready with the comms.

"Fire in the hole!"

Shailene covered her ears and closed her eyes to protect her night vision. She heard the boots of the body search/demolition team clomping on the hard-packed surface of the dirt and gravel road as they ran toward where she and Chris lay, just inside the tree line. A couple seconds later her eyelids glowed red and she felt as much as heard the boom of the grenade simulator, representing an explosive charge destroying the weapons and communications equipment they'd taken off the bodies of the "enemy," Shailene's pals in Tactics Club.

The next task was leading the patrol to their pick-up point, which was actually just a couple kilometers—klicks in Army slang—further down this same road, but they had planned a covert five-klick movement through the woods to stay hidden and safe. Chris got to his feet and Shailene followed suit, glad to take her body away from the snow that was melting through the front of her pants. Her body was OK—chilled, but not wet thanks to the insulation of the field jacket, but everything from the middle of her thighs down was numb and felt weird and foreign as she brought her legs under her.

"Ranger Opitz!"

Shailene looked in the direction of the voice and saw Sergeant Pike, his slim silhouette readily identifiable because it carried a long walking staff instead of the M-16 rifle or M-60 machine gun all the Ranger candidates carried on patrol.

"Yes Sergeant!" Chris responded.

She saw Pike alter course slightly and come toward them. "Ranger, put your patrol on the road and take them out of here. After the noise of the ambush, there's no point in moving tactically any more—speed is security now, so get everyone on the road and high-tail it out of here."

"Speed is security"? Shailene thought. She supposed it made sense, but something didn't feel right.

"Yes Sergeant."   Chris turned and called out "Team leaders, point, on me!"

Something felt really wrong to her, and she put her hand on Chris' shoulder to get his attention. He half turned toward her. "Chris, I got a bad feeling about the road."

"What?"   He leaned closer, but sounded impatient. "What are you saying?"

"I think putting us on the road is a bad idea—it's not tactical. I don't buy that 'speed is security' business. If this were real and the enemy were sending someone fast to intercept us, they'd probably use the road, and then we'd run right into them. We should stick to the plan."

"Pike said to take the road—the exercise is over and he just wants to move things along, get us back for the intelligence debriefing. We're takin' the road."

She knew as well as Chris did this wasn't real, just an exercise, but by now she'd learned to immerse herself in field exercises and treat them like real missions. Pike had taught her that in Tactics Club: "Always train like it's the real thing, because in the blink of an eye, it is." He told about when he was with his Ranger battalion, and his unit was called back early from an exercise. They were issued real ammunition and parachutes, and less than 24 hours later were dumped out of a plane flying over Grenada, where they seized an airfield from Cuban troops. *In the blink of an eye...*   That matched with Shailene's own experience of violence: at any time, in any place, without warning. *In the blink of an eye.* For now, though, she didn't say anything about always training like it's real. She already had a reputation as a Tactics Club geek which, on top of her gender, annoyed most of the guys in ROP even more. Instead she said, "The mission isn't over until we're home. As long as we're out here, following the rules protects us."   She realized immediately that word choice wasn't any better.

"Shailene, that's all well and fine, but we're *not* in enemy territory, OK? You don't have to prove anything, all right?" The others were drawing near now.

"What's up, Chris?" Mark Taylor, who was the compass man, asked. "I've got the next azimuth ready," he said, referring to the compass bearing they were to follow.

"We're takin' the road—Pike said speed is security and we should use the road to get the hell out of here. I want point in front, then the rest of the ambush line to just come forward onto the road. Ten-foot spacing between individuals, on the shoulder, alternating sides, weapons facing out. Any questions?" No one said anything. "Let's do it. I'll be down on the road." Chris turned and walked out of the tree line.

Shailene, a growing sense of apprehension in her gut, followed him onto the road, stepping quickly so she could pull even with him. He turned to look at her as she came alongside. "Chris, let's at least put security out front of us on either side of the road in the woods, just in case there's an ambush set for us." He opened his mouth to speak, but before he could she added, "It won't slow us down much and it makes sense. Pike will like it," she added, hoping this last would persuade him, since the truth of the statement was obvious to anyone who knew Pike.

He paused, considering her suggestion, then looked around before walking up to the two guys who had been the rear security team while they were waiting in ambush, but who were now in the center of the column they were forming on the road. Shailene heard Chris send them forward to where the point man, Eric, and Mark were standing, and to the left, into the trees. Then she followed him as he jogged forward and sent what had been the ambush's right flank security forward and into the trees to the right. He turned to Mark and Eric. "OK, let's go," he said.

Chris and Shailene held their place on the road as the patrol filed by them. They resumed walking when they were once again in the middle of the column, falling into place on the left shoulder. The patrol continued almost silently down the packed dirt strip. Shailene glanced back and saw Pike about twenty feet away, the only person walking down the center of the road.

They'd been going about five minutes when there was gunfire to their right front. "No shit!" Chris whispered, then shouted "Everyone break right!" and headed for the trees on the right side of the road. Once in the trees he shouted "60's!", calling the two M-60 machine gun teams forward, then turned to Shailene. "Call the team leaders, tell them to take their people and circle around to our right, away from the road. Ed's in charge—have him call you and when he's in position to assault. I'll have the '60's lift and shift toward the road when he's ready to attack."

Shailene nodded, put the handset to her face and keyed it. "All teams, this is Romeo Zero-Six: Move one hundred meters southwest, then one hundred meters southeast. Stay online parallel to the road and await orders to assault. Alpha team leader is in command of this element. Confirm you understand, over." While she was on the radio, she watched Chris turn to the machine gun teams and send them forward to reinforce the security team which made initial contact. She also noticed Pike standing nearby, watching Chris, but saying nothing. Chris moved up the line behind the machine gunners, directing the guys in the middle of the column deeper into the woods. Shailene followed Chris, both of them crouching low as they weaved their way through the trees and deadfall, reaching the embattled security team just as the machine guns opened up. Even with the metal adapters on the muzzles to enable the weapons' mechanisms to work with blank rounds, the flare coming out of the barrels was impressive. There was actually now a cacophony of gunfire as the Tactics Club's would-be ambush fired back. Shailene could hear them shouting, re-arranging themselves to return fire, since they would have all been oriented toward the road. This gave the ROP patrol the advantage of surprise and some time to put their own plan into action. She and Chris crawled the last few yards and lay prone on the ground behind a large tree trunk.

"Remind Ed to call us when he's ready to assault!" Chris shouted to her over the jackhammer pounding of the machine guns before firing his own weapon at the enemy's muzzle flashes.

Shailene spoke loudly into the radio handset while watching for anyone approaching behind them. A few seconds later she heard Ed tell her to stand by. She looked toward Chris, who was talking to Sergeant Pike.

"...We're developing the situation. I set up a base of fire here, and sent the rest of the patrol around to attack the flank. I'm waiting for their call telling me they're in position, and then we'll shift fire away from them toward the road, cutting off the enemy's retreat."

"Pretty fuckin' good, Ranger, if it goes like you planned. That was a good move sending out security on your flanks."

"It was Ranger Campbell's idea—she—"

"Romeo Zero-Six, Romeo One-Six, in position, over."

"Chris, they're in position!" Shailene shouted.

"Tell 'em to start their assault!" Chris whipped around. "Shift fire!" he shouted before crawling forward to ensure everyone got the word.

"One-Six, this is Zero-Six, begin assault, say again, begin assault, out."

Shailene saw a burst of gunfire to their right front as Ed and his team opened up. This was followed by wild yelling as the assault charged the OPFOR positions. Pike passed quickly and silently between the machine gunners, heading for the action. The shouting and shooting continued for another minute, and then she heard Pike's voice:

"Cease fire! Cease fire! All right, everyone in the OPFOR is dead."

Chris shouted for the soldiers near him to stop shooting. In the sudden quiet he heard Pike say "Now what, Ranger Schroeder?"

Ed's voice: "Search teams, search the dead! Everyone else, take up a position facing out!"

There was a pause and then Shailene heard Ed's voice: "Zero-Six, One-Six, objective secure, over."

"Zero-Six, roger." She rose to her knees and turned to the others.   "Chris, they're done, we can consolidate on the objective." They stood and began gathering their equipment and putting their rucksacks back on.   As Shailene was cinching up the shoulder straps on her backpack, Chris stepped near her. "Thanks. You saved our asses, mine especially."

She shrugged. "I'm big on survival."

* * *

I start running for home again, this time with no noise from my little gym backpack.

I never made any really close friends at West Point, but I definitely had a sense of belonging to the community, of being among friends, even if I wasn't close enough to keep in touch with any of them after graduation. I definitely had mixed feelings the morning I graduated from West Point, realizing, even as I was finally reaching the goal of the previous four years, I would miss the people and the place. Since leaving there, in the absence of enforced togetherness and the bond of shared trials and troubles, I've been pretty much alone, even more than after transferring to the public high school in Cambridge when I was fifteen. Miranda had been the one exception to my isolation, the only real friend I've had since the Bad happened.

Eight

As I round the corner and come down the last bit of walkway to my apartment's door, I hear my neighbor's wife screaming.

The first time this happened, I was about to pound on their door—I actually had my fist raised, about to slam it into the center—when she switched from inarticulate screaming to say "Oh god, *yes!*" I stood frozen for several seconds, fist stopped in mid-air, before turning and going back to my apartment. Since then I've been woken up a couple times in the night, my bed vibrating with their bouncing transmitted through the floor that runs beneath both our apartments, and I've learned his name is either God or Brian, or maybe both.

It's rare for them to make this much noise in the middle of the day, but I just ignore it. Sex, even the self-inflicted kind, really isn't an option for me. I'm still not sure how that first time with Miranda went so well. If I knew, I'd have repeated it. Maybe it was the dressing up; that seems like an obvious thing to try, now that I'm looking back on it. Then again, maybe the newness of it had something to do with my success that day, or the surprise, the way I just fell into the moment and forgot myself. Whatever the reason, it was a big, beautiful firework, exploding and lighting up my world, then gone. *If only I were a lesbian*, I think sardonically, but there's more truth than humor in the wish.

When we broke up, I badgered her into agreeing to continue as friends. Of course, that didn't work. We had one really awkward dinner out after that, both of us trying hard to be cheerful and easy like before, and by dessert we were fighting back tears. Neither of us called the other after that, though I found myself hoping for a message on the answering machine every time I came home. Recently I disconnected the machine and put it away in a big box on the floor of my closet where I store stuff I almost never use. I don't really care if I miss anyone else's calls.

I slide the deadbolt home. After I sit on the chair I keep by the door to take my shoes off, I stand and wedge the chair under the knob. On the way to the bathroom I stop by the set of drawers built into the same wall-mounted unit that houses some bookshelves and my bed. I get a fresh pair of panties and a stretchy cotton tank top from the underwear drawer. All my underwear is the same: plain, white, cotton, and cheap. I open another drawer and pull out a pair of jeans. In another month it'll be too hot for these, but I prefer to cover my legs, so I'll wear these as late into the hot weather as I can stand. Finally I open a third drawer and, after a moment's deliberation, pull out a dark gray T-shirt.

I carry the clean clothes into the bathroom and turn on the shower. I undress while the hot water is arriving, and hang the gym clothes on their hangers before stepping under the spray. I take my time soaping up, covering the familiar territory at a leisurely pace; one thing I have lots of now is time. I close my eyes and focus on the tactility of my skin, the feel of the bar of soap and the palm of my hand running over my body. This isn't sexual or exciting, but there is something satisfying about it, at least in the moment. I open my eyes and look down the length of my body: the gentle, shallow swelling of my breasts, and below them the pink ridge of scar extending down a few inches from the bottom of my sternum to the top of my abdomen. I'm good at not thinking of the scar's origin now, and usually just see it as another part of me, a familiar terrain feature on my personal landscape. Below my abdomen is the small mat of dark yellow hair, which is almost brown now that it's wet. And finally there are my legs, thickened with muscle from all the running and weight training. Since my goal is to be less attractive, especially to men, I don't shave my legs, but it's hard to tell unless you look closely. I don't shave my armpits either, but I don't have much more visible hair there. I put the soap in its dish and rinse off, then cut the water and towel myself dry, rubbing my skin until it glows pink and tingles.

I put the panties on and then the stretchy white tank top. I like these undershirts better than bras—they fit better and give my undersized breasts all the support they need. I buy my T-shirts large; this gray one is baggy and the hems on the sleeves reach to my elbows. My jeans are cut for men and hang loosely off my hips.

I pad into the kitchen area and pause, thinking of lunch while gazing absently at a picture I taped at eye level to one of the cupboard doors. It's a photo I took in the fall of my second year of high school not long before the Bad, while I was still at Byfield Academy. It shows a building we students called The Tower which, despite the name, was really a small house with a two-story stone turret as its main body. The round turret gives the impression of height since it contrasts with the low aspect of the wooden part of the building, and it sits isolated from any other human structures. The Tower stands on a bluff overlooking a broad expanse of salt marsh, on the edge of the forest which surrounds the school. I took the picture from the little-used and poorly-maintained road which crosses the marsh, so the scene includes the emptiness of the marsh and the bright fall colors of the woods behind The Tower.

Making up my mind, I bend and open the half-sized fridge, and take out a quarter loaf of wheat bread and a jar of kosher dill pickles. I get the peanut butter from the cupboard, and spread some on a piece of bread. Using my sharp little paring knife, I cut a couple pickles into lengthwise slices and lay them on top of the peanut butter. A second piece of bread makes the sandwich, and I sit down with it and a cup of tap water.

I'm not sure how the peanut butter-dill pickle combination even occurred to me, but it wasn't so long after I became a vegetarian, and I remember clearly how *that* happened.

The first meal I had in the hospital, after I came out of the fog of nightmares and anesthetics, was roast beef. Nothing fancy, of course, just hospital chow: a couple thin slices of meat, roasted potatoes, and mixed peas and carrots. And that creepy wiggly jello stuff that was always dessert in the hospital. My stomach was still a little wonky from the drugs and the pain, but I was hungry too, and glad to see food. As soon as I picked up the knife from the tray, though, I felt uneasy. I cut into the beef, and a thin, blood-tinged liquid seeped out onto the white plate. I stopped cutting, but the liquid's flow increased. Becoming redder and thicker, it filled the plate, then overflowed onto the tray. I dropped the knife and fork and closed my eyes. I felt the blood spraying me in the face, running into my nose and ears, matting my hair, the wet, metallic stench of it choking me.

When I'd last used a knife, in the pre-dawn hours of the day before, this is exactly what happened, and it saved my life. But to say I was glad to have used it, or even that I did not regret using it, would be way too simple. I was certain I would use the knife again if I, unthinkable as it was, had to repeat what I went through, but it changed how I saw things. That evening in the hospital, the blade was no longer just a utensil, and the meat was flesh from a corpse. It didn't matter the corpse wasn't human: dead was dead. The tray ended up crashing to the floor, and I had to be sedated again.

I'm less visceral about this now: tableware and roast beef don't give me panic attacks anymore. What began as instinctive revulsion has evolved, with reflection and the healing of passing time, into principle. It's simple: I don't unnecessarily harm anything with the mental capacity to suffer or value its life. After I'd thought about it, I was surprised it had taken so much to bring me to this point. For most of my childhood my family had a cat. I named him Sammy, loved him like the sibling I never had, and felt like my heart had been ripped out when a speeding car cut him almost in half. But I never gave a thought to all the dead animals I was eating. Animals were animals, and meat was food; I'd never harm an animal, but really liked bacon with my pancakes. It took my own pain, my own will to live when faced with a predator's attack, to make me appreciate similar feelings in others, human and otherwise.

At first I only gave up meat. This was hard enough on my grandmother, who didn't understand how you could build a meal without some kind of flesh, fish, or fowl. I ended up buying some cookbooks and doing a lot of my own cooking. I found I actually liked it, and felt better physically—sort of lighter and cleaner. Later I came across a book about the abuses of the factory farm system. I learned egg-producing chickens spend their entire lives in cages so small that, once the birds are fully-grown, there isn't room for them to open their wings or even turn around; and veal calves are confined in similar conditions, kept deliberately malnourished and sedentary to produce better-tasting meat. Stuff like that put me off anything joining animals with industrial food production, so now I don't eat anything from animals if I can help it.

Anyway…peanut butter with dill pickles. I guess what I like is the combination of sweet, sour, and salty. That and the crunchiness of the pickles and the super-chunk peanut butter. Somehow it works, even if it does sound weird.

While I eat, I listen to the radio. I used to listen to a classic rock station, but now I mostly listen to Public Radio. I miss talking to Miranda, and listening to the voices and ideas is a substitute for conversation. It gives me more to think about than music. I heard the show that's on now the first time it aired, but I keep it on anyway, half-listening and wondering what to do with the rest of the weekend. Last weekend I spent several hours working on Stacey—changing her oil, rotating her tires, washing and waxing, cleaning the interior. This weekend, though, I don't have any projects and, except for maybe a run tomorrow morning, I don't have any more physical training planned either. I wonder if there's any studying I can do, but I'm already ahead on my assignments for the two grad school courses I'm enrolled in this quarter.

Besides, I just don't feel like studying programming syntax or computer processor architecture this weekend. My choice to major in computer science is based more on job opportunities than personal enthusiasm. Miranda made the same claim, but I could tell she really was interested in the stuff. I don't know exactly what I want to do when I become a civilian again, but I'll need to take care of myself, and something with computers seems as good a job as any, and more appealing than a lot of other careers I can imagine, including staying in the Army. The military has been fine, and good to me, but the culture and lack of freedom regarding where I live and how long I live there chafes, so I'll probably get out sometime in the next few years.

I finish my sandwich and the cup of water, rinse my plate at the sink, and place it and the cup on my makeshift drying rack. *Now what?* I already cleaned this place last night, even though I'd also cleaned it last weekend and could barely see any dust to wipe up. I've been re-reading Camus' *The Stranger*, but if I'm going to spend the afternoon reading, I really want something new. I don't know what exactly, but maybe I'll know it when I see it. I consider going to the library, but in my current frame of mind Fort Rucker's little library seems so...lifeless. Then it comes to me: the mall.

OK, not exactly momentous or inspiring, but... I could browse the big chain bookstore there and most likely find something interesting to read. And, since I no longer have access to Miranda's music collection, I could also look for some swing music CD's of my own at the music store. It seems like such a great idea—so normal, positive, and obvious—I wonder how I didn't think of it before. *Maybe I'm finally getting my shit together again.*

I shove my wallet into one hip pocket and my keys into the other, pull on my black and white Chuck Taylor high tops, and head out to my car. It's around noon, and the sun is beating down fiercely—surprisingly so for April. Fortunately, I always leave a folded piece of corrugated cardboard with a picture of a big watchdog on it in position under the windshield, where it keeps the interior a little cooler and deters really stupid car thieves.

I get in and, since Stacey has no air conditioning, I roll down both doors' windows. I put on the sunglasses I keep under the parking break lever. They have black wire frames and small, round, very dark lenses that do a good job of mitigating the intense glare of Alabama sunlight. The inside of the sun screen has a handy "NEED HELP—CALL POLICE" message printed on it in big letters and, in smaller letters, to help really stupid drivers, a warning to remove the screen before putting the vehicle in motion. I fold the screen up and tuck it away.

The nearest mall, Wiregrass Commons, is about forty-five minutes away over a fast road which mostly traverses flat fields. By the fall many of these fields will be white with tufts of cotton, but now they're mostly brown or green, spread out under a perfectly blue sky showing not a hope of cool relief in the form of rain or even clouds. I regret choosing the jeans over a pair of shorts. It's too warm to shut the windows, so it's too noisy for the radio. Instead I listen to the wind and the sound of Stacey's engine.

All the shady places in the mall parking lot are already taken, so I deploy the sun screen again and leave the windows slightly open. Inside the mall, the sweat in my shirt and pants dries quickly in the air conditioning. I wander down the main thoroughfare, past the food court and a Radio Shack. It's not really crowded, but there's enough people around to make the place feel busy. I've been to this mall before, but don't remember exactly where the book and music stores are located. I'm in no hurry, though, and content to walk around and look at all the store fronts and displays until I find what I came for. In the walkway in front of one of the anchor stores, a major clothing retailer, I notice a special display with three amazingly life-like mannequins. Surprised at the realism, I slow down to look, searching for seams or chips in the faces as I pass until I see one of them blink. I freeze, confused for a moment before realizing I'm looking at an actual teenage girl. I look at the others: all girls. *Weird.* One of them smiles faintly at me, and I look away quickly and start walking again, leaving them behind. I pass several more stores—men's clothing, women's clothing, athletic shoes, toys. I pause briefly at a pet store where eager puppies put their front paws on the other side of the window and look out at me excitedly. I smile a little at them, but also feel worried, wondering if they'll find good homes, wondering what happens to the ones nobody takes home.

I move on, and the central corridor opens out, both laterally and vertically, into an atrium. This part of the mall is a big circular space with a domed skylight above it. There are more stores around the edge of the circle, but I find myself looking up at the tinted sunlight, the blue sky muted to a grayish purple. I look down again to keep an eye on where I'm going. One time I came through here when they had a bunch of new sports cars on display in this area, but today there are no special events. Even the fountain in the middle is turned off and the pool drained, for maintenance I guess. There are a few people sitting near the trees and bushes planted around the edge of the empty pool, and a small child runs awkwardly but quickly across my path. I break stride to avoid running over him or her—I can't tell which—and hear a parent call "Jimmy!" I step behind the kid and continue on my way.

Past the atrium I find the music store, and realize I'm not even sure where to look. I wander around for a while until I decide swing would have to be part of the jazz section, but even then I don't really know what I'm looking for. Since it was Miranda's music, she handled selecting discs and putting them in the player. I remember her poster for the Birmingham Bruisers, but don't find any of their CD's. Discouraged, I give up and move on to the book store, which I now see is pretty much at the opposite end of the mall from where I entered.

Book and video stores always offer plenty of distraction: there are so many things to look at, so many stories to dive into, so many opportunities to forget. I stand in front of the magazine section first, looking at the dispatches from other worlds—cars, sports, fashion, show biz…men, women, hunters, investors. I already subscribe to a weekly news magazine, and I see the issue I finished reading earlier this week in the rack, along with its competitors' offerings, but why read more of the same news? I flip through copies of *Scientific American* and *National Geographic*, but there's not enough interesting stuff in either of these issues to inspire me to buy.

I move on to the new fiction section. As usual, I find it a little overwhelming—so many voices asking to be read, trying to be heard above the din. I get tired of looking for something to jump out at me and move on to what I guess is the "old" fiction section. I look for some of the writers I've enjoyed in the past, but see nothing appealing to me there either. I'm reaching that point of discouragement where nothing sounds good; I can't even describe to myself what I'm looking for. I leave the fiction section and turn down a nearby aisle.

Cooking. I like to cook, and I've gotten pretty decent at it—at least good enough to keep myself happy. But cookbooks aren't what I had in mind. I go to the next aisle and look down it: Gardening. I guess that makes sense: growing the food kind of goes with cooking the food, but still no help for me now. I look around and spot a sign for Philosophy and Religion.

This being small-town Alabama, the philosophy and religion section of the store is heavy on Christianity and light on everything else. It's too bad the focus is so narrow. The reading about Far Eastern religion I did while I was stationed in Korea was really interesting and rewarding, and it got me into a more disciplined and regular practice of meditation. I doubt I'll ever achieve any kind of enlightenment or surpassing peace like the Zen literature described, but regular meditation does seem to smooth out my emotions somewhat, especially the angry ones. Christianity, on the other hand, was useless and misleading. I scan the Judeo-Christian titles on the shelves in front of me: *Lies. As if there were a God.*

I could be wrong about that: God might exist. If he does, though, he's not what Christianity says he is. What kind of loving father would put his children in *this* world? My parents loved me, and died trying to protect me. God, on the other hand, was deaf to my pleading for help, and I had to save my own ass. I guess a lot of Christians would say God *was* there, and helped me get my hands on the knife, helped me open the big blood vessels in my attacker's throat. I hate when people say things like that. If God were there at that moment, then why not show up an hour or so earlier and have the monster die in a car wreck on his way to our house? Why make the monster in the first place? Save us all a lot of trouble. The bottom line is, I was there and I know: I was alone with the fucker when I killed him. And if I'd turned the other cheek like the *Bible* instructs, I'd be long dead now. And not just me: in all probability, there would other dead girls and murdered families by now. The police investigation tied the one I killed to similar incidents in Tennessee, West Virginia, and Pennsylvania. It was a career with him.

So, yeah, God might exist, but given the choice between believing in no God, and believing in the demented, sadistic God that would create this world, I'll take the former. I sleep better that way.

I turn away in frustration, still at a loss for something to read. The next aisle over from philosophy and religion is science. *There's a combination*, I think. *Maybe that's what I need.* I've always found science interesting, and there's something comforting about it too. I like the honesty empirical evidence and reproducible results imposes on the search for truth, and the unquestioned value of understanding for its own sake. My eye catches on a black spine with a picture of a planet on it, and I pull the tall, thin book from the shelf. It's filled with big glossy color photos and diagrams: planets, galaxies, and nebula. It even has an orders of magnitude diagram similar to one I had in my bedroom as a kid. I close the volume and hang on to it as I resume browsing. A title on a book with its front cover facing out catches my eye: *The Mind of God*. I wonder why this book is here instead of in the other aisle. The subtitle is *The Scientific Basis for a Rational World*, and it occurs to me that right there, with "rational world," the book is already on the wrong track. Still, I'm curious, so I take the book from the shelf and, tucking the other book under my arm, I flip to the table of contents. It's not a big book, and it's obviously not a text book, probably not even scholarly, but the chapter titles sound interesting: "Can the universe create itself?" and "Why is the world the way it is?" I look for something about the author, Paul Davies, and find a note on the back saying he's a professor of mathematical physics at a university in Australia, which sounds like he could be credible. I flip through the book and see a few diagrams but no pages dense with equations, so I decide to give it a try.

I carry the books to the cashier, barely registering a light itch just south of my sternum as I do. After I finish paying, I leave the store, and begin traveling back down the mall's main avenue toward where I came in, ready to go home and read.

I scratch at my scar, but the itch doesn't go away.

Oh shit.

* * *

Seoul, Korea
June 1994

Shailene stood while she read a small book on Zen practice and philosophy written by Zen master Shunryu Suzuki. By two in the morning even the uncomfortable chair at the staff duty officer's desk in battalion headquarters wasn't enough to keep her awake, so now she was standing up. At the Military Academy it had been standard practice for cadets who were having trouble staying awake during class to stand up behind their chairs, and that's what she thought of now as she swayed a little and tried to stay focused on the reading.

The private first class who was assigned as her driver for the night, PFC Blalock, was not required to stay awake the entire shift, so she'd told him to take a nap on the couch in the commander's office. He actually seemed to feel a little guilty about sleeping while she had to stay awake, but she reminded him he would have to work the next day, while she wouldn't, which is why he was allowed to sleep, and she was not. She was secretly glad he'd given in since she really didn't want to try to read while he watched another low-budget horror movie on the cart-mounted TV and VCR he'd wheeled out from the conference room.

The phone's ring was jarring and reverberated slightly in the near total silence, making her jump. She put down the book and picked up the handset. "Staff duty officer, First Battalion, Five-Oh-First Aviation, how may I help you sir?" she said, reciting the prescribed phone greeting.

"Ma'am, this is Specialist Marroni, Delta Company, Third Military Police," the male voice said over the line, referring to one of the MP units stationed at Yongsan, the main American base in Seoul. "I have Private Dexter Williams here, and I need to transfer custody of him to CID at your headquarters."

"Uh, OK. Thanks for the heads up," she said, still absorbing the information. She had never heard of Dexter Williams, but he must be from her battalion, maybe from Bravo or Charlie Company, which were both assigned to outlying airbases.

"Yes ma'am, out here," the MP said, using radio jargon even though he was on the phone. She encountered that a lot, and even caught herself doing it sometimes.

She replaced the handset and logged the call as required, glancing up at the big clock over the desk and noting the time. She considered waking Blalock, but decided there was no point, then wondered if she was supposed to call the Criminal Investigation Division to have them send someone over for the transfer, or if the MP's would have already done that. She had a number for them in the binder that came with the SDO job, so she called. The sergeant who answered the phone told her in that technically respectful, but actually disrespectful and exasperated way mastered by sergeants and older warrant officers, that yes, *ma'am*, he had contacted the investigator on call, who would be there shortly. "OK, just checking," she said, considering saying more and deciding it would be pointless before hanging up.

She stood looking around for several seconds, then returned to her reading. About ten minutes later a government sedan pulled up in the brightly-lit area in front of the building. A man, probably in his thirties, wearing a dark business suit and carrying a small briefcase, came through the door. His pale face was clean-shaven, and his brown hair was barely short enough to conform to military standards. "Can I help you?" Shailene asked immediately suspicious.

"Good morning, ma'am." he said in a voice as smart and no-nonsense as his attire. He produced a small black leather rectangle from his jacket and unfolded it to reveal a badge and military ID card to her, and then laid it on her desk. "Sergeant Allridge, CID. I take it they haven't arrived yet."

"No, not yet," she replied as she studied his credentials, glancing up to see if the face matched the photo. Satisfied, she recorded his arrival on the next free line of the duty log form, copying the correct spelling of his name from the ID card before handing it back to him.

"Thanks," he said, pocketing the identification folder. "A real winner, this guy they're bringing in."

"Oh?" she responded automatically, but not really wanting to know details.

"Yeah, MP's picked him up from local police, who arrested him for beating the crap out of a hooker in Itaewon," Allridge said, referring to the shopping and sex district frequented by U.S. servicemen in Seoul. "Apparently her pimp heard the screaming, tried to stop the guy himself, then called the cops."

Shailene tried to deflect the conversation. "Wasn't the pimp afraid of getting arrested himself?" She didn't really care about the pimp, but it was the best segue she could come up with on the spot. "Or is prostitution legal in Korea?" She noticed the scar on her upper abdomen had begun to itch. *Oh shit, not now*, she thought. *I really don't need this now.*

"No and yes. Prostitution is technically illegal, but Korean law is written to allow the sale of sex in certain areas."

"Like Itaewon," she said, absently nodding while thinking about excusing herself to go to the bathroom. The itch had rapidly turned into pain which was going deep and getting sharp now, probably, she figured, because of this conversation. "I—"

She broke off as they both heard a vehicle pull up. Their heads turned toward the window and, in the illumination cast by the flood lights outside, they saw two military policemen exit a camouflage-painted utility vehicle and then help a handcuffed young man out of the back. The jeans and a short-sleeved collared shirt he wore were badly wrinkled, untucked, and too big for him. Shailene didn't recognize him, but he had that scrubbed, skinny, gangly look typical of many young soldiers she'd seen. His hair was cut in a "high and tight": the sides and back of his head were nearly shaved and the hair on top was slightly longer. This haircut was unusual for soldiers in aviation units, but not unheard of.

"Here's what we're doing, ma'am," Allridge said as he opened his briefcase and extracted some paperwork from it. "The MP's are turning Williams over to you, as the unit's representative, and then you're turning him over to CID— me."

The door to the building slammed open and the three new arrivals entered, the MP's boots sounding loud on the tile floor.

Shailene swallowed hard as the pain intensified until, if she didn't know otherwise, she'd have been sure she was being stabbed all over again. *It's not real, it's not real...* she repeated silently in her head as she forced herself to stand straight and keep her face neutral. "OK," she said, focusing on the forms the CID agent was laying out on the duty officer desk. She sat down to try to ease the pain, but of course sitting down didn't help. *Just focus, get this done and send them on their way.* She picked up her pen and logged the prisoner's arrival on the log sheet, noting the time according to the big clock on the wall. Then she looked back at the forms. "OK, what do I do here?" she asked, managing to keep her voice level and controlled as she did.

Allridge had Williams produce his ID card and handed it to Shailene. She looked at the photo on the card, then looked up at the young soldier. The eyes that met hers were flat and cold, and their darkness was in sharp contrast to the paleness of the face around them. The calm emptiness she saw in them reminded her of— She quickly looked back down at the ID card. Except for slightly longer hair in the photo, the face was clearly the same.

"Record the prisoner's name here," Allridge said, pointing at a space on the first form, "and here"—a space on the second form.

She did as instructed, and then, after quickly reading through the text on each document, she signed, adding date and time, in the spaces the CID agent pointed to. Finally she logged the prisoner's departure with Allridge, noting that Williams would be held at the Central Detention Facility on Yongsan's main post. It was all over in a couple minutes, and she was alone again as her pen inscribed Williams' time of departure. Almost as soon as the vehicles pulled away from the building, the pain in her dropped off dramatically, and continued diminishing until, several seconds later, even the itching was gone without a trace.

"What a relief," she muttered under her breath as she rubbed the scar below her sternum through her flight suit and T-shirt, enjoying the absence of hurt, and wondering why it had lasted so much longer this time. In the past, the peak pain had never lasted more than several seconds. But, assuming the pain was some kind of flashback, it made sense she would re-experience the trauma the entire time someone she knew to be dangerous was nearby. It certainly made more sense than years ago when she was driving alone on Interstate 95. That time the pain came and went without any obvious provocation, but it had been so brief it had been easy to shrug off.

Anyway, it's over now.

She looked at her list of required duties, and noticed she had one more arms room check coming up in about an hour. She'd have to wake Blalock for that one since he'd have to drive her there. The headquarters company didn't have its own arms room and instead shared space in a big one on the main post. She could drive the vehicle herself, but he had signed for it at the motor pool and, anyway, it was procedure for them to make this check together.

She went back to her book, glancing at the clock after a while, then every few pages. After about forty-five minutes she decided she should start getting Blalock awake, and went down the hall and into the commander's office. Blalock's boots were off his feet and on the floor as she'd instructed him, and he was on his side, snoring softly, one arm bent under his head as a pillow, his knees bent so he could fit between the couch's armrests. For a moment she felt almost like a mom, looking down at the soldier who, although probably only about four years younger than her, appeared very young as he lay sleeping. She reached down, placed her hand on the upward-pointing shoulder, and shook it gently. "PFC Blalock," she said quietly. "Blalock..." The deep breathing continued. "Blalock!" she repeated more loudly.

His eyes popped open, looking a little startled. "Huh?"

She straightened up and took a step back. "It's time for another arms room check."

He looked puzzled for a moment, then his face cleared. "Oh, OK ma'am." He rotated to a sitting position and looked around blankly for a couple seconds.

"Your boots are over here. I'll be out front," she said, and returned to the duty officer desk, where she started the arms room entry on her log. A few minutes later Blalock came clomping down the hall, and she heard the jingle of keys.

"Sorry I was so clueless when you woke me up, LT. I was in the middle of a dream."

"Anything good?"

He smiles. "Yes ma'am—I was talking to my wife."

His wife? He can't be much over nineteen. "I didn't know you were married."

"Oh yes ma'am—we got married right after I got out of AIT. I just wear my ring here," he said, pulling the bead chain with his ID tags out of his shirt and showing a gold wedding band alongside the small imprinted metal plates. "It's a bad idea for a mechanic to wear any kind of jewelry on his hands or wrists."

"Good thinking." He'd probably gotten the same scare lecture she had, the one with the color photo of the "degloved" finger—bloody bones in lieu of a ring finger, attached to an otherwise normal-looking hand, with the bruised flesh sheath, complete with fingernail, on the table beside the hand. Later, she'd met a guy who'd actually had his finger re-attached after his high school ring, caught between slats on a truck while he was jumping off, pulled his finger's flesh, tendons and all, off the bones. The re-attached finger was twice as big as its companions, and purplish in color.

"We had about a month together before I had to come over here. But I took a couple weeks for my mid-tour leave and went back to Chicago to see her."

She locked the door to headquarters while Blalock started the utility vehicle's diesel engine. They drove over the steep hill separating Camp Coiner, a sort of military subdivision, from Yongsan, the main part of the sprawling U.S. military complex in the heart of Seoul. The streets were dark and empty of traffic as they drove the same route they'd taken several hours earlier to the arms room. About halfway there, as Blalock chatted about his high school courtship of his wife, Shailene noticed the itch growing in her midsection again. Instinctively, though she knew there was no reason to, she pressed the fingertips of one hand into the scar as the scratch became a burn, then sharp cramps. She breathed deeply, trying to ignore the hurt and keep it secret from Blalock. Mercifully, the pain didn't get as bad as it had when Williams was in the room with her, and then it actually tapered off again as they continued down the street.

By the time they arrived at the arms room the weird sensation was gone. Shailene jumped out and checked the lock on the door while Blalock watched from the vehicle. She walked down to the corner of the building, looked at the barred window on that side, saw it was still dark and the bars were still in place, then returned to the SUV. "OK, that's our last check. Only what—an hour and a half until we're relieved?" she said cheerfully.

"Yes ma'am—although then I have to go to work."

"Yeah, that's true. Maybe you can get some more sleep when we get back."

Blalock turned the vehicle around and they headed for battalion headquarters. Soon the pain on and under her scar was cranking up again. This time, as they rolled down the street, Shailene stared out her window, wondering what could be causing this. It couldn't be anything about Blalock—she'd been around him almost all night. The sensation was once again going from a ripping feeling to a severe cramp behind the scar when she noticed a building unusually lit up for that time of night. A light near the entrance illuminated a small sign on the wall there. She watched it as they approached until she could read:

BUILDING 2380
CRIMINAL INVESTIGATION DIVISION
Headquarters
Judge Advocate Offices
Central Detention Facility

As they continued rolling down the street, the hurt inside her quickly abated, and perhaps ten seconds after leaving the jail behind the last itching vanished.

Weird.

Part Two

Alan and Denice

Nine

Topeka, Kansas
November 1971

He felt the warmth spreading over his legs, and at first it was a good feeling, until he remembered what it was and jolted awake, trying to clench his dick shut as he did. But it was too late: the sheets were wet—really wet down there. *Oh no, not again...* he thought as he scrambled to his knees and began pulling the sheets up and throwing them off before the mattress got too wet. "Oh no, oh no, oh no not again." He whispered over and over as he worked, draping the sheets between the mattress on the floor and the dresser, where he trapped a dry section of the sheets in a drawer, hanging the wet part in mid-air. He didn't know what time it was, but hopefully there would still be time for the sheets to dry before morning. He would just have to stay awake and check them until they were dry enough to put back on the mattress, and then Mom wouldn't notice.

He changed his underwear and spread the wet one out to dry on the floor. It was chilly in the room. Alan knew this would make things dry slower, and it made him feel cold as he sat on the edge of the stripped mattress, wondering how long this would take.

After what seemed like an hour, but he knew was probably much less since time almost always seemed longer than it really was, he checked the sheets again. Still wet. He checked the underwear he'd taken off: wet. He sat on the edge of the mattress again. As he waited, dressed only in his underwear and his Rocky and Bullwinkle T-shirt, he started to shiver. He thought about putting on more clothes, but he was tired and really just wanted to go back to sleep, not get dressed. Instead, he pulled the blanket around him, making a small tent over his body as he sat cross-legged on the mattress.

Checked the sheets again: still wet. Maybe a little more dry—it was hard to tell. The pee on them was definitely cold though, and Alan knew things dried faster when they were warm, so this didn't look good, but he couldn't think of what else to do. A hair dryer would help. Mom had one she kept in the bathroom, but it was really noisy and would wake up her and his sisters if he tried to use it. He sat back down on the mattress and pulled the blanket around him again.

After a while all he could think about was lying down, as if the mattress were pulling him toward it. He resisted, afraid he would fall asleep, but after checking the sheets a third time and finding them still wet, he decided he would lie down for just a few minutes.

"Alan!"

Alan's eyes popped open. The room was bright with daylight. A sick feeling got big in his stomach.

"What the hell is going on here, you little shit?" She sniffed the air. "Did you—oh, *shit*! You pissed the bed again, didn't you?"

He thought about denying it, but couldn't think of another way to explain the sheets being draped across the room and the smell of pee, so instead he said nothing and closed his eyes again, wishing the whole situation would go away.

"Get up you little shit! Goddamn it, I don't have time for this! I said get *up*!" She yanked the pillow out from under his head and hit him with it.

Alan knew if he didn't get up now, things would only get worse. He opened his eyes again and sat up, hoping if he looked at her and she saw he was sorry then she'd stop yelling at him. "I tried to dry—"

"I don't care!" She stepped to the draped sheet and felt it. "Uh! It's fuckin' *soaked*!" She grabbed it, almost pulling the dresser over as she pulled the end free of the drawer Alan had shut on it. Turning to Alan, she gathered up the wet part and pushed it in his face. Alan leaned back, away from the peed on sheet, but his mother grabbed his head and held it while she wiped his face with the damp cloth. "Is this what it's gonna take to teach you?! Do I have to treat you like a fuckin' puppy? Do I have to fuckin' *house*break you?!"

Alan tried not to, but the tears came anyway.

She let go of his head and stepped back with the balled up sheet. "Yeah, you better cry, you little baby. I'd put you in diapers again if they weren't so goddamn expensive. I'm sick of this! I am not gonna make a special fuckin' trip to the laundry to get these clean. You're just gonna have to sleep on them until we go again. You'll prob'ly piss on them again anyway. Honestly, seven years old and wetting the bed! When are you gonna grow up?"

"Alan wet his be-ed!" The older of Alan's two little sisters, Missy, appeared in the doorway, smiling her gummy, two-front-teeth-missing smile and looking at him with a mean gleam in her eye. "Alan wet his be-ed!" She looked right at him so she could see her song hit home.

"Honest to god, Alan, she's younger than you and she doesn't piss in her bed. Angela's *four* and *she* doesn't piss the bed! You're just like your father: a fuckin' immature bastard. Why are all the males in my life such fuckin' retards?"

"Re-tard! Re-tard! Alan's a re-tard!"

"I just wish he'd taken you with him when he walked out on us, but no, that woulda taken too much maturity. All right, get goin' Missy—go get your sister dressed."

"Bed-wetter!" she shouted and ran from the doorway. He could hear her across the hall in the room she shared with Angela. "He did it again! Even you don't wet your bed, do you?"

"Alan, stop sitting there looking dazed and get going!" She threw the wadded up sheet at him, hitting him in the face.

"Did you change your underwear at least?" Without waiting for a response she stepped toward him again and slid her hand under his butt. "At least you had that much sense," she muttered. Alan couldn't tell if she were talking to him or herself.

"Alan wet the be-ed! Alan wet the be-ed!" his sisters chanted in their room.

"Missy, I told you to get her ready! Now shut up!" She stormed across the hall.

Alan stood up from the mattress and started getting dressed.

A half hour later Mom dropped Alan and Missy off at the bus stop on the way to take Angela to day care. It was a cold, overcast day. There'd been no rain, but the sky was very dark. Alan stood gazing across the street at a pawn shop but not really seeing it. He didn't want to, but kept replaying that morning, which was a re-run of a lot of other mornings since Dad left. He didn't know why he'd started peeing while he slept, and he definitely didn't know how to stop it. If he did he would. He knew he was too old to be wetting the bed, and he hated the way his mother and sisters acted when it happened. He looked over at Missy, who was chatting with the other first grader girls. At least he knew she wouldn't tell anyone about his peeing the bed since she wouldn't want anyone to know she had a bed-wetter for a brother. He looked around at the other kids. Some were talking with each other, some, like Alan, weren't, but no one was standing near him, as if there were some invisible wall around him.

Good, he thought, and turned his head to look down the street, not in the direction the bus would come from, but where the bus would go. About a block down he could just make out an empty lot behind the parked cars, stores, and trash cans. Alan saw this lot every morning from the bus as it drove by. It was filled with tall grass, which had still been green back in September, but now it was all turned brown. There was trash in the lot too—cans and bottles, pieces of newspaper, fast food wrappers, and other junk. As he looked down the street, picturing the lot in his head more than actually seeing it, he stuck his hands in his pockets. The fingers on his right hand found the little plastic lighter he'd taken off the kitchen table yesterday. He felt the hard, smooth shape of it, and the grooves in the wheel on top, the wheel you spin to make a flame. He stood that way for a minute or two, pressing the tip of his thumb against the wheel and wanting to spin it, before turning and walking away from the bus stop. He didn't look back, and no one said anything.

Alan walked half a block from where they waited to catch the bus to school, then crossed the street and continued walking on the other side. Glancing back once, he saw no one, including his sister, seemed to care he'd left. He put his hand in his pocket and felt again the slim, smooth lighter. He continued walking right into the vacant lot they passed on the bus every day, following a path of trampled grass and packed dirt which cut diagonally into the middle of the area. The grass on either side of the path was taller than Alan, and though he could still hear the noise of the street, he couldn't see anything but dirt, grass, and sky after he was a few steps in. Picking up a big scrap of newspaper, he kept going until he reached what seemed like the center, though there was no way to tell for sure. He stopped and knelt on the ground, and pulled out the lighter.

It took a few tries, the lighter's wheel making the tip of his right thumb tingly, but he got a flame started and held the little button down to keep it going. He touched the tiny fire to a corner of the newsprint, watched it spread up the paper, then dropped the sheet as the flames quickly climbed toward his hand. Soon the entire sheet was going up in an orange blaze. First he imagined the sheet of paper was his wet bed sheet; then he imagined it was not just the sheet, but the mattress and pillows and blankets too. As the flames spread to the dry grass, he saw the fire taking his bedroom—no, the whole apartment they lived in, along with his mother and sisters. His sisters, who were chanting about him wetting the bed, were suddenly choking on the smoke, then screaming as their clothes caught fire. His mother was on fire too. The fire was turning her and his sisters black, turning all of it black, turning it to smoke, which blew away on a morning breeze.

Alan heard crackling behind him and turned to see flames there too—somehow the fire had spread behind him, and now it was on all sides of him, hot and sounding like the train that ran behind their apartment's building, except without the horn. Realizing he might be on fire soon, Alan ran further down the path—now the only way out. The path took him to the sidewalk of the next street over. He turned and saw clouds of gray smoke and approaching orange flames. The fire cleared the grass and trash out of the lot, making it disappear in smoke, like magic. A fire engine, horn blasting and sirens wailing, pulled up and firefighters piled out and began opening a fire hydrant a few feet away. Alan ignored them. He only hoped the fire would get everything before they put it out.

Ten

Alan opens his eyes, and finds himself looking at the pale purple sheet with the pattern of dark violet fleur de lis on it. Denice hung this on the wall to "brighten things up." Alan is OK with it. There's a cracked dent in the drywall behind the sheet, so at least this covers that up. If he lived alone he would have used some spackle to repair the damage, but the sheet is easier, and it maybe looks better than just a bare wall. Denice is pretty good like that, making things better.

The bedroom is softly lit with early morning sunlight, which suddenly seems to get brighter when he remembers their plan to go down to Panama City Beach today. It's been months since they went to Mobile, weeks since they made today's plans. There were a lot of days when he thought he'd explode with the waiting, but now it's here. Today. He's excited, but there's also a peace in knowing the wait is pretty much over. He thinks about what else they'll do today, since they won't leave for PC Beach until this afternoon. Something fun—no work today, just fun things.

Alan rolls over and looks at Denice. She's still asleep; even without looking at her, he would know this from her breathing—that deep, slow sleeping breathing. He studies her face, a face he knows at least as well as his own since he's been looking at it almost every day for nearly three years now—three years next month. For some reason, though, he never gets tired of looking at her. Her lips are slightly parted now, her plump lower lip relaxed. When her mouth is closed and she's not smiling, she looks a little pouty because of this fat lower lip. That's one of the little details he loves. Her brown eyes are closed, of course, the dark lashes of her upper eyelids fanned out over the skin under her eyes. His gaze touches the familiar landmark of the tiny freckle under her left eye, then wanders up to her forehead. A few whispy locks of her hair, blonde now to please him, stray across her forehead, partially obscuring a couple of small scabs. She still has a little trouble with her complexion, at least on her forehead, even now that she's twenty-six. That doesn't bother him though; she still looks great.

It amazes him that he didn't pay any attention to her the first time they were in the same room together. He was at the Waffle House with some of the other guys from work. As usual, they were talking about sports shit—start of baseball season or something. Alan was pretending to listen, but not saying anything because on the inside all he could think about was how stupid it was for guys making ten bucks an hour to be obsessing over a bunch of millionaires who get paid to play games. It made him angry, and he looked out the window to avoid making eye contact and risking them realizing what he was thinking. He figures that must be why he didn't notice her then. Denice says she noticed him that time, but didn't say anything.

The second time they crossed paths—the first time he noticed her—was in the restaurant again.

* * *

Dothan, Alabama
May 1992

Bullshit, Alan thought as he followed the guys into the Waffle House. Harry, who owned the contracting business, insisted on all of them having breakfast together most mornings. It wouldn't be as bad if they all didn't have to kick in for it. But if there was one thing Alan had learned, it was when to shut up. Not shutting up had gotten him kicked out of school a few times as a kid, and then the Marines. He reminded himself this was just a means to an end. Eventually, after he'd picked up some experience and some dough, he'd start his own contracting business, and then he'd tell Harry to go fuck himself.

That had been the good thing about the trucking gig: no one telling him what to do most of the time. Sure, he always had an assignment, but once he pulled out of the lot it was up to him how he got his load to its destination on time. He'd done that for about five years, but it finally got too damn boring. The repo job had been OK, since there too he was on his own a lot of the time, following people around and then stealing their cars back, but the pay sucked, and it was pretty boring too. Anyway, the one thing keeping him going here with Harry was the plan to someday have his own business. Then he'd be in charge, and people would have to do what *he* said.

Inside the restaurant the familiar smells of bacon and waffles engulfed him. He wasn't particularly hungry, but since they would end up splitting the bill evenly four ways he figured he might as well get something for his money. He realized too late that, by being the last to enter, he would end up on the outside of the booth, away from the window. *Shit.* They all slid in, and Jesse passed menus out. Alan stared at his glumly.

"Their problem is they got no bullpen. They should never have traded Ortiz away—he was the only decent pitcher they had, him and Jefferson."

More sports talk. Alan hated sports. He tuned them out, focused on the menu.

"Hey guys, how y'all doin' today?"

Alan looked up at the waitress. She had brown hair; Alan preferred blondes. Still, she was slim, not bad looking except for too much makeup—typical of women down here in Alabama. He looked back down at his menu while the other guys flirted with her.

"Hey Denice, what's shakin'?" Bobby said, as if he knew her. They must have had her as a waitress before. Alan looked up at her again and decided her face was a little familiar. And she was, in fact, pretty good-looking, for a brunette. *Why didn't I notice her before?* When he ordered, Alan made a point of catching her eyes, and he got a smile in return before she left for the kitchen, leaving him wondering.

The other guys didn't seem to notice, and he wondered if he were reading too much into it, but when she returned with their food a several minutes later, she seemed to set his plate down a little more carefully, accompanying it with a quiet "here you go" as she did, and another quick little smile.

While he ate his breakfast, and the others talked about freakin' NASCAR of all things, his thoughts stayed on her. When she came back to check on them, she looked directly at Alan when she asked if everything was all right and if she could bring them anything else. Alan gave her his smile before replying "everything's great, thanks," and got a warm back-at-ya smile in return. He'd learned a long time ago he could rely on the smile to open doors and legs.

Soon it was time to go. Not wanting to give the guys a show, he walked out with them, but then pretended to want the bathroom before they went to the job site, and went back inside. He met Denice coming over to clear the table. "Hey, listen, my name's Alan," he said, giving her the smile again.

"I'm Denice," she said, smiling awkwardly since he obviously already knew her name.

This moment of social weirdness only made him want her more. "Maybe we could go out sometime..."

"I'd like that," she said. She pulled out her order pad and jotted a phone number on it. "Call me, OK?"

Eleven

He had no idea then that he'd still be looking at her face almost three years later. That had never happened before. As a rule, he didn't get attached to anyone. Normally he couldn't stand being close to anyone for more than a couple weeks. But Denice broke that rule. He's not sure what makes her so different, but somehow, she is. Somehow, he has only grown closer to her. He can't even remember them ever arguing, not really.

Still watching her face, he goes back to making their plans for the morning. He'll wake her up at—he turns and looks back over his shoulder at the clock. It's six-thirty-three now. He'll let her sleep until seven, then he'll wake her up and they can have sex, work up an appetite.

Then breakfast. They should eat out—all three meals today. They'll have breakfast at…Joseph's. That's a good place. They'll have eggs and…pancakes, but no bacon. Well, maybe Denice can have bacon, if she wants. It's sort of a holiday after all, so she can decide if she wants bacon or not.

Then they'll come home and watch a movie on the VCR. He let Denice rent one of those romantic chick flicks she likes sometimes. Usually her taste in movies is better than that, but sometimes… They won't watch that this morning; she can watch that on her own. Today they'll watch a James Bond movie. Alan likes Bond movies. Bond is always in charge, always ready for anything. *The coolest.* That'll put him in a good frame of mind for tonight.

Alan continues planning the rest of their day, but soon finds himself reminiscing again.

* * *

Dothan, Alabama
May 1992

"Ah don't want you to think Ah normally give out my phone number to customers at work, or to anyone, for that matter." Her voice was pure rural Alabama, all the long I's coming out as ah's, the other vowels drawn out, the cadence leisurely and the syllables heavily inflected.

Her dialect was nothing new to Alan. He'd been living in Alabama for almost four years, and what used to be interesting and even amusing had long since become ordinary and even grating at times. But it was different with Denice. As he listened to her voice on the phone, he kept seeing her smiling at him in the restaurant, kept remembering the way her uniform blouse hugged her breasts, which were on the small side, but seemed at least to be perky, though it was hard to have any idea what they would be like without the support of a bra. "So why'd you give *me* your number?"

"Ah don't *know*," she said through a smile he could hear, and really drawing out the last word. "You just seem different—Ah don't know. You're quiet, lahk you know where you're at and don't need to tell everyone else. Ah lahk a guy who's sure of himself. What about you?"

"I'm not into guys," he said, grinning.

She laughed. *"No!* You know what Ah *mean!* You make a habit of asking out waitresses?"

He considered this for a moment, then answered truthfully, "No, I don't. There's something about your smile—I really like your smile."

"Thank you," she said, the smile still very apparent in her voice.

"So, listen, I don't like talking on the phone. How 'bout we meet for dinner tomorrow night?"

The next night he picked her up from in front of her apartment building in his Ford Econoline van. Alan would have preferred to have still had the repo'd Camaro he'd bought at auction, but he'd traded it in for the van when he started working for the contractor. The van was better for driving onto construction sites, and he had plenty of room for his tools inside. Denice didn't mind; she actually seemed impressed with the vehicle.

They went to a little Italian place—not a chain, but an actual, semi-swank place with checkered tablecloths and a little candle in a metal and glass lamp on each table. There was even a separate menu for wine, though fortunately the people here knew not to take the whole snooty thing too far. For example, Alan didn't have to wear a jacket and tie—he probably could have even worn jeans, but he had on his good pants, the tan Dockers, and, still clean and pressed from the cleaners, a shirt with a buttoned-down collar. This place had worked out for Alan before—he'd banged two other women after dinner here.

They spent some time looking over their menus. Alan was just deciding on the chicken parmesan when Denice closed her menu. He looked up. "You know what you want?"

She smiled and shook her head. "Ah can't decide. Whah don't you order for me?"

Alan raised his eyebrows. "Yeah? Well, what do you like?"

She shrugged. "Ah don't know—Ah don't eat out much. You pick for me."

He looked at her for another beat. It wasn't that he didn't like the idea, but this had never happened to Alan before. He grinned a little—not a perplexed or fake polite one, but a real smile. He dropped his gaze to his menu again, considering the options. He'd chosen the chicken over the veal because of the price, but veal seemed like a good idea for her.

The waiter came over. "Are y'all ready to order?" he asked, glancing at Alan, then looking at Denice, expecting her to speak first.

Alan spoke up. "She'll have the veal parmesan, with angel hair on the side."

The waiter looked at Alan, then down at his pad, nodding. "That comes with a salad—what kind of dressing would you like?" he asked, then looked up at Denice expectantly.

Alan looked at her. She looked back at him and raised her eyebrows slightly. "She'll have Italian dressing."

The waiter looked back at Alan, a slightly bemused expression on his face, then jotted a note on the pad before looking at Alan again. "And for you, sir?"

"I'll have the chicken parmesan with linguine on the side, and ranch dressing on my salad. And bring us a bottle of the house red wine." Alan didn't know anything about wine, but after a slightly awkward moment the first time he'd come here with a woman, he'd learned to simply ask for a bottle of the house wine and be done with it.

The waiter nodded once more, finished the note on his pad, and headed for the kitchen.

"So…you and those guys you come in with sometahms—y'all build houses, raht?"

"Yeah, sometimes." Alan shrugged. "Mostly we do work on houses that are already built—new roofs, decks, siding—stuff like that. That's most of our work."

"Do you like it?"

Alan shrugged again. "The work's OK, but I want to have my own business eventually."

She nodded, and there was a sparkle in her eyes as she said, "Ah knew it. Ah figured you'd want to be in charge. You don't really much lahk those guys you work with, do you?"

"What makes you say that?"

She tilted her head to the side and looked down. "Ah can tell. Ah see a lot of folks come through the Waffle House, and Ah got so Ah can tell what's what with most of 'em. Plus, you don't talk much—they're all chattin' away about sports or whatever, and you're in your own world."

A small laugh escaped Alan's mouth, surprising him. He looked down then up again, and laughed more openly. It felt good. "You're right about that—really perceptive. I guess I'm not what you'd call a people person."

"Yeah, me neither. Ah got a couple girlfriends, but, you know, they're OK sometahms, but mostly Ah just hang out with them when Ah don't have anything better to do, you know?"

"Yeah, I keep to myself most of the time—when I'm not working, I mean. I like to read sometimes, maybe watch TV. I like movies a lot—that's mostly what I read about—movies."

"Ah really lahk movies too. What kahnd do you lahk?"

* * *

Staring at the purple sheet hanging in front of the wall, Alan remembers at first, when she told him horror movies were her favorites, he thought she was just trying to make it look like they had stuff in common. But she could describe and go on about her favorite scenes just as well as he could his. She was partial to stuff from the eighties, like the *Friday the 13th* films. Alan favored older, classic flicks from the early seventies like *Texas Chainsaw Massacre* and *The Hills Have Eyes*, but he'd seen the Jason movies too and knew she wasn't faking her familiarity with or love of them.

Alan remembers all this in the minutes before seven a.m., before it is time for him to wake her. He rolls toward her and props himself up on his right elbow. Watching her and waiting, he remembers the rest of their first date.

* * *

Dothan, Alabama
May 1992

As they left the restaurant and were walking toward his van, Alan considered his chances. His main interest in dating was sex, but sometimes inviting a woman back to his place didn't go over so well on a first date, unless the woman was drunk, which Denice probably was not. They'd finished the bottle of wine, and she seemed a little happy, but still in control of herself. Anyway, trying for sex on the first date could backfire and permanently kill any chances he had with her. Plus, he was actually enjoying her company, and didn't have to fake interest in the dinner conversation like he usually did, so he definitely didn't want to blow this.

But then, as they neared the van, Denice veered close to him and hugged his right arm, pressing her breasts against his elbow. "Thanks for dinner, Alan; Ah'm having a great tahm with you."

"Me too. So, uh, would you like to come back to my place? Hang out together some more?"

"Ah dunno—you tell me. Would Ah?" she asked, giving his arm a squeeze and looking up at him.

He looked over at her and smiled.

"Tell me. Please?"

They stopped walking and he looked down at her, met the eyes that were looking up at him imploringly. "You're coming home with me."

She smiled broadly. "Yes sir!"

At the time he was living in a studio apartment in what passed for downtown Dothan. It wasn't much, but he kept it clean and had given it a fresh coat of paint and done some minor repairs, so it looked fine. When they got inside he locked the door and turned to see her standing a few feet away, not looking at his place, but keeping her eyes cast down toward the floor. He followed her gaze, but saw nothing remarkable about the low-pile carpeting. "What?" he asked.

She turned her head and, pushing her dark hair back behind her ear, said quietly, almost too softly for him to hear, "You can do whatever you want to me."

He felt his cock almost instantly go hard against the inside of his pants.

What he wanted was rough—that's his preference, but he was not as rough as usual. When she let him choose her meal, he felt almost protective of her, wanted to do right by her, and it was the same now. She trusted him, gave him control, and that made him feel, for lack of a better word, *responsible*.

Twelve

"Time to wake up, baby," he says, gripping her shoulder firmly, but not too hard.

Her eyes pop open, then shift to look at him. As happens most mornings when he wakes her, she smiles when their eyes meet.

"We got a big day ahead of us."

Her grin broadens. "Ah know," she says, her voice still sleepy.

Alan releases her shoulder and Denice rolls away from him and gets out of their bed, the sheet and light blanket slipping from her naked body as she stands. She's still in good shape: her back tapers subtly to her waist, then her hips flare dramatically, complementing her full, round, firm ass. He watches it move as she walks to the bathroom—a little jiggle and a lot of back and forth.

She doesn't close the bathroom door, of course, and he watches as she sits and pees. She does this unselfconsciously, paying no attention to him, or anything really. She simply sits, focused on the middle distance, her face neutral. When she's done, she tears off some toilet paper and wipes between her legs. This strikes him as amusing since she's about to get in the shower.

When the shower begins to run, he pushes aside the bedclothes and gets out of bed. He feels the weight pressing lightly against the front of his boxer shorts as he walks toward the bathroom, where he strips off his underwear. Denice is standing beside the tub, testing the water temperature with her hand. While he adds his urine to hers, he looks down at her round, perky ass standing there under the entwined blue, green and red vines and thorns tattooed across her lower back.   He flushes.   Although he has just relieved himself, his erection remains undiminished at half mast.   He turns to see Denice looking over her shoulder at him, her eyes smiling.   She turns from him, pushes back the shower curtain, and steps in.   He follows her, and as he enters she smiles while she backs up to make room for him.   Her eyes flick down to his crotch, and even before she brings her eyes up again to meet his, her smile is broadening.   When their gazes meet he reaches out with both hands and grasps her hips, pulling her toward him.   Their open mouths meet and he kisses her hard, their teeth clicking together briefly as he drives his tongue deep into her mouth and encircles her body with his arms.   He feels her breasts' yielding pressure against the bottom of his rib cage, and runs his hands over the water-slick skin of her back before dropping them to her butt and pinching her hard.

She yelps, then smiles at him as she grinds her body against his.   "You're so *rough*.   Hurt me some more."

He bites the skin over the muscle running from the left side of her neck down to her shoulder.   As he does, he feels her fingernails dig into his back, scratching shallow furrows in his skin.   The resulting burning sensation intensifies his senses: the smell of her clean, wet skin, the slippery feel of it against his body, the sound of her little gasps and moans.

They've had sex in the shower before, but this morning he just wants a blow job—there'll be time for the other stuff tonight.   She seems to intuit this, and gradually works her way down his body, licking here and biting there until she's on her knees and gazing up at him past his fully erect cock.

Seeing her at his feet in this position of subordination always reminds him just how devoted she is.

* * *

Dothan, Alabama
June 1992

The lamp on the bedside table cast a soft, slightly yellow glow through its shade. Alan didn't want spotlights, but he did like to see what he was doing, and who he was doing it to. Especially when she had as nice an ass as Denice did. He also liked her tattoo—about a six- or eight-inch length of blue, red, and green design, all twists and curls and points, like the scrollwork on some old sword or piece of furniture, or maybe thorn-covered vines, running across her lower back, just above her ass. He traced the design with his eyes to distract himself and avoid coming too soon.

Looking at her ass as he fucked her, he decided tonight was the night. They'd been seeing each other for almost a month, and had had a lot of sex already, but, maybe because he could imagine himself spending time with her, *being* with her for more than a few weeks, he'd been more restrained than usual. This despite the fact that every time they began to lead in to sex, she told him straight out: "You can do whatever you want to me." Tonight, he decided, he would find out if she meant it. He pulled out before he reached the point of no return.

She was still breathing hard, her dark hair partly obscuring her face, her mouth open, as she turned to look back at him. She said nothing; she only watched him attentively. He opened the drawer in the bedside table someone down the street had put out with their trash. The table was small, shiny, and made of wood, with a small glass knob on its lone drawer and a couple not so obvious cigarette scorch marks on top. It was still fine as furniture, and Alan had carried it home to his apartment without hesitation. Now he took from the drawer the tube of KY jelly he'd put there a week ago, anticipating this moment. He removed the cap and, holding the index and middle fingers on his right hand extended and pressed together, he squeezed a generous dollop onto them. The gel felt very cool and wet. Without waiting for it to warm, he pressed the lubricant-bearing fingers between her spread butt cheeks.

Denice let out a barely audible gasp as the chill, wet lubricant hit her hot flesh.

Alan worked the lube in, insinuating his index finger, and then his middle finger too, into her rectum, gradually getting the sphincter to relax, and lubricating the passage thoroughly. This too was a departure from his usual way with women. He found lubricant was more or less essential for anal, but usually he didn't take so much time preparing the woman.

He could tell this kind of penetration was new to her; he felt the tension in her, and thought he heard her swallow hard a couple times, but she said nothing, and she did eventually loosen up. When his fingers had penetrated their entire length, he withdrew them. They were a little dirty, and there was some smell, but that was part of the appeal, though he couldn't say exactly why.

His cock was still fully hardened; even this prep work was a major turn-on for him. He now pushed the head of his dick into the gapped hole, felt the sphincter tighten around him and then relax slightly again. He slid himself the rest of the way in.

It took all his concentration and every trick he could think of to distract himself from coming, so intense, and so anticipated, was this act. Control was essential, though, because he didn't want to come yet. He had one more test for her after this. He fucked her ass for what seemed a long time, but was probably only a minute or two. Then, still in control, and still pre-orgasm, he withdrew and got off the bed. Like his fingers, his penis was a little soiled, and there was some smell of shit.

Denice looked back at him again. She knew—apparently instinctively—she knew better than to question him. Instead, she looked back, her expression a mix of passion, expectation, and eagerness.

"Come here," Alan said, taking another step back away from the bed.

Denice, still on all fours, backed off the bed, then turned to face him.

"On your knees. I want you to suck me clean."

Without hesitation; in fact, he thought he noticed a trace of a smile once she heard what he wanted, she dropped to her knees and grasped his shaft with her right hand while touching herself with her left. He watched as, eyes still locked with his, she opened her mouth and moved her head forward.

She's going to do it. "Stop."

She obeyed instantly, the head of his penis actually inside her open mouth, but she did not close on it.

He was suddenly, bizarrely, reminded of a Bible story he'd been told as a child, about how a man (*Abraham?*) was told by God to kill his son. Then, at the last possible moment before he slit the boy's throat, God told him to stop. The man had proven his loyalty, and earned God's favor. "Get back on the bed, like you were a minute ago, you slutty angel." He knew then he'd found the perfect woman, and more than ever before, he wanted to do right by her. He'd never felt this way about anyone or anything else, but she was his, and he wanted to do right by her.

Thirteen

After she sucks him off, they soap up and take turns washing each other's back. She finishes rinsing and steps out of the tub. Before closing the curtain and finishing his shower, Alan watches as Denice, standing on the small rug in the center of the tiled floor, bends forward and begins toweling dry her long hair. Seeing her naked, wet, and preoccupied, he starts to smile.

Suddenly, out of nowhere, a thought of her father appears in his head. He closes his eyes and the shower curtain.

* * *

Dothan, Alabama
November 1992

Alan and Denice watched Leatherface doing his chainsaw dance at the end of *The Texas Chainsaw Massacre*. Alan, smiling and thinking how he never got tired of this movie, glanced over at Denice. Her eyes were wide, and there was a faint smile on her lips. Her eyes shifted to look at him and her smile broadened.

"*Damn!* That was *way* scary! She's just lucky that truck came along, or she'd have been up on the hook in their kitchen!"

"Did you like it?"

"Yeah, that was *way* cool." She got up and turned off the VCR and the television, leaving them only with the light of the low-watt bulb in the ceiling fixture. She rejoined Alan on his battered couch, snuggling up close and pulling his arm around her.

He cupped her breast and smelled the shampoo on her hair.

"So, Alan, do you have Christmas off?"

"Uh, yeah—you?"

"Ah think so—Ah think the Waffle House is closed on Christmas Day. How 'bout the day before Christmas?"

"I don't know—I guess I could take it off—why? Hey, we're not going to have to do some weird family get-together for Christmas, are we?"

Denice let out a short burst of laughter, but it didn't sound like her usual laugh. "*Hell* no!" More off-key laughter. "That'd be the day. Ah hope Ah never see them again."

"Yeah, I feel the same way about mine. Families are for shit. The only thing I remember about my dad was him taking off his belt so he could hit me with it."

"That sucks—parents suck. Did he hit you a lot?"

He tilted his head and frowned dismissively. "I don't remember how often it happened. When I was six he went out for a pack of smokes and for all I know he's still looking for them."

"What do you mean?"

"He never came back—just disappeared. We never heard from him again. I think he just got tired of us. Good riddance as far as I'm concerned. My mom wasn't much better, but she didn't hit me much."

"Ah wish *mah* dad had left."

"He hit you?" Alan asked, feeling a spark of anger ignite in the back of his head.

"Ah wish," she said quietly.

"What?"

He felt her go tense, and she said nothing. The spark burst into flame. "What did you say? What did he do to you?"

"Shit, Alan, Ah—"

"Denice."

She was quiet.

Alan moved his hand from her breast up to her shoulder and squeezed a little—not enough to hurt, but he wasn't going to tell her again.

"Mah dad, he...he used to...do things with me, lahk, things a father shouldn't do with his daughter."

Alan didn't know what to say.

"Alan, you're—you're hurting me."

He realized his hand had tightened down hard on her shoulder and immediately relaxed his grip. He got up, crossed the room to the table. "Let's go." He picked up his keys and looked down at her as he headed for the door. There were tears in her eyes, and that just made him want to get the daughter-fucker even more.

She got up and left his apartment with him, waited on the landing while he locked the door, then followed him down the stairs. Alan held the passenger door on the van for her while she got in. He circled around the front and got in on his side, put the key in the ignition, and started the engine. "So how do I get there?"

She looked over at him.

He glanced back at her, then looked out the passenger side window at the mirror to check the position of the car parked behind them. "Which way?" He backed the van up, put it in drive, and started turning the wheel to pull out onto the street.

"To—to my apartment?"

"What?" He put his foot back on the brake. "What? No, to where your parents live—why would we be going to your apartment?"

She blinked, and a tear rolled down her cheek. "Ah—Ah thought you—you didn't want to be with me anymore on account of what he did."

He looked at her hard. "Huh? Aw, no way, Denice! No! We're gonna go fix your dad."

A slightly hysterical smile spread across her face, and her shoulders began shaking. At first he thought she was crying, but then realized she was laughing.

"What are you laughing about?!" he said, starting to feel confused and more angry.

"It's just that he beat you to it—he's been dead for somethin' lahk—Ah dunno—eight years now." She got the laughter under control, stopped it. "Doctors said it was his liver—too much booze."

Alan didn't think he should, but he felt stupid for some reason. "Well, why didn't you say somethin'?"

The smile dropped from her face. "Ah'm sorry, honey. Ah didn't know what you were fixin' to do. Ah—Ah thought you were breakin' up with me, takin' me home."

"Why would I want to do that? Never mind. Shit. OK, get out."

Denice exited the van and stood on the sidewalk while he repositioned the vehicle back in the center of the parking space and shut off the engine. He put his hand on the door handle, then it occurred to him. "Hey!" He rolled down his window and shouted to Denice, on the other side. "Hey, what about your mom?"

"What?"

"Get back in!" he said, feeling really exasperated now. He leaned over and unlocked her door again.

Denice climbed in and closed the door, then looked over at him expectantly.

Staring out the windshield and keeping both hands on the wheel, he took a deep breath then said calmly and quietly: "What about your mom? Where was she when all this was going on?"

"At home with us."

"And she let him do that to you?"

"There wasn't anything she could do!"

"She could have taken you out of there."

Denice shook her head. "No—she's…she's weak. She—Ah don't know that she *did* know what he was doing."

That last part sounded unconvincing. "Oh, c'mon—don't bullshit me, Denice!   She must've!   How could she not? We're gonna get her. How do I get there?" He reached up to turn the key again, but Denice grabbed his wrist and held it midway on its journey, surprising him.

"Alan, she's not worth it! Please! Please, honey—she's shit, she probably convinced herself it wasn't happening, distracted herself by ignoring me and focusing all her attention on Jeremy."

"Who's Jeremy?"

"Mah little brother. He was her favorite. She barely noticed me, so it's not so crazy to think she didn't know what was happening." Denice swallowed. "And even if she did, forget her—if we do something to her, the police'll figure it out, and she's not worth going to jail."

He looked at her, thinking it over.

"Please, Alan," she said softly, "Ah'm begging you. Please, let's just go back up to your apartment. Please."

* * *

Now, knowing what screw-ups the cops are, it doesn't seem so likely they would have been caught. He'd brought it up once more after that first time, but Denice pointed out she might not even be able to find them again anyway, since she hadn't had any contact with her mom or her little brother for about eight years. So who knows where they are now. Still, he'd like to make them pay, maybe set them on fire like that cat he torched, only without killing them first.

Fourteen

Kansas City, Missouri
March 1980

Alan's stomach was in knots. At first he'd thought maybe he was just hungry, but three slices of take-out pizza hadn't helped. It was definitely nerves making him feel this way. He looked over at Judy, her big, frizzy dark blonde hair mostly obscuring her face as she sat cross-legged on the couch, her head bent over the history book open in her lap. The hair didn't hide the thick, black plastic frames of her glasses, and he focused on them. *She's just a nerd—nothing to be afraid of there. You can do anything and she won't know if you're doing it right or not.* He'd only kissed her a couple times before this; the last time had included tongue and she'd let him squeeze one of her little boobs, but tonight he was going all the way for the first time. He put his hand in his pocket and touched the foil-wrapped circle of the condom.

Well, shit. He realized he should get going. His mom and sisters were all in Independence tonight for Missy's Junior Miss Pageant or whatever—they wouldn't be back until midnight or later—but he wasn't sure how much time he'd need. Maybe she'd want to screw for hours. It suddenly occurred to him maybe the one condom wouldn't be enough. *Maybe I can just keep it on until she has to go home.* Fortunately, her parents were pretty cool and didn't care when she came home, and even let her borrow their car so she could drive herself home.

He realized she was looking at him, her brown eyes magnified by the thick lenses in her glasses. "Earth to Alan, come in please," she said in her somewhat nasal voice. "You're not even listening to me."

"What?"

"The debate over the structure of Congress—I just summarized the whole thing and how they solved it, and you weren't even listening."

"You mean the Connecticut Compromise?" Mild surprise registered on her face, telling him he was right. "See, I'm listening. Look, let's take a break, OK?" he said, closing his notebook and putting it on the coffee table, pushing the pictures of his sisters out of the way and actually knocking a couple onto the floor. They were both sitting on the threadbare cushions of the sofa; now he slid closer.

As he did this, Judy looked back down at the open textbook with the little "what are you doing?" smile on her face. She wasn't really what anyone would call hot, but the smile definitely made her cute. He put his arms around her waist. "C'mon, break time," he said, hiding his nervousness. She looked up at him through the nerdy glasses, a more mischievous smile on her face now.

"Um—take off your glasses."

The smile faltered for a second, but she did as he asked, placing the specs on the coffee table and then smiling more broadly. Her eyes looked strangely small without the glasses, but removing the glasses was probably an improvement. He leaned in a little closer like he'd done the last time and, like the last time, she closed her eyes and met him with her mouth open.

As they kissed, he felt a thrilling quiver move through his stomach, and he hugged her tighter before moving his left hand up to cup a breast. He began kneading it, feeling its soft firmness—

"Ow—take it easy!" she said, pulling back and putting her hand over his on her breast. "Not so hard."

He felt embarrassed and irritated at the same time. He loosened his grip and began caressing more lightly, and she moved in to kiss again. Kissing was fun, but it wasn't anything new, so he moved his free hand down from her breast, over her side, then down to the tight jeans covering her right thigh. *So far, so good.* A few more seconds and his hand was on the inside of her left leg and moving up to her crotch.

She stopped kissing and pulled back. "What are you doing?"

"What?" he asked, putting a note of protest in the word.

"Exactly: what are you doing?" She grabbed his hand and shoved it back to the outside of her right leg.

He left it there.

After a few seconds of studying his face, she closed her eyes and they started kissing again.

A few more seconds and he tried again.

"Alan! Knock it off!"

"Oh come on—what's the big deal?"

"The big deal is I don't want your hand there," she said and grabbed his hand more roughly than before and shoved it toward him.

Something clicked over in his head. Although he knew it wouldn't work, he forced his hand back where it was, hard against the crotch of her jeans, only a couple layers of fabric between his fingers and her pussy.

"That's it! I'm outta here!" she said, pushing his hand away and standing up. She grabbed her books and glasses off the coffee table and headed for the front door, taking her coat from the back of the couch as she went.

"What?! No way! C'mon!" he shouted, leaping up from the couch and running after her. He reached her at the front door and put a restraining hand on her shoulder.

"Get away from me, you perv!" she shouted, shrugging away violently. She started to open the door, but he slammed it shut again.

"Alan! What the hell are you *doing*?!"

"Just sit back down on the couch!"

"No, I'm leaving!" She opened the door again.

He slammed it shut again. "No you're not!" Suddenly his left shin erupted in pain and he staggered back a step, as much from the shock as from the sharp hurt. He regained his composure in the next moment, but by then she was out the door, leaping over the three steps to the front walk. He bolted out after her.

At the door to her parents' car she turned, key in hand, to confront him. "Alan, if you touch me again, I swear I'll scream so loud the whole street will turn out to see!"

He grabbed her arm anyway, intending to pull her back to the house.

"EEEEEEEEEEKKKKK! Get your hands OFF ME!" The scream was piercing and actually hurt his ears.

Instinctively, Alan let go and turned to go back inside, gesturing violently as he went. "Fine BITCH! You UGLY BITCH!" He heard the car door open and shut. The engine started just before he slammed the front door closed.

Inside, Alan stomped through the living room and ended up in the kitchen. Not sure why he'd come in here, he grabbed the back of the nearest chair and thrust it to the floor. The back of the chair bounced off the linoleum, and the legs clattered against his legs. He kicked at them, got his leg tangled, and almost went over backward before his hand found the table top and he was able to steady himself. His fingers curled around the edge of the table, and for a second or two he seriously considered demolishing the entire kitchen.

But he didn't want to hear his mother and sisters pissing and moaning about it, and he definitely didn't want to be asked why he'd done it. Breathing hard, keeping himself from exploding, he looked around the room. His eyes fell on a disposable Bic lighter near the middle of the kitchen table— his mother's, since no one else smoked, though he knew Missy had tried it a couple times because he smelled it on her. Alan took the lighter and, clenching it in his fist, he stormed out of the apartment, grabbing his keys off the table by the door as he went and letting the door lock behind him.

Like Judy, he vaulted from the porch over the three front steps. He hit the short front walk running and kept going, without any specific destination in mind, until he found himself behind a strip mall. Here he found what he'd been looking for: trash cans and stacks of discarded newspaper from the coffee shop there. Pocketing the lighter and his keys, he grabbed several sheets of newsprint, violently balled them up, and threw them into a half-filled battered metal garbage can. He grabbed another section of newspaper, unfolded it, and balled up several more sheets, allowing the other sheets in the section to drift around him like oversized autumn leaves. He continued this process until the can was filled above its rim with loosely crumpled paper.

He noticed his hand was shaking slightly from the adrenalin as he held the lighter out and spun the wheel. The flame appeared on the first try, but it was small. He allowed the flame to go out, used his thumb nail to rotate the flame size control as high as it would go, then spun the wheel again. This time the flame stood a good three inches high. Keeping the fuel tab depressed, he touched the tongue of flame to a mangled edge of paper, which immediately caught fire. The flames spread and soon the can was roaring with the conflagration, and he could feel the intense heat of it on his face.

Something brushed against his leg. He jumped back and looked down.

A cat, light gray in the dim illumination cast by the security lights over the doors and the blaze in the trash barrel, looked up at him and meowed, then stepped closer and rubbed itself against his leg. Something about the way it moved—the quiet smoothness as it walked back and forth—reminded him of Judy. Despite her awkward appearance, she did have a certain grace about her, a quiet confidence he thought he recognized in the cat. Alan squatted down to get a closer look. The cat paused in its motion, watching him as he came closer to its level. It meowed again and drew nearer to sniff at where Alan's jeans stretched over his knee. Slowly, cautiously so as to not alarm the animal, he reached out and touched its head with his fingers. It reacted by pushing its head into his touch, apparently expecting to be scratched behind the ears. Instead, Alan drew his hand along the top of the head and down the back of the neck, following the lay of the fur there. The cat wore no collar, but its fur was sleek to the touch. He repeated this motion, but this time he ended by grabbing the loose skin behind the cat's shoulders, as he'd seen an animal control officer do once when capturing a stray cat years ago back in Topeka.

The cat was lighter than he'd expected, and he hoisted it easily with one hand, amused by the startled yowl he got in response. Holding it out at almost the full length of his arm, as the animal control officer had done, he was safe from its flailing clawed paws and hissing, toothy mouth. "Fuck you Judy you fuckin' bitch," he said, then turned, hauled back, and slammed the cat head first into the brick wall. "Fuck you, you cunt!" he shouted, and slammed the now limp bag of bones into the wall again. He imagined her face bloody and broken as he slammed her into the bricks, her nose flattened, her lips cut, her forehead skinned, and blood everywhere. He continued this, cursing so hard he saw flecks of spittle flying out in front of his hot, swollen face.

After a while he realized he was hitting his own hand as much as the limp bundle of fur, so smashed was the cat's head and neck. Disgusted, he threw the body into the smoldering interior of the trash can, piled more crumpled paper on top, and restarted the blaze. "Burn you fucking cunt."

* * *

That night was the only time he'd ever harmed an animal. It wasn't that he regretted it; each of the other two times he'd broken up with girls in high school he'd gone looking for a cat to vent his frustrations on, but never again found one when his rage was boiling.   Looking back on it now, he sees how pathetic that was.   After all, the cat had nothing to do with Judy, even if it did sort of remind him of her.   The animal had just crossed his path at the wrong time, and he'd done to it what he'd wanted to do to the bitch but hadn't because he was afraid he'd get caught and punished.   He wouldn't kill a cat that way now.   He doesn't particularly like cats, or any animals, really; he doesn't get the whole pet thing.   But animals are innocent—they can't help the way they are. People are different.   Even kids, once they get to a certain age, know right from wrong, but do bad things anyway.   The adults are even worse.   Fathers beat and rape their kids.   Mothers make their sons feel like shit or look the other way while the fathers do bad stuff.   Alan has no sympathy for people, but attacking animals for fun, or just because you're pissed off, is wrong.   It's loser kid stuff, and he's put all that behind him. He was weak then—a different person from the man he is now, a man who is in charge of his life, who in another couple years will have his own contracting business, and who has a good woman giving him sex whenever he wants it.

Fifteen

They have the windows down as Alan drives the van through central Dothan. It's clear and the air, while cool, has a certain edge to it. Maybe it's a smell or a kind of pressure on his face and neck—he can't pin it down, but it portends a very warm day, probably in the mid eighties. On the hot side for April, and good because it means he and Denice will be able to lay out on the beach down in PC this afternoon, get a little sun. It'll be their first trip to the beach this year. *Today just keeps getting better and better.*

Today is special—a fun day, and dining out for all three meals is part of that. Usually they don't eat out all that much. Soon after Alan got involved with Denice, he stopped going to breakfast with the crew. He didn't like to see Denice waitressing, bringing meals to all those people, dealing with their bullshit. Now he has breakfast at home with Denice. And he's pretty much always packed a lunch. Denice used to get a couple meals at the Waffle House when she still worked there, but he had her quit that right after she got her GED, and now she works in the office of the collection agency he used to do repo work for. That's a better job for her, and it'll pay better too when she gets a raise, which Terry will no doubt give her after she finishes her first year with them.

There are plenty of parking spaces on the street, and Alan is able to drive right into one without having to parallel park. He kills the engine, gets out, and walks around to Denice's side. As always, he opens the car door for her. He opens the door to the restaurant too.

They've been to Joseph's before. It's a clean, comfortable little place, with lots of light pouring in through the big windows in front. The walls are plain white, but there are always lots of paintings hanging up, most of which are for sale by local artists. Alan isn't really into art, but he thinks the paintings in here look good. They're mostly brightly colored, and mostly abstract. The trouble with paintings that try to show things in the world is they're just poor imitations. If he wants to see a house or a tree, he's not going to look at someone's attempt to draw it; he's going to look at the real thing or, if he has to, a photograph. If someone's going to make a picture, then he should make it of something interesting, something people don't normally see. Abstract paintings are good because they show what's in the artist's head.

The small sign just inside the door says "Please Wait To Be Seated." Alan looks around, sees several openings, and decides they should sit at a table on the left side of the room, under a painting with broad, bright slashes of red and orange paint.

There's a flapping and rustling sound, and Alan turns his head to see a waiter walking by with a large sheet of paper, which he places over a table as a tablecloth. Alan remembers this is the place where they cover the tables with paper and give you crayons so you can draw and write. *This day just keeps getting better and better.*

"Hi, just the two of you?" The person asking is a young woman—fairly attractive, for a brunette, though not so much as Denice when she had dark hair. This woman does have interesting blue-gray eyes, though—very pale, like on summer days around here when the sun bleaches most of the blue out of the sky.

"That's right," Alan nods and smiles, warming up for later.

"Smoking or non-?"

Alan had forgotten about this. He glances over at the table under the painting he likes, and the tables around it, and sees no ashtrays or smoke. *Of course—things are going my way today.* He looks back at Gray Eyes. "Non-. We'd actually like to sit under that red and orange painting over there."

"Um," she says, looking over at the painting and table in question, and seeming a little confused. "Uh, sure, OK, right this way, please." She walks over to the table and hands them menus as they take their seats.

Alan sits with his back to the restaurant so he can look at the painting over Denice's head. He really likes the bold slashes of bright color.

Without opening it, Denice puts her menu down to the side and picks up a mug sitting in the middle of the table. "Hmm—not a big selection, but we have crayons," she says, peering down into the container.

"Spill them out—see what colors we have."

The crayons are somewhat battered and worn-down, but still serviceable. Alan returns his attention to the menu. They'll have two eggs each, scrambled, a short stack of pancakes each. And what the hell, an order of bacon for each of them too. He closes the menu and puts it down.

"Brown, red, blue, silver, and burnt sienna, whatever that is," she says, her hands bracketing the wax sticks, which she's arranged neatly in a row.

"Coffee?" a young man—probably about twenty, asks, proffering a pitcher of black liquid.

"No thanks," Alan says.

The waiter looks at Denice, who just shakes her head and looks at Alan.

"I'll have a glass of tomato juice, and she'll have pineapple juice—do you have pineapple juice?"

"Uh, yes, um-hmm."

"OK, pineapple for her, tomato for me. And we'll each have two eggs, scrambled, short stack of pancakes, and side of bacon."

"All right, same for you ma'am?" he asks, looking at Denice, who keeps her eyes on Alan, a small, closed-mouth smile on her lips.

"That's right, she'll have the same as me," Alan says, putting a slight edge in his voice.

The waiter looks back at Alan, then down at his pad. "All right." His tone rises on the second word.

"What's that mean?" Alan asks quickly, interrupting him. The edge in Alan's voice is sharper now, and it causes the waiter to pause momentarily as he's picking up the menus.

"Uh, what?"

"Your tone—you sounded as if you'd just heard something that sounded crazy. Or did I misinterpret that?"

The young man looks surprised and uncomfortable. "I—no—I mean, no, I was just saying that, OK, everything's good, and I'll just go and get your juices."

Alan shrugs and smiles broadly, and deliberately puts a casual, friendly sound in his voice. "Oh, OK, just wondering. Thanks."

The young man smiles, nervously, and his shoulders drop noticeably as the tension suddenly leaves his body. "Sure, be right back with your juices."

After he leaves, Alan looks across at Denice and smiles. "What a smartass."

"More like a *dumb*ass—he had no *ahdea* how to react to you. People suck."

He smiles big at that and lays his forearms on the table, his hands palms up and reaching out to her. She runs the tips of her long fingers over the shiny, hard calluses he's accumulated from wielding hand tools at work, then settles her slender hands in his. He closes his thumbs and fingers and gazes at the face that's become so familiar to him, but he never tires of looking at. "I'm glad we found each other."

"Me too!" she says, smiling big and showing almost all her upper teeth. She has beautiful teeth; the only thing a little off is her lower jaw sits a little too far forward, and this is more obvious when she smiles. Her chin sticks out, making her look spunky, like she's got a little of the devil in her. Alan has always loved this about her, but it took him a while to figure out what gave her that look.

Neither of them looks up when the waiter returns with the juice and sets the glasses on the table beside their outstretched arms. After he leaves again, Alan gives her hands two quick squeezes, then releases them. He tries his juice, which is thick and rich with flavor, just like tomato juice should be. "How's the pineapple juice?"

"Excellent," she says. "Want some?"

"No thanks." Alan selects the blue and silver crayons and begins rubbing them on the paper table covering. These colors are clean, hard, and cold, and even though the lines are rough as crayon lines always are, the colors make Alan think of polished metal. He makes smooth curves across the table top, pushing items out of the way as he proceeds from left to right. When the waiter returns, Alan notices he is careful to avoid putting the plate on Alan's work. Alan smiles to himself, then puts the crayons back in the middle of the table. He pulls the plate over, picks up his fork, and starts eating. As he expected, the food is great. It's been a while since they came here, but he remembered this as being a good place, even if he couldn't recall exactly what they'd had last time. He looks across at his woman. Denice has already put away most of her eggs and is starting to work on the pancakes, while he's had only a bite of each; she's a fast eater. "How do you like it?" he asks.

She looks up, smiles a big, tight-lipped smile and chews, nodding. She swallows and smiles bigger, still nodding. "Really great. Ah lahk this place."

"Me too." He bites into a crisp strip of bacon and savors the salty, dark crunchiness.

"So," she says, then pauses as she swallows again, "Ah don't know why, but Ah keep thinking about what you told me yesterday, about what you read in *Fangoria*—"

"You mean about the new *Friday the 13th* sequel that's coming out this summer?"

"No, no, although that was cool too. No Ah mean about Leatherface—what's the actor's name, the guy who played Leatherface in *Texas Chainsaw Massacre*?"

Alan smiles. "Oh yeah, Gunnar Hansen. You mean how he wrote that book about the coastal islands?"

"Yeah, Ah mean, how random is that? That the big, hulking guy hanging people on meat hooks and chasing 'em around with a chainsaw wrahts books about nature."

"Surprised me too. I guess that's why they included it in the article, because it's not what you'd expect. According to what he said, though, the gig as Leatherface was the part that was out of character for him. He was going to college at the time to be a writer or nature guy or whatever, and did the movie as a summer job. But because we saw the movie first, we've always thought of him as some big scary killer. Really, though, Leatherface doesn't exist at all outside the movie, so it's not like Leatherface wrote a book. The guy who *played* Leatherface wrote the book, so if you think of it that way, it's not so weird."

"Yeah, well, you're raht, but Ah still think it's pretty funny."

"I think *you're* pretty funny."

Denice rolls her eyes and finishes her breakfast. Alan is still barely halfway through, as usual. She pushes her plate aside and goes back to drawing.

Just then there's a slight commotion as a group of four middle-aged women sit at the table next to Alan and Denice's—just a couple feet away. He glances over and takes in the graying hair, white faces, large jewelry, and conservative dresses. This tells him all he wants to know about them, and he immediately loses interest, but not before accidentally making brief eye contact with one.

"Good morning," she says brightly, and he looks back to see her smiling at him.

He nods and smiles the reliable smile, just for practice. "Hi."

"Oh, good morning," and cheerful "hello's" from each of the other three float over.

Alan says "hi" again and looks over at Denice, who is smiling but keeping her eyes down on her drawing. She looks up and meets his eyes, and her smile gets a little bigger. Alan smiles back, and takes another bite of pancakes. While he chews, he stares at the painting on the wall over Denice's head, then shifts his eyes down to her side of the table. He notices she's drawn a cluster of red blossoms with what must be sienna centers. The flowers are different sizes and shapes, but all with the same colors. "What's with the flowers?" he asks. "You're not wimping out on me, are you?"

She shrugs. "Ah dunno, Ah couldn't think of anything else to draw."

"I think they're lovely, dear," coos the lady who is basically sitting next to Alan.

Denice smiles briefly at her, barely looking up, then changes crayons and starts drawing on another part of the table top.

"I haven't drawn anything in *years*," one of the women next door says.

"Oh, give it a try, it's *fun*," another encourages.

Alan continues to eat, glancing up occasionally at what Denice is drawing. It begins as a row of vertical brown lines, then she adds sienna circles on top of each one. When she adds the jagged red lines at the base of each circle, and some stray drips of red below, he knows what she's drawing and smiles.

"Look, she draws like I do," one of the women at the next table says, her voice smiling and friendly.

The woman sitting next to Denice looks over at the row of figures. "Are those your children?"

Denice smiles and looks up at Alan, then over at the women. "No, they're severed heads on poles."

This shuts the women up right away.

In the silence that follows, Alan says to Denice, "Are you scaring the neighbors again?"

Denice smiles broadly at him, her eyes bright and happy.

Alan turns to the old women: "You never really know who's sitting next you, do you?"

Sixteen

Alan's arm is around Denice's shoulders as they sit on the couch, and her legs converge with his on top of the coffee table. They're watching Sean Connery's James Bond fight Odd Job in the bowels of Fort Knox, near the end of *Goldfinger*. Alan owns most of the Bond movies on tape—all of the ones starring Connery. He doesn't know how many times he's seen this one, but enough that he doesn't need to pay attention to know exactly what's going on. He still enjoys the movie, but now it's enough just to see and hear it without really following the plot closely.

Instead, his mind drifts. His life now is so different from when he was a child, belittled by his mother, mocked by his younger sisters. Now, like 007, he gets the respect he deserves.

He thinks about that morning he walked away from the bus stop. One minute he was standing there, feeling miserable. The next he realized there was nothing stopping him from walking away, from simply stepping off and heading down the street. It was the first time he'd ever taken charge of his life. If he hadn't been only seven, he would have kept walking that day.

Instead, he set that vacant lot on fire. Alan still likes fire, but the only fires, besides the barbecue grill, Alan starts now are the cars he torches, and there's a practical reason for burning those. Not that he doesn't enjoy seeing them burn, from a safe distance. But he hasn't torched anything purely for fun since he ignited the trash in a can behind his barracks when he was in boot camp. That fire got him kicked out, which was fine with him. He'd been fed up with all the asshole drill instructors giving him shit. If he'd wanted shit, he could have stayed home with the bitches. He'd joined the Marines so he wouldn't have to take shit anymore, not so he could get more of it.

Anyway…he hasn't started a fire for fun since then. He's thought about it a couple times, and he still occasionally goes out of his way to follow the fire engines to the smoke. He even thought about being a firefighter a few years back, but decided he wasn't all that interested in extinguishing flames. He smiles while picturing himself as a fireman, with the helmet and big coat, getting to the fire and telling the guys with the hose to hold off: "Just let it burn a little longer! Just a little longer!" he'd say. Some fireman; more like a *fire*-man. But starting fires for fun is behind him now: that's kid stuff. These days, with Denice beside him and things going his way, there's nothing in his life, other than the occasional inconvenient vehicle, that needs incinerating.

Goldfinger ends and, as usual with Bond movies, Alan himself feels a little like James Bond: totally cool and utterly confident. He clicks the TV off, then gets up from the couch and ejects the tape from the VCR.

Unfortunately, although this is mainly a fun day, he does need to get the lawn mowed. This prospect puts a damper on the James Bond feeling—it's pretty much impossible to imagine 007 pushing a lawnmower—and he wishes he'd planned the day differently and they'd done the chores right after breakfast, before watching the movie. There's no avoiding it now, though, since it's supposed to rain all day tomorrow. Wet grass doesn't cut as well and the clippings tend to end up in messy clumps which have to be picked up before they kill the grass underneath. The yard isn't very big, though, so it hopefully won't take too long, assuming the mower isn't acting up again. A ripple of dread passes through him at the thought. Although he's actually disassembled and cleaned the mower's carburetor, and replaced the spark plug, it remains temperamental. He should probably just junk it and buy a new one, but mowers are expensive, and it seems crazy and even weak to throw out a mower which does, eventually, work. Doing so would amount to admitting he's not skilled enough to fix the machine.

He looks at his watch: it's about eleven a.m. "I'm going out to cut the grass," he says to Denice. "You clean up in here, and noon we'll head over to the mall for lunch." Alan has Denice clean their place every weekend. This has been true since they moved into this half of a duplex together about a year ago. She wasn't so skilled at housecleaning initially, but she has always been eager to please him, which makes her a fast learner. Most weeks now he just does a cursory inspection of her work—she's that consistently good. She won't have time to finish this morning, but she'll make a decent start on it.

"OK, sounds good Chief," she says with her cute little smile. The first time she called him Chief it surprised him, and he wondered if she were being insolent. But that first time she hadn't said it in response to him telling her to do something; it had just come out naturally: "Hey Chief, you want spaghetti for dinner tonight?" He let it go, and since then he's realized it's a term of affection, and she almost always has this little smile—not a mean smile, but a happy, safe smile—when she uses the name.

He looks back down at the videotape and fits it into its protective sleeve before shelving it with the other Bond flicks, all arranged in chronological order from *Dr. No* to *License to Kill*. He's heard that, after six years, there's finally going to be another Bond movie this summer, but with that Remington Steele guy as 007 and a woman as the new M. Alan isn't sure how to feel about this: on the one hand, he's glad there's finally going to *be* another Bond flick, and the new guy can't be any worse than Timothy Dalton, who he's never really gotten used to. On the other hand, replacing M with a woman sounds really bad. He knows, though, there's no way he won't go see it, probably on opening weekend.

But now he has to cut the grass. The mower is in the basement. He doesn't like going down there because it's a spider kind of place, and he hates spiders. Whenever he goes down there, he first goes around outside and opens the metal bulkhead he'll have to carry the mower through. Then he goes back inside, flips the light switch at the top of the stairs leading down from the kitchen, and checks the ceiling as he descends and enters the unfinished space. Once he saw, blocking the bottom of the stairway, a big orange spider with really long legs climbing a thread to the ceiling, and it was like someone had poured a bucket of ice water down the back of his shirt. Luckily the can of bug spray he got from the kitchen had pretty good reach, because as soon as the poison hit, it dropped to the floor and started running around crazy fast. Alan sprayed it some more from the stairs until it stopped moving, all the while feeling the chills up and down his spine, and scratching the back of his neck at the thought of a spider dropping down on him. Once the thing stopped moving, he came down the stairs, sprayed it again, and when it didn't move he quickly stomped it to be sure. It was weeks before Alan's skin stopped prickling whenever he entered the basement.

Today he sees no spiders.

The mower, which was left in his half of the basement by some previous tenant, or maybe the landlord, is a pretty basic, old gas-powered job, with no extras like self-propulsion or mulching settings, but it does have a catch bag. Alan squats down and checks the handle for spiders, finds none, and then pulls the machine up the plywood ramp someone installed over the few concrete steps leading up to the bulkhead. The mower is heavy, and he has to lean back to haul it up the steep ramp. As he does, he hears the fuel sloshing around in the tank, reminding him it might be time to add more gas. *There should be plenty left in the can downstairs.* It also occurs to him that he has yet to change the oil in it, even though he used it all last summer, and has no idea when or if the oil had been changed before he moved in. *Maybe next weekend.*

As he backs out into the sunlit yard, he hears a whirring sound, accompanied by a soft clacking. Once he gets the mower settled on level ground, he looks around to see the guy who lives in the other half of the duplex pushing a wheeled device—some kind of seed or fertilizer spreader—around on the other side of the small hedge which divides the yard. *Shit.* The guy, a tall, skinny man who looks to be in his mid-twenties, moved in next door about three months ago, but Alan has so far managed to avoid him.

Before Alan looks away again, the other man looks up, smiles, and waves, stopping the wheeled device and walking toward the low hedge between them. "Hey, neighbor! I thought we'd never get a chance to meet." As he walks, he tosses his head a little to get some of the longish, slightly wavy brown hair out of his eyes.

Although he is cringing on the inside, Alan is actually pretty good at making nice with people when he needs to. He smiles and walks over to his side of the hedge, hand extended. "Hey, how are you?" Alan grips the other man's hand hard. "Alan Hayes."

"Scott Oldham."

There's a moment of surprise in the other guy's brown eyes, and Alan eases up a little. The return grip is firm, but not the equal of Alan's. Point made, Alan releases the hand.

"Perfect day for this kind of stuff, isn't it?" Scott offers, absently rubbing his right hand with his left.

"Yeah, great weather. Have to get this stuff cut before the rain tomorrow."

Scott nods. "By the way, if you want to borrow my mower, let me know. I noticed you had a hard time getting that old clunker started a couple weeks ago. You'll never have that problem with mine," he adds, smiling broadly and gesturing at the device he'd been pushing a minute earlier.

Has he been watching me? Alan wonders, feeling a small fire ignite deep in his head. *Watching me look like an idiot trying to get that mower started? And mocking me now?* Alan feels his smile fade as his eyes track toward the device Scott is pointing at. He sees now it's not a spreader after all— there's no bin for seed or fertilizer on it, just long, gently-curved metal bands arranged in a horizontal cylinder with the wheels as the end caps. "That's a mower?" He looks back at Scott, liking him less with each passing tick of the watch on his wrist. Considering he didn't like him to begin with, any more than he likes anyone besides Denice, Scott was now inscribing his name on Alan's shit list.

"Oh yeah—it's a *reel* mower—R-E-*E*-L, like a fishing reel. The rotating blades on the reel meet a straight, fixed blade on the bottom, and work like a scissors, snipping the grass. Pretty cool, right?" Scott is obviously all about the ingenuity of this device.

Alan actually does find the mower interesting. He might even like it if he didn't now associate it with this dickhead. The idea of never having to put gas or oil in it, or having to fuck with the engine when it won't start is appealing. But there's no way he'll use one while this guy Scott is around. "Yeah, that's great, but I think I'll stick with what I got. Have fun!" he says, waving and turning, glad to be breaking the conversation off quickly. If the mower starts up like it's supposed to then in a few seconds it'll be too noisy for Scott to talk to him.

"Nice meeting you, Alan!" he hears Scott say.

"Same here," he calls over his shoulder, trying to keep up the neighborly façade but still walking toward where his mower squats on the concrete pavers in front of the bulkhead.

Fortunately, the mower does start right up today, and Alan feels a sense of deep satisfaction in having fixed it up to work properly.   A little of the James Bond feeling of competence reasserts itself.   He begins in the backyard, and after he finishes it he empties the catch bag's load of grass clippings into a big paper yard waste bag.   During this pause he   notices   What's-His-Name—Scott—carrying   the   reel mower in one hand as he takes it down the steps under the bulkhead on his side, and Alan is surprised at how light it must be.

While he wheels the mower down the driveway to the front yard, Alan thinks about their plans for the evening.   He and Denice only do this once every three months, give or take. There are practical reasons, but it also keeps these trips special, and the anticipation is part of the good in this.   It's hard to believe, and sad, that for most of his adult life this wasn't part of him.   If it hadn't been for Denice, he might never have realized this about himself.   What's more, the discovery was mostly an accident, and he wonders if, had things happened differently, he might never have understood what he needs.

* * *

Dothan, Alabama
September 1993

Alan stared at the driver leaning back against his dusty race car.   Alan paid particular attention to the broad smile, the whiteness of his teeth breaking through the dirty gray of the man's face.   Even across some forty years of time, through the medium of a black and white photograph, the man's absolute happiness was obvious.

Alan looked away, his eyes skimming over Denice sitting on the other side of the little round table from him before gazing out across the bar's interior.   The Saturday night crowd, the new country music that tries to sound like top-forty rock, the old-time dirt track racing memorabilia—checkered flags; old signs advertising oil, cars, and gasoline; posters advertising races—all of it helped distract him. Denice would have been fine staying home, watching TV or whatever, but if he stayed home when he felt this way, he'd end up picking a fight with her, which was really saying something with Denice. It's not easy to start a fight with someone so eager to please you, so quick to agree with you. In fact, their fights weren't really fights; they were more him yelling and Denice getting more and more pouty and quiet.

He knew he had a good thing in Denice; she was better than any other woman he'd ever known. And it wasn't just the sex, either. The sex was great, but his appreciation of her went way beyond that. He usually felt so right when he was with her, so good about himself, so confident. He had no idea what made him want to get pissed off at her so he could feel the anger and lash out. He would understand if attacking her felt good, but instead it made him feel like shit. Even as he was being a jerk, he *knew* he was being a jerk, which made him hate himself, which somehow made him more angry at Denice. Alan knew this was crazy, but there it was. So when he felt hungry for rage, he took them out someplace where he could be distracted from what was going on inside him.

Usually they came here to Boomer's, because it was convenient and didn't charge a cover, and the sensory overload of the place, especially on the weekends, was just what he needed. For a while. Lately, though, this hadn't been working either.

He looked over at the bar. The light was murky, especially when looking all the way across the big room, but even so the woman at the bar stood out. Maybe it was the cowboy hat with the blonde braid dangling out from beneath it. Or maybe it was the white tank top over the tight jeans, the clothing advertising the body underneath by selectively hiding and revealing. Whatever, she was clearly hot.

He hadn't said much to Denice since they sat down, but now he leaned over the small table and, still staring across the crowded room, he nodded at the cowgirl. "Check out the ass on her." He glanced at Denice, took in the jutting lower lip, the vertical lines between her eyebrows, and was at once pleased and filled with self-loathing. She squinted a little as she looked through the smoky haze. "The one in the cowboy hat," he said. "Looks like she had to stuff that ass into those jeans, they're so tight."

"You think she's fat?" Denice asked.

"What? *Fat?* Hell no. Look at the curve of her ass, look at how narrow her waist is. I like the hat, too."

"Ah could get a cowboy hat." She was quiet for several seconds, staring across the room. "What about the one to the raht of her, three people over—the one in the black T-shirt? You think she has a nahce body?"

That was the thing about Denice. Even when he deliberately did things to piss her off, she went along with it; she would do anything for him. *So why am I doing this to her?* "Yeah, she's pretty good too. I don't like her ass as much, but she has nice tits—not too big, not too small." He glanced over at Denice, saw her eyes were cast down, looking at something in her lap, which he guessed was the shredded remains of the little napkin that came with her beer. "Does that worry you?"

She looked up at him, met his eyes with hers. She was holding her eyes open wide, the picture of innocent blankness, but there was a shininess to them that gave her away. "Does what worry me?"

He smiled with half his mouth, looked back at the cowgirl. "You have to learn to trust me. If I want to talk to someone, even a woman with a sweet ass, then I'm going to do it. Don't think you can tell me what to do."

"Ah don't! Ah mean, fahn. That's cool. Ah'm cool with, you know, whatever."

"You say that, but I can see you gettin' all pouty over there, and it's not gonna work. In fact, I'm goin' over to talk to her, just on principle. If I want you to join us, I'll push my hand through my hair; that's your signal. Don't come over before that, got it? You don't do anything until you see my signal, or until I leave. If I leave, then you can leave. Got it?" He looked over at her, hating himself for this but wanting to do it too.

Her eyes looked angry, hard, and hurt. "OK, Chief," she said, and nodded once.

"Good." Alan stood and walked casually over to the bar, assessing the situation as he approached Cowgirl.

With the exception of Denice, Alan was a consistent failure in maintaining relationships with women. He was, however, really good at picking up women. Part of it was his smile. He'd practiced it in mirrors, but mostly he'd refined it in response to the reactions he got. It was a real movie star smile. He'd never worn braces—hell, even if his mother could have afforded them, which she couldn't, she'd never have sprung for them. Not for him. But he hadn't needed them; his teeth had naturally grown in straight, and Alan had never taken up smoking or drinking a lot of coffee, and was pretty good about brushing, so they'd stayed very white. It didn't hurt that the rest of him was attractive too: bright blue eyes in a face that tanned easily, dark hair which still showed no signs of receding or thinning, and a six-foot-even lean body made muscular from the work of building houses.

But the most important factor in his success wasn't his looks or his smile. He couldn't really lay out specifically what he did, how it translated into actions, but the key to bedding women was his attitude. He'd discovered this when he'd arrived in San Diego just prior to starting Marine boot camp. Feeling nervous, unsure of himself, and alone, he'd had a couple beers to calm down a little. It hadn't been enough to make him drunk, but the beer, combined with the nervous anticipation of reporting for duty, and being in an unfamiliar city, had resulted in a kind of apathy toward everything else. When he'd found himself next to a woman in short shorts and a pink halter top while ordering another beer, he'd automatically begun chatting her up, mainly to take his mind off of what he'd gotten himself into by signing up for the Marines. He'd had no expectations with her beyond a few words while they ordered drinks, but he'd ended up spending the night in her apartment, which had been a hell of a lot better than his original plan of stretching out on a bench in the bus station. Since then he'd realized he didn't need the alcohol; the key was the mix of self-assurance and apathy.

Alan wedged himself in next to where Cowgirl was sitting, made eye contact, flashed the smile, and complimented her on the hat. From there it was clear sailing. He'd noticed on the way over that the guy on the other side of her had been trying to chat her up, but the poor bastard didn't stand a chance. After about twenty minutes she started touching Alan's arm lightly and briefly while she was speaking to him, and he knew he could bed her. He glanced over at Denice to make sure she was watching him and ran his fingers back through his hair. Then he threw some bills on the bar to cover the drinks he'd bought.

Several seconds later Denice was walking up to where Alan was leaning on the bar. Not caring that Cowgirl—actually, her name was Tina—was in the middle of saying something, Alan turned and smiled at Denice. "Hey Beautiful."

Denice, clearly troubled and confused, managed to respond with a weak smile and "Hey."

"You're really somethin', you know?" he said to her, registering but not acknowledging Tina's sudden silence.

Denice shrugged, looked down.

"No, I mean it—did you just get here?"

Denice looks at him, clearly confused, but with the hint of a real smile just beginning to form on her lips. "Um, sure..."

"You must have, because otherwise I'd have noticed you by now."

"Do you two know each other?" Tina asked, trying to get Alan's attention again.

"No," Alan replied, his eyes still locked with Denice's, "but I'm hoping that's about to change." He turned his head and looked at Tina. "Sorry honey—one way or another, I've got to go." He turned back to Denice, who now really was smiling. "Can I take you someplace a little less crowded, maybe buy you a drink?"

"Um, *yes!*"

"By the way, I'm Alan," he said, holding out his hand to shake.

She put her hand in his. "Denice—pleased to meet you, Alan."

"Wait—*what?* What—?" Tina sputtered.

Alan considered staying longer to enjoy Tina's confusion and outrage, but instead, still grasping Denice's hand, he led her out to his van. When they got home they fucked like mad, then fell asleep in each other's arms.

* * *

When he's done, Alan shuts down the mower. The sudden quiet feels like pressure on his ears. He thinks again of the reel mower which, now that Scott has gone inside, seems more appealing. He wonders if it really works, and glances over at the yard on the other side of the front walkway, which does look neat and mowed.

After he puts the lawn mower away and closes the bulkhead again, he goes inside and finds Denice wearing rubber gloves, her blonde hair pulled back under a red kerchief with little curly black and white designs on it, scrubbing out the kitchen sink. "How's it going?" he asks.

"Pretty good, Chief. I finished the living room and the kitchen is just about done."

Alan checks the clock on the microwave: 11:45. "Finish this up and then get ready to go—we'll leave for the mall at noon."

Seventeen

The parking lot at the Wiregrass Commons Mall is already crowded, but someone pulls out as Alan drives down one of the aisles. He swings the van smoothly into the newly-opened spot, nailing the alignment and spacing perfectly on the first try. *James Bond.* The sunlight is cascading down, splattering everywhere, splashing off the cars and light trucks all around them and filling the front of the van. "Leave your window open a couple inches—let some of the heat out."

Denice does as instructed, and Alan does the same with his window before they get out. They had the air conditioning on while driving over here, but now Alan feels the heat and humidity on his face, and finds it pleasing. It'll be a good first day at the beach.

Denice is waiting for him as he rounds the back of the van. He takes her hand and they walk together across the parking lot and up to a set of double doors leading in. Simultaneously, Alan grasps the door handle on the right and Denice the one on the left, and they pull them wide. Still holding hands, they repeat the process with a second, inner set of doors, and stride into the cool darkness of the mall. Despite the big breakfast, he's hungry again. "Let's get lunch first."

"OK."

"I'm getting Chinese, but you can pick whatever you want." Out of the corner of his eye he sees her turn her face toward him, and he turns and looks back, sees the question in her eyes. "Sure—why not? It's a special day."

She smiles back. "I think I'm going to Burger King."

"OK, wherever you want," he says, grinning and walking a little taller with her by his side.

The entrance they chose is actually very close to the food court—diagonally across the mall's central corridor from it. Alan and Denice stride past a grouping of trees and shrubs which Alan suspects are fake, and into the food court. As they enter, Alan immediately notices the carousel. Like any mall food court he's ever seen, the restaurants here are arrayed on either side, with chairs and small tables in the big open area in the middle. But the carousel is new. Alan and Denice both stop at the edge of the dining area and take it in. The carousel is made to look old-fashioned: the seats are all traditionally-painted horses and there's not much flashiness beyond the painted bright colors and a row of oval mirrors about two feet high and one foot wide around the central column. Even the music is traditional—old-time carnival music is how Alan thinks of it. At times, though, it's almost drowned out by the excited shouts and laughter of the children on the ride and lined up waiting. "Shit," he says quietly.

"Yeah," Denice agrees.

Alan is as indifferent toward children as he is toward animals, as long as they remain irrelevant to his life. When he ends up someplace where he has to hear their noise and see their manic running around, however, his apathy rapidly converts to the contempt he feels for people in general. Most people see children as innocents, but spend any time around kids and it's easy to see in them the adults that bred them, and the adults they'll undoubtedly grow up to be: loud, obnoxious, and self-centered. As with adults, this is especially true when you get a herd of them together, like now around the carousel. Alan watches two little boys contort their faces at each other bizarrely. Next to them a little girl is flapping her arms and occasionally screaming. It's the interior of a mad house. If he'd known about this he wouldn't have planned to eat here, and he seriously considers turning them around and heading out. But they were also going to the music store to see if the new Danzig CD is out yet, and they were going to look at new

TV's too. If they leave to eat somewhere else, they'll just have to come back later. Besides, he's hungry and he doesn't want his life dictated by a bunch of breeders and their yard monkeys. "Well, fuck it—we'll just sit down here—there's enough free tables." He glances over and sees the Burger King line is pretty long but, on the opposite side of the food court, the line for Great Wok of China isn't bad at all. "Still want to go to Burger King?" he asks.

Denice looks over, then back at him. "It's OK with me if it's all raht by you. Ah'm not that hungry anyway."

Alan shrugs. "OK, I'll save you a seat."

There aren't that many good Chinese restaurants around here, but this place has excellent pork spareribs and shrimp fried rice, which he's been anticipating all week. Once he gets his food he goes looking for a table. Unfortunately, now the tables which are furthest from the carousel are all taken, but there's still a few which are a fair distance from the noise. He picks one that's clean and sits down. There's a family with three kids nearby, but they're oriental, and usually their kids are pretty well-behaved, so that should be fine. For a moment he considers waiting for Denice, but he can see she is still four or five people back from the front of the line. Plus the smell of the food is literally making his mouth water, so he digs in and forgets about the people around him until Denice sits down across from him and starts tearing open her bag.

"I *love* these *frahs*," she says, drawing out the second and last words in her Alabama way as she tears open the paper bag to make a kind of place mat and dumps the contents of a large fries onto it.

He smiles as he watches her tear open three ketchup packs at once and squirt their contents all over the french fries. She repeats this twice more, until the potatoes are dripping with the red sauce.

She looks up and notices him watching. "Got to have mah ketchup!"

He shakes his head a little and returns his attention to a spare rib.

"So how is it?"

"Pretty decent," he says, looking up and nodding. "No, better than that—they're pretty damn good. Not as good as the ones I had in San Francisco," he says, recalling a stop he'd made there years ago when he was a long-haul trucker, "but I guess that's not surprising."

"Let's go there someday!" Denice says, suddenly excited. "Ah've never been anywhere besides Alabama, Georgia, and Florida. You think maybe we could travel sometime, go someplace new?"

"Sure Baby," he replies, but has no idea when they'll do anything like that. Denice doesn't realize how much something like that would cost, both in terms of money spent and money they would miss earning while being on vacation. Fortunately, she doesn't dwell on it.

"Ah wonder if that new Danzig CD is out now—Ah hope it is! Wouldn't that be cool, to have that for tonaht?"

He smiles and nods. "Yeah, it'd be good road music for the drive down too." Suddenly he remembers something. "Speaking of tonight, don't let me forget to bring the toolbox up from the basement and put it in the van. That'd be pretty lame, to not have it with us tonight," he adds through a smirk.

Denice laughs, "Yeah, pretty lame!" She holds up a french fry which somehow escaped most of the ketchup flood. "Here, trah this."

He swallows a mouthful of fried rice, then leans forward. She places the french fry in his mouth and he bites down on it, tasting mostly salt and fat, with a hint of potato. He knows this isn't good food, but has to admit there is something about it that makes him want to eat more of it. He resists, declining a second offering and instead finishing his own meal.

After lunch they empty their trays in the big trash receptacles on the edge of the seating area and then head further down the mall's main corridor to the music store.

In the heavy metal section Denice goes right to the D's and, after few seconds, hisses "*Yessssss,*" and holds up a darkly-colored square—the new Danzig. They hunt around some more and Alan buys a Pantera CD which actually came out last year, but for some reason he hadn't picked up yet. They continue to browse, but end up buying just the two discs.

After that they stop off in a department store and look at TV's. Alan would like to get a newer, bigger set, but they really can't afford one yet. They wander through the display area, checking out all the different screens, each one with a slightly different version of the colors in a music video featuring some hottie of the moment with a nice, fuckable ass. A salesman moves in on them like a shark smelling blood, but Alan tells him to get lost, and the guy moves on. Salesmen are annoying, especially when he can't afford to buy. Alan notices, and not for the first time, how frustrating it is for him to look at what he wants while being unable to get it. He stores this feeling away for use tonight.

Tonight. It's time they got going; he turns to Denice, who is watching a screen with rapt attention; so much it takes her an extra second or two to notice he is looking at her. When she does realize this, she immediately turns her face toward him, an expectant look in her eyes. "Let's go," he says.

Part Three

Worlds Collide

Eighteen

Oh shit.

I freeze in the mall's main concourse. The itch below my breastbone, which has been intensifying as I headed back toward where I entered the mall, is suddenly joined by a sick feeling lower, in my stomach, and a tightening in the back of my throat. This is the first time I've gotten the scratchiness in the scar below my sternum since that time in Korea, since realizing these flashbacks might actually be more than psychological bruises.

The first time I experienced this sensation in my scar was almost a year after the Bad happened. I was waiting for my bus home at the underground Harvard Square station in Cambridge, looking at the West Point catalog the school guidance counselor had just given me. Then, too, the pain had begun as an itch. It had been some time since the deep incision in my upper abdomen had healed and the concomitant itch of mending tissue had stopped, but that's what this was like. Then the itching became scratching, then cutting, and the hurt continued to amplify until it felt like I was being torn open and stabbed all over again. I thought there must be some complication from what had happened to me, something the doctors had missed. I staggered out of the public transit station and went to the school nurse's office, but long before I got there the pain, which had been diminishing since soon after I began moving, had completely evaporated. Even the itching was gone. Still, the nurse made me an appointment with my doctor. The initial examination found nothing wrong, so Dr. Zahir ordered an MRI of my torso. That also revealed nothing out of the ordinary. Zahir explained that in cases of post traumatic stress disorder people might re-experience the incident, sometimes with all their senses, and sometimes with only one or two. This is commonly known as a "flashback," and he referred me to Sarah, my shrink. Eventually we concluded someone or something on the bus platform must have triggered my memory of the Bad. Maybe a guy standing nearby was wearing the same cologne as the monster, though I couldn't remember *him* wearing any artificial scent. I can remember a lot of other smells from that night—I wish I could forget them—but cologne or aftershave isn't among them. Still, it could have been a sound, or even nothing, just a memory boiling up from my subconscious. Could have been.

I experienced the sequence of itching through full, painful flashback again a couple years later, while on an evening trip to New York City with a bunch of other cadets from the Military Academy. Recognizing it as an illusion, I was more embarrassed than scared, and hid my distress as best I could. It helped a little to at least know there wasn't really anything wrong with my body, and if I just walked and waited it out, it would pass. And so it did, within two or three minutes of its beginning. I went with the same explanation when I was driving south on Interstate 95 after graduating from West Point. I couldn't figure out what would have triggered the sense memory of the Bad when I was alone in my car, just listening to the radio and driving along, but there was no other explanation, and anyway that time the pain came and went in a matter of seconds.

But that night in Korea, when Private Dexter Williams was arrested and brought in for transfer to CID, made me begin to doubt the flashback theory. Not at first—at first the situation made total sense: being in the same room as a known sexual sadist would be expected to trigger a reaction in me. What was bizarre and confusing was later that night when my body, or my subconscious, knew before I did that I was passing close by the detention facility where Williams was

being held. It's possible I already knew at some level where
the detention facility was, but remembered it only
subconsciously when we drove by it. Possible, but I really
didn't think so. I wondered too about the gradual ramping up
from an itch to a scratch to mounting pain. The same
sequence happened in reverse each time we passed the
detention facility and left it behind. There was no itching or
scratching during the Bad, just horrible pain, so why were
those precursors to pain part of my flashbacks? And the
sequence was so consistent, as if my body were aware of and
reporting on exactly how far away Willams was from me. Not
knowing what to do with the experience, and without any
better explanations, I filed the memory away as a mystery. I
didn't forget about the incident, but I've barely thought about
it because I haven't had any flashbacks since that night.

Until now.

If what happened that night in Korea was what it seemed
to be, then there's a predator here in the Wiregrass Commons
Mall with me. My mind reeling, I turn around and walk
quickly back in the direction of the bookstore, trying to
diminish the sensation and put as much distance as possible
between me and the source. Incidentally, this also means
putting distance between me and the end of the mall where I
parked, but so what? I can exit the mall somewhere on the
other end and circle around through the parking lot *(but what
if he's out there?)* back to where Stacey is waiting. Then I'll
lock myself in, drive home fast, and slide that deadbolt into
place. Now I'm beyond the bookstore I just left; the itch
persists, but it's gradually fading. I'm getting away.

Stop.

It takes a few more steps before my feet get the message,
but I stop mid-concourse.

Fear feeds fear; I know this from experience. Fear takes
control, turning retreat into panic, stealing the ability to act,
and making me vulnerable. The only counter to this is to take

back the initiative. My car is *that* way, and I'll be fucking damned if these bastards are gonna push me around.

Besides, I don't *really* know what's causing this pain. Maybe it's nothing. Maybe I was running from my own imagination. Maybe if I *follow* the pain…

Slowly I turn and look down the length of the mall: the filtered sunlight from the glass dome and skylights high above softly illuminates the multi-hued crowd of people continually stirring itself, the window displays, the living mannequins, and, somewhere in all this, the source of my pain, whatever or whoever it is. The idea the bastard who attacked me left something behind in me, something that more than nine years later is still hurting me, is unspeakably revolting, but all the same I want to know about it if that's true. Whatever the reason for the pain, it's part of my reality now and I need to understand it.

But what if there is *a monster on the other end of this pain? Better to just get away now.*

The first step is an act of sheer will, but each succeeding step gets easier as I push aside the fear and focus on finding answers. It feels good to confront this instead of running; I'm back in control. The itch builds to pain, but I separate myself from it, hold it inside me, reassuring myself my body is fine, no matter how bad it feels. I observe the intensifying sensation and follow its increase through the swirl of shoppers and commerce. By the time I reach the food court the cramps are severe, but I keep my posture straight and my face neutral.

I stand on the edge of the food court and scan the tables and serving counters. I notice there's an old-fashioned carousel at the far end of this area, with a crowd of children and their parents around it. I study the cluster of people with a dawning dread, wondering if there might be a predator among all those kids. Instinctively I walk toward them, but by the time I reach the carousel, although the difference is slight, I notice a small reduction in the hurt. *I'm moving away from the source.* I turn and look behind me. Nothing seems unusual—just people having lunch, chatting with friends, ordering food, cooking, a few sitting alone and reading. Confused, I follow the only guide I have and begin backtracking along the edge of the table area in front of one bank of restaurants, paying close attention to the pain inside, like a sadist's "warmer/colder" hints. I enter the table area and, when the pain is going right through me, sit down a couple tables away from a man seated alone, eating Chinese food. He is clean-shaven, his light brown hair trimmed, his clothes tidy. He looks a little older than me, in his late twenties or early thirties.

I take one of the books out of my bag and pretend to read while casting furtive sidelong glances at him. *Why him?* He looks completely innocuous: just sitting, eating his lunch. *Is he a rapist? A murderer? Can I, I don't know,* smell *it on him?*

As I consider this, another person, a woman who is maybe my age, sits down across from him. She has a tray with food from Burger King.

"How is it?" she asks him, pulling her long bleached hair back into a ponytail.

"Pretty decent," he says, looking up at her and nodding.

The two continue chatting with easy familiarity: "I wonder if that new Danzig CD is out now," "Help me remember to get the toolbox out of the basement and put it in the van when we get home." At one point, she feeds him a french fry. Watching surreptitiously, I see neither wears wedding rings, but the body language, their way with each other, indicates closeness, even intimacy.

It can't *be him, not if I'm sensing a rapist or something—she wouldn't be with him if he were, would she?* I realize that's naïve—women sometimes stay with violent men, but still, this is not what I expected. I look around at the other people nearby: an Asian family with three young children, an elderly couple, a group of four giggling adolescent girls. None of these people, including the happy couple eating french fries, seems even remotely dangerous. The pain in me continues to scream away, though I find myself becoming somewhat adapted to it. I discreetly press my fingertips through my T-shirt against the scar, but this of course does nothing to change the hurt. Eventually, their lunch finished, the man and woman stand and take their trays to the trash receptacles, emptying the debris and stacking the trays on top, then walk away hand in hand. I watch them go and feel the pain ease. Completely baffled, I get up and follow them at several paces. As I do, the pain remains at a constant level. I watch them purchase CD's at the music store I was in earlier, and then look at TV sets in an electronics store, but they don't buy anything there. I back off in these places, gazing at them from a distance that mitigates the hurt.

I'm scarier than they are. The pain is definitely related to them, but it beats me why. I follow them back past the music store and the food court, to one of the mall's exits, and out into the parking lot; after all, my car is this way too. In fact, they're walking toward the same general area where I parked, but a couple aisles over from Stacey. They get into a large, mostly windowless white van which has been modified with a fiberglass cap on the roof to make it taller. It could be a commercial vehicle except it's free of logos. It's clean and looks to be in good shape. Trying to be inconspicuous, I continue walking as I pass the van, but there's really nothing more to see; the vehicle is as unremarkable as the people in it, right down to the standard-issue Alabama license plate. I stop a few cars past them and, as I hear the van's engine start, I spot Stacey and walk toward her, accepting the experience as proof that, as weird as it is, there's nothing to this pain: it really is just a random flashback. I reach my car and get in, ignoring the blast of heat inside, ready to go home. I pull out, the steering wheel and gear shift as hot as everything else in the car, but not hot enough to burn thanks to the watchdog sun shield.   The van is still waiting for the traffic light at the parking lot exit.   The hurt in me ramps up again as I pull into line a few cars back, just as the light turns green.

We both turn right, but then they immediately cross over to the left lane and then a left turn lane.   There's not much traffic, so on impulse I follow them.   Even as I'm doing this, I couldn't say why.   The escalating strangeness of this situation is apparent to me, but I don't address it any more than to think it might be interesting to see where they go next or, if they go home, what kind of place they live in.   Besides, it's not like I have any schedule to keep—it's still early afternoon and my weekend is wide open, so why not?

We travel a couple miles to a modest residential area within Dothan.   I continue driving past the place where the van pulls in, circle the block and come back down the couple's street, parking by the curb a few houses up from theirs, in the shade of a large tree.   The neighborhood is clean, and very quiet: everyone is either away or indoors.

I get out of my car and walk down the cracked and buckled sidewalk past their house, a light green duplex with a driveway on either side of the building.   Looking for any information, any clue to the significance of these people, I note the house number, but there's no mailbox to carry a name, just a slot in the front door.   The van sits in the driveway and—big surprise—hasn't changed in the few minutes since I last saw it up close in the mall parking lot. No bumper stickers, no logos, ordinary license plate, cap on the roof making it taller, white…   I notice there aren't many windows in it.   Besides the windshield and door windows in the front, the only others are a small, dark, square window near the top of each of the two back doors, and two small skylights sticking up from the roof.   There's a sliding side door on the passenger side, but there aren't any windows in it. I try to remember other vans I've seen and decide the lack of windows isn't so unusual, at least, not in vans that are primarily used for carrying stuff and not people, but maybe the guy is an electrician or plumber or something. I keep walking down to the end of the block, read the street name off the sign there, take a left, and continue around the way I drove a few minutes before. As I do, the pain fluctuates; I observe it like I would a science experiment, noting the changes in intensity as my distance from the home varies, just as it did in Korea when Blalock and I approached and then receded from the Army jail.

When I get back to Stacey, there's nothing left to do but leave. I consider staying until dark so I can maybe see some activity inside the house, but how long am I going to watch nothing? How long am I going to stalk these people like some kind of crazy predator?

Maybe this is how it starts.

I don't know if I should react to that idea with humor or horror. I look at the part of the van I can see once more. *Why them?* I shake my head and turn, get in my car.

I roll down the driver side window, then lean over and roll down the other window. I start the engine and shift from reverse to first when I look up and notice the doors on the back of the van are now open and the man is lifting a heavy-looking metal toolbox into the back, while the woman appears carrying a garment bag and a small cooler. I shift back into neutral and watch. The man takes the luggage from her and steps up into the van, and she goes back to the house. After several seconds the man emerges from the back again and closes the rear doors, then he goes back to the house. I don't see any more activity for a few minutes, but from here the front half of the van is obscured by the corner of the building. Suddenly the van backs out and heads down the street away from me. I shift back into first and pull out, following as far back as I can without losing them, both to minimize the pain in my scar and to be inconspicuous.

We end up heading south on Highway 231, which connects Montgomery, Alabama, to Panama City, Florida, by way of Dothan.   Between Dothan and Panama City the highway is mostly long stretches of straight road, with two lanes each going north and south, crossing the low, flat countryside.   There's not much of interest along the way— some planted fields beside tree-shaded farm houses, some abandoned fields with the mandatory decaying shack, its wood turned gray, metal roof rusted, and windows broken or missing.   Around the rivers and creeks the highway crosses there are small areas of forest.   Occasionally there are groups of tired-looking houses with a gas station and convenience store.   The van stops once for fuel at one of these places. Stacey's tank is still more than half full, and I don't want the couple to see me again, in case they remember seeing me at the mall, or notice me later, so I drive past the gas station.

How long is this going to go on?

I turn right on to a cross street, then left on to a street parallel to the highway.   The houses here could have been anywhere in suburban or small-town America, except for the spreading pecan trees, which are probably pretty unique to the southeast.   I park in a patch of shade and shut off the engine.

It's quiet here, and I listen to the lack of wind and engine noise.   The silence is a tangible pressure in my ears after an hour of driving fast with the windows open.

How much longer are you going to do this?   I ask myself.

I gaze across a grassy yard at a tire hanging by a rope from a tree branch.   Well, what else do I have to do anyway?

Maybe you're just bored; maybe your mind invented the pain as a distraction from the empty monotony of your life. Maybe you're going crazy.

If this is just me going crazy, would the pain be so consistently responsive to what's around me, increasing and decreasing predictably?   The pain is just an itch now.   I stare at the tire swing, feeling that itching, waiting for an answer.

I'll just see where they end up. Then, if it doesn't mean anything to me, I'm going home.

This is ridiculous.

This might be the only chance I get for a long time to try to figure out what causes the pain. I sit a few more minutes, and then feel the itch become a scratch, then an itch again, and I know the van has pulled out of the gas station and is back on the highway. I start the engine and follow them.

Nineteen

Cruising down 231, Danzig blasting out of the van's speakers, Alan feels his excitement grow. What began as a stirring in the pit of his stomach when he woke up that morning is now radiating throughout his body, from the slight tightness in his chest to the tingling in his fingertips, from the mild vertigo in his head to the warmth in his groin and heaviness in his cock. There are still several more hours of anticipation ahead of them, but now the focus is on the day's main event, and all the distractions are behind them. He looks over at Denice, and she looks back and smiles at him, her chin seeming to jut out when she does, her brown eyes catching the sunlight that's all around them. He looks back at the road ahead, then glances at the mirror on his side. There are a few cars around, but not enough to hold them back or slow them down. Still, he keeps his speed below 65, within ten of the posted limit, just in case there are speed traps.

What they do on these trips began that night a year and a half ago at Boomer's when he flirted with and then discarded Tina the Cowgirl at the bar. But that was just a first, blind step in the right direction. He didn't realize what he really wanted until several months later.

* * *

Dothan, Alabama
February 1994

Alan parked the van in the driveway next to their half of the house and got out. The night air was chilly, but Alan barely noticed. Part of the warmth in him was from the alcohol—especially the two shots he did, straying from his usual strict beer habit. Mostly, though, it was the anticipation of Tracy.

Just then she pulled in behind the van, with Denice riding shotgun to provide directions to their place. Tracy killed the engine and the women got out at the same time, both smiling and giggling.

Alan stood on the little path leading to the front door and waited as they came to him, one on each side. Their bodies felt warm against his as he pulled them close, and he felt his dick stir inside his jeans and boxers. Tracy started playing with the buttons on his shirt, and he felt Denice's hand squeeze his ass. Stumbling a little, he turned the three of them as one unit and they walked somewhat unsteadily up the path and the few steps to the front door, where he actually had to struggle to get free of them and get his keys. He held the door as the two women walked through, then followed them in.

Even as he was shutting the door they were both on him again, taking his jacket off and fumbling with his shirt buttons. One of them, probably Denice, had turned on the light, and the sight of the two of them, both beautiful and blonde, Denice's hair long and wavy, Tracy's shoulder-length and more curly, caused Alan to swallow hard and his heart to thump almost audibly.

Denice reached up, put her hands around his neck, and pulled him down for a deep, hungry kiss, as if she were trying to consume him.

Normally at this point he would put both his arms around Denice and forget all about the other woman. That was the pattern they'd established, their game. Tracy would be the fourth woman to be suddenly ignored and pushed aside. Eventually, if she didn't catch a clue and leave, but instead started mouthing off, as two of the other women had, they would tell her to get the fuck out. But this time, Alan kept one arm around Tracy and, after a long minute, pulled away from Denice and turned to kiss the other.

He kept his right arm around Denice even as he turned from her, and he felt her stiffen: confusion and, he was pretty sure, fear running through her. He tightened his right arm around her a little more, holding her close, hoping to reassure her, silently telling her to trust him and requiring her loyalty. Then his tongue was sliding over Tracy's. She kissed differently—more jaw movement, with little bites at his lips. His cock pressed against the front of his pants, and he felt his power coursing like an electric current through his body.

He pulled back from Tracy, looked at Denice again and smiled, trying to reassure her. "OK, now you two kiss."

Denice searched his face, her eyebrows drawing together, worried, but then Tracy was leaning in, smiling, eyes closed. Alan dropped the smile and gave Denice a stern nod. She hesitated another moment, then shifted her head and returned Tracy's kiss. Alan watched up close as the two pretty faces pressed into each other, and then he pulled his arms away and took a step back. "Undress each other," he ordered.

Denice opened her eyes and tried to look at Alan, but he just nodded at her again. *Just go with it, Denice,* he thought as he kicked off his shoes.

Tracy already had Denice's jeans unsnapped and was working at the zipper, all while still kissing her greedily. Denice pushed Tracy's leather jacket off her shoulders and Tracy straightened her arms momentarily to let it slide off and drop to the floor. Then, having gotten the zipper down, Tracy slid the jeans off Denice's hips. Denice hiked up the short red dress Tracy was wearing, bunching it around Tracy's waist to reveal silky black panties at the top of smooth, gently-curved thighs which ended in a tight, jutting ass even nicer than Denice's.

Alan realized then he wanted nothing more than to fuck that perfect ass. He moved around behind Tracy and, putting his hands on her hips and bending his knees to lower himself, he pulled the firm roundness into his crotch and pressed his dick, still reined in by his clothing, against her crack. He slid his hands up and pulled the red dress over Tracy's head, then undid the clasp on the bra, which matched the black panties, and slipped the straps off a pair of creamy, lightly-freckled shoulders. He took a step back and undid the buttons on his jeans, letting them drop to the floor, and finished opening his shirt, exposing the front of his body.

Denice had stepped out of her shoes and jeans and was pulling off her T-shirt as Tracy bent to her breasts and began biting and licking through the white lace of Denice's bra. Tracy's bra was on the floor now, and Alan moved in from behind again to complete the Tracy sandwich, causing Tracy to straighten up and lean her head back for a kiss, which he gave, but then he broke away to peer over Tracy's right shoulder and see her perfect breasts culminating in distended pink nipples. He brought his hands up and stroked the hard points with his finger tips, eliciting from Tracy a sharp intake of breath followed by a moan.

Denice undid her bra, which clasped in the front, and shrugged out of it before going to her knees and pulling Tracy's panties down to the floor. Alan felt Tracy step out of them and, with Denice's help, her shoes while he was kissing her. He slid his right hand down to the short, trimmed hairs of her bush. Then he felt a hand on top of his, followed by the brush of Denice's hair. Tracy leaned back into him and spread her legs further to allow Denice access, and he heard wet lapping sounds as Denice began tonguing Tracy's snatch. Tracy let out a moan that was halfway to a yell and leaned more of her weight against Alan. He hadn't thought it possible, but her kissing actually became more urgent, her mouth so wide he thought she must be trying to swallow him whole. Alan pinched Tracy's nipples between his thumbs and forefingers, and she began to undulate, waves of passion literally washing through her body. She broke off kissing him and began panting and moaning.

Alan's erection had by this time found its way out of his boxers and was now pressing into Tracy's naked back. If they kept on with what they were doing, Tracy would probably come, but he didn't want her satisfied; he wanted her still hungry and quivering with need, like she was now. *Time to fuck her ass.* "Denice, go get the KY."

Denice immediately pulled back from Tracy's pussy, wiped the back of her hand across her mouth, and headed for the bathroom.

Tracy let out a little coo of disappointment, but seemed to get over it quickly as she straightened up and turned to face Alan. She grasped and squeezed his penis, then carefully worked the waistband of his boxers over it and down his legs to the floor. She looked up at him with a mischievous gleam in her eyes before taking his cock in her mouth. She blew him expertly, with one hand encircling the base of his shaft, pulling the skin tight, and the other stroking his balls.

I'll have to teach Denice to do this, he thought, then looked up to see her returning from the bathroom, her firm breasts bouncing slightly as she came down the stairs, the green and white tube of lubricant in her right hand. Alan savored the blow job a little longer, enjoying both the sensation of Tracy's mouth on his dick and the anticipation of reaming her ass.

Denice stood by obediently and watched, her face neutral.

Alan reached down, took a handful of hair on the back of Tracy's head, and tugged her head away from his crotch.

Her eyes opened and flicked up to Alan's, a momentary look of concern in them, quickly replaced by the gleam from before. She moved her head back and smiled. "Getting close?" she asked, a tiny hint of mockery in her voice.

"I hope you like it rough," he said, and pulled the hair straight up.

The smile left her face, replaced by furrows of pain. "Ow," she said as she quickly got to her feet.

He released his grip on her hair. "I'm sorry," Alan said. "Personally, I like a little pain—it intensifies everything. Are you OK?"

Tracy nodded, rubbing the back of her head. "Yeah, you just surprised me is all."

Alan smiled. "That's good, isn't it? Nothing worse than boring, predictable sex. So, you ever been butt-fucked?" he asked, making it sound like "So, you ever been to Albuquerque?"

"Uh, no," she said, shaking her head. "I'm really not into that."

Alan glanced over Tracy at Denice, who was already watching Alan's face as she stepped up close behind Tracy. *Good girl*, he thought. Alan shifted his eyes back to Tracy's face. "You are now," he said, still smiling, still with the happy, conversational tone in his voice. He took a step toward her.

Tracy smiled nervously. "Uh, no, maybe next time." She took a step back, and Denice grasped Tracy's upper arms from behind. Tracy jumped and started to twist away from both of them, the smile gone. "All right, what's go—"

Before Tracy could break free, Alan was on her. Together, he and Denice wrestled her to the floor. "Let's get her over to the coffee table," he ordered, and they half dragged, half carried her, kicking and grunting, across the carpet and pushed her face and shoulders down on the scattering of *Popular Mechanics* and *Fangoria* magazines. Alan got behind Tracy and knelt down on the backs of her lower legs. He put his hands on her shoulders and pressed her down onto the coffee table.

"NO! Let me go!" the bitch screamed.

"Shut up, you cunt!" Alan yelled. "Denice, get my belt out of my pants over there. I've got her."

Denice let go of her and ran across the room to where Alan's clothes lay piled.

The cunt thrashed around, trying to get loose. "Get *off* me you son of a bitch!"

The body struggling beneath him intensified his hard-on and his anger. He shifted his left hand over so it was pressing squarely between her shoulder blades and then grabbed the front of her throat with his right hand, slipping his thumb and forefinger under the corners of her jaw and pressing up. That stopped the shouting, replacing it with a high keening sound.

Denice trotted over with the cloth belt in hand.

"Work the part of it near the buckle into her mouth, then tighten it as hard as you can in back of her head," Alan instructed. "That'll keep her quiet."

Denice complied, and Alan helped by forcing his thumb and forefinger deeper into the soft flesh under the jaw and ordering her to open her mouth.

"OK, now come around to my side and kneel on her shoulders." He moved his hands as Denice climbed onto the gash's shoulders from behind. He looked at Denice's ass and noticed she was still wearing her panties, but he decided to let it go. "If she starts thrashing around again, press her face into the table, got it?"

"Sure thing, Chief," she said from her perch.

He smiled when he heard "Chief," then looked around for the lube. "Where's the KY?"

Denice looked over her shoulder. "Sorry—Ah guess Ah dropped it when we were grabbing her. You want me to go get it?"

"Nah, fuck it." He didn't want to delay any longer. Instead, he spit on his fingers and wiped them on his throbbing penis, repeating several times. Then he spread the cheeks of that sweet ass as wide as he could, like splitting a peeled orange, and pushed his rod into the gapped hole. The friction pulled at his cock's skin initially, but he wanted this so bad it was worth it. He kept driving and, spurred on by her grunts, spasms, and muffled screams, he forced his way in. After that, her blood made the path slicker, and he gained momentum. The cheeks jiggled a little every time he slammed home into that perfect ass. The more he fucked it, the more he wanted to fuck it so hard it would stay fucked forever. He found himself almost chanting "Take it, take it, take *that* you little cunt!" He wasn't sure why he was saying this, but it felt good, justified. He squeezed her hips harder as he approached climax, until the crescendo ended with him jackhammering her hole.

He stayed in her a while after he'd come, catching his breath, letting his heart slow down a little. When he finally pulled out, his dick was both still erect and filthy with blood and shit. As he stood, he realized he'd been kneeling on her calves the whole time, and now there were red and purple bruises the shape of his knees there. "Damn," he said, smiling, noting also that the legs didn't move.

Denice looked over her shoulder at him.

"Damn," he said again. Then: "Climb off—see what she does." He moved close to the slut's right side, and Denice climbed off on her left. Alan noticed another pair of bruises, one over each shoulder blade, where Denice's knees had been. The cunt didn't move, but he could hear her ragged breathing around the gag. He reached down and grasped the loose end of the belt where it came out of the buckle at the back of her head. He pulled. Only her head came up. He felt the dead weight of it, but he could still hear her breathing. He increased the tension until she pushed herself up off the coffee table. He stepped around and looked at her.

The face was wet and streaked with tears mixed with eye makeup. The watery eyes were shut at first, but opened as he was watching. They shifted in a brief search and found his. Her lips moved around the gag, as if she were trying to speak.

"Undo the belt," he told Denice. "Lower it so it's around the neck."

Even with the gag out, she still seemed to have trouble getting her mouth to work. Finally she managed to whisper "Please."

"Please? Please what? Please fuck me again? You're a horny little *cunt*, aren't you?"

More tears rolled down both cheeks. "Please…just let me go. Please." She whispered hoarsely.

"Oh, we'll let you go, all right, but first you have to suck me clean. I mean, look at this—it's disgusting! Your shit and blood all over me. Clean it off," he said, standing with his partially erect dick inches from her mouth. "Clean me off, and then we'll let you go." She started to reach up with her hands, but Alan slapped them down. "Not like that you stupid gash! With your *mouth*! Suck me clean."

More tears, then she closed her eyes and slowly leaned forward, her mouth slightly open, her lips and chin trembling.

"Oh, you're going to have to do better than that!" He grabbed her head with both hands and pulled her face against his cock. "I know you know how—you were doing great a little while ago."

She made a ridiculously weak attempt to comply.

Frustrated, Alan grabbed his half-erect, glistening penis and put it in her mouth. "Now clean it off!"

She worked her mouth around him, but her tongue was sticky instead of slippery. Still the sight of her on her knees, going down on his filthy root was enough to get him fully hard again.

He made her blow him for a good twenty minutes or so, until he actually came again, the second orgasm even more intense than the first. After that, though, he was spent. He pulled his boxers on and sat on the couch, watching his slave.

"OK, please, can I go now?" she asked meekly, not meeting his eyes anymore, but staring vacantly at the magazines strewn across the coffee table.

Now what? he wondered. He hadn't planned any of this; it had all just happened. Not that he was complaining, since he'd gotten his rocks off twice, but now he really had no clue what to do with this little fuck bunny in his living room, and would like her to just disappear. "What do you think, Denice? You ready to let this little vixen go?"

Denice, who had been standing by awkwardly the whole time he was getting sucked off, looked at him uncertainly, obviously searching his face for the right answer. *What* is *the right answer?* He considered letting her put her clothes on and walk out—get in her car and get out of the way. She'd been fun, but now having her here was a pain. *But then what?* He slowly shook his head at Denice.

"Uh, no—no!" Denice replied, unsure at first but then more confident. "No way! She comes in here, fucks my man, and expects to just walk out of here like nothin' happened?! No way!" She wound up and slapped the back of the gash's head as hard as she could, knocking the kneeling figure forward, back down onto the coffee table. "Fuck that! She has to pay!"

Alan couldn't tell if Denice had actually hit hard enough to throw her onto the table, or if the slut was just cowering. *No way*, he thought. There was no way they could just let her walk out of here. She'd go to the police, or at least to the hospital, which would probably go to the police after they saw the bruises and what he did to her asshole. *No way can she walk out of here.* He stood, walked around behind the slumped figure, and picked up the loose end of the cloth belt, which was still cinched around her neck. He held the fabric strip in his right hand for several seconds, considering, watching the pussy's back shaking—she was crying again. He thought about strangling her, but then, on impulse, he jerked her head back and simultaneously shot out a kick, his heel connecting with where her neck met her shoulders. He'd meant to hit higher and break her neck, but he'd hit low, and that sent the bitch into a frenzy of panic. She leaped up and lunged against the belt, but he held tight and yanked backward. She stumbled—almost fell—backward, then got her feet under her and lunged against the belt again, this time almost tearing it out of his hand. Alan grabbed on with his other hand as well. "Get the hammer!" he shouted to Denice, who immediately ran for the kitchen. Alan had a good hammer in the van, but they kept a cruddy old hammer in a drawer in the kitchen for little jobs like hanging pictures. It took all his strength to reign the bitch in. At least she wasn't screaming—the people in the other half of the duplex would only be able to hear so much of that before they'd stop dismissing it as normal sex noise. No, instead she was making a weird gagging—sort of a suppressed coughing—sound, and Alan figured the noose around her neck was partially strangling her. *Where the fuck is Denice?* He wondered as another lunge pulled him a step closer to the front door. Bitch still had a lot of fight in her, he'd give her that. He felt like a sport fisherman trying to reel in a whopper.

Denice returned, holding the hammer out to him, handle first like he'd taught her. but he was afraid to lessen his grip on the belt. "You do it! Whack her in the head!" he said, consciously holding back from shouting, worried the people next door might wake up. Denice hesitated. *"Do it!"* he shout-whispered, and Denice turned the hammer in her hands and stepped toward the slut's head. Another lunge brought them all another step toward the door. *"Fuckin' do it!"* he whisper-shouted again.

Denice, holding the hammer in both hands, raised it above her head and brought it down on the back of the cunt's head.

It was only a glancing blow, though, and the fuck actually did manage to scream, and struggled some more.

"God damn it, Denice, hit her!" he whisper-shouted louder.

Denice glanced at him, her face worried, then back at the bucking, grunting woman, who was now covering her head with her hands and arms. She raised the hammer with both hands and this time she got a better hit in, on the unprotected base of the skull, just above the neck. The gash went limp and hit the floor.

Still holding the belt in his left hand, Alan stuck out his right. "Give me it," he snapped. He took it and stepped up to the slut's head, kicked her arms out of the way, and took a couple shortened practice swings aiming for a spot just behind an ear. He brought the hammer down, and there was a sort of crunching sound. He swung again. And again, until the head was like the cat's head all those years ago: smashed and indisputably dead.

* * *

That night, messy, unplanned, and *extremely* risky, was a moment of clarity for him. Because as perfect as Denice is for him, there are some things he just can't—*won't*—do with her. *Because* he loves her. And because she'd do anything for him; the complete obedience is normally great, but sometimes you just want to make somebody do what she doesn't want to do. He and Denice had tried some stuff, pretending he was raping her, but it just wasn't the same. Looking back, he sees he'd been heading for that night for months and just hadn't realized it.

After that night his restless moods mostly went away, and his relationship with Denice got better and stronger. But to maintain that, he needs to blow off steam every so often—every three months has been fine, though he's thought about changing that to every two months, since three months seems like such a *long* time. Anticipation is one thing, but...

Anyway, they've refined their techniques, improved their planning. That first night had been all improvisation, but fortunately he's a quick thinker. He checked the papers for a while afterward, and never did see mention of anyone finding the body. For all he knew the Chattahoochee River carried the body down to Lake Seminole, if the gators didn't eat it first. Someone surely found the car, or what was left of it after they wiped it down and turned the gas tank and interior into a gasoline-fueled firebomb. They'd left it burning on a concrete pad in an abandoned trailer park Alan had passed one day on the way to a job site, and that was the last they saw or heard of anything to do with that first one.

Alan smiles. The music, the road hurtling beneath them, the landscape scrolling by—he looks over at Denice, and she smiles back at him. *Good times.*

Twenty

We end up at the waterfront in Panama City Beach, arriving at about five p.m. The van turns into the large parking lot in front of a sprawling club called "Breakers". To not draw attention to myself and Stacey, I keep driving past the club. My scar's itching vanishes several seconds later. I end up about a quarter mile down the road at a little dive of a seafood restaurant built to resemble a fisherman's shack. Or maybe it was a shack someone turned into a—well, "restaurant" is a strong word. *Now what?* I feel exasperated, but realize it's probably partly due to being hungry, the peanut butter and pickle sandwich having long since evaporated. I kill the engine and go in.

This being a seafood place, there isn't much for a vegan to order, but I'm not likely to find any better options around here. I decide to go with a fried oyster sandwich, fries, and unsweetened iced tea. Obviously shellfish are animals, but lacking a brain or even much of a nervous system, they can't be much more aware of pain or their lives than a plant, so it seems OK to eat them. As I wait by the counter I notice a large bottle of Tabasco sauce, so when I get my sandwich I sprinkle it liberally. I carry my food to the small deck out back, and eat in the spotty shade of a faded and torn umbrella. The cool breeze off the Gulf of Mexico and the cold tea feel great after the heat inside the car and the extreme cold of the air conditioned interior of the restaurant. I savor the lack of discomfort and the satiation of hunger.

Eventually, as I sit sipping the last of the tea while gazing at the sunlight glittering off the waves, I wonder if maybe the couple will be gone by the time I get back to the club.

Actually, it's more hope than wonder that I feel, and I decide if they are gone, then that will be it and I'll just turn around and go home. I could be home before nine.

After finding a gas station and refilling Stacey's tank, I head back to Breakers. At first I try to deny it, but the familiar itch along my scar intensifies the closer I get to the club. "Shit," I say softy. I turn and park on the other side of the Breakers lot from the white van, nose out so I can see it as I sit. The parking lot quickly becomes boring, though, and isn't telling me anything about why this ordinary couple triggers this bizarre sensory flashback in me. I lock Stacey's door and walk across the pavement to the club.

As I get closer I can hear Jimmy Buffet singing *Cheeseburger in Paradise* over the club's outdoor sound system. Hearing Buffet's distinctive voice reminds me he is, ironically, a fellow native of Massachusetts. I don't remember where I picked up that piece of trivia. I don't think he mentions it much himself—images of autumn leaves, snowy landscapes, and puritan forebears doesn't really mesh well with the tropical beach bum stage persona he's cultivated.

There's no cover and no bouncer at the door, so I walk right in. The interior was designed and decorated to look like a big beachside hut, with large, airy spaces under exposed wooden beams and palm fronds. On my way through I notice a mounted swordfish, casting nets, dive flags and equipment, coconuts, and wicker furniture. There's a bar on one side and what looks like an area where food is served on another, but there aren't many people in here now, so I don't slow down much to look around. Instead, I follow the mounting pain out the broad openings in the ocean-side wall and onto a deck which stretches the length of the building.

A few feet below me is the beach, which at this time of year and at this hour is sparsely populated, so the couple is easy to spot. They've spread a blanket out and are lying together, surrounded by the white sand this part of the Florida coast is noted for. I descend a few wooden steps and walk out onto the sand, but keep my distance. Even from forty or fifty feet away I can see they look reasonably fit and, I suppose, attractive in their swimsuits. They aren't reading, and don't seem to talk much; they just lie on the beach in the fading, cooling sunlight, ordinary and innocuous. *What is it about them?* After a while, I get up and walk close by them, but above their heads so it would be hard for them to see me. Predictably, the pain cranks up to an intensity that almost takes my breath away as I pass within a few feet of them. I swallow and master the suffering, and observe it diminish as I continue walking down the beach. I find a new, more comfortable vantage point about a hundred feet away, and sit again to watch them and listen to more Jimmy Buffet songs. At this range my scar feels like it's glowing and stinging at the same time, as if the scar tissue, and only the scar tissue, were badly sunburned.

After about half an hour they get up, fold their blanket, and head for the parking lot. I follow at a distance and watch them enter the back of the van. I return to Stacey and watch as, a few minutes later, they re-emerge in dressier—but still casual—clothing: a short maroon skirt and crimson tank top for her, and khakis and a loose-fitting short-sleeve light green shirt for him. They enter the club and after a few minutes so do I.

I find them in the restaurant part of the club I noticed earlier. It's much busier now, with people ordering sandwiches and small items like nachos and chicken fingers. Not hungry and not interested in watching them eat dinner, I find my way upstairs to another big open space with broad picture windows overlooking the beach and the ocean. Recorded music, not Buffet but something pop-sounding I can't identify, is playing over the sound system, but it isn't extremely loud and I have no trouble hearing a waitress when she stops by. I've been to clubs only twice before, but I know about needing to buy a drink, so I order a tomato juice. Fortunately, there was still no cover to get in, and I have some cash on me, so I can afford the exorbitant charge and a tip for the waitress.   I decide to make the drink last as long as possible.

Sitting and watching the sunset is pleasant. My mind rests more or less empty, aware of the sharp cutting and tearing sensation below my sternum, but otherwise content to wait quietly and listen to the music, which is actually not bad—mostly classic rock like Van Halen, ZZ Top, and Aerosmith, and some newer stuff like Guns N' Roses and Red Hot Chili Peppers. I don't listen to music much anymore, but I still like hearing this.

After about half an hour I feel the pain go deeper into me. It's useless, but I knead the scar with my finger tips as the cramps behind it sharpen. As an experiment, based on what I've seen earlier today, I guess they're maybe fifty feet away, then turn and look back across the broad expanse of dance floor and seating space to search for them.   There are considerably more people out here now than when I first arrived, but after a minute of studying the crowd I see them, as I anticipated, about fifty feet away at the bar, ordering drinks. Beverages in hand, they walk to a small table and sit down across from each other. Between sips from their glasses, their heads and eyes are swiveling, taking in everything around them.

I move to a more shadowy location where I can watch without turning and without, I hope, being obvious. Occasionally either the man or the woman leans in to the other and speaks, and then they usually both look in one direction or another, sometimes laughing, sometimes nodding appreciatively.   People watching—more ordinariness. Probably that's what they like to do for fun when they go out. Maybe they're looking to make new friends or something.

That sounds weird and foreign to me, but I've heard people do that.

Eventually I feel pressure in my bladder and, abandoning my now empty glass, I head for the bathroom.

Twenty-One

They are close now, and Alan feels the strange mix of excitement and calm that comes over him at these times. He and Denice lean forward on their little table, scanning the room and sipping their beers.

"OK, your four o'clock, Jeff—Red at the bar," Denice says, using Alan's alias for practice.

Alan turns to look at a big-breasted young woman with flaming red hair down to her shoulder blades, standing at the bar ordering. "Interesting—a red head would be new. I've never had a red head." He watches as the bartender puts three drinks in front of her, which she carries back to a table where two other women wait. "Oh well," he says, and sweeps the room with his eyes. He notices a pretty blonde—her hair is short, but her face is striking—sitting off towards a wall, alone, with a single, mostly empty glass in front of her.

"Oh Jeff, you've got to check this guy out—your seven."

Alan flicks his eyes back to Denice, sees her smiling, then turns to follow her sight line. A middle-aged guy—late forties, minimum—with a Hawaiian shirt and jet black hairpiece over a salt and pepper fringe, is standing at a table talking with two women who look like they're probably still in college. "That's just embarrassing, Diane," Alan says. "I'm embarrassed for him. So, check out your four. Short blonde hair sitting alone."

Denice shakes her head, smiling at Hairpiece. "Whah do guys do that? Who do they think they're fooling? Same with those comb-overs—*yuck*!" She leans back in her chair and looks casually around over her left shoulder first, then her right, while stretching, then leans forward on the table again.

"She's pretty," she says, turning back to Alan and meeting his eyes.

"And alone."

"I can try bumping into her in the bathroom, Jeff."

"Sounds like a plan to me, Diane," he replies, smiling. He leans forward and kisses her briefly, the tips of their tongues touching for a moment.

Alan looks again at Red, sitting with her two friends, and thinks about ways they might split her off to be with them.

Denice says "Sometime we should take two at once; we could handle them."

He looks over at her, sees she is looking straight ahead at a pair of women, who are in turn checking out some guys at a pool table and giggling. "I'm sure you're right, Diane." He watches the girls and thinks about it. "That would open all kinds of new possibilities, wouldn't it?" He turns his head and sees Denice looking at him, the wicked gleam in her eyes matching the grin on her lips. "You're a bad girl, Diane," he says, laughing quietly.

She shrugs. "It's just hard to find someone a—"

Movement in his peripheral vision catches Alan's attention and he looks up to see the solitary blonde walk past them. "There she goes," he whispers, interrupting Denice.

Denice tracks her visually. "She's headed for the bathroom—I'm on." Her eyes widen briefly and she takes a deep breath. "OK, Jeff, see you in a few!"

"I'll be here."

Twenty-Two

I gaze blankly at the door to my stall, enjoying the solitude while I feel the liquid drain out and the pressure on my bladder ease. *At least it's a decent bathroom*: clean, well-lit, and stocked with toilet paper. I look down at the array of inch-square tiles, mostly white with some black thrown in, and I try to make out if there is a pattern to the placement of the contrasting colors.

I wince as the hurt under my heart quickly mounts. Surprised and alarmed, I look up at the stall door again. *Why is he coming this way?* Just as I'm reminding myself the men's restroom is immediately adjacent to the women's, the door to the bathroom opens and the pain peaks. *Is he in here?* I wonder, panic reasserting itself. *Is he coming after me?* I strain my ears, listening. The person who came in hasn't gone to a stall. *He's out there waiting for me. Fuck! I should have listened to the pain and stayed the fuck away from him!* There are little clinks and rustling noises, like someone rummaging in a purse. *No, calm down—maybe it's not him. Or he's next door in the men's room, and this person coming in here was just a coincidence.* Silently, I ease myself off the toilet and look under the stall's door. A pair of slender legs ending in strappy, stylish women's shoes with fairly low, broad heals stands facing the sinks. I don't actually do it, but mentally I breathe out a huge sigh of relief. I sit on the toilet again. He must be in the men's room, just the other side of the wall behind me—that would account for it, right? *Either that, or I really am going insane.*

I finish up and exit the stall, crossing to a vacant sink to wash my hands, managing with great effort to keep my posture erect and my face composed despite the intense hurt. *It's not real, it's not real...*

The woman at the sink is the female half of the couple I've been following. She's leaning in to the mirror, applying lipstick. Her eyes flick toward mine in the mirror, making contact before I can look away. "Hey," she says, pausing long enough from applying the lipstick to flash a bright smile.

Still surprised at the coincidence, I manage to nod slightly. "Hi." *Does she know I've been following her? Is she going to confront me?* I look away and turn on the water, putting my hands in the stream from the tap, wishing the liquid could cool the pain in me.

"You are *sooo* lucky!" The voice is pure South.

I pause in mid-reach for the soap dispenser and look at the other woman's reflection. "What?" The word comes out sounding a little like a gasp.

The woman has put her lipstick back in her purse and now is opening a compact. "Your bone structure—those cheekbones—you don't need to do this," she says, making eye contact in the mirror again and holding up a tiny brush before using it to apply a dusting of color under her cheekbone to create the illusion of more shadow. "Wearing your hair short like that shows them off even more—Ah'm kahnd of envious. Ah'm just glad Ah'm married so Ah don't have to compete with you!" she says, smiling broadly.

I look back at the soap dispenser and press the lever, feeling embarrassed, wishing the pain would stop. I force a deep breath and then speak carefully to keep my voice level and natural sounding. "Thanks. Um...I don't think you'd have anything to worry about." I start soaping my hands quickly, eager to be done with this and out of here.

"Oh *raht*, Ah'm sure," she says ironically. "Amazing cheekbones and modest too."

I rinse my hands, pull a paper towel out of the dispenser to my left, and dry them as I head for the door, desperate to get away.

"Bah the way, mah name is Diane," the other woman says, offering her hand as I'm stepping past. She pronounces her name *Dah*-ann.

I stop and automatically grasp the offered hand, squeezing too hard at first, but quickly relaxing my grip when I feel the lack of pressure in hers. "I'm Shailene."

"Shailene?"

Diane holds my hand for another beat while I nod, making me feel even more uncomfortable, on top of the sensation that I'm being stabbed. *It's definitely her that's causing this pain.*

"What an interesting name. Say, you're not from around here, are you?"

I guess she's basing this observation on my lack of a southern accent and not on my cheekbones, modesty, or name, but what is this about? "No, just visiting."

"You here with your boyfriend? Or looking for someone new?" she asks with a conspiratorial grin.

What? As much as I want to put distance between us, I decide to go with it, just a little, to see what I can find out. After all, this is probably my last, best chance to understand the pain. "I don't have a boyfriend, so I guess the second thing," I say, forcing myself to smile back as convincingly as possible. "Really, though, I'm just hanging out."

"You want to hang out with mah husband and Ah? We're pretty much doing the same thing—just came down here to go to the beach, have a couple drinks and relax."

"Sure, that would be nice," I say, going completely against everything I want to do and hoping that's a good idea. I follow Diane back to the little table she and her *did she say "husband"?* had taken earlier. As we walk, I wipe some sweat from my forehead with the back of my hand. Then I glance down at Diane's left hand and see it still lacks rings.

"Honey, look what Ah found in the bathroom," Diane says, smiling broadly.

I inwardly roll my eyes at this, and wonder if the pain is some kind of annoying people warning. *No, I'd hurt all the time if it were that.*

The man is smiling even before his wife announces me. Now he half stands and sticks out his hand. "Hey, Jeff Lind."

"Shailene," I say, gripping back.

"Whew! Strong grip!" he says.

I let go and force a smile, not sure what to say to that, feeling completely awkward, and having a hard time concentrating because of the continuing torture in my midsection. We all sit down; I try to sit as far back from them as I can, but it's not far enough to ease the pain at all and makes it harder to hear. *This is just going to hurt, and I'm just gonna have to take it.*

Jeff signals to a passing waitress. "I'm buyin'—what'll you have, Shailene?" he asks.

"Uh, just uh, I don't know, a Coke, I guess."

"Aww, c'mon, relax!"

I shake my head, but decide to not mention I don't drink. "No thanks—I've got to drive home, and I already had one drink."

Jeff nods once, then turns to the waitress. "One Coke, a beer for me, and," he looks at Diane, "daiquiri?"

She looks from him to the waitress and nods, and the waitress heads for the bar.

"So where *are* you from?" Diane asks.

We make small talk like that for a few minutes, mostly me answering their friendly questions and listening to their polite comments about my responses. They're surprisingly easy to talk to. I carefully avoid mentioning my last name or being in the military, giving out only the student part of my identity which is, after all, true. I try to be discrete as I wipe away the perspiration that keeps forming on my upper lip and forehead. I feel it running down my back too. *Damn this hurts.* Fortunately, it's not long before the conversation takes an odd turn.

"So you're between boyfriends, hunh?" Jeff asks casually. "I remember the dating scene—lot of lonely nights before I met Diane. Course, just because we got married doesn't mean we have to stop having fun." He looks at his wife.

As if on cue, she says, "Yeah, we're pretty open-minded about the whole marriage thing." This bit of dialogue somehow sounds canned.

I have no idea what to say to this. "Yeah, well I see you're not wearing wedding rings, if that's what you mean."

They both laugh. "Very observant! What did you say you were going to school for? Private investigating?"

"No, computer science," I say, unable to think of any other comment. I get that he's trying to be funny, but I find it grating.

"What we're getting at, Shailene," Diane says, leaning closer, "is sometahms we lahk to invaht someone over to party with us—sort of a date, but with both of us."

I stare at Diane, wondering if I'm hearing this right.

"I swear we're both clean," says Jeff will holding his hands up on either side of his head, as if showing me how clean his palms are. "And we always use protection, for us as much as our dates."

"And you can trust us—we won't do anything you're uncomfortable with." Diane rests her finger tips lightly on my arm as she says this, setting off alarms all over me. Instinctively I pull my arm back a few inches, breaking contact with her.

Him again: "It's really just for fun, and if you haven't tried the group thing before, it's a chance to experience something new." The back and forth is like some kind of rehearsed tag-team sales pitch. If the words were different, I'd think they were trying to enroll me in their Amway scheme.

I hit my weirdness limit. "Uh, I'm sorry," I say, shaking my head in surprise as much as to indicate "No." I look up from the table at Jeff and then Diane. "I'm sure it's a lot of fun, and you both seem like nice people, but I'm just—I guess I'm kind of old-fashioned that way. I'm not interested. Sorry." As I stand up I pull some crumpled bills from my pocket. "Let me pay for my Coke," I say, pulling out a five.

"Don't worry about it," are the words Jeff uses, but his tone says "Fuck off, bitch."

Startled, I shove the money back into my pocket. "I'm sorry," I say quickly and walk as fast as I can to the stairs leading to the first floor, find the exit, and leave the building.

Twenty-Three

"And you can trust us—we won't do anything you're uncomfortable with." Denice/Diane lies.

Alan/Jeff notices she touches the small blonde woman's arm as she says this, which is normally a good move, but the bitch almost immediately pulls her arm away. She's even sweating despite the air-conditioning. It's obvious they've lost her, which is frustrating, and not only because of the additional delay and need to continue searching. If he'd just seen Shailene in passing, a face in the crowd somewhere, he probably wouldn't even notice her. The characteristics obvious from a distance—flat chest, very short hair, and lack of makeup—would not have caught his attention. Now that he is sitting across from her, though, he can see how pretty she is: the clean lines of her face, the blonde slashes of eyebrows angling down toward the center, the well-defined cheekbones, and the clarity of her skin make her really attractive. He wants badly to see that beautiful, balanced, appealing face contorted in agony, and then to cut it open. "It's really just for fun, and if you haven't tried the group thing before, it's a chance to experience something new," he says, giving it one last try, but he knows he's lost her, and he wants to throttle her right here in the bar.

"Uh, I'm sorry," she says, shaking her head *no*. She looks up at Jeff, then shifts her eyes quickly to Diane. "I'm sure it's a lot of fun, and you both seem like nice people, but I'm just—I guess I'm kind of old-fashioned that way. I'm not interested. Sorry." As she stands up she has the audacity to pull some wadded money from a front pocket in her jeans. "Let me pay for my Coke," she says.

As if he gave a flying fuck about her fucking Coke. He wants to come across the table and slam his fist into that perfect, narrow nose, but *he* is in control and he won't let this prissy little bitch goad him into making a scene and ruining his plans. "Don't worry about it," he says, keeping his anger in check, but letting enough of it through to get rid of her.

She gets the message and shoves the money back into her pocket. "I'm sorry," she says quickly and practically runs for the stairs leading to the first floor.

Scared her the fuck off, he thinks with short-lived satisfaction. He looks over at Denice.

She smiles weakly, reaches out and grasps his hand. "Hey, don't worry. We've missed before, but we always get someone."

Denice—*Diane*—is right.   He takes a couple deep breaths, dispelling the rage, purging the violent thoughts, getting back into charm mode. Her hand on his helps with this; her touch calms him. Sure, it would've been fun to take that cunt apart, but... "It's cool," he says, "No problem." He takes a sip of his beer, the act of which makes him feel more calm, more back to normal. He takes another sip and sets it down. He gives her hand two quick squeezes, then lets go and leans back. He turns his head and eyes to his far left and resumes scanning the room for likely prospects.

Twenty-Four

Outside, I hurry across the parking lot, my mind racing to catch up. Even though I know from the diminishing pain that the distance between us is growing, I find myself looking over my shoulder, wondering if Jeff might be following me to act out the anger I heard in his voice. I get in the car, lock the door, and sit staring out the windshield. The absence of pain, replaced by the mild itching, tells me he's not coming after me, but I still want to start the engine and get the hell out of here.

But I don't; I stay right where I am. I think again of Private Williams and his flat, expressionless eyes, and about discovering how the pain responded to his proximity. Then I think of Diane and Jeff: I see their faces in my mind, hear their friendly, carefree voices, and then the way Jeff sounded when he made that last comment. *This is crazy. How can it be? It's impossible.* I wonder what would have happened if I'd gone with them. Then I think about them still in there, most likely approaching another woman. I look across the parking lot—I can see the raised top of the white van over the mass of cars that arrived since I got here.

At least, I *think* that's the van. I start the car and drive slowly around the parking lot until I confirm the van's identity by its license plate and find a better parking space from which to watch it. I back in and cut the lights and engine.

There is no rational explanation for what I am experiencing. The most obvious explanation seems simply wrong: I didn't know Jeff and Diane were at the mall when I walked out of the bookstore, and I didn't realize I was near the detention facility in Korea the first time I passed it. How can a flashback be triggered by something or someone unavailable to my senses, by someone I'm otherwise completely unaware of? And what kind of flashback varies so predictably and consistently with physical proximity to another person, the way this pain does? The ability to sense at a distance the threat posed by certain people fits nowhere in my framework of thought.

Actually, that's not quite accurate. Flashbacks aside, since the Bad I've found I *can* sometimes sense danger. Like the time when, for no particular reason, I had a bad feeling about my car. This wasn't Stacey, but rather the car I had in flight school, the hand-me-down station wagon my grandparents gave me when I graduated from West Point. I'd been driving the car without incident for several months, but one morning, for the first time, I had a bad feeling as I unlocked the door and started to get in. I got back out, walked all around the old vehicle, and saw nothing wrong. I was about to get back in when, on impulse, I squatted down and found a fresh puddle underneath. It turned out to be brake fluid—a seal had failed and much of the liquid had seeped out overnight. And then there was that mission during the Ranger Orientation Program when I sensed Sergeant Pike was setting us up to walk into a simulated ambush with his "speed is security" line. That wasn't real danger, obviously, but maybe because I took those missions so seriously, it seemed real to me on some level. Incidents like these might have seemed a little spooky to me when they happened, but mostly I was just glad to have anticipated the trouble when there was still time to deal with it.

So maybe this relived pain is another piece of the same puzzle, just scarier because it's a lot less subtle, and because it's more obviously connected to the Bad.

Oh fuck... I think, and feel like throwing up.

Twenty-Five

"**I** actually did a group thing last year with a couple at Florida State—they had an apartment off campus. I was kind of nervous and wouldn't have done it except they were really nice like you and Diane."

Jeff nods, really believing he is inviting Kristen to have sex with him and Diane. That's the key: really believing your own lies while you tell them. There's always time to remember the truth later. "So it went well, I take it—I mean, you seem interested."

"Oh yeah, it was really fun. We did it a few times. I was sorry to see them go after they graduated."

Her eyes—they're pale, though he can't tell exactly what color they are in the dim club lighting—her eyes smile along with the rest of her face as she says this. She's obviously turned on by her memories and the anticipation of making new ones with him and Diane. He notices again what a great smile she has—almost as good as his own—and the contrast of her dark hair with the paleness of her eyes is compelling in an almost exotic way. She has a great body too—he was able to check that out when she was standing at the bar with her girlfriends, before he peeled her away and lured her back to the table to meet Diane. Though she's sitting down across from him now, he can still see how really big her breasts are thanks to the tight tie-dyed tank top she's wearing. Breasts that big tend to sag under their own weight, and he wonders if they'll still look good naked. But she can't be more than twenty-one, so they'll probably be fine. In fact, he's glad that chick with the short blonde hair turned out to be such a frigid bitch since this one has a much better body and is almost as pretty.

"Ah totally know what you mean about the first tahm," Diane says. "Jeff and Ah talked about it ahead of tahm, of course, but Ah was still kahnd of nervous. It helped, though, that she was really sexy, lahk you."

She touches Kristen's hand lightly as she says this, and Kristen smiles and almost squirms in her seat. She's ready to go now.

"Plus, being bah, this is pretty much the only way Ah can be with a woman now that Ah'm married."

Jeff knows they should get gone now since more talk only risks saying something to change her mind. "Listen, I don't know about you two, but I'm ready to get out of here." He knows Diane will follow his lead, so he looks at Kristen, who smiles broadly and nods eagerly. He turns to Diane. "Why don't you ride with Kristen—" he breaks off as he feels a light touch on his hand. He turns to look at her, worried he's just set them back by misjudging and moving too fast.

"Call me 'Krissy'," OK? I like that better."

Jeff notices her smile is a little sloppy, and is glad they're getting out of here now before she has any more to drink. The last thing he wants is for her to be anesthetized. "OK, Krissy it is," he says, managing to smile convincingly again. He turns back to Diane. "So like I was saying, Diane, I think you should ride with Krissy so if we get separated in traffic you can still give her directions to our place. Sound good?" It felt weird asking if his instructions were OK, but he quickly got back into Jeff mode and looked questioningly at the girl, as if he were looking for her consent as well.

"Sure, that sounds great," Krissy says, nodding eagerly again. "Let's go!"

Twenty-Six

Now, watching the white van in the parking lot outside Breakers, I have both the sense of impending danger *and* the itching in my scar. Thirty minutes pass; cars and people come and go. Another half hour goes by as I sit listening to fragments of music from the club, voices of people walking by, traffic noise on Front Beach Road, the street running by the club. Finally, after more than ninety minutes all together, the pain in me ramps up, and a minute or two later Jeff appears in my field of vision. He walks up to the driver door on the van, unlocks it, and gets in. *Just him?* I start Stacey's engine, but keep the lights off. The van backs out, then heads slowly for the street. I turn in my seat to watch it and see it pause at the parking lot exit, and then another car—something small, red, and sporty—approaches the van. I can just make out a dark-haired woman driving, and someone else, Diane I guess, in the passenger seat. As the red car draws near to the van, Jeff pulls out onto Front Beach Road, heading west. The sporty car follows behind, and I pull out of my space and leave the lot right after that. Fortunately, even at night the tall van is easy to pick out in the moderate traffic along the restaurant and hotel-studded strip of beach front, and I see it take a right on Highway 79.

In less than a mile we leave the lights and activity of the shore behind, and are plunging into the dark forests and swamps of the interior. The highway is dead straight, and I slow to allow more distance between me and the other two vehicles, but just as I'm doing this I see a brief splash of white light on the road, and then the van turning. Then the tail lights on the car draw together and the white light of its headlights appears to the left momentarily as it turns. I try to keep my eyes on the point where they left the highway, but it's hard to do on an unlit road devoid of visual reference points. I hit the accelerator to catch up. Fortunately, there seems to be only one turn off to the left in that stretch, so I kill my headlights and take it. The new road, though smaller, is also straight, and I manage to see them just as they take a right up ahead. As soon as the car leaves the road, I turn on my headlights again and speed up until I reach and take the turn. I turn off my lights again, but this road is not as straight, and I don't see the lights of the others any more. Without headlights it is really dark here—too dark to see where I'm going—so I have to turn them back on. I pass a crossroad, but continue on and speed up some. I drive for a few minutes past a couple more side roads, but without seeing any vehicles, before I notice the itching on my scar has completely vanished. *Shit.* I reach a second crossroad and stop. If they came this far, there's no way I'll find them. I know nothing about these roads, where any of them might lead or how far. But I'm more relieved than disappointed to have lost them.

Twenty-Seven

Alan squats down beside their prisoner, his face inches from the skin on her arm, smelling the terror coming off her, *feeling* it like a vibration in the air. He examines her naked body closely, savoring the reality of the moment. He barely hears Denice's taunts, but listens closely as the prisoner tries to appease them, to gain their pity and compassion. She won't, but he enjoys hearing her try. He notices the plastic ratchet ties pinning her wrists to the tops of the rear chair legs are already chafing at the skin: there's a thin, raw, red strip just above the milky white of the thin plastic strap. Still squatting, he side steps and looks at her left ankle, sees chafing there too, just under the small rose tattoo. He turns and looks at her large breasts with their broad, pink nipples. Her breasts, big and firm to begin with, are made to seem larger by the way he has her arms pinned back behind her. He raises his eyes to her face, meets her pleading, tear-filled eyes and smiles, not to be mean, but sincerely, because the moment is so perfect. He is in control, and she is *not*; *she* must submit to *him*.

"C'mon, Chief, let's do this!" Denice says, agitated, impatient.

He turns his head and looks at Denice's face, which is red and angry. By contrast, he feels incredibly calm now that they finally have the gash tied to the chair, now that all the waiting and preparation and anticipation are over. Now he is completely in the moment, experiencing it totally to make up for the long months since the last time, and the long months before the next. He says nothing; he swivels his head and sees the cunt's eyes flick from looking at Denice, back down to meet his.

"Please, sir, please…" Her voice is hoarse and more tears roll down her cheeks. Her big breasts quiver; her whole body is trembling.

Slowly he stands, and her eyes stay locked with his, following him as he rises above her. The roof over the main part of the van was already removed and replaced with a truck cap when he bought it, so there is just enough headroom to stand up. He cups her chin in the palm of his left hand, letting her believe she is getting through to him. With the fingers of his right hand he combs her dark, almost black hair back from her face and marvels again at how light her gray-blue eyes are. He strokes her hair some more, gazing into her eyes.

"Alan…" Denice says, sounding impatient.

"Shut up," he says quietly, assured in his authority, now enjoying Denice's discomfort as well as the bitch's.

"Please, sir, please, just let me go…"

He smiles down at her, looking kindly on her. His fingers flow through the hair, this time combing it back behind her left ear, which he then grabs and twists as hard as he can while watching the shock and pain light up the gray-blue eyes. Keeping his eyes on hers, he lets go of her chin and holds his left hand out to Denice. "Hand me the vice grips."

The vice grips, he's learned, inflict acute pain both when they are applied and when released, while the soldering iron's effect seems only to diminish as it destroys the underlying tissue. Still, he likes to employ both. The advantage of the soldering iron is its shape; its similarity to a penis has not escaped him.

Her screams are like foreplay in their effect on him.

He supposes that's why what he does has evolved the way that it has. The first time, back at the house in Dothan, his initial intention really had been just sex—vanilla sex except for the threesome part. And except for the forced rear entry and the part at the end when they had to kill her, that's actually all it was. The next time he knew from the start his goal was to hurt and eventually kill, but it had still started out with sex. But with the last couple bitches he couldn't wait to start making them hurt, and discovered doing this stuff first actually makes the sex better.

"Please, God, please, NO! *Pleeeeease!*"

"Go ahead and scream, bitch! Ain't no one out here to hear you except us!" Denice holds her face inches from the cunt's when she shouts this as loud as she can. She likes to yell at the fucks now that he has them using the van parked in a remote place instead of getting a motel room.

Her tears are mixed with sweat now as he holds the soldering iron under her chin, not touching the skin yet, but close enough for her to feel the intense heat coming off the metal. Then he realizes he is sweating too. The interior of the van, which had been cool from the breeze generated when they were driving, is becoming really warm and humid now that they're stopped. This is only the second time they've used the van—the last time was in January, so heat wasn't a problem. He considers starting the van's air conditioner, or maybe just opening the side door.

All this is in the back of his mind, though, as he holds her head by the hair and moves the tip of the soldering iron into her nose. Even his tight grip on her hair is unable to prevent her thrashing her head around, but with the smoking rod actually in her nose, she is only making things worse for herself by moving. He smells the burning flesh, and thinks again of fire consuming all the bad stuff, the things he hates.

"Wooo, yeah! Burn baby, burn!" Denice whoops, leaning forward at the waist, her hands balled into fists, her shouting competing with the crazed screaming.

Alan pulls the iron out, notes the blackness on the end of it, then looks at Denice. "Punch her! Punch her nose as hard as you can!"

Denice gets quiet as she winds up and throws a slightly wild punch which only grazes the nose, landing mainly on the left eye.

"*Please! Please stop! Please stop!*" the cunt sobs.

Twenty-Eight

It occurs to me that maybe on some subconscious level I *let* them get away from me, and the relief I was feeling gives way to guilt. I'm still worried for the woman who was driving that red car, afraid my dread and the weird, painful sense were right, and she is in real danger. *And now I've let her down. I was her one hope, and I let her down.* I shake my head and reassure myself it was all in my imagination, and she's probably having a great time enjoying three-way sex with a weird, scary couple who trigger flashbacks and fear in me. Before I can stop it, my mind is replaying the memory of what happened to me that night—the Bad—and I wonder how different things would be now if someone could have helped my parents and me.

Maybe someone could have, but she just gave up and went home.

Fuck. I decide to backtrack and go a mile down each side road I find between here and the first crossroad, using the pain to look for them. The plan sounds weak, but I don't have any better ideas and there *is* the proximity component to my flashback or whatever it is. It doesn't reach very far: when we were on the highway the itching would fade out all together when I was a few hundred feet back—maybe a little more than a football field. But if I can get within that distance of wherever they went, assuming they stopped somewhere around here, then I can use the pain as a sort of homing sense to track them down. *A reconnaissance by pain.* If I still don't find them after exploring these roads, I'll just go home. *What more can I do? The alternative is to wander aimlessly all night and probably get lost.*

What if I do find them—what then?

The question comes suddenly and, not having an answer, I dismiss it almost as quickly. I doubt my plan has much potential for success anyway. But I can't just drive away without at least trying.

I continue one more mile beyond the crossroads I just came to, then backtrack and investigate a mile down each of the side branches of the crossroad. Finding nothing, I continue retracing my journey, detouring to follow another side road on the left when I come to it. The pain still does not return. The next side road is on the right. After about half a mile I am both relieved and terrified to feel the scraping itch along my scar. I turn off Stacey's lights and slow to something like twenty miles per hour, following the light gray swath of road illuminated by the sliver of moon. Soon, the itching turns into more painful scratching. I slow further, just creeping along, leaning over the wheel, straining my eyes. Something on my left catches my attention; I stop and look. Seeing nothing, I ease the car forward again in first gear, looking at the woods on my left as I do, and see a yellow light about fifty yards off. I realize I'm looking not at woods, but only a line of trees between the road and an open field. I pull over as much as possible on the shoulderless road, stop, and cut Stacey's engine.

I immediately notice the night sounds all around me— frogs and insects, the hooting of an owl. These had been audible before, but with the engine running and my focus on finding the others, I hadn't consciously registered the noise, which is actually pretty loud.

So now what? Just thinking this increases the nausea, which is lower than the other pain, and more diffuse, squeezing everything from my stomach to my crotch, making me feel like I need to pee and maybe shit too.

I look out my window at the van's interior lights shining through the passenger side window at the front of the boxy vehicle. I turn back to the dark road in front of me, then to the deeper darkness on my right, and wish I could wake up from this nightmare and find myself at home in bed, weirded out, but relieved and safe.

Shit, this is fucked up.

As a cadet at West Point, I jumped from a thirty-foot platform into a swimming pool while wearing my combat fatigues and boots. I don't like heights, and jumping from the platform wasn't mandatory—jumping from a lower platform was the requirement—but I made myself jump from the highest one. To overcome my fear, I muted my consciousness and just focused on doing what had to be done, moving my legs to walk to the edge of the platform, positioning my arms as I'd been taught to protect my face, and then stepping off into the air. I do much the same thing now, silencing my inner voice and focusing on my actions. I carefully open the door, then close it without latching it. I turn and walk purposefully toward the van.

I go a few steps when I notice the emptiness of my hands. I want *something*, just in case this really is as bad as I think it might be. But what? I always carry pepper spray in my pocket, but I want a *weapon*. I stop and mentally inventory the contents of the car: books, pen, extra quart of oil, emergency blanket, spare tire, *lug wrench...* It has a telescoping handle to provide extra leverage. I retrace my steps, find the wrench behind the driver's seat, and remove it from its soft plastic case. I don't fit one of the sockets on it— just take the metal bar and extend the handle to its full length. I turn and, feeling like I've already taken way too long, walk briskly through the tall grass toward the van, hefting the weight of the wrench in my right hand. As I cross the field, the pain increases, but by now I'm used to it, more or less, and carry it along without allowing it to impede me.

"Please, God, please, NO! *Pleeeeease!*"

The woman's scream stops me dead about forty feet from the van, freezing the entire length of my spine. My mind reels, recoiling from the reality, as a heavy, glistening ball of ice slips down and drops with a thud in my stomach.

"Go ahead and scream, bitch! Ain't no one out here to hear you except us!" A woman's voice—Diane, I guess.

I want to vomit, and then I'm running toward the van, rage overriding everything else, even the stabbing below my heart.

As I near the van, there's inarticulate screaming, and Diane again: "Wooo, yeah! Burn baby, burn!"

Then Jeff's voice: "Punch her! Punch her nose as hard as you can!"

"*Please! Please stop! Please stop!*"

The handle of the van's sliding side door is in my hand and I jerk it hard toward the back of the vehicle.

Twenty-Nine

Denice gets quiet as she winds up and throws a slightly wild punch which only grazes the nose, landing mainly on the left eye.

"Please! Please stop! Please stop!"

Alan doubts she even knows what she's saying anymore. "You can do better than—"

CLUNK.

The sound stops him mid-sentence, but it takes another second to register what the sound was: someone outside yanking on the locked side door handle.

"What the f—"

"Help me! Help! Hel—"

"Shut up!" Alan orders as he backhands the bitch's face before taking a step toward the front of the van and grabbing the Beretta semi-automatic from the console between the front seats. "Stay here with her," he barks at Denice then flicks the lock on the side door and hauls it open while holding the Beretta ready in his left hand. He scans the small area illuminated by light from the van interior and hears rustling to his left. Switching the weapon to his right hand, he leans out and aims.

Thirty

CLUNK. The door is locked and remains shut. All the voices inside stop instantly.

"What the f—" Diane's voice, cut off by

"Help me! Help! Hel—" cut off by

"Shut up!" Jeff shouts. He says something more as a couple heavy footsteps thud on the van floor. I hesitate: *shit—now what?* Two more heavy footsteps inside, then a metallic click from the door. Instinctively I turn and start to sprint for the nearest cover—the front of the van. My ears, straining backward, hear the door sliding back.

BLAM! The gunshot propels me in front of the van, knocking me to the ground below the van's grill. It takes me a second, but I realize it was not a bullet but the force of the sound and the reflex it triggered in my muscles that threw me to the ground in front of the van; I'm actually not hurt, other than the consistent stabbing sensation. I hear legs swishing quickly through the tall grass beside the van, following me, and instinctively I roll under the front bumper. I keep on crawling, dimly aware of the sound of the van's idling engine and scraping my back on some part of the van as I pass under it. I move through the grass on my belly until I come back to where I sprinted a moment before, beside the van but forward of the sliding door, *and behind him.*

I glance quickly back toward the side door, but see no one. I crawl out from under the vehicle and turn toward the front, hefting the weight of the wrench in my hand as I start to sprint through the trench of broken stems I and my hunter made. Now I am silent fury running. I raise the metal bar over my shoulder and round the front of the van again. Jeff is in front of the darkened driver side headlamp, peering down the other side of the van. He starts to turn back toward me, and in a moment of exhilaration I realize I have him. I bring the bar down on the side of his skull as hard as I can, knocking him to the ground.

And then it isn't Jeff at my feet, but that other bastard from nine years ago. There's a whoosh in the air as I bring the iron bar down hard on his head. Years of hate and fear move me, and the bar hums through the air again.

The sound of cracking bone brings me back to the present. The crack is accompanied by a different feeling in the wrench as it hits: the head is softer—*wetter*—and absorbs more of the energy of impact, reducing the vibration coming back up through the handle.

"Alan?"

Who's Alan? Is there another man out here? I look at the inert body by my feet. There's not much light, but he seems to be wearing Jeff's clothes.

"Help! Help me!" The voice is screaming and sobbing at the same time.

Got to help her.

"Shut the fuck up! A-*lan!*"

"Help! Please!"

Gun. I shift my eyes from the battered head to his right elbow, follow the arm out to his hand. A few inches from his fingers, nestled in a crater of bent grass stems, is the black shape of the weapon.

Thirty-One

Denice sees the flash from the gun; the bang bounces off her chest and ear drums. Alan jumps out of the van, and she wonders if she should close the door. *He didn't say.* She decides to leave it open, but stands inside looking out at the darkness and twisting her hands together, suddenly feeling afraid, wishing Alan hadn't left her alone, wondering what she should do.

"*Help! Help me!*"

"Shut up you *bitch!*" she yells, still focused out the doorway, trying to hear what's happening outside. Instead, Denice hears her father's voice shouting in her own. *Shut up you bitch.* No, not shouting—his voice isn't loud, but the tone carries enough threat to more than make up for the lack of loudness. *Shut up you little bitch.* His lips touch her ear as he says this, as his weight presses down on her in her bed in the darkness of her bedroom, and she wants to scream and hurt someone.

She refocuses on the doorway and, blocking out the sobbing and loud breathing behind her, she strains to hear what's happening outside. All she can hear are frogs and bugs and shit, and she wonders what that means, wonders if whoever it was ran away, because if they were still here Alan would be shooting them. *Wouldn't he?* She glances around inside the van and sees the big hunting knife, still sheathed, laying on a shelf near her. She picks it up and grips the handle tightly before pulling off the sheath.

She hears something outside, slightly metallic, like metal hitting something that isn't metal—a kind of thud followed by a brief tone—from the front of the van. She hears it a few more times, then there's another sound, sort of like a stick breaking. "Alan?" she calls out tentatively, wishing he'd let her go with him when he left the van, hating the uncertainty of being alone.

"*Help! Please!*"

The sudden renewed shouting from just a couple feet behind is magnified by her straining ears and makes her jump. She spins around. "Shut the fuck up!" Then, over her shoulder, "A-*lan!*"

"*Help! Please!*" the bitch screams; she just won't shut the fuck up.

Denice steps behind the chair, grabs a handful of the bitch's hair with her free hand, and wrenches the head back.

"*Please help me!*"

Denice, as she brings the knife up, sees the cunt's eyes are clamped shut, but her mouth is open to yell again. "Shut up you *bitch!*" Denice just wants her to stop screaming.

"*Hel—*"

Denice shuts her up, plunging the knife into the center of the stretched throat as hard as she can. The blade is sharp and penetrates deep, through the windpipe, and the screaming stops. Instead, the breath comes out the new hole in the neck sounding wet and gurgly. Denice has to saw a little to cut back out through the side of the neck, and suddenly a big gout of blood shoots out, and feels hot and wet on Denice's face. Instinctively she closes her eyes and backs away, the knife passing through the last inch of throat as she does. Somehow she manages to pull the chair back with her and the bitch goes down with it, hitting the floor. Denice looks down and sees the girl on her back, her neck pumping lots of blood, her eyes open and rolling in their sockets.

Thirty-Two

More screaming: "*Please help me!*"
         "Shut up you *bitch!*"

"*Hel—*"   The voice is cut off, ending in an
incomprehensible wet choking sound.

I drop the tire iron, grab the gun and run with it, my
momentum causing me to swing wide around the side of the
van. I arc back in toward the sliding door, which is still open,
yellowish light spilling out. Suddenly, a woman appears in
the opening, backlit by the interior lights, her bleached hair
down and wild, her face too much in shadow to see. She
launches herself from the van at me and I instinctively bring
the gun up, cradling the firing hand in my left. I pull the
trigger automatically: three rounds in quick succession. The
impact of the bullets alters Diane's trajectory, causing her to
land in a crumpled heap on the ground between me and the
van.

The dark-haired woman. I move to enter the van, but just
as I'm stepping over Diane's body I feel a surprisingly strong
hand grasp my ankle. Panicked, I aim down and fire twice at
the mass of blonde hair. The grip on my ankle goes slack, and
I quickly enter the van and look around, weapon ready,
looking for another man named Alan.

But there's only one person left in the van. "Oh no oh
fuck no!" I whisper as my eyes fall on the young woman
attached to an overturned metal chair in a large pool of blood.
I go to her, kneeling in the red puddle and cradling her head
carefully, trying to close the gaping wound in her throat at the
same time. The woman's light blue eyes are open, but it's

obvious they're no longer seeing anything. "I'm sorry I'm sorry I'm so sorry," I sob until I start choking.

There's no response, no evidence the woman hears my apology. I look at her imploringly, but the dead floppy weight in my arms tells me she is already gone. It's hard to tell, but I guess she looks twenty, maybe twenty-two years old—a little younger than me. I try to close the lids over the dead eyes, but they won't stay completely shut. I lay her head gently on the floor and stand, looking around as I do. I find a beach towel nearby on the floor and drape it over her body as best I can given she's still tied to the chair. As I do, I try not to see her nakedness, or the torn, bruised, and burned skin. I notice for the first time the smell of the interior—the wet metallic odor of blood, the acrid lingering trace of burning solder, the sour stenches of urine and sweat. My head swims; I stumble for and fall out the van's side door, going to my knees and vomiting nothing but stomach acid in the matted grass, burning my throat and in back of my nose, and pulling a muscle I didn't know existed in my crotch.

After the retching stops, I look up and see Diane's corpse. *I have to get the fuck out of here.* I get my wobbly legs under me, trip over my feet, and start heading for the road and Stacey.

Shit, this is a crime scene. Obviously, since it's Florida in April, I'm not wearing gloves, so my fingerprints must be all over the gun and the tire iron. *What else did I touch?*

I have to go back. No—oh fuck no. I stand hesitating, torn between wanting to get away and needing to protect myself. *Just get it over with.* I turn and stagger back to the van, realizing I must have left the gun inside. *Shit!* I give Diane's body as wide a berth as I can and pause at the open door. *Shit.* Holding my breath, I step up into the van and scan for the weapon, figuring I must have laid it down somewhere, and finding it next to a pair of vice grips with something stuck in the closed jaws. Without intending to, I glance at the towel-draped body, then I pick up the gun and step back to the doorway. I pause briefly to look at Diane's corpse on the ground and check either side before stepping back outside.

I take a couple deep breaths, trying to clear the miasma from the vehicle interior out of my lungs. I can hear the squishy thudding of my heart, still racing, beating against my ribs. *The pain is gone.* I look down at the body on the ground again, but feel remorse only for the woman in the van. Other than that, I feel surprisingly numb now. *I want to go home.* But I still need the tire iron.

As I approach the front end of the van, it suddenly occurs to me I never checked to see if he were dead. The hairs on the back of my neck prickle as they try to uproot themselves from the skin there. *What if he's still alive?* I look nervously over my shoulder, the gun now held up, ready to fire. *But the pain is gone; does that mean they're both dead?* Not taking any chances, I approach the ground in front of the van slowly, weapon in both hands, arms partially extended and head canted forward, trying to aim down the barrel, though it's too dim to see the gun's sights. I barely see a pair of feet in the matted grass. Then legs. I circle outward, moving my aiming point up the body as I see more of it. I step closer when I think the muzzle is pointed at his brain case, then fire from about six feet away. The head jumps with the impact. I aim and squeeze again, but nothing happens, and I realize the action on the gun has slid back, indicating the last round is gone. I step closer, then avert my eyes. I look around the body and find the wrench. I pick it up by the handle and wipe the gory business end of it a few times on a clean patch of grass.

Alan? I slowly look back at the corpse. He's definitely dressed in the clothes Jeff was wearing at the club, and he's the same size and build. *It has to be Jeff—he was the only one to get in the van back at Breakers, and there's no one else around. Must've been fake names.*

I shake the questions off and refocus. *What else did I touch?* I remember yanking on the door handle. *Just that, I guess, right? Nothing* in *the van, except the towel and—* My face contorts and my eyes fill. "Fuck this—fuck it!" but a hot tear rolls down my cheek, mixing with the sweat. I force myself to walk to the side of the van, past the opening, but not looking in, and past the body on the ground, but not looking at it. I focus on the door handle and go up to it. Holding both the gun and the wrench in my left hand, I pull the front of my T-shirt up and use it to scrub the door handle. As I do this, I register the sound of the van's idling engine. I automatically want to shut it off, but that would mean going inside again. And touching things. I leave the engine running and walk quickly back to where Stacey is parked, scuffing my shoes in the tall grass as I go. I wipe my right hand on the front of the thigh part of my jeans before pulling open the door. I pick up the plastic bag of books and shake my purchases out before putting the gun and tire wrench in the bag.

The bookstore seems a lifetime ago.

I wipe my now empty hands, which are still sticky, on the front of my jeans again, and scuff my shoes on the packed dirt of the road, then get in and drive away.

Somehow I manage to find my way back to Highway 231, and then drive the speed limit all the way home. I stop only once, on the bridge connecting Panama City to its beach, and then just long enough to throw the gun and tire iron into the bay.

Part Four

Reckoning

Thirty-Three

"OK Honey, say your prayers so you can get some sleep."

I clasp my hands, close my eyes, and bow my head. "Our father, who art in heaven, Harold be thy name." I say the rest of the prayer, finishing with "Amen."

I wait for Mommy to say "amen" too. When she doesn't, I open my eyes and look up, but she isn't there. "Mommy?" I look around the room—my bedroom when I was a child—but I don't see her. I feel my face scrunch up: my eyebrows dip down toward my eyes, and my chin wrinkles spasmodically. I bite my lower lip, knowing something's wrong; something bad has happened. I know this, but...if I can just find Mommy maybe it'll be all right. I scootch over to the side of the bed, swing my little pajama-clad legs around, and shove myself off the edge of the mattress. My feet hit with a *splat*. I look down and see I'm standing in a patch of carpet saturated with warm red wetness. My mother is lying in the puddle, her throat split open, her glassy eyes staring at the ceiling.

"Mom!" I shout and drop to my knees on the floor beside her, suddenly feeling older. I cradle her head and try to close the wound in her neck. I look at her face, only now it isn't my mother, but the dark-haired woman, and I'm not in the bedroom I had as a child anymore. Now I'm kneeling on the hard floor of the van, and the young woman's dead eyes are staring sightlessly at me.

My whole body spasms awake.

I lay very still, moving only my eyes around the room, orienting myself, visually touching my points of reference. The deadbolt latch on the door is in the locked position, and the chair is in place under the doorknob. The apartment is brighter than it usually is when I wake up, but it is definitely my little apartment in Daleville, Alabama, and I'm in the bed that folds out of the wall. I flip over and look at the other side of the room: I'm alone and safe. And sweaty. The sheets are sticking to my skin. I wonder if I screamed or not, and decide I don't care, for all the noise the couples in the apartments on either side of mine make when they have sex.

Then the nightmare, and the events that preceded it last night, catch up with me. *Oh shit.* My stomach cramps and my chest tightens. I close my eyes tightly and pull my knees closer to my body, compacting myself.

My mind races, sorting history from dream. Sarah, my counselor right after the Bad, taught me to attend to my dreams as a way of dealing with the internal demons. I've gotten lax about doing that over the last few years, but now I instinctively deal first with the more fleeting memory of the nightmare. That's also easier than confronting the reality of multiple killings. I can't remember much before the prayer. For years I'd thought God's name was Harold, until one night at bedtime my mom noticed I was mispronouncing the word "hallowed" and corrected me. *Harold.* I shake my head and feel like crying at the girl's innocence. I give the little girl saying her prayers and her mother a moment of mental silence before moving on.

I acknowledge the images in the rest of the dream. I do not like to do this, but I need to make up for all the times I've skipped it. I know from experience repressing dreams only gives them power and leads to emotional trouble later. The images aren't entirely unfamiliar anyway. Memories of the Bad: my childhood bedroom where it happened, my mother's corpse, blood—standard stuff for my nightmares. Except for the young dark-haired woman. I feel dizzy at the memory, as if the bed is moving under me.

I want to escape last night so much my body fairly vibrates with the yearning, like the leg muscles of a sprinter in the starting blocks, as if I could outrun the reality of what happened. If only I'd had something else to do yesterday, and hadn't gone to the mall. Or if I'd just ignored the pain of the flashback. After the Bad, I promised myself I would do everything I could to protect myself from violence like this, and there I was yesterday, rushing headfirst into it.

But what happened in that field in Florida is part of my life now, inescapable and immutable. Without wanting to, I see again the dark-haired woman, nameless to me, her dull, dead eyes half shut, the muscles in her face slack. I pull the covers over my head to hide from the memory, but it follows me, along with the sadness and—worse—the guilt. If only I hadn't gone for the gun—if I'd gone back to the side of the van faster, then maybe it would have gone differently, maybe I could have saved her life.

Or been stabbed by the same knife that cut her throat.

I start replaying every moment in that field, but then the images really start getting to me. I pull the covers back off my head and roll onto my back, staring up at the ceiling, trying to displace the pictures in my head.

"I'm sorry—I did try though." I immediately realize how pointless these whispered words are, and I feel stupid. I lie still, feeling bad and studying the whorls in the plaster on the ceiling.

You can't change what happened; just deal with it.

Should I have reported this to the police? I know the answer is, at least from the perspective of the police, an unequivocal "yes," but what would have happened to me? I killed two people. Sure, I'd been trying to defend a third person, and myself, but what if the police, and ultimately a jury, didn't see it that way? Or if they did, but still sent me to jail for some lesser murder charge like manslaughter? I realize I know almost nothing about the law, despite two mostly boring semesters of it at West Point; I don't know if the term manslaughter is even possible in this situation. I do know reporting this to the police puts me at the mercy of a huge bureaucratic system known for making mistakes, and I'm not going to jail because of those fucked up bastards Diane and Jeff, or whatever their names were. All anyone needs to know to convict me of some kind of premeditated murder is how I followed them all afternoon and evening, across state lines, and actually went to their van carrying a weapon to confront them. I don't even know how to dispute it; I definitely can't explain the thing that caused me to follow them. I don't understand it and barely believe it myself. And I am *not* going to jail because of them. Or to the electric chair—this is Florida I'm thinking about, after all. I've got to clean my clothes, the car, make sure there's nothing connecting me to those fucks.

My mind flashes to the image of the vice grips lying on the table in the van and whatever was left clamped in their jaws, and I shudder. How did this happen? How is this shit in my life again? That poor woman. I close my eyes, wanting to cry, but apparently unable to.

At least you stopped them. They needed killing.

I've heard the phrase somewhere before, but hearing it in my own head scares me. Even so, it's true. If only someone had killed *him* before he...I stopped him, and I don't regret it. My conscience has always been clear about killing him, and this, what I did to those two last night, is no different.

Except I need to make sure no one knows I killed them. This imperative helps shift my attention away from the murdered woman I failed. I get out of bed dressed only in the clean underpants and tank top I put on after showering last night, and pull on a fresh pair of jeans and a faded gray T-shirt. The clothes I wore yesterday, sitting in a heap on the bathroom floor, are obviously unwearable now. The T-shirt and jeans have blood on them from the dark-haired woman *(don't think about it).*   The rest of it—underwear and the rest—smelled bad when I was taking it off. I'll take it all to the laundromat this morning.   I stuff them in the blood-streaked plastic bag from the bookstore. I considered leaving the weapons in the bag when I chucked them, but hoped fully exposing them to the bay's sea water would accelerate their destruction and make them useless as evidence. Maybe I should have wiped my fingerprints off them before I threw them out. But it's unlikely anyone will think to look there for the weapons, and even if they do, the bay is a really big place to search. *Right? Do fingerprints wash off when submerged in water?* Well, it's done now. I'll throw the bag in a dumpster somewhere after I put the clothes in the washer. There might even be a dumpster behind the laundromat. I think of the car: there would have to be blood on Stacey's steering wheel—my hands were sticky with the stuff. I pull one of the socks out of the makeshift laundry bag, soak it with water, and go outside. I notice it's beginning to cloud up, and hope it'll rain soon on the dirt road and the van and the bodies down in Florida, and help erase traces I left—tire tracks and anything I might have missed.

There's not as much blood on the door handles, gear shift, and steering wheel as I thought there would be, and what is there comes off easily when rubbed with the wet sock. I go back inside and put the sock back in the plastic bag.

A half hour later, at about ten-thirty, I'm sitting in a plastic chair waiting for the washing machine to finish with my clothes. I'm flipping through the book about the universe I bought yesterday, just looking at the pictures and registering maybe half of what I see. I give up and close the book, hugging it to my body and crossing my arms over it while staring out the windows over the bank of washers.

OK, calm down and focus. Only two things about last night matter. One is never getting caught, and you're taking care of that now. Go down the list: fingerprints on the van—

scrubbed off, weapons—dumped in the ocean, blood on you and the car—washed off, bloody plastic bag—in the dumpster out back of here, bloody clothes—washing them now.

That seems to be everything.

So there's no evidence, no reason to connect you to what happened. There are probably tire tracks on that dirt road, but there's nothing you can do about them, and it'll probably rain soon anyway, and then they'll be gone too. Done.

The other thing that matters is the woman they killed.

I pause at that, once again running the mental tape of what happened, wondering how it would have gone if I'd skipped getting the gun.

OK, look, you did the best you could—you have to give yourself that. It didn't work out, and now she's dead and there's no changing it. All you can do is learn from what happened.

So what have I learned?

What the pain means.

It doesn't make sense, but there it is. The pain is apparently a sort of early warning system for—what? Bad people? I would have to feel it a lot more often if it were that simple. Everybody is at least a little bad. *Really* bad people? I think about the dead eyes of the arrested soldier in Korea, the only other person I've identified as triggering the pain. Then I think about the couple I killed. *Diane and Jeff.* They seemed so friendly, normal. But all that meant was they were good at getting what they wanted. And now I've seen what they wanted. Like the one who attacked me, they actually sought and enjoyed pain in others. They liked the power to inflict that pain, and ultimately death, for their own amusement.

I learned a little about this in a psych class I took. The professor described the phenomenon as the "asocial" or "soulless" personality, and called the people who exhibit this complete absence of compassion "sociopaths." They used to be called psychopaths, but at some point the American

Psychological Association decided to change the name.   In that same class we were shown a short movie documenting an experiment in which researchers manufactured a sociopath monkey by taking it at birth and isolating it from all experience of love and social interaction with any other living thing until it reached adulthood.   When finally put together with others of its kind, this monkey was unable to interact normally.   Instead, it alternately feared social contact and lashed out with extreme aggression.   Sociopaths are unable to understand the feelings of other people, and so see others as objects rather than fellow creatures capable of emotion and suffering.   In some cases, I think, this might be because sociopaths themselves have empty emotional lives, but this is just a guess; I'm no psychologist.

Maybe that's what triggers the pain; maybe sociopaths throw off some smell or energy or something I can pick up on. My psych professor said as much as one-percent of humanity might be sociopaths.   If that's true, I'd be in pain a lot more, but maybe there are degrees.   Possibly it's only the really dangerous, predatory ones that set me off.   But how?

I don't know, but something is definitely happening here.

So what do I do with this?   The lifeless face with the half-shut eyes appears in my mind again.   *Oh fuck, no.*

Thirty-Four

I can't, I tell myself again. This is, of course, absolutely true; it's practically self-evident. I've spent the past nine-plus years protecting myself against violence, mainly by avoiding it. I'm a pilot and computer science student, not a vigilante or a hero. I'm not emotionally equipped and probably not qualified to do this.

I've been making these points with myself since the laundromat this morning, but they're not sticking. It's a rainy day, perfect for the reading and studying I've been trying to do, but I keep catching myself staring out the window, thinking about a lifeless body under a beach towel in a van in Florida, the rain drumming on the roof over it, splashing into the tall grass just outside the van's open door. I keep coming back to those thoughts, and what it means to be able to sense bad things coming.

Now, as I'm waiting for my pasta to cook for dinner, I'm still fighting the irresistible, repellant idea.

No way, no fucking *way. I'm not going to do it.*

And I don't have to. One of the first realizations I had after the Bad, when I was eventually calm enough to think rationally again, was that my parents, my Sunday school teachers, and the minister at my church, had all been wrong about God. It was obvious: either God doesn't exist at all or, if he does exist, he isn't anything like I'd been taught. There was no way an all-powerful, caring being who loved me and my parents would have allowed that—that *monster*—to do what he did. In fact, if the creator of everything *were* good, then the monster wouldn't have existed in the first place. So either there is no God, or God is not all-powerful, or God is not the kind, compassionate guy people like to believe in. The last possibility was the most disturbing. Nobody wants to live in a universe created by a sadistic, malevolent God. Embracing the middle explanation would have required me to create some elaborate alternative mythology, maybe including a devil or other competing gods, and I was done with all that bullshit. The first explanation, that there simply is no God, seemed the most rational and the easiest to accept. So there's no one telling me what I have to do. Except me.

But getting rid of God doesn't mean throwing out morality... Ideas of good and bad still exist for me; it comes with the human being package. The monster that killed my parents, that I killed to save myself, was Bad, and I distance myself from what defined him. The monster intentionally harmed others, so I avoid harming anything that can feel even an approximation of what I endured from him. I became a vegetarian. I try to treat the world kindly, and to consider others and respect them. I try to be the opposite of the monster.

Isn't that enough?

I use a spoon to fish a rotini from the boiling water, carry it the one step sideways to the sink, and run it under some cold water before sampling it. I go back to the stove and turn off the electric element, back to the sink with the pot to get rid of the water.

"Do no harm" doesn't mean I have to stop others from doing harm, does it? This is where religion would come in handy—clear rules and checklists for achieving salvation. There's a commandment to not kill, but there's nothing about having to stop others from killing. In fact, Christians are supposed to "turn the other cheek," right? But as an atheist, I have to figure it out for myself, and I don't get the salvation and eternal happiness perqs, either. All I have is my conscience and this fucked-up place I've found myself in.

I finish draining off the water and pause, the pot's handle in my grip.

Beyond respecting others, my only obligation is to myself. I try the words on for size, mentally tugging at them to coax a better fit.   After all, with God and my parents out of the picture, and my grandparents pretty much out of my life, *someone* has to take care of me. And that includes keeping me safe in this jungle of a world. Looked at this way, this thing, this *sense*, is actually a great resource. If I understand it right, it means no human monster will ever be able to surprise me again. I'll feel them coming from hundreds of feet away, and be ready, or better yet gone, when they arrive. So I should be psyched.

Right?

I dump the pasta on my plate, pour some tomato sauce from a jar over it, and sit down to eat. My table is the island which divides the kitchen from the rest of the apartment, so I have a view out the window of the small tree just outside and the landscaping and other apartment units beyond. It's as if last night didn't happen. It did, but everything else keeps going just like always.

I see the young woman's half-closed glassy eyes again; my fork stops in mid-air. Out of nowhere I wonder what she would be doing now if she weren't dead (and probably still lying in that van, in a field, in the rain). I put my fork and the food on it back down on the plate.

"Stop it!" I whisper loudly, my hands twisted together in my lap. "Just stop it! It's done. You did all you could, now let it go."

I really did do all I could. When I started out yesterday, I wasn't sure what the pain meant. In fact, I didn't even know the pain would be part of my day—I just meant to go to the mall, buy a book or two, see something other than the walls of my apartment. Then, when I suspected there might be danger to the woman, I investigated and intervened. *I did my share—*

what more could I do? I'm no hero: I did the best I could with what I had. I didn't even have to do that much. I could have—should have—gotten away rather than risking my own neck. She *put us* both *at risk by going with them—how stupid was that?*

I stare blankly at the pasta and tomato sauce, my hands still clenched.

Who am I kidding?

"Oh...shit," I whisper through a tightening throat. I push my plate away and, elbows resting on the table, hide my face in my hands. The tears finally start and I let them come.

If someone else had this...sense or whatever it is and could have saved my parents and me... If I'd been better prepared, I could have saved that woman and she wouldn't be lying in the van in the field in the rain now.

"God *damn* it!" I slam my fists down on the table top and make the plate with its pile of food jump. "Why the *fuck* do I have this?" Fists again. "Harold, you son of a bitch! Haven't you done enough to me?" Fists and tears.

I remind myself I don't believe in God, but it still feels better to blame someone.

Thirty-Five

The high-pitched beeping sound wakes me at 4:30 a.m. I feel around beside my pillow on the mattress and locate my wristwatch. Years of practice helps me quickly find the correct button on the watch's edge to silence the insistent beeping.

I like to lie in bed when I first wake up and take stock of things, but it's Monday, my helicopter platoon is on the day shift this week, *and* I have to get in a workout at the gym before going over to the airfield, so I have to get my ass in gear. I will myself out of bed and stumble around the room, putting the bed away, pulling on my gym clothes, and sitting for a half hour of poorly-focused meditation.

Any number of thoughts can intrude while I'm trying to keep my mind blank, but today I'm not surprised to find the events of the weekend still haunting me. Today I just give in to these thoughts, but try to displace the sadness and guilt over the young woman I failed with the more bearable and constructive, but still kind of overwhelming, reality of the sense. I don't know what else to call it, but the responsibility it imposes on me is inescapable. I'm done resisting that anymore; now I just sit with it, try to accept it.

After I unfold my legs and put the cushion away, I make myself a cup of instant coffee and wash an apple, then sit down for the pre-training snack. While I sip and eat, I wonder if the bodies have been discovered yet. Suddenly my guts clench, and I look up at the window, half-expecting to see police officers outside, hear them pounding on my door. *But there's no evidence pointing to me.* I even chucked the jeans and T-shirt I wore on Saturday into the dumpster behind the

McDonald's on Daleville Avenue. I washed them, but pitched them anyway in case there was trace evidence the laundering didn't get rid of. *It's pointless to keep worrying about it— either they'll come for me or they won't.* I have enough to worry about besides that.

I drive to the gym because it's faster than running. Inside the weight room, since it's a weekday morning, I see Lou, one of my gym buddies. I never see these guys outside the gym, and for some reason I almost never see them in here on the weekends.

He spots me at about the same time I notice him and calls out "Hey, Cory!" from across the big room. This is a high compliment since by calling me Cory he's likening me to the several-times-over Ms. Olympia, Cory Everson. I actually look nothing like her, and I'm no where near as big and muscular as her; Lou is being friendly, not accurate. I return the compliment by calling him Franco, after Franco Columbo, another bodybuilding champion, whom Lou actually does resemble a little. Lou is only a couple inches taller than me, but seems almost as broad as tall. He took steroids in college while he was competing as a power lifter, but is off them now that he's an Army officer, and also older and wiser. I tense a little as he crosses the room toward me, his short legs striding as long as they can, his broad shoulders rolling with his gait. I know what's coming, but I also understand it's a gesture of friendship, so I don't protest when he throws his arms around me and slaps me on the back.

"Hey!" he says loudly next to my head, still slapping my back.

"How's it going, Lou?" I never return the embrace, but he doesn't seem to notice, and his enthusiasm at seeing me makes me smile a little, which is saying something since he's touching me, and I hate being touched.

He releases me and backs up a couple paces. "How you doin'? How was your weekend?"

The truth flashes through my mind, but I manage a generic "Fine, it was fine. How 'bout you?"

"Not bad. Played rugby on Saturday, kicked some big ass. Went to that bodybuilding competition in Dothan yesterday. It was a pretty good show—you should have come."

I remember now he'd mentioned it to me last week. "Yeah, I actually wasn't feeling well yesterday—kind of a 24-hour thing."

A look of concern comes over his face. "Yeah? That's too bad. How are you now?"

"Oh, I'm fine," I say, fudging the truth before changing the subject. "So did your girlfriend go to the competition with you?"

"Yeah. She was a good sport but doesn't really get it, so afterwards I made it up by taking her out to dinner."

"That sounds good."

He shrugs his massive shoulders. "I guess. She's always wanting to go out dancing, but look at me—can you imagine me dancing?"

I feel a smile tugging at the corners of my mouth as my mind produces an image of what has to be over 200 pounds of body packed onto a five-six frame trying to move like Fred Astaire.

Lou smiles too, then laughs. "You see what I mean—for you, that smile is laughing! So I took her to a little Italian place. I guess that was OK, but the portions were small. She didn't seem to mind, though."

"That's too bad." The portion size was probably fine. One time I did run into Lou at the gym on a Saturday morning, and afterwards we went to breakfast at a place with an all-you-can-eat breakfast bar he said he visits all the time. Maybe it was just coincidence, but when we walked up to the buffet a bunch of the staff came hurrying over with more trays of food. Lou picked up some of the smaller containers set into the warming rack and dumped their entire contents on his plate. He went back twice more, and finished everything he took.

He shrugs again. "It was OK—we went to her place afterwards and she had some leftovers in her fridge. She's Cuban too, and makes a great *ropas viejas*."

I nod, not really sure what old clothes have to do with food, but figuring it must be the name for some Cuban dish. Lou could make this conversation continue indefinitely, but I have to get my butt home for breakfast and a shower in two hours, so I steer the talk back to lifting. "So what are you working today?"

"Legs. In fact, you're just in time—I've maxed out the sled again and need another hundred pounds."

"One-twenty." I've done this before, so I know what he's getting at.

"Even better."

I follow him over to the leg press machine, also known as "the sled," where he has completely filled the weight-bearing bars on both sides with forty-five-pound plates. I don't count them, but it must be at least nine-hundred pounds all together. I put my stuff down and climb up on top of the sled part—the moving frame that holds the weight—while Lou sits down at the bottom and braces his feet against the metal pressing plate.

"You ready?" he asks.

"Just a second." I find a stable perch and something to grip while avoiding the rails the sled rides on. "OK."

He closes his eyes and takes a couple deep breaths. His face tenses as he begins applying force with his legs. The sled and I travel upward smoothly until his legs are almost straight out and vibrating slightly. With his hands he retracts the supports that hold the sled in its resting position, and then lowers me until the tops of his thighs are against his chest. He pauses a second, then grunts loudly as he sends the sled up the rails again. He repeats this five more times before bringing the supports back in and letting the sled rest against them again. I climb down off the machine. As soon as I'm clear he says "thanks," then does another bunch of repetitions without me.

I get my stuff and go off to a quiet corner of the room to figure out what I need to do today. I'm working shoulders, chest, and biceps, and I look at my notebook to set some goals before deciding to start with shoulder press.

As usual, I train alone, and on the breaks between sets I continue the line of thought I woke up with. While I accept the obligation the sense imposes on me, I really don't know what that responsibility means in practical terms. It's not like I have some psychic ability to know where and when violent sociopaths might be operating; I just know when I'm close to one. In the past, I've gone years without experiencing this pain, so who knows when—*or even if*, I think hopefully—I'll feel it again. By the time I'm done lifting and on my way home, it seems clear my only obligation is to be ready. If I do run into trouble again, I need to be better prepared to stop the monsters and save whoever the intended victim is. This doesn't seem so bad at all; in fact, it's pretty much what I've been doing all along anyway. Looking at it this way, yesterday's agonizing seems almost ridiculous. *I don't know what I thought I would do.*

So how to prepare? What else can I do that I'm not already doing? I sit at a traffic light, pondering that one, and then it comes to me: Better weaponry. *And a new tire iron—I need to replace that.* Maybe because I'm an American, the first thing that occurs to me, after remembering my lack of tire iron, is a firearm. But I'm not even sure what the rules are or the procedure to get one is. I suspect it's not that hard, especially in Alabama, but then I remember I already have a weapon at home. It's been a long time—probably a year or more—since I even looked at it, but it should still be there in my box of junk.

When I get home my neighbors are at it again: I can hear the headboard beating a fast rhythm and her crying out excitedly. *At least they'll be done soon.* I go to my closet, push aside the hanging clothing, and take out the cardboard box my microwave oven came in. I use this to store stuff I don't access much: some of it junk I might need someday, some of it emotional things like the photo album with pictures from before: my parents, me as a kid. Kneeling on the floor, I open the box and take the album out, laying it aside. I rummage around, through other stuff which is not emotional, just seldom used. There's an "I *heart* Massachusetts" plastic travel mug with a lid to keep the beverage from slopping out in a moving vehicle. I last used it when I drove south after graduating from West Point. And there's my Army-issue lensatic compass, which I haven't used since the last time I went backpacking, which was while I was still a cadet. An old thermos, a scarf, a knit wool cap, a pad of water-proof paper. My answering machine is here—that's a combination item: emotional junk I might need again someday. But as long as I still hope to get a message from Miranda, it's staying in the box where it can't cruelly raise expectations. At the bottom, under all this stuff, is a polished wood case, about a foot long and maybe four inches wide.

* * *

West Point Military Reservation
May 1991

Shailene watched as Sergeant Pike wielded his electric clippers over another scalp, wishing she could get a haircut like the others. West Point was all about short hair, but not "bizarre hairstyles," and a high and tight, while fine for a guy, would be considered bizarre on a female. Even so, she'd just as soon be rid of her hair, in spite of *(or because of)* all the compliments it used to get.

Pike was giving Ranger haircuts to each of the seventeen guys who had completed the cadet Ranger Orientation Program—the ROP—and would be leaving for Georgia the next day. They were already wearing the combat fatigue uniform they would be wearing for the next nine weeks, and Pike and Shailene were wearing them too, since it was West Point and everyone needed to be in the same uniform. It was a pretty warm day, though, even for late May, so they all had the fatigue shirt removed and were wearing only the brown T-shirts over the mottled black, green, and brown pants.

"I can't get over the fact that, after all we've been doing for the last five months, the real work hasn't even started yet," said Doug. He was reinforcing the cover of his Ranger handbook with green hundred-mile-an-hour tape, which civilians would know as duck tape, but for some reason went by this much longer name in Army circles.

"Thanks, Doug—putting it that way really makes me feel psyched for the next two months," said Eric, who was laminating labels to be used with sand tables—three-dimensional models used in mission planning.

"You guys will do great, in part *because* of the past five months," Shailene interjected. She was helping Eric with the laminating. "I doubt anything in Ranger School can be harder than the ruck races."

The ruck races were Pike's creation. Seven miles, much of it over rock-strewn dirt trails, over the top of the West Point ski slope, down the other side, and then back again. They'd run, walked, staggered, and even slid down the ski slope's icy snow on their butts, in full combat equipment minus rifle. For the first race, the backpacks—or rucks, as they called them—weighed forty pounds, and the weight went up each race after that, topping out at fifty-five. Shailene, under the terms of her agreement with Pike, carried the same weight as everyone else.

"Yeah, those were pretty bad," Eric said, nodding while concentrating on keeping air bubbles out of the clear sticky film he was applying to a cardboard tag before looking up at her. "But you completed all of them, Ripley."

Shailene wasn't sure who started it, but about halfway through ROP she'd become associated with the tough heroine from the *Alien* movies. She didn't really like or dislike the nickname; by now everyone in the program had a nickname, and she supposed it could've been worse. Maybe there *had* been worse names she didn't know about. She sensed the resistance from the guys at the first physical fitness test. No one interacted with her more than necessary, and she got a lot of looks, especially from the guys who hadn't been in Tactics Club with her. Beating some of them on the two-mile run, and doing more sit-ups than some of them seemed only to incur more resentment. But she kept her mouth shut and busted her ass at whatever they were doing. The tide began to turn when she completed the first ruck race. She'd been dead last—she always finished last in the ruck races—but she didn't quit and she made it in under the hour-thirty-minutes time, the same standard they all had to meet. That seemed to count with a lot of the guys. Plus, there was definitely the "shared suck" factor: that group cohesion born of mutual hardship endured. Somewhere in the midst of it all someone had called her Lieutenant Ripley, and the name, shortened to just Ripley, stuck.

"Fuckin' A," said Doug. "You should be going with us."

"I think the majority of people at the Ranger School would not agree with you," she replied.

Doug opened his mouth to reply, but was cut short by Sergeant Pike's voice.

"All right, Rangers, gather 'round!" Pike snapped the old bed sheet he'd been draping over the cadets, rolled it up, and climbed into the back of his battered van. He appeared again seconds later holding a narrow wooden case about a foot long and maybe four inches wide. Standing in front of the open back of the van, he waited as they gathered in a semi-circle.

Sergeant Pike looked them over for several seconds before beginning, a tight little smile on his lips and in his dark eyes. It occurred to Shailene in that moment she was looking at someone who was exactly where he wanted to be. "First of all, Captain Paladen wanted me to let you know he's really pissed off he couldn't be here this afternoon, but they've already got him preparing for the new crop of cadets starting this summer, and he couldn't get out of his planning session today. He wanted me to tell you, which I was going to anyway, that you're a great bunch of soldiers, and we've both really enjoyed training you over the past five months. Personally, I'd be glad to have any—*any*—of you as my lieutenant. Now seventeen of you are flying down to Georgia tomorrow morning to start Ranger School, and one of you isn't, but you all did the same training with me, and you are *all*," he paused, finding and holding Shailene's gaze for the next four words, "ready for Ranger School. Those of you going down, I know you'll do great, and you'll be wearing Ranger tabs in August—" He was interrupted by a spontaneous chorus of "hoo-ahhs" from the cadets, and paused, smiling, until they quieted down again and he could continue. "But Campbell here doesn't get that chance.

"Now I have to say, when she first spoke to me last December about doing Ranger Orientation, I was against it. But I've known Campbell since she joined the Tactics Club when she was a plebe, and she's been part of the opposing force for the program's training patrols the past two years, so—" He suddenly stopped and, shaking his head and rolling his eyes, his tone changed. "Ahhh, that's bullshit. The truth is, she arm-wrestled me for it and won, so I had to let her in." There was some laughter, and Shailene smiled. "She did it, knowing she wouldn't be able to go to Ranger School, and with the agreement that if she couldn't keep up or meet the same standards as the rest of you ugly fucks, she would be dropped from the program, just like anyone else." He paused again, looking down and shaking his head slightly before returning his gaze to the faces around him. "I thought for sure the ruck races would do her in, especially since that last ruck had to be more than half her body weight."

There were smiles and some quiet laughter. Shailene smiled again, but looked down, embarrassed as she sensed this was leading up to something that would make her the center of attention.

"But she stuck with it, did all the patrols, all the ruck races, and even beat some of you in the 10K road race. She met the same standards as everyone else here. So when Opitz came to me with this idea, I just wished I'd thought of it. But since I didn't, I'll let him take it from here."

Chris Opitz, who had been appointed section leader for the trip down to Georgia, stepped forward and took the polished wooden box from Sergeant Pike, who stepped to the side.

"I think we each have a moment or incident when we realized Ripley was for real, and not just trying to make some political statement or whatever, but was actually serious about the training. I think for more than a few of us it was when she completed that first ruck race and then apologized for making us wait. But for me it was that cold dark night when we had just completed an ambush and Sergeant Pike uttered those infamous words—"

"Speed is security!" someone shouted, triggering more laughter through the group.

"You said it," Chris continued, smiling. "At that point I was so cold I could barely feel my legs, and I was ready to buy that line and get the hell back to someplace warm. It was Ripley's idea to put out the flank security elements in front of the column, and you know the rest.

"Anyway Ripley," he paused a beat and looked at her directly, "Shailene, I think I speak for all of us when I say we wish you were going with us. If you were, I know you would end the summer with a Ranger tab on your shoulder. We felt you should have something to recognize that, and though we can't put a tab on your shoulder, we can still give you a Ranger tab of your own." Chris paused a moment before coming to attention. "Ranger Campbell, front and center!" he commanded.

Shailene's face felt hot with embarrassment. She was also aware of a certain wateriness in her eyes. She found herself standing at attention in front of Chris, saluting him. He returned the salute, smiled, and their right hands grasped as their left hands transferred the wooden case to her. Chris did a right face and walked over to the side where Sergeant Pike was standing, leaving her alone. She became aware of clapping and slowly turned to face the group. She glanced up at the smiling faces, then down at the box, which she now saw bore a small brass plate on its lid, engraved

RANGER CAMPBELL
"RIPLEY"

"Open it up! Open it!" The applause continued.

There was no latch, but the hinge was stiff. Grasping the top with one hand and the bottom with the other, she pried it open. The inside was lined with black crushed velvet, and she immediately recognized what was set into it: a Fairbairn-Sykes commando knife. The blade, which was as black as the handle, but sort of dark gray compared to the velvet lining, was engraved with a small Ranger tab.

Her Ranger tab.

She felt her chin wrinkle, and before she could stop them the tears came. She felt her face flush even hotter, and she couldn't stop her mouth from smiling or the water from flowing out of her eyes, but she managed to look up and choke out "Thanks guys" in a hoarse stage whisper. Mercifully, she felt an arm around her shoulders and looked up to see Pike congratulating her. Then they were all coming up and shaking her hand, and she felt something she hadn't felt since before her parents died.

Thirty-Six

By the time I reach the post library, sweat has soaked through my T-shirt and shorts. It's September, but in southern Alabama that's not much cooler than May, June, July, or August. After the long hot summer, I'm pretty well sick of sweat and heat, but resigned to it too. Instinctively I walk slowly, minimizing my effort and the amount of heat my body produces.

The air conditioned atmosphere inside the library almost feels solid, so abrupt and extreme is the difference in air quality. My wet clothes are suddenly cold and clammy, and I suppress a chill that runs through me. I've been coming here every weekend all summer, though, so I know from experience I'll be dry in a matter of minutes. I walk over to the periodicals area, where there are racks of magazines and newspapers, and several large armchairs. The chairs are nothing fancy, of course, but they're comfortable enough, although they are upholstered in some kind of fake leather plastic, which would be too cold, and kind of gross, to sit on before my clothes have dried. I take the *Atlanta Journal-Constitution*, mounted on a wooden rod, off the rack and over to a tall table, where I lay the paper down and begin visually scanning it, page by page, while standing and waiting for my damp clothes to finish drying.

As usual, I find nothing about unsolved but apparently related strings of killings. This is routine, and good. I'm fulfilling my obligation by being vigilant for opportunities to help, but also finding my help is not needed.

When I first became aware of the sense, back in April, I thought I might carry around the dagger the guys in ROP gave me—figured I'd buy some kind of shoulder harness-mounted sheath for it, but I realized before I did that it wouldn't work. At eleven inches long all together, placing the handle a few inches down from my armpit put the tip of the blade squarely in the middle of my hip. When I was standing. Holding the knife in place against the side of my torso, it stabbed anything I sat on. So I kept it under the driver's seat in my car, but then worried it might get stolen if someone ever broke in. Not that my little Geo Metro with her bottom drawer sound system is much of a thief magnet, but I would really, really feel bad if I lost that knife. So the dagger went back in its wooden case, which went back in the old microwave box in the closet. I still intend to buy another knife, one with less sentimental value, but I haven't gotten around to it yet, probably because it seems so unlikely I'll run into another monster around here. How many serial killers can there be in rural southeastern Alabama? And I already got rid of two.

I don't like to think about this, but I also have to wonder how realistic carrying a knife is. I mean, would I *really* be willing to use a blade to kill someone again? If I'm going to be completely honest with myself, carrying the knife was a dumb idea.

But that was the only concession I'd made to the sense, and when I stopped keeping the blade in the car and put it away in its box again, it was as if nothing had changed as a result of that night in Florida. While part of me would have been content with that, at some level I still felt I had to do *something* with this newfound ability. The idea of checking the major regional newspapers occurred to me while I was in the shower one morning after getting home from the gym. So, for the past four months or so, I've been visiting the library every weekend and going through the *Journal-Constitution*, the New Orleans *Times-Picayune*, the Jacksonville *Florida Times-Union*, and Birmingham's *Post-Herald*, which are all the major papers the Fort Rucker library gets, besides the *Wall*

Street Journal, which seems irrelevant to what I'm doing, and *The New York Times*, which seems both redundant and remote after looking at these other four.

I read the Sunday comics in the Atlanta paper, then put the newspaper back on the rack, exchanging it for *The Times-Picayune*. I carry it over to one of the chairs and sit down. Even though my clothes are completely dry now, the plastic skin of the seat and backrest still feel very cold, but that lasts only seconds. I run my eyes down the front page, hitting each article's title and finding nothing about murder. I turn the page and continue scanning.

Second Couple Murdered

The headline on page three stops me. I don't recall reading about a first couple being murdered, but the article fills me in: both couples were shot to death in their parked cars in central New Orleans. Over the summer I did some research into serial killers, figuring the information could come in handy, and this story in the paper immediately makes me think of David Berkowitz, better known as Son of Sam. I read the article twice before my surprise converts to the sick realization this is probably what I've been looking for. Still, the police chief is quoted as saying they're still searching for a connection between the two couples, and refusing to commit to the possibility this was the work of a person targeting strangers. I try to remember the cop TV shows and movies I've seen, but ordinarily I avoid that stuff, so there's not much help there in reading into the chief's statement. Common sense, though, tells me he would be slow to admit he had a crazy roaming the streets of his city shooting random couples. That might create panic and would probably cut into the tourist trade. I don't know much about New Orleans, but I know they're big on parties like Mardi Gras, and famous for their food and music, so I suspect tourism is important there.

But maybe it is something else—maybe the couples were buying drugs from the wrong people or something. Whatever the reason, they weren't robbed: the article is clear about that.

Well, shit...what am I gonna do?

I look up from the newspaper and gaze around the room, waiting, frankly, for a plan to materialize on its own. I wait about a minute, but no plan shows up. *I don't know.* My mind remains blank, and I wonder why this doesn't happen when I try to meditate. I decide I should at least take some notes, or better yet make a photocopy of the article. There's a copier in the library, and I manage to wrestle the newspaper and its wooden pole into position on the glass scanning bed. A quarter in the slot and pressing a button finishes the job—the two-column piece fits on one standard-sized page.

I go through the rest of the papers like usual. These yield nothing remarkable, nothing on the killings in New Orleans. After I finish I start the walk home with my sheet from the copier.

As I go, the debate in my head cranks up again. What would I do if I did go to New Orleans? And what if this isn't the work of a sociopath?

Are you really willing to wait and let another couple die before you try to do something to stop this monster?

I go back and forth with this for a while, and by the time I cross the bridge spanning the railroad gap just outside the Fort Rucker gate I'm feeling lost and overwhelmed.

I can take the leave—I certainly have the vacation time saved up, but I still don't know what I would do once I got there. And he's *shooting* people. What am I supposed to do against that? Maybe I'm not supposed to do *anything* except protect myself, and what better protection than staying right here in Daleville?

I pass the Taco Bell where it's possible for me to get two bean burritos—an entire dinner—for less than a dollar. I consider stopping in since it is almost time to eat, but keep walking. I have food at home.

So I let another couple get shot, and then how would I feel? Would their blood be on my hands because I could have possibly done something, but instead stayed home?

But what can I do?!

I want to become two people so I can grab and shake myself, shout demands at myself until I get a satisfactory answer. But that doesn't happen. Instead the argument in my head just gets louder and less rational, the same mentally shouted questions over and over.

Stop! Fuckin' stop. I actually stop walking and, standing there on the sidewalk with the light Sunday evening traffic passing by, I close my eyes and enforce a moment of quiet in my head.

After a few seconds I start feeling conspicuous. I open my eyes and resume walking home, silencing all questions and retorts until I engage the deadbolt on my door and wedge the chair in place under the knob, locking myself in. I sit down on the couch and lean forward, resting my elbows on my knees and my face in my hands so I can go through it all quietly and sensibly.

OK, whether the police say it or not, something is going on in New Orleans when two apparently unrelated couples are violently killed in the same way. I might be able to prevent a third pair of people from being killed, and I have the means to try—I have plenty of vacation days saved up, and I can afford to drive over there and get a hotel room. But what will I do once I get there? There's no point in going if I don't know what to do. Even if I figure out how to find him and actually *do* find him, what can I do against someone with a gun? Should I get a gun of my own? So I can do what? Gun him down because he triggers psychosomatic pain in me? I sit with these questions for several minutes before my thoughts wander back to what I read about Son of Sam. He was caught when a parking ticket in the area of one of his shootings was traced back to him. As soon as he was confronted by police, he pretty much confessed. If I can find out who the killer is, and even where he lives, I can give that information to the police, and if they confront him, maybe he'll just give himself up. Or if he doesn't, the police can tail him or whatever and catch him that way.

I think about it some more, but I can't come up with anything better. I also like that this plan doesn't include me fighting with or even confronting the killer. I can use the pain to find him, then follow him around to find out stuff the police can use to identify him—a license plate, where he works, where he lives, a name on a mailbox. If I can find him soon enough, no one else will get shot. I'll save someone's life—how great would that be?

But how do I locate him? After all, New Orleans must be a big place. I remember reading something about serial killers preferring to work in certain areas or kinds of places because they find those areas more comfortable, or because they're good places to find the kinds of victims they seek. I pick up the photocopied article from where it is lying by my feet and scan it again, finding the locations of both shootings. Of course, knowing almost nothing of New Orleans, I still have no idea if the locations are in the same neighborhood or the same kind of area. I think about where I might get a map, and I remember that my AAA membership, which I have for the emergency road service, also offers maps and guide books. The map department must be closed today since it's Sunday, but I'll call them first thing tomorrow and have them send a map of New Orleans and a guidebook to help me find someplace affordable to stay. Once I get the map, I can plot the two shooting sites, and maybe that'll narrow my search area. The sense seems to have a range of about a block, so maybe, if I know what neighborhood to look in, I can find him.

And then I tell the cops about him and get the hell out. Hopefully I can do that part anonymously. I'll have to— otherwise they'll want to know how I know, and there's no way I can explain that.

Part Five

New Orleans

Thirty-Seven

I pocket my change and carry a couple croissants, today's copy of *The Times-Picayune*, and a glass of fresh-squeezed orange juice back out into the stone-paved courtyard. Even more than the room I'm renting, this café has become my refuge, my base in New Orleans. I stumbled across it three days ago on my first morning here, drawn in by the glimpse of light and greenery at the end of a dimly-lit twenty-foot passageway off of Royal Street. I've found it's not all that unusual to see something like this in the French Quarter, but most courtyards belong to private residences and entry is barred by locked iron gates. This one's gate was wide open, and a varnished wooden board propped up at the entrance on the sidewalk advertised the place as the Royal Blend Coffee & Tea House. Intrigued, I followed the brick passageway, weakly illuminated by lights made to look like gas lanterns, into an elongated courtyard surrounded by the old brick walls of the encompassing buildings, but open to the sky and filled with shady, indirect sunlight. It's this airy but sheltered space which keeps me coming back every morning. The pastry and juice are very good too, but more important is the food for my spirit. There's a fountain here, and several small trees with lots of low, leafy branches and other plantings down one long side of the yard. The eight or so round, black metal tables and matching chairs make it always possible for me to get one to myself and spread out the newspaper. The tables have folded umbrellas poking up out of their centers, but there hasn't been any reason to use them in the three days I've been visiting. Potted plants are suspended by chains from a second-floor balcony running down the long side opposite the trees, and small birds flit from these to the tables and ground, then up into the trees, and back again, chirping as they go. The courtyard is cut off from the rest of the world except for the arched passageway through the surrounding building. The length of this corridor, the trees and plants, and the sounds of the fountain and birds dampen out most of the noise from the street and block the sight of it.

I choose a table about halfway down the enclosure, set down my purchases, and locate the section of the paper with the comics in it before sitting. I've been buying the newspaper for information about the murderer I'm here to find, but I always like to start off with something fun before getting down to business. I split one of the croissants with a metal butter knife and spread some strawberry jam from a little plastic container on it, then read the comics. A couple of them make me smile before I put them aside and turn my attention to the front section. I find nothing about random shootings of couples in parked cars. There have been no more incidents like the two that started me on this quest, and I think again maybe he's done and I won't find him, and I can go back to my life. *Maybe.*

According to what I've read and plotted on my map, both shootings took place in central New Orleans. The first was in the Business District, the more modern section of town just across Canal Street from the Quarter, and the second was on the opposite side of the Quarter in a quiet adjacent neighborhood called Farbourg Marigny. Since my plan is to try to put myself within sensing distance of the killer, I'm renting a relatively inexpensive room in a home that's set itself up as a small inn in Marigny, and spending my days and evenings roaming central New Orleans, waiting for the pain to start up in me. I do this until around one in the morning, well past the time of both shootings, so I don't get up until about eight a.m.—pretty late for me.

All this searching has turned up nothing. I signed up for nine days of leave, but with three of them already gone, I'm beginning to wonder if it will be enough. Part of my problem is with only two incidents so far, and each in a different neighborhood, I can't focus on one area the killer has clearly settled on. My feet ache from crisscrossing the French Quarter and the hours-on-end patrolling of the Business District and Marigny. Yesterday, Tuesday, afternoon I went back to my room and traded my usual Chuck Taylor high tops for running shoes. I love my Chucks, but they're light on cushioning and walking on concrete all day is taking its toll on everything from my lower back down. The running shoes help, but I'm still pretty tired.

Of course, I still can't be sure there really *is* a sociopath behind these shootings, but it seems likely, and I'll continue on that assumption until the police prove otherwise or I run out of time here. *What else can I do?*

Thirty-Eight

*A*t least it's an interesting place to walk around in, I think as I make my way down Bourbon Street through the growing crowd of evening pedestrians. I find the French Quarter, also known as the *Vieux Carre* or Old Quarter, especially appealing. This half square mile or so rectangle was the extent of the city before it was even called New Orleans, when it was a sixteenth century Spanish colonial outpost clinging to the edge of a vast, unknown world. The preserved centuries-old architecture extending block after block has the same old-style charm I remember experiencing in Boston, but here it's more concentrated and, in many cases, better preserved. In Boston you have to hunt for the interesting old buildings among skyscrapers, subway stations, and that eyesore the elevated Central Artery, although I read somewhere that piece of work's days are numbered.

Damn, I'm hungry. Besides the preservation of history, this city's other pleasant surprise for me has been the food. Much of it is no good to me because of its meat content, but every place seems to serve something I can eat, and everything I've tried so far has been delicious. A lot of it is pretty hot with chile pepper too—an added bonus for me since I developed an addiction to hot stuff when the Army started packaging tiny bottles of Tabasco sauce in the field ration packets. Also, I've decided that crawfish, or mud bugs as people here sometimes refer to them, are OK to eat since they're not much different from insects, and probably about as emotionally advanced and self-aware. I'm not entirely comfortable with this distinction, and would have preferred to stick with a completely vegan diet, but it seems a reasonable assumption, so I'm going with it for now. My favorite dish is something I'd never heard of before—crawfish etoufee. This is a thick stew of peppers, onions, celery, and crawfish served over white rice. I tried this my first evening in New Orleans, and have had it twice more since. I also really liked the gumbo I had for dinner yesterday—a dark, thick, almost smoky stew with a slippery texture, filled with okra, shrimp, oysters, rice, and crawfish.

I walk another block down Bourbon Street, eyeing the restaurants before wandering into one with a rustic look which advertises balcony seating upstairs. One of the staff, a thin guy about my age, shows me to a small table overlooking the street I just walked down.

I normally don't eat out much; I feel conspicuous dining alone in anything above that bottom tier of restaurants, the fast food franchise. But in this town the great cooking, omnipresent music, and anonymity of the crowds of people make it easy for me to forget myself. I really enjoy meals here. Unfortunately, the costs of dining out, plus the rate on my albeit no-frills room, are beginning to add up. Tomorrow morning I'll stop by a small grocery store I remember passing on Royal Street and get some bread, peanut butter, and jelly so I can at least have lunch on the cheap in my room.

I read over the menu and decide to try this place's gumbo, see how it stacks up against what I had last night. The waiter stops by, takes my order, and leaves with the menu. I turn my eyes on the street below, and watch the continually changing show, accompanied by cajun music from the band on the first floor of the restaurant and blues from the open door of a club across the road. I've noticed almost no vehicles travel Bourbon, which is instead dominated by masses of strolling people, many of them carrying "go cups"—large plastic cups provided by the bars for take out alcoholic beverages. Despite all the booze, the crowd is surprisingly good-natured. The sheer variety of people is equally remarkable—every shape, size, color, and age seems to be present.

For a while I watch a young man selling strings of shiny, brightly-colored beads to passers-by. Despite his best efforts to attract attention to himself, the vast majority walk by without even a glance, and I begin to feel sorry for him. After a while, though, another man about the same age stops by, and Beadman drops his sales persona and retreats a few paces from the river of people to chat and laugh with this friend for several minutes before they part company and Beadman resumes his pitch.

It occurs to me this man I've been feeling sorry for probably has more friends than I do. To be honest, I don't have any real friends—some *friendly acquaintances*, but no one to confide in, to have a memorable conversation with, no one to really *be* with. With Miranda gone from my life I am even more aware of an incredible *quiet*. Without the noise of friends and social interaction, I'm more aware than I want to be of the bare fact of my life.

My dinner arrives, and I dig in enthusiastically, my hunger displacing the existential moodiness. The gumbo is spicy, but after a couple spoonfuls I take advantage of the bottle of Crystal hot sauce on the table, and make the food hot enough to cause my nose to sweat. There's a side of cornbread too, and this provides a little relief whenever my mouth starts burning too much. As I eat, I continue to gaze at the shifting scene below. The bead seller has moved on. Across the street a small group has gathered at the blues club's open door, their ears catching the hard-driving music spilling out. Five young men in shorts and T-shirts, some wearing over-sized, ridiculous hats, stumble along laughing loudly and spilling liquid out of their go cups. A white-haired couple strolls arm-in-arm. The people keep coming; it's like having a god's eye view of humanity with all its variety, in all its stages from youth to old age. The people pass by, on their way to somewhere or nowhere, and then they're gone, replaced by others like them.

Life really isn't much, is it? Some pleasure, some pain, and eventually oblivion. I wonder what the point is, if maybe the idea is to maximize the pleasure and minimize the pain until it's over. *In that case, what am I doing here?* Actually, I like New Orleans—the problem is what brought me here, what I'm doing; this would feel completely different if I were here simply as a tourist. *I guess I'm here to minimize pain for other people.* But doing that means I have to confront the last thing in the world I want any contact with. And, I realize, if I'm successful it will also mean increasing the pain of the monster doing these shootings.

Fuck him—he started it.

The more I think about it, though, the more complicated it becomes. I'm trying to do God's job of deciding how happiness and hurt ought to be handed out. *Well, someone should, but when did this become my responsibility? How is any of this my problem?* Maybe each person is supposed to take care of himself. But that's what the bastard I'm hunting is doing—taking care of his deformed needs. Maybe there are no oughts or shoulds. *But I'm here, alive—there's no getting around that. I have to do something.* Sartre coined a phrase that sums it up nicely: "condemned to be free." Like a miracle, we pop into existence and spend perhaps seventy-some years trying to figure out why, before popping back out of existence, like an elaborate practical joke.

I notice my bowl is empty, but don't remember finishing the food. I take a sip of iced tea, lean back, and look up at the night sky, which, because I'm in the city, is an orange mist of light superimposed on bland, unremarkable blackness. The artificial lights hide the reality I know is out there, the stars and planets, the incomprehensible vastness of the universe. I look back down at the river of people. *Maybe "joke" is giving us too much credit. Maybe "accident" is the right word.*

But even sitting here having this conversation with myself seems to undermine that idea. *Hell of an accident— sort of like dumping out a box full of puzzle pieces and having them land more or less put together. It's theoretically possible, but if it ever happened you'd wonder what was going on.*

The waiter comes by to clear the table and asks if I want dessert. I say "no thanks" and he leaves to get the bill.

If it's not an accident, then something caused all this— me, the people down in the street, the world, the stars out there in space. Even if it is an accident, it had to come from somewhere, right? Something had to dump out the puzzle pieces. Something had to make the puzzle pieces, make the cardboard, make the wood, make the trees, make the— I see the infinite regress. *But if everything, accident or not, comes from something, where does it stop? Harold? Back to him?*

The waiter returns and gives me the bill. I pull out my wallet and leave money on the table. Back on the street, I resume my pre-dinner direction of movement, but the crowd has become too dense. *He's not going to be in this mess of people anyway—too many witnesses.* I escape down a side street, following it all the way to Decatur, then stop, debating left versus right. One seems as good as another: three nights in both areas of the shootings hasn't turned up anything. Before dinner I had been headed for the Biz District, so I turn right, heading for Canal Street. I soon come to a Y intersection. I have my map with me, but I don't need to look at it to know the left branch would take me between the river and downtown, into the Warehouse District where there have been no shootings. But that doesn't mean the shooter can't live, or at least walk around, there. Maybe I haven't found him because I've been looking in the wrong area. I wait for traffic, then cross the road and start down what I see from the sign is North Peters Street.

There are plenty of people on these sidewalks too, but it's easier to breathe here. I walk at the steady, moderate pace I've become accustomed to, past souvenir and T-shirt shops. Up ahead I see a small crowd of people clustered around an open door. The large sign jutting out over the entrance has a light shining on it. I read "Tipitina's" in flowery cursive letters. Judging from the music I can already hear, I figure it's a club or bar.

As I walk toward the sign, I hear one song end and another start. I try to make out what kind of music it is, but it's confusing—pounding piano keys combined with electric guitar, and a rough male voice singing. When I reach the door I can finally make out the words of the song:

> *A man ain't nothin' but a face in the sand,*
> *Wave comes along and washes the land,*
> *There's a soul untouched by human hands,*
> *Untouched! Untouched by human hands!*

The words stop everything else for me, and I feel a prickling on the back of my neck. I can hear several voices backing up the lead singer, all practically shouting *untouched by human hands* over and over again. That's the part that gets me. A smile spreads across my face and my eyes feel full. I realize I'm holding my breath, listening:

> *A man ain't nothin' but a barrel of tears,*
> *I'm gonna dance for a million years,*
> *There's a soul untroubled by human fears,*
> *Untouched! Untouched by human hands!*

I stand rooted, oblivious to everything but the music and the words they keep shouting to me. I can't stop smiling, nor do I try. Standing there, lost in the sounds and those words, I actually believe them, believe *he* never touched me, could never *really* touch me, touch the *real* me. The tune eventually ends and, amidst wild clapping and cheering from the audience, the band goes right into another. The change of songs breaks the spell, but I stay immersed in the music, hiding from my history a little longer.

"Hey, *chere*, c'mon in."

I register someone is talking to me and look around. The other people who were gathered in front of the club have either moved on or entered—I don't know which—and now it's just me and a white man with a face weathered by at least fifty years of intense living standing by the door.

"Umm, what's the cover?" I ask, reaching into my pocket for my wallet.

He waves dismissively. "Ah, forget it! You already made my night—I haven't seen a reaction like dat to music in I don't know for how long." His dialect is warm, compelling, and unfamiliar to my ears.

"No, really," I say, feeling embarrassed and taking out my wallet.

"*Lagniappe*—on the house. For true. C'mon in." The lilt and cadence of his voice make his speech a kind of music.

I put my wallet away. "OK, thanks. Uh, what band is this?"

A surprised look crosses the man's face. "You never heard dem before? Da way you look just now, I figure you must be deir biggest fan. Dem's Da Radiators."

"The Radiators?"

"Yeah, dey're a home-grown band, from right here in N'awlins."

"Oh—thanks!" I feel I should say more, but can't think of anything.

"Enjoy, miss," he says, waving me through, and I enter the club.

It's a little smoky, but I soon forget that as I get caught up in the music again. I buy a Coke and find a place to stand and listen. The band is five men, mostly somewhat older—in their forties, I guess. Their music isn't exactly rock, but not jazz or blues either—it's hard to categorize, especially for someone as ignorant of music as I am. I really like it, but can't really explain why. Somehow, the whole package of vocals, keyboard, two guitars, bass, and drums connects with me. The set ends, and as the crowd is calling for an encore I suddenly remember I'm supposed to be hunting for the shooter, not hanging out in a bar. I want to stay—The Radiators are taking the stage again, but I look at my watch and realize it's after ten—both shootings occurred between ten and midnight, so this is my main time for patrolling. But I also need to empty my bladder, so I hear most of the encore number while I'm in the bathroom and then leave hurriedly, my ears straining backward as I walk out the door and into the warm night.

"Leavin' so soon?"

I look back and see the man who let me in. "Yeah, I gotta go." I let the reluctance come out in my voice. "Thanks, though—it was great!"

"You come back again sometime soon *Petite*, all right?"

"All right—thanks!"

I continue down North Peters for a few blocks until I reach the bright lights and crowded sidewalks of Canal Street. Beyond this busy thoroughfare, the streets of the Warehouse District look relatively dark, quiet, and intimidating, but it seems absurd to be put off by dim streets when I am, after all, looking for a serial killer armed with a handgun.

I go four or five blocks down Tchoupitoulas Street and am about take a right toward Lafayette Square when I feel the dirty itching on my scar. My throat constricts and my tongue is suddenly too big for my dry, sticky mouth. After seeking this for four days—four months if you count all the weekends I scanned newspapers—I wish it weren't happening. But I remind myself the plan is to just follow the guy, find out something about him, then phone it in to the number I looked up for the police—no contact required. I take a deep breath, hold it and try to calm myself for a few seconds, then let it out faster than I intended. *OK, which way?* I decide to continue my original course and head for Lafayette Square. The itching holds constant for several steps, then fades to nothing. I reverse course, heading toward the river. The itching increases and evolves into the painful scratch. I exhale a tremulous sigh. *Here we go.*

I spot him when I reach Commerce Street, which intersects with the street I'm on near a plaza filled with artfully-lighted fountains and stone columns. It's not hard to pick him out—Commerce is a narrow, one-lane street, empty of cars now, and he's the only person on it, walking confidently down the sidewalk, heading right for me. Panic rises in me, but I contain it and turn to gaze through the iron fence surrounding the plaza, as if interested in the fountains and unique architecture there. I hope my hammering heart isn't audible outside my body and remind myself he targets couples in parked cars, not solitary women on sidewalks. As the distance closes, I resist the temptation to look at him, letting the growing pain keep watch. I concentrate on standing up straight and keeping my face relaxed, while holding on to the knowledge that despite the hurt, no real damage is being done to my body. The pain is as strong as the other times I've experienced it, but I'm getting better at handling it.

I look back over my shoulder at Commerce Street just as he's reaching the intersection with my street. By the glow of the street lamps I see he's only a few inches taller than me— five-seven or five-eight, I guess—and kind of doughy looking, though not excessively heavy. His wavy hair is a little messy, maybe a medium brown, and long enough to cover his ears. His pale face is clean-shaven. He pays no attention to me, but pauses briefly at the corner before continuing down the street I've been following. I look at his clothing as he walks away. He's wearing a loose-fitting short-sleeve blue shirt with a collar, but no tails—it's meant to not be tucked in and hangs over dark-colored pants which I don't think are jeans, but probably aren't dress pants either. Dockers or something. I let him get to the next cross street before following, looking everywhere but directly at him so he doesn't feel the weight of my gaze. The streets here are closely-spaced, so even though I'm leaving the full length of a block between us, the sense continues to scratch away at me.

He continues toward the river, then leads me on a meandering walk past most of the convention center before heading away from the river again, paralleling an elevated highway. We roam like this for about half an hour, wandering the streets just south of the Old Quarter, and I wonder what he's up to. When I imagined how this plan would work I always saw myself following him to maybe a couple destinations—stores or whatever—and eventually to either a car, and I would get the plate number, or to a home, and I could get an address and maybe a name off a mailbox or door buzzer to pass on to the police. This aimless wandering is making it hard to follow him inconspicuously.

Shit! It occurs to me suddenly: *He's probably* hunting. The small muscles up the length of my spine tense. *Shit, shit, shit.* A fresh batch of nausea in my stomach joins the deep cramping sensation below my heart. *Of course he's hunting— what did I expect? I've been looking for him in the places he's hunted before!* The magnitude of my stupidity astounds me. But where else could I look? *Yeah, but I might have anticipated this. Now what am I going to do?* My mind is blank on that one. *Maybe he won't find anyone he wants to shoot*, I think with hope born of desperation. Approaching from behind, I look at him as he waits to cross a street, wondering where he's hiding the handgun. *It's got to be in his waistband, under the shirt.* I suddenly realize I've nearly pulled even with him, and he's looking back at me. Trying not to be obvious, I allow my gaze to wander casually away from him, hoping he'll assume I was just looking around, not looking at him.

We resume our wanderings, but now, when I occasionally glance at him, he is sometimes looking back, obviously aware of me. I wonder if, on the next deserted stretch of street, I might come under fire. The small canister of pepper spray in my pocket won't stop a lot of bullets. I decide to call the police, and start looking for a payphone. A couple blocks later we pass a hotel and I duck into the lobby.

Ignoring the front desk clerk staring at me, I look around and quickly spot a bank of three wall-mounted payphones off to my right. I change course and speed-walk up to the one furthest from the clerk. My hand stops in mid-air, halfway to the phone's handset. *What am I going to tell them? That a man is wandering the streets of the Warehouse District?* There's nothing I can say to convince them he's the killer, and I sure don't have a name, address, or license plate number to give them. I decide to take the tact that I "just know," and they can invent whatever reason they want for this knowledge. I grab the handset and reach into my back pocket for the scrap of paper I wrote the phone number on. Cradling the phone between my shoulder and head, I unfold the piece of paper and spread it on the small horizontal surface under the phone set. When I look at the number, it occurs to me I should really be calling 911, given that the fucker could find someone to shoot any minute now. I punch in the three digits and stuff the paper back in my pocket.

"911 operator, what is your emergency?" a calm, professional-sounding male voice asks.

"I'm calling about the—uh, the guy who shot those couples—I've seen him; I think he's going to shoot someone…tonight, like, any minute now," I say, realizing I already sound crazy but having no clue how to fix it.

There's a momentary pause, then "So, someone is threatening people with a gun?" he asks.

"Yes—well, not yet, but I think he's going to. Tonight."

I hear crisp and professional giving way to weary and dubious: "OK, ma'am, what is your name?"

Crap. I should have expected this, but I didn't think about them wanting information about me. Maybe it's because of what happened in Florida last spring, or because I know I can't explain to anyone my source of knowledge and so don't want to be questioned in detail, but I balk at giving my name, and just drive on with my message. "Never mind that. The killer is walking around in the Warehouse District now—I just saw him heading down South Peters Street, away from the Quarter. I think he's looking for his next targets."

"OK ma'am, slow down please. What is your name?"

"Look, he's out there right now! He could be killing someone *right now*! You need to send someone to South Peters Street right away, and they'll see him. He's wearing a light blue short-sleeve shirt and dark pants. He's a white guy, clean shaven, with brown hair to below his ears, maybe five-eight, and a little heavy. He's walking all over the Warehouse District—I've been following him for almost an hour. I think his weapon is in the waistband of his pants, under his shirt."

"Ma'am," the operator says, his irritation plain in his voice, "I'll be happy to help, but first you need to give me some more information. Let's start with your name—"

"Just send someone! South Peters Street!" I hang the phone up hard. *Fuck!* I knew it'd be a hard sell, but...*shit. Now what? What am I s'posed to do now?* I walk quickly out of the hotel, ignoring the clerk who, I see with a glance, is really staring at me. *Was I that loud?*

Back out on the sidewalk, I look in the direction I last saw the guy traveling, but now there's just a group of four college-age women moving toward me, talking loudly and laughing. The itching is there, just barely. I guess he's within a block or two of me. I head in his last known direction. The itching becomes briefly painful before fading away again. I stop, looking around uselessly, trying to imagine what combination of movements would account for what I felt. Worried I'm going to lose him and free him to do whatever he wants, I walk quickly back up the street. The itching holds steady, but there is still no sight of him. Clearly he is on another street nearby, probably a parallel street, but which one? I pass the hotel I was just in and follow the sense for another block before ducking down a side street and, anxious to find him, actually run toward Commerce Street. Before I even reach Commerce, though, the fading itch tells me I guessed wrong. I reverse direction and run back down the cross street, past South Peters. When I near Fulton Street the stabbing sensation is ramping up fast. I slow to a walk just before reaching Fulton, and immediately spot him standing on the sidewalk next to a parked car about twenty feet away, reaching under his shirt. By the time these images register with my brain, he is bringing the gun up to fire into the vehicle.

"NO!" I shout.

He spins around, pointing his weapon at me.

Oh shit! I turn to run back the way I just came but it's like the faster I try to go the harder it is to move, as if I'm immersed in water. Something punches me really, really hard in the back of my right shoulder and suddenly my face is inches from the brick sidewalk. I hear four shots in quick succession, along with the shattering of glass. My Army education kicking in, I instinctively roll a few feet toward the building on the corner, putting it between me and him before pushing off from the ground and sprinting back up the cross street. The street is lined with parked vehicles on both sides; I duck between a couple cars and cut diagonally across the street. Just as I'm passing between the parked cars on the other side, the sound of another shot sends a jolt through my entire body. I crouch lower, make the sidewalk, and keep running. At the corner I turn right onto South Peters without breaking stride and duck between parked cars to leave the sidewalk. A quick glance backward shows no vehicles coming up behind me. I run across the street, leap on to the sidewalk, and continue sprinting, turning hard up the next cross street. I cover half the block before an amplified voice sends a shudder through my adrenaline-loaded body.

"Stop, this is the police," a loudspeaker blares.

Relieved, I whirl around and run toward the cruiser, which has its blue strobes flashing. This street is narrow and there are no parked cars along it, so I can run right at the driver window on the cruiser.

"Stop where you are—do not approach the vehicle!"

The words penetrate and I stop abruptly, instinctively raising my hands above my head. The sensation of a red-hot spike being hammered through my right shoulder surprises me and makes me dizzy. My knees buckle; I stagger but manage to stay upright. I lower my right arm a little to ease the pain and hold it there while fully extending my left arm. "Please!" I shout.

The driver window comes down to reveal a uniformed police officer.

"Please—the shooter is near here—we might be able to find him."

"Are you injured?" asks the officer looking out the window as the car pulls up next to me.

Maddeningly, they don't seem to get the urgency of the situation. "Yes, but we need to go back and find him—"

Both cops get out of the vehicle and the one nearest me— Driver—asks where I'm hurt.

What are you guys doing?! "My shoulder, but please, we need to go *now*—can I get in and give you directions?" Tears of frustration and pain are welling up. I fight them, wanting desperately to appear rational. "Please!"

Driver steps behind me. "Jesus," he says under his breath, then "I think she's been shot," to the other officer, Passenger Side.

"That's what I'm trying to tell you—the guy that's been shooting people here shot me, and he was chasing me—he might still be around here," I say, though now I'm losing hope.

"Get her in the back," says Passenger Side. "We'll make a quick search on the way to Charity."

"Shouldn't we call EMS?" Driver asks.

"This is faster anyway."

Driver, still standing behind me, frisks me quickly. My whole body goes tense at his touch, but the search is brief and legit. "All right, you can put your hands down," he says as he steps around me and opens the back door.

As I duck to get in I feel his hand rest lightly on the top of my head, and then I'm in the seat and the door is closed. As soon as I sit down a wave of vertigo washes over me, and a chilly sweat breaks out all over my face and body. I struggle to stay focused and conscious, and to keep the gunshot wound off the seat back. "He chased me up the next street over," I say, pointing with my left hand so Driver can see me in the mirror.

"Girod Street?"

"I don't know the name of it—the next one over that way."

"Yeah, that's Girod," he says, driving up to the corner and taking a left, followed by another left.

"He shot me two streets down from here," I tell them as they turn onto Girod, "and chased me up this alley."

"What happened?" Passenger Side asks. "Why'd he shoot you?"

"He was about to shoot into a parked car, and I shouted at him. He turned, I ran, I got hit." We cross South Peters Street and I scan both sides of the alley I just ran up a few minutes ago, but there are no people around.

"What made you think he was going to shoot into the car?"

"He reached under his shirt and pulled a gun out while he was standing next to the car—this is where I got shot—if you take a right we should see where—there! I think that's the car he was standing next to. It was one of these..." *But why is it still here?*   I assumed the people would have driven off when they heard the shooting, and I wonder if the car had been empty after all.

Driver moves the cruiser slowly up the line of cars, the spotlight mounted on his side turned on and shining across the hood at an angle into the parked vehicles.   "You say it was one—oh Jesus!"   Driver stops the car.

"What?" I ask.

"Shit," says Passenger Side, before turning toward me.   "I thought you said he chased you."

"He did," I answer, but remember I didn't actually see him after I started running.   I strain to look around Passenger Side at the car and glimpse a red splash on the passenger window of the car in the spotlight.   My head swims, the seat back drops away from me, and I fall backwards into a deep darkness.

Thirty-Nine

Daylight is streaming in through a window, but I don't know where I am. I shift my eyes and roll my head on the pillow: bare light green walls, TV mounted high up on a bracket, two more beds, unoccupied, a few feet from mine. The beds have wheels and aluminum guard rails. My bed has guard rails too, and the pillowcase feels brittle and a little rough. "Oh fuck no," I whisper, tears welling up. *Mom, Dad...* I bring my right hand up and gingerly touch my upper abdomen, but there are no stitches there, no hurt, just a slightly raised scar. *Wait—what?* I remember running through the streets, and think hard to remember more. *New Orleans. It's 1995—September.* I realize this is the first time I've woken up in a hospital since the Bad, and work hard at reminding myself where and when I am, bringing up and mentally examining every detail I can recall from the last few days. Doing this helps me hold it together until I remember the car window covered with blood. I shut my eyes tightly. *Not again. You fuck-up! Not again, not again...* Since he targets couples, there must have been two people in the car, two people he killed. The image of the dark-haired woman's bloody neck appears on the insides of my eyelids. *That makes three you've allowed to be killed now.*

Not counting the first two people you got killed.

A couple tears leak out of my scrunched eyelids. *Fuck.*

But it's not like I didn't try. I open my eyes and bend my elbows to raise my hands so I can see them. Both palms are covered with gauze dressings, crusted through in places with dark reddish-brown dried blood. There's more gauze on my right forearm, and a needle attached to a tube is plugged into the vein where my arm bends. The thought of the tip of the needle scraping around inside my vein makes me feel woozy, and I straighten my arms out again. My right shoulder is throbbing a little, and when I reach my left hand around to explore it my right shoulder moves too, causing a flare-up of pain. It doesn't feel so intense, but something tells me I should respect it, so I put my left arm back where it was. These wounds are the proof: I *did* try. It's not much, but I hold on to that.

Soon a nurse walks in. "Oh—you're awake," she says.

I nod, then wonder. "How—" I have to pry my tongue off the roof of my mouth to say that first word. I try to swallow while the nurse looks at me sympathetically and steps closer. "How long have I been here?" I manage, my voice sounding hoarse.

"You came in last night—it's about 10 a.m. now."

Her voice sounds a little distant and echoes slightly. I nod again, absorbing the information.

"How 'bout some juice? How's that sound?"

I intend to nod eagerly, but I seem to only be capable of slow motion.

She operates the motorized bed to get me propped in a sitting position. My shoulder hurts in that weird, muted way as my weight redistributes, but it's worth it to be sitting up and feeling a little less helpless. She places the bed control by my left hand. "I'm supposed to let the police know when you wake up, but I can put that off for a while if you like."

It takes me a moment; the synapses in my brain are firing slowly. *The police...maybe I can help them catch the bastard?* "Oh—oh, no...I can to talk—talk to them now...I want to...talk to...them." *Was that too many "to"s?*

"Sure?" the nurse asks.

"Yeah...I'm sure," I say, my swollen tongue and groggy mind forming the words at their own pace. *Shit they must have me on dope.* I hate that and decide to refuse any more of the stuff.

About half an hour and two cups of apple juice later I'm feeling more coherent when the cop arrives—coherent enough to wonder if it was a good idea to speak to him while my thinking is still muddled by the pain killers. But I need to make amends…to help stop that shooter mother-fucker.

The detective is maybe in his forties. He's wearing a navy blue business suit with a dark purple shirt and dark blue tie. His nose is narrow and jutting like a hatchet blade coming out of his face, and as if it weren't already sufficiently prominent, he has underlined it with a neatly-trimmed moustache. Like the moustache, his hair is medium brown. He wears it combed straight back, but not slicked down. "I'm Detective Baudoin," he says, showing a badge. "New Orleans Police Department."

"Hi detective," I say, and wonder if I sound dopey.

He turns and retrieves a chair from the corner and sits down next to the bed. "Mind if I record our conversation?" he asks.

I shake my head. "I don't mind—go 'head."

He pulls out a small recorder and switches it on, says the date and time, and has me give my name, address, phone number, and information about where I work. Then he says "Tell me what happened, starting with what brought you to New Orleans, and what you were doing before you encountered the man who shot you."

I am distinctly uncomfortable with being less than candid, but explaining about the sense and how I came to understand its meaning is out of the question, since it would mean talking about what happened in Florida. It would just sound crazy anyway. Instead, I leave those parts out and tell the minimum: I'm on leave for a week, visiting New Orleans, enjoying the food and music and walking around.

"Alone?" he asks, sounding not surprised so much as just trying to get all the facts. "You came here alone?"

I nod. "Yes."

"OK, and what were you doing last night before you were shot?"

"I left a club in the Quarter and was wandering around, when I noticed this man. There was something strange about him that caught my attention."

"What club?"

I try to remember. "Um, something like Tip—Tipina..."

"Tipitina's?"

"That's it—I think that's it."

"And you were at the one in the French Quarter—on North Peters Street, correct?"

Obviously I had no idea there was more than one, but I nod, "Yes, that's right."

"OK, so you left there and were just walking around in the Warehouse District?"

"Um-hmm."

"Alone?" Now he sounds a little surprised.

I nod again.

"The witness is nodding affirmatively," he says for the tape. "Do you realize that can be dangerous?"

I look down at my bandaged hands.

"Let me re-phrase that: *Did* you realize that could be dangerous?"

"I had my pepper spray."

"Why were you walking around there?"

I study the bandages on my hands some more, trying to think of an excuse. "I'm interested in old buildings—I like to look at them."

"At night?"

I'm the one shot here—why am I getting interrogated? I look up at the detective and shrug—a bad idea since it causes a flare of hurt behind my right shoulder blade. "I felt like walking around, getting some fresh air, and wanted to see a different part of town."

Baudoin looks at me with arched eyebrows for a moment, and I resist the urge to say anything more until I get another question.

"You said there was something about the man that caught your attention—what was it?"

I hesitate, then say truthfully, "I had a bad feeling about him—I'm not sure what caused it, but something seemed bad about him."

"Can you be any more specific?"

What can I say? "I guess it was something about the way he was walking around, like he was looking for something, and he kept going up and down the same area, the same streets."

The detective stares at me for several seconds. I stare back, sensing he's deliberately creating this awkward silence. *What is this?* I drop my gaze to my hands, but manage to keep silent, my resentment building.

Finally, "Go on, what happened next?"

The question seems obvious, and I feel stupid for keeping silent and waiting for him to ask, instead of just going on with the story. *Maybe it's me—maybe the painkillers and my conscience are making me paranoid.* My hostility, though, continues to simmer, confusing me. *I should have waited until my brain felt clearer.* I look directly into his gray eyes and work to keep my voice level and emotionally neutral. "I followed him around for a while, at a distance, just to see what he would do. Like I said, he seemed to be looking for something—he kept wandering up and down various streets, looking at all the parked cars. Well, I'd read about the murders—in the newspaper—about those people killed in their cars, so I found a phone and called 911." I make a point of mentioning the phone call, in effect saying "no vigilante here." I figure the phone call will eventually come up anyway, since they'll probably recognize my voice and I was, after all, in the area I referenced in the call.

"Where did you call from?"

"A hotel on South Peters Street." Again he's looking at me as if expecting more, so I add "I don't know the name of it. I saw a hotel and went in to find a pay phone."

"What did you tell the person who answered?"

"Just that I saw this man walking around and thought he might be dangerous, that he might be the guy who's been shooting people."

"Did you identify yourself?"

I wonder if this is some kind of a trap to check the veracity of my story. I pretend to think about it, as if trying to remember. "Nnnoo," I say slowly. "No, I guess I didn't. The man on the phone seemed to want to talk a lot, and I was worried the guy would get away—he'd been walking around a lot, and I didn't know if he would be on South Peters Street for long. I just wanted the police to get there quickly." *No vigilante here.*

"So after you got off the phone—"

"I immediately went looking for the guy again—I didn't want to lose him. As it was, I almost did, but somehow managed to find him just as he was pulling his gun out. He was looking at a parked car as he did it—I thought maybe there was someone inside, so I shouted at him. After that, things happened pretty fast—I think he just turned and shot me, because next I knew I was on the ground. There were more shots...I thought he was shooting at me. I rolled behind the corner of the building I was next to, then ran up the cross street." I pause as I watch and listen to the replay in my head. "I think he shot at me again, but...he missed me. I ran down that street, crossed South Peters, ran down another street, and that's when the police car picked me up. That's about it."

The detective nods and seems to be studying my face. *Why does he keep looking at me like that? Like he's trying to see* through *me.* I look down at my hands, then back up at him.

"So when you were lying—"

How—?!

"—on the ground and you heard those shots, you thought he was shooting at you."

I nod. "Yes," I say quietly.

He does the silent staring thing again, and, getting the hang of this, I look down and wait him out.

"There must have been something that made you want to follow this man around—how long did you say you followed him?"

I wonder if I did say, but I'm not sure. I silently curse myself again for not waiting for the pain meds to wear off more before talking to the police. I stick with the truth—there doesn't seem to be any point in lying about this part. "I'm not sure—maybe half an hour?"

"You tell me."

"I guess about a half hour or so," I say, fighting to keep the edge out of my voice and wondering if I should have fudged the time shorter.

"So what made you so concerned about this stranger that you would take half an hour out of your vacation to follow him around a fairly deserted part of town late at night? There must have been something."

I look at him for a few seconds, trying to remain calm and to get my fogged brain to think clearly, check for danger. Finally, "Gut feeling." He raises his eyebrows and opens his eyes wider, but I stick with my answer since it is, in fact, literally true. "Gut feeling. I thought he might be dangerous, and I felt obligated to keep an eye on him."

"Didn't it occur to you this might be creating a dangerous situation?"

What is this? "Sure, but I kept my distance, didn't confront him or anything—look, are you saying I did something wrong? Because I thought I was doing a good thing."

He sits back in the chair. "You did, but you should have called us sooner."

"Hey, I did the best I could, all right?"

He looks at me with mild surprise.

"Even as it was, I felt weird calling," I continue. "I didn't really have anything concrete, but after following him around for a while I definitely felt I had *something*."

The detective looks at me several more seconds.

I want to tell him to knock it off—I know what he's doing and it's not going to trip me up or get me to tell him more. Instead, I remind myself that, regardless of how I feel about this momo, I still have a mission. "Anyway, I think I can describe him."

"I was about to ask you that. I'll have a sketch artist come by, and you can work with him." He clicks off the recorder and puts it in a pocket of his suit jacket. "Miss, you *did* do a good thing, especially since we'll have a description of him. You're apparently the first of his intended victims to survive."

"I'm big on survival," I say absently, relieved the questioning is over.

He leaves his business card on the table by the bed, telling me to get in touch with him if I think of anything else which might be helpful, and predicting the sketch artist will be by in about an hour.

Forty

After the sketch artist gets done, I lie back and close my eyes, but the throbbing in my shoulder keeps me from sleeping. The pain meds have worn off, but I'm trying to do without them. I lie still for a while, glad to be, by luck, the only patient in a three-bed room. I look out the window at strands of cottony clouds stretched across a bright blue sky, and try to get past the surrealness of the past 24 hours.

There's a soft knocking on the open door. *Now what?* I wonder, hoping more needles aren't involved and rounding up the willpower to refuse more pain meds. Then I hear whispering.

"I think she's asleep. Let's just leave the flowers and go."

I turn my head and see two uniformed police officers crowded into the doorway. One of them is holding a vase filled with brightly-colored flowers. "Um, hi?" I say.

"Oh, you're awake," the one not holding the flowers says awkwardly.

We stare at each other dumbly for a couple seconds. "I'm not sure who you're looking for, but I'm the only one in this room."

"These are for you," the one not holding the bouquet replies, then turns to the other cop and says, with a hint of exasperation, "Tell her, Remi."

Officer Flowers nods. "Yeah, we, uh, thought you should have something to brighten up your room." He pauses, then says, "You know, because we heard you were from out of town, thought you might not get flowers right away."

"Thanks," I say, nodding because I'm not really sure how to respond. "Maybe you should put those down on the table next to the bed," I say, looking at the small, wheeled piece of furniture that has my cup of juice on it.

Officer Flowers smiles and carries the arrangement around the foot of the bed. As he sets the vase down, I recognize him as Driver from the previous night, the cop who'd wanted to wait for an ambulance instead of letting me direct them to the killer. "Is this a standard New Orleans Police thing—bringing flowers to crime victims? I mean, that is *really* nice."

"Uh, well, not usually…" Officer Flowers stammers.

"What Officer Menard is trying to say, Ms. Campbell, is no, but we think what you did was really brave. Most gunshot victims wouldn't care about chasing down the bad guy before getting medical treatment, and most unarmed people wouldn't have tried to intervene when someone was pulling a gun out."

"You've got a lot of spine, Ms. Campbell," Officer Menard says, nodding.

I notice myself starting to smile, which feels a little strange. "Thanks guys—that's very sweet, but I don't feel like I did much good, since I didn't save anyone but myself."

"He had a gun, you didn't—what could you do?," Menard retorts.

"That's what I keep asking myself."

"You did great, Ms. Campbell."

This is getting embarrassing. "I feel terrible about what happened, but let's just leave it at that, OK? Second, thank you for the flowers. Except for the guy who shot me, everyone in New Orleans has been great to me, and I appreciate it."

"I don't think you should take that guy's shooting you personally, ma'am," the cop who is not Menard says.

I smile. "Maybe not. And just call me Shailene, OK? I get that ma'am and last name stuff all the time in the Army, but I'm really not into all that formality."

"Shailene, I'm Paul, Paul Minicucci," the slightly older, heavier cop with the dark hair says, holding out his hand.

I forget my wound for a moment and automatically lift my right hand to shake. Pain erupts behind my right shoulder blade and I wince and drop the hand.

"Oh, I'm sorry!" he says quickly, dropping the proffered hand and standing awkwardly. "I wasn't thinking."

"I guess I wasn't either," I say, reeling a little from hot, sharp spike of pain. *The pain meds are definitely wearing thin.* The awkwardness is contagious, though, with the two of them standing over me, looking like they want to do something to make me feel better, but afraid to do anything. Careful to not move my body, I hold up my left hand. "Let's try this hand."

He smiles a little and shakes with his left. "Sorry about that."

"Don't worry about it." I turn to the younger-looking cop. He has wavy light brown hair and is skinnier and shorter than Paul. "Remi Menard," he says, taking my left hand in both of his and holding it gently, as if it were some fragile piece of china. My left hand fits into a normal handshake with his left, so I squeeze like I normally would—maybe a little harder—to let him know I'm not some delicate flower. He looks briefly surprised, then smiles and gives me a little squeeze back before letting go.

"So you're in the Army?" Paul asks. "Where are you stationed?"

"Fort Rucker—in Alabama. Have you heard of it?"

He nods. "Yeah, I was in too, for a few years. Spent most of my time at Fort Bliss—there's a misnomer for you. So Rucker is the aviation center, right? Do you fly?"

"Yeah, I fly Hueys—UH-1's. Nothing fancy, but I like flying. The rest of it I'm not so sure about, but flying is fun."

"Yeah I get that. It was a good way to get started, but I didn't want to stay in."

"So have you guys caught the bastard yet or what?" I ask.

They look at each other, then back at me. "Uh, no—"

"I'm kidding," I interrupt, mentally cursing myself for trying to be funny. I'm just no good at that.

Remi speaks up, "But now that you've described him to a sketch artist, everyone will be looking for him."

"Yeah, I don't know. I mean, your artist was great—it's not his fault; I just had a hard time remembering the details of the guy's face. If I saw him again, I'd recognize him, but to get the shape of his nose right, the spacing of his eyes, stuff like that, from memory—it was hard."

"You probably did better than you think, and anyway, it's more than we had before," Paul replies.

"Yeah," Remi adds.

I look at Remi, expecting him to say more from the way he said "yeah," but he just smiles and looks a little embarrassed, which makes me feel embarrassed. I look down at my gauze-wrapped hands.

"Well, look, we really should get going," Paul says. "We just wanted to stop by and check on you. It was nice meeting you, Shailene."

"Same here, guys. Thanks again for the flowers."

"C'mon, Remi."

"Bye Shailene."

"Bye Remi. Be safe, all right?"

"OK," he says, nodding and smiling at me as he sort of side-steps toward the door.

Forty-One

Hoping for distraction from all that's happened and the pain in my shoulder, I tried watching the TV for a while. I don't have a set at home, so I wasn't sure what to expect, but after flipping through the channels and watching pieces of programs for a half hour or so, I use the remote control to turn it off. Apparently I haven't been missing much.

There was one show which was mildly interesting—a drama about government cover-ups of extraterrestrials visiting Earth and shadow organizations being the real power behind the government we think is in charge. I don't doubt there's more to the government than we ordinary citizens get to see, but I've always thought it was giving federal employees way too much credit to believe Washington could actually keep aliens visiting the planet a secret for decades. After all, I'm a federal employee, and work with lots of them, and while we're generally a good bunch of people, we're not uniformly much better at keeping secrets than any other large group of people.

I can see the appeal of a show like that. I think a lot of people would rather believe the universe is a busy place full of intelligent, and even malevolent, life rather than what it actually is: vast stretches of cold emptiness punctuated by harsh, barren, lifeless planets and stars—our home being a rare and possibly unique exception. Most humans don't like to be alone. I also get the conspiracy theory angle: People don't like the idea that bad things just happen, like a crazy person really can kill a president for no good reason. The scary truth is very bad things happen unpredictably and without rationale all the time, and none of us is completely safe. I *really* get that.

I sit in silence, thankful again to have gotten a three-person room to myself. I look at the bunch of flowers sitting on the table next to my bed. Sometimes good things happen unpredictably and without logical reasons too.

My shoulder is throbbing, and I consider turning the TV back on. I could've had more pain meds, but I'm still holding off. If it gets really bad, I'll probably change my mind, but the drugs were making me feel weird—fuzzy and sluggish. I don't like that; I felt vulnerable. I don't trust anything that impairs my mental alertness; if I didn't have to, I wouldn't sleep. For now, at least, the pain is manageable so, except for some ibuprofen, I'll stay drug free.

The doctor called me lucky, which is one way of looking at it, I guess. The way the bullet hit, and the way my body was moving at the time, my shoulder blade deflected the round before it hit anything vital, and the bone didn't even crack. The muscle there is torn up pretty well, but they were able to stitch it back together and, barring any complications, I should be cleared to leave in the morning. Lucky. Of course, if I'd *really* been lucky, I wouldn't have gotten shot in the first place. If I were lucky, I wouldn't be able to find these bastards and wouldn't even be in New Orleans now. But that's a dead end I won't go down.

The sharp drilling in my shoulder doesn't feel so different from the pain I got under my scar when I was near the shooter last night, but it seems to hurt more because I know my body really is damaged. I try something I read once in a book on meditation, and actually focus on the pain. I put myself in the pain and try to really experience it, to savor it. This just makes it worse—so much for that bright idea. I quickly change tactics and try to think about something else. I end up exchanging the physical hurt for mental torment: I think about the couple in the car last night.

Two more dead, thanks to my fuck up. Detective Baudoin was right: I should have called the cops sooner. *But the plan was to get more information on the killer before calling. The plan was to intercept him before he was on the hunt.* I pause, considering that. *I guess no one told the killer about the plan.* If people hadn't died because of this, that might be funny. Instead, there's a yawning, empty, helpless shame inside me. Add two more corpses to the list of people I was supposed to rescue. "I'm sorry," I whisper and instantly regret it. Apologizing doesn't help the dead; it's just me trying to make myself feel better, and failing even at that.

But beating myself up, while it might be justified, doesn't help the dead or the living either. At this point the best I can do is figure out where I went wrong and how to not make the same mistakes again. I messed up by trying not to get my hands dirty and hoping I could somehow get the police to handle the bad guy for me. It never occurred to me that by the time I found the guy, it'd be too late. For all I know, I can only sense these bastards when they're close to doing something bad. Or maybe he doesn't even hang out in New Orleans except when he's hunting. It was irresponsible to leave so many opportunities for failure in my plan. Even if the plan had worked, it was weak from the start; I see that now. Even if I had found the shooter earlier, and gotten all kinds of information about him, what would I have told the police? And assuming they did take me seriously, which is probably a stretch, all he would have to do is act innocent when they came knocking. I realize I was banking on him surrendering and confessing like Berkowitz, the Son of Sam, had when confronted, but there was no reason to expect things to go that way. And I doubt the police could get a search warrant based on an anonymous, baseless tip. Waiting to come up with something clearly incriminating—well, that's what I'd ended up doing, and by then it was too late to get the police involved. At that point, the only person in a position to stop him was...me.

Crap.

But what was I supposed to do against him? In fact, I *had* tried to stop him; that's how I got shot.

The answer is obvious: Carrying a gun would have made all the difference in Florida too, and the dark-haired woman would be alive now—fucked up *(like me)*, but alive.

The idea isn't so far-fetched. As a pilot, my assigned weapon in Korea was a handgun; I'd qualified with a Beretta nine-millimeter at the firing range. I also fired .22 caliber target pistols while I was on the intramural triathlon team at West Point, and was a pretty decent shot. Hell, last night I could have just waited until one of the times when he and I were alone on a street together, and then I could have taken him out right then, before he could threaten anyone.

The image of that in my mind, of shooting the guy without any provocation beyond the weird, impossible sensation in my upper abdomen, is alarming. *Isn't he doing the same thing—shooting people he thinks deserve it, for whatever fucked up reason his mind has concocted? What if I'm crazy? What if this pain is some kind of psychotic hallucination?* But Florida—the pain was so reliable, so predictable in its increase and decrease. And I saw what they did—I held that dying woman in my arms, had her blood all over me. That was no hallucination. *Was it?* I wonder how I would know if it were. But then there was last night—the bullet wound in my back is real, and the police saw the victims in the car. It can't all be in my head. No, the sense is real. I don't understand it, but it *is* real. Still, the idea of coldly gunning someone down just because of the sense...

Hold on—I'm actually sitting here seriously considering killing people—what the hell has happened to me?

Well, I *am* in the Army—killing people, at least indirectly, kind of goes with the job. But that seems pretty academic until there's a war; in fact, it had been literally academic at West Point. We talked about and practiced killing a lot there, but that's a long way from actually doing it. I know that from personal experience. Even *those* times I'd been defending myself; that's different from walking up and assassinating someone.

I see the doors closing, channeling me: Not only am I obligated to use my ability to stop these monsters, but I have to be ready to resort to killing them myself. But even that's not enough, because I can't just murder them when it's convenient and safe for me. No, I have to wait until there's real danger, and only then can I resort to violence myself. *This just keeps getting worse, doesn't it?*

"Fuck it. Just fuck it." I shake my head and want to punch something, but that would be pathetic and stupid, and would aggravate the pain in my shoulder, so instead I just shake my head some more. "Fuck."

The remote has a button on it for controlling the overhead light, and I use it to make the room dark. The door is already closed, and only a little light seeps in under it, combining with light from the city coming in through the window. I find myself gazing emptily at various objects in the dimness, not so much tired as tired of thinking.

Maybe it's some adaptation, an instinctive reaction to what happened. Like my ability to sense predators isn't so crazy, but is actually a prolonged survival response, a heightened sensitivity to danger which triggers a flashback in the form of the pain I felt during the Bad. Looking at it this way, my ability doesn't seem so far-fetched. Another one of those "accidents" that makes sense, that seems too rational and convenient to be an accident, making me wonder if there is some intelligence or order behind the world. It occurs to me that even looking for a rational explanation implies an expectation. Human behavior aside, the world does work in understandable, even predictable, ways. Science and technology bear that out; my own ordinary everyday experience bears that out. And so does my extraordinary sense.

Of course, the one time I really needed the sense, I didn't have it. That's typical of Harold isn't it? Harold can create a whole universe based on consistent, predictable laws like gravity and relativity, but can't protect a girl and her family from a monster. *A monster he created.*

I realize, for the first time in something like ten years, I seem to be buying into the whole God thing. It's hard to avoid the idea, though.   Just sitting here thinking about this is compelling evidence for the universe being more than a random collection of matter and energy. Somehow elements forged in exploding stars light millennia away ended up coming together to make me. Somehow the three pounds or so of glop in my skull are weaving these thoughts. *Talk about crazy. And yet, here I am.*

I guess the theory is that given an infinity of time, almost anything can happen by chance. But this world, and even just my brain, seem a lot to ask of random occurrence. And here's another thing—evolution gave me and my ancestors the ability to adapt to danger by learning to sense its presence, but why did it also give me the impulse to risk my own neck to try to defend others? Where's the survival advantage in that? I guess if I thought about it long enough I could come up with an explanation, but here I go again with expecting explanations, intuiting the order around me.

So...is there a God? Is Harold real after all? I feel the right side of my mouth tighten into a bitter smirk. *Well, if Harold does exist, he's a real bastard. And he apparently has it in for me.*

My smile fades as I think of all the other people he apparently has it in for. Really, I've gotten off pretty easy, if you think about— Thoughts of the couple killed in their car yesterday, the young woman in the van in Florida, and my parents pop into my head in rapid succession, taking me by surprise and setting off a fresh wave of guilt. I shut my eyes tight.

But if Harold *did* create this world, then he created the monsters that killed all those people too. *Harold you fucker, if I have to go after these monsters, then I'm coming for you too—if you do exist, then this is all your fault, and that makes you even worse than these bastards I have to hunt.* I open my eyes and realize I've clasped my hands like I used to when I prayed as a child. I pull my hands apart; I haven't prayed since I pleaded for help and received none, and I'm not going to start now, even if there is a God.

Forty-Two

The two-lane road crosses a bridge over the Choctawhatchee River, which is really more of a stream than a river, and hidden under a dense canopy of trees and vines. This road is familiar territory; except for two weeks ago when I was in New Orleans, I've been taking it at least a couple times a week for the past year, going to grad school at a campus on the northwest edge of Dothan. While Highway 84 is a better route to the mall, this much quieter, narrower road winding through the trees and fields and a couple hamlets is a slightly quicker, more direct route to the Troy State Dothan campus. Plus, it's a more interesting drive than the flatter, straighter, faster road over the mostly unbroken fields to the south.

The road ascends away from the river, and now there are breaks in the woods every so often where there is a house. These houses mostly look at least fifty years old, some in bad need of paint and with rusting metal roofs. Although there is still a lot of farming in this area, these buildings imply there used to be more, since some have the large but modest appearance of old farm houses, and there are also a few barns sagging back to earth, quietly waiting for gravity to finish with them.

Another sweeping curve and the trees give way to open ground on my right as I pass an iron arch with a Pepsi-logo-adorned sign proclaiming "Newton Town Park." The first time I saw this sign I was struck by the contrast. There's a Newton back where I come from in eastern Massachusetts, but that Newton is a small upscale city of something like sixty thousand or so. The Alabama version has at most one tenth that number of people, and a much quieter, more rural personality.

Besides the park, the first thing I see as I follow the curving road around is George's Discount Grocery, which shares its sign with the Coke logo, right above a vending machine for the same. Squatting on the ground beside George's is a semi-portable sign with a letter board like they use on theater marquees so the message can be easily changed. Today it reads:

GEORGE'S GROCERY
UPTOWN NEWTON ALABAMA
GREEN BOILED PEANUTS
WE BUY RATTLESNAKES $1.00 E

George's is the first store in a block containing perhaps ten different establishments, including a general store, a law office with a shingle out over the sidewalk in front, a diner, and, at the opposite end from the grocery, a two-story building with used furniture arrayed on the sidewalk. All have weathered brick or stucco fronts, detailing in the tops of their facades, and the smaller scale typical of buildings that are at least fifty years old. I've seen this look in small New England towns too—streets where all the new construction stopped decades before. I prefer the look of these older buildings, but there's also a sense that the money and energy has gone out of this place.

There are only a couple cars parked along the street, one over by the park and one in front of the diner. Since it's mid-morning on a weekday, I guess that's not so surprising. There are also no pedestrians. I pull over when I don't see any signs for Nell Street and find myself parked in front of the Newton Baptist Church, a newer-looking brick edifice with a more permanent and prominent version of the George's Grocery sign. This one reads:

JESUS CHOSE TO DIE FOR YOU
YOUR CHOICE IS HEAVEN OR HELL.

I go back to looking for a street sign and checking my road map.   There's no sign, but the cross street running between the end of the block of stores and the big red brick warehouse which comes after them seems to be in the right place.   I glance over my shoulder before driving across the street and down what I hope is Nell, passing a faded advertisement for Jefferson Island Salt painted on the brick wall of the used furniture store as I go.

I love these old painted ads, which surprise me with their durability, often outlasting the companies and products they pitch.   When I see these I think about how, for an instant, I'm sharing the same experience as all the other people in other times whose eyes took in essentially the same image.

I follow the road for about a quarter mile, past some more woods, which suddenly give way to a dirt lot on the right.   I pull in; the dirt is packed so hard it feels no different from the pavement as I drive on to it.   The building is set back from the road under the spreading branches of some massive old oak trees hung with Spanish moss.   The building itself is a combination of unpainted concrete and clapboards faded to a dusty slate blue.   There are two large windows, each with a set of heavy bars bolted over it.   The windows look dark to me, but that's probably just because I'm still in bright sunlight. Between the two windows is the front door, which is glass on a dark metal frame.   An outer metal gate is propped open to one side.   The sign over the door reads "Lee's Gun Works." Coming off the left side of the structure there's a windowless wing which I take to be the indoor shooting range the Yellow Pages ad mentioned.   There's only one other vehicle in the lot, parked to the right of the building: a Ford flatbed with Harley-Davidson and NASCAR stickers on the back window and two bumper stickers: "My other car is a Hog," and the ubiquitous yellow and black "MOTORCYCLES ARE EVERYWHERE." I pick a spot a couple car widths down from the door and get out.

Buying the cell phone was no big deal, though I'm not too keen on the monthly payments. Fortunately, I have some financial wiggle room since I don't really do much beyond the essentials with my salary, and I have yet to touch the savings my parents left me. Mainly, though, it's just a cell phone—practically everybody has one these days. A handgun, though...buying one of those is another big step down that road I never wanted to be on in the first place.

I'm also worried about the bureaucracy around purchasing a firearm. Isn't there some kind of background check now? Will anything that's happened to me show up on that? Will any of it matter? I look at a wall of trees across the street, then turn and approach the front door, walking toward an image of me in my small, dark sunglasses, oversized T-shirt, jeans, and canvas sneakers.

An electronic chime announces my entrance. I remove the sunglasses and look around the interior which, with the fluorescent fixtures and the sunlight from the albeit tinted windows, is pretty well-lit. The counter, running most of the length of the room, is a glass case filled with handguns, knives, and, surprisingly, some old-style hand grenades and a couple modern grenades painted light blue—training models. The glass counter is interrupted in the center by a cash register, behind which, on the wall, is displayed a picture calendar from last year, but opened to this month, with a picture of a bikini-clad woman, her bulging breasts barely restrained by her swimsuit top, reclining improbably on a large motorcycle. *What is it with guys and big breasts?* I wonder idly. Above the calendar is a very old-looking long gun. I'm no expert on antique weapons, but I think it's some kind of muzzle-loader, maybe a Civil War-era rifle. On either side of this are several bayonets arranged in order of length with the two longest ones—each maybe two feet long—on top. The rest of the back wall is covered with hunting rifles and shotguns.

I hear footsteps coming from the back room.

"Hey, how you doin' today?"

The smiling speaker fills the doorway leading to the back room. He's about six feet tall and has a black T-shirt stretched over a thick body which is not really muscular but not completely flabby either. His arms are big in the same way, so big that the short sleeves are stretched smooth. He's wearing a Pennzoil baseball cap, with lots of curly brown hair practically exploding out from around the bottom of it.

"Hey," I say, "good morning."

"It is that," he says, still smiling but now looking past me out the window and stroking the long, slightly straggly chin whiskers which put a point on what is otherwise a very round, kind of pink face. "Ah love this tahm of year, air starts coolin' down, actually pleasant to go for a walk outsahd."

His voice is soft, almost gentle—not what I expected, but kind of a relief. "I'd think you'd be used to the heat by now; I mean, you're from here, aren't you?"

He looks back at me and his smile broadens. "Tell bah the way I talk, hunh? Yeah, well that's fair 'nough since Ah kin tell bah the way you talk you aren't. Where're you from?"

When I came down to Alabama for flight school three years ago, it was the first time I'd been in the South, and I felt some concern, wondering how people here would react to me. Nothing bad ever happened, and Miranda, a life-long resident, and I had, obviously, hit it off pretty well. But sometimes I still feel like the outsider. "Massachusetts."

"Really? I was up that way about fahv years ago, 'bout this tahm of year, too. Beautiful—love them autumn leaves ya'll got up there."

I smile a little. "Yeah, me too. So were you there on vacation?"

"Yeah, sorta. A couple cousins of mahn live in New Hampshire."

I feel my eyebrows go up. "Yeah?"

"Yep. Was kahnda a family reunion. They're good people up there, though Ah don't know how they stand all that snow. Guess the fall makes up for it. That and bike week at Laconia."

"Oh yeah, that's right."

"See—you know what Ah'm talkin' about. You rahd?"

It takes me just a second. "Uh, no, sorry."

He shrugs. "Figure it doesn't hurt to ask. So what brings you here today, ma'am?"

"You can call me Shailene."

He smiles and puts his hand out. "Nahce to meet you. Ah'm Lee. So, Shailene, what are you lookin' for today?"

"A—" I almost say "gun," but stop myself as my eyes again skim over the collection in the glass case and on the wall in front of me. "A handgun. Semi-automatic, nine-millimeter, I think."

He looks thoughtful and strokes the little beard again. "Um-hm. Have you purchased a gun before?"

"Um…no."

"OK, well, if you're interested, Ah can probably he'p you pick out something to your lahking." He shifts his eyes to meet mine, his eyebrows raised questioningly.

I nod, grateful. "Actually, that'd be great."

"So it sounds lahk you've already given it some thought—what makes you say 'nahn millimeter'?"

"Well, I qualified with a Beretta in the Army."

His eyebrows go up. "Really? You in the Army?"

I nod again. "Why does that surprise you?" I ask, not offended, but curious about how other people see me.

"Ah dunno," he says, shrugging, looking a little nervous. "Ah mean, you just don't look lahk the Army tahp to me—small, kahnd of—well, what do you do?"

"I fly helicopters."

"No kidding? That's way cool. All raht, well, OK, so you qualifahd with a Beretta nahn-mil—that'd be the M-9, which to us civilian folks is the 92FS. An excellent—and very popular—handgun. Trigger reach maht be a little long, though, for you, and trigger pull can be heavy, especially for that first double-action pull. Did you fahnd it uncomfortable or awkward to shoot?"

I'm not following all the gun lingo, but I think back, trying to remember the day at the range in Korea, the only time I actually got to fire the weapon. "Um, I don't remember it being a problem, but to be honest I didn't fire many rounds with it."

"Um-hm, Ah think you might fahnd it tahring after a wahl, but Beretta makes a variant of that model Ah think would be better suited to you." Lee walks down the length of the display case. "They actually rolled it out just recently, mainly for law enforcement and special military applications, but Ah think it maht be good for you." He squats down and opens the back of the case. "Here we go! And Ah'll bring you a standard FS too, so you can see the difference." He walks back over to me with the two weapons and lays them side by side on a plastic pad advertising ammunition. "See, the Vertec has a thinner, straighter grip and a shorter trigger reach than the regular model. It's also a couple ounces lahter, which doesn't hurt. And it has this rail you can use to mount a laht or a laser saht, if you're interested in that."

"Is there much benefit to that?"

"What? A laser saht?"

I nod.

"Well, depends. Ah don't use 'em much mahself, but mostly Ah target shoot, and laser sahts aren't really sporting.

They're desahned for real world use. Are you bahying this for self-defense?"

I nod, glad that he brought it up since I wasn't sure if or how I ought to work it in to the conversation. The way he says it so matter-of-factly, I feel less weird about this.

"For self-defense a laser maht make sense. They're definitely better under low-laht conditions since you don't have to worry about seeing the ahrn sahts on the barrel. Also makes it easier to keep your ahs on the bad gah."

"Would the laser add a lot of bulk?"

"Used to be they would, but now they have ways to build them in to the body of the weapon.

"Now usually when women come in looking for a self-defense weapon, Ah recommend a small revolver, like the Smith & Wesson Model 642, also known as the Chief's Special." As he speaks, he walks a few steps down the counter and bends to reach into the display case again, coming out with a small, shiny handgun, which he carries back and lays on another plastic pad beside the two Berettas. "Go ahead and pick it up, see how it fits into your hand."

Ordinarily I'd be a little irritated by someone making assumptions of physical weakness based on my gender, but I feel really ignorant about this stuff and am glad to get the advice. Plus, I'm already liking Lee—he seems like a good guy. I pick the revolver up and look it over. It does feel good in my hand, but—

"See, the hammer is enclosed, so it won't snag on anything."

"Um, yeah, that's good, but—how many rounds does this hold, anyway? Six?"

"Fahv. But really, how many would you need?"

I automatically think of the van in the field in Florida—how many shots did I fire there? Five? Six maybe? I remember wanting to put another bullet into his skull, to be absolutely certain he was dead, but having no rounds left.

"Well, probably, but better to have more rounds than I need than not enough, right? The Beretta holds more than that, right?"

He nods. "It takes up to a twelve-round magazine, and you can have one more chambered too. The thing about pistols, as opposed to revolvers, is they're more complicated to operate and disassemble, but Ah guess you're more comfortable with maintaining and operating fahrarms than your typical civilian. Let's trah them out in the range. Lee takes the guns off the counter and puts them underneath, then sidesteps a couple times to his right. "We'll need nahn mil for the Vertec," he puts a box of rounds on the counter, "and these for the Chief's Special. Ah know you said you weren't interested, but just humor me and trah it out, for comparison." He walks over to the cash register, flips up a section of counter top with no cabinet underneath it and comes through. He locks the front door and grasps a plastic sign hanging from the door handle. The sign has a clock face with the words 'Gone Shooting—Back By:' printed above it. He glances at the clock on the wall behind the counter, then looks at me. "fifteen minutes sound all raht to you to do some shootin'?"

"Sure, that sounds great." It occurs to me that maybe I should be nervous, being locked in, alone with this big guy and all his weaponry, but one good thing about the sense is I can spot the really dangerous ones. *Right?*

He smiles and looks down at the plastic clock face and moves the hands to show fifteen minutes from now, then flips it around so it hangs facing out of the glass door. "OK," he says, turning and picking up the boxes of ammunition, "let's go next door."

He steps past me and pushes open the door marked RANGE. He pauses in the doorway to flip a light switch, and the inky darkness is immediately displaced by lots of cold white light. Lee lets out a satisfied sigh. "Ah love coming in here. It was a lot to add the range onto the building, but it's one of the best things Ah've ever done."

The air is a little stale, but comfortably cool and dry. The room is about forty feet long and thirty feet wide, with, near our end, a wooden counter divided by thick vertical timbers into five sections. The walls are all painted white. Looking to my right down the length of the hall, I see a couple paper targets, each roughly the size and shape of a human torso and head and riddled with holes. The clamps holding the targets are attached to loops of bicycle chain running the length of the room. Behind the targets, the far wall has five large, rough circles of chipped gray concrete, standing out in contrast to the whiteness around them.

"Ah make a lot of money just off the range fees folks pay when they come here and shoot. And, a couple tahms a year, Ah have competitions here—great publicity for the store, and Ah sell a lot of ammo and a few weapons to folks bahying on impulse." Lee walks over to the second section of counter, sets the boxes of ammunition down, and hits a button mounted on the column to his left. A motor above our heads begins humming and the target comes toward us while he reaches into a bin below the counter and pulls out a fresh target. When the used target reaches him he hits the button again and the motor shuts off. He exchanges the targets, tossing the used one into a trash can by his feet, then activates the motor again, which this time runs in the opposite direction, taking the target back down the lane. He stops its movement over a red line on the floor labeled 5 YARDS. Then he turns and, unclipping the large ring of keys from his belt, he unlocks a heavy wooden cabinet behind him and opens its door to reveal several small shelves, each with a handgun on it. "So let's see: FS and Vertec," he takes them off the shelves and holds them out to me. "Just put these on the counter over there."

I do this while he squats down. "Chief's Special is…here." He carries this last over to the counter.

"We'll start with your pick—the 92FS." He sets the weapon, a box of ammunition, and an empty magazine in front of me. "If it's all raht by you, Ah think you should load each weapon yourself, so you get a feel for all of it."

I nod. "Sure, good idea." I've loaded a lot of magazines, so it's familiar to me. But when I pull the slide back in preparation for inserting the magazine, the two-week-old bullet wound in back of my right shoulder erupts with pain. The surprise and intensity of it makes me wince and wobble a little, and I put my hands and the weapon on the counter in front of me.

"You all raht?" Lee asks anxiously.

I blink a couple times and nod. "Yeah, I, uh, I got hurt a couple weeks ago, and it's still kind of tender. It's been feeling a lot better lately, but I guess that movement was a bad idea." I pick up the gun with my right hand and brace it on the counter before working the slide with my left. There's another little twinge from the injury, but nothing like before. "I'll be fine—just have to do some stuff left-handed for a while." I load the magazine, hit the slide release button to chamber the first round, flip the safety off, then put the pistol back in my right hand and carefully raise my arms to fire. This hurts some, but it's not too bad, so I just ignore it and start firing. The target is only fifteen feet away, but I'm still pleased when I place nearly all the rounds I fire in the center of the target silhouette.

Lee changes the targets for me, and I continue to do all the loading and operating of each gun. After I fire the 92FS, I try its modified cousin, the Vertec, and find Lee is right about the fit. While I can fire the 92FS, the Vertec's smaller handle and closer trigger feel better in my hand, like I have more control of the handgun. The revolver is even easier to fire, though I'm not significantly more accurate with it. And why carry five rounds in the weapon when I can carry thirteen? "I'm gonna go with the Vertec," I say after finishing up.

Back in the store, I mention the other item I came in for. "So I'll also need a holster…" I say as he flips the "gone shooting" sign back around and unlocks the front door.

He looks at me as he walks back through the counter to his side. "Do you want me to explain to you about concealed-carry permitting? Or are you just going to use the holster at home and at ranges?"

I already knew, from movies I guess, that there was some kind of additional licensing required to carry around concealed firearms, but I want to draw as little scrutiny as possible from the government. It's bad enough there'll probably be some kind of background check telling them I'm buying the gun without also telling them I plan to have it with me in case I need to kill someone. If I do use the gun, it's probably going to be in some incident I don't want associated with me. *Like Florida last spring.* "Um, I'm just interested in the holsters right now."

He nods. "OK, what kahnd are you thinkin' about? Shoulder? Hip?"

"Over in Korea I carried my sidearm in a harness that went across the back of my shoulders, with the holster tucked under my left arm."

"Sure, OK, a shoulder rig. Nylon or leather?"

"Um, nylon, definitely," I say, trying to avoid dead animal-derived products as much as possible.

He nods and ducks through the doorway to the back room.

While I'm waiting, I pick up the Vertec from the counter and heft it. It feels heavier than it did a few minutes ago in the range room, or over a year ago in Korea. *My weapon.* It's surreal, in a bad, nightmarish, "is this what it's come to?" way.

Lee emerges from the back room, and I put the gun back down on the pad on the counter.

"Now let's see," he says, fiddling with the straps on the harness. "Ah've got it as small as it'll go—the thing is, not many women buy handguns this sahz, so the rigs that fit a Vertec are a little big, but Ah've got this one cinched down pretty good...here ya go."

I take the equipment from him and quickly start to put it on, first my left arm, then an explosion of pain as I move my right arm the wrong way. I wince before I can stop myself.

"Here, Ah'm sorry—mebbe Ah kin help..."

He steps toward me and reaches out, and instinctively I back away, regretting it as I do, but still not wanting to be touched.

He freezes then drops his hand and steps back again. "Ah'm sorry, Ah just—"

"It's OK," I say, waving my left hand dismissively and shaking my head. "I just—don't like to be touched."

"Ah just saw—you're in pain—"

"Yeah, it's OK—you'd think I'd remember by now—it's been two weeks. It's a lot better now than it was, and I think because it feels better most of the time, I'm not being as careful with it."

"What happened?"

"I'd rather not talk about it," I say as I try to take the rig off my left shoulder and finding now even that hurts. "Look, uh, maybe you *can* help. Uh, would you just take this off so I can figure out how to put it on?" I take a step toward him.

Gingerly, he lifts the harness off my left shoulder and I pull my arm out of it. "Mebbe if we lay it out on the counter, you can sort of back into it," Lee suggests, spreading the webbing out on a section of glass-topped display case.

I look at it, thinking.

"Put both hands into it behind you, then get it over your right shoulder first."

The right side first makes sense, and I mentally kick myself for not thinking of it to begin with, since that's how I've been getting into my clothes. I do as he suggests, then take the Vertec from the counter and put it in the holster. The bottom of the holster, containing the muzzle of the gun, is actually resting against the crest of my hip bone, and I feel like I did as a little kid when I'd step into my mom's shoes. I look up at Lee, whose lips are pressed together like he wants to say something, but is restraining himself.

"Feels kinda big. I guess the Beretta I had in Korea must have sat the same way on me, but this feels kinda big now."

"Well, yeah," he says nodding soberly, "it *looks* kahnda big on you. Not that it matters unless," he tilts his head to one side and raises his eyebrows, "hahpothetically speaking, you wanted it to be inconspicuous."

"Well, crap. Maybe I should go with Chief's Special like you said."

"There's lots of different models—plenty of smaller ones. Let me think…Sig 232…Walther PPK…" Suddenly his eyes light up. "Wait—hold on a second. Ah didn't think of this because it's really new, but Glock just came out with a really cool little gun—Ah mean," he added hastily, "it's a real handgun, a nahn mil, and it holds thirteen rounds, but it's a lot more compact than the Berettas you've looked at." He ducks down behind the counter, and I hear him open and close one door, then another. "Here it is—Ah think this is the gun for you, Miss Shailene: the Glock 26."

I look at the gun. It's black and compact—even smaller than the revolver. "That holds thirteen rounds?"

"Yep," he says, holding it out to me grip side first.

I take the gun from him. After the Vertec, this one feels light.

"Let's try it out," he says, coming up with another box of ammunition and going over to the door sign again.

Inside the range, while I'm loading the magazine, Lee explains some of the unique aspects of the pistol. "One thing about Glocks, is they don't have no safety. It's funny, because Glock will tell you their guns have *three* safeties—a mechanism to prevent accidental discharge if the gun is dropped, and a couple other things, but they all amount to saying the gun will only fahr if you pull the trigger. Hmmm, who'd a thoughta that? So Ah guess the trigger guard is the only real safety. Obviously you already understand this, but with Glocks it's doubly important you don't put your finger inside the trigger guard until your fixin' to shoot. Some folks don't lahk that, but then again, a lot of cops are carrying Glocks now because they don't have to fuck—sorry—mess around with a safety—it's always ready to shoot. And as if that weren't enough, the trigger travel is pretty short and the pull is laht."

All this is sounding really good to me, and I wonder why he didn't mention this weapon before. "So what's the bad part?"

He smiles and hands me the weapon. "Well, maybe there isn't one, Calamity Jane. Trah it out."

I insert the magazine and press the slide release to chamber the first round. Aiming down range, I squeeze off the first shot, and it surprises me. "You're right—this trigger is really easy." I squeeze off the other nine rounds in rapid succession, and manage to hit well in the black target silhouette with all of them. I lower my arms and look over at Lee, who has a huge smile. I smile back.

"Ah believe we've found your weapon, Miss Shailene."

Forty-Three

Having that weapon isn't much comfort back in New Orleans two weeks later when I spot the killer across a street from me, walking along the iron fence bordering a small park, not far from the place where I'm staying in the Marigny neighborhood. I wouldn't have noticed him if the pain hadn't first told me he was nearby. In the six weeks since I last saw him he's grown a full beard and a moustache, and changed the way he combs his hair. I immediately think of the sketch I talked a police artist through, which ended up running on the front page of *The Times-Picayune*. I'd felt bad, thinking I wasn't able to describe the son of a bitch well enough to create a decent likeness. I worried I was misleading people more than informing them, but apparently the killer had been impressed with his portrait. Full beard or not, now that I'm looking across the deserted street at him walking through the pools of light cast by the street lamps, I can tell he's the same one I followed before. Seeing his build, height, and the way he moves, he is clearly the guy I saw draw his weapon on two people in a parked car, the one who killed those people, and tried to kill me.

Alone on the quiet residential street with him, I suddenly feel exposed and vulnerable. I duck into the covered entrance area of an apartment building and pretend to push a button on the call box by the door. I keep my back to the street, but my ears strain backward, listening for the shot. I wonder if he noticed me, and think about the Glock in its holster under my left arm, concealed by an oversized button-down work shirt made of thick cotton fabric. Then I think about the potential consequences of a shootout. Like getting shot. Or getting arrested for shooting him. I glance back over my shoulder and see him continuing on his way, now receding from me.

Instead of drawing the gun, I pull out Plan A—the cell phone. I already saved a few relevant numbers as speed dials, including Detective Baudoin's office and mobile numbers, and the general number for the New Orleans PD. But with the killer right here, I use the phone's tiny keys to dial 911 and put the phone to my ear, waiting for the ring.

I follow the awning from the building entrance almost to the curb and look down the street, but the bad guy is gone. *Shit.* I begin walking quickly in the direction he'd been headed. As I near the corner, I wonder why there's still no sound of ringing from the phone. I take the small device from my ear and slow my walking so I can examine the lighted display. I can see the 911 digits are still there, but nothing seems to be happening. Then, briefly rolling my eyes, I remember: *You gotta push the send button, dummy!* This is my first cell phone, and I've only made a couple calls with it since I got it, so I guess it's an understandable mistake, but I'm not long on patience right now. I use my thumb nail to mash the send button, then put the phone back to my ear and look around anxiously.

I realize I stopped walking while I was looking at the phone's display, and now I notice I'm standing on the corner of Frenchmen and Royal. I look down Frenchmen and see him heading away from me and toward a great little restaurant I ate at a couple times called The Praline Connection, which is now closed and dark.

"911 operator, what is the nature of your emergency?" a woman asks in a near monotone.

"Hi, the, uh, the guy that's been shooting people, he's walking down Frenchmen Street."

"Has anyone been hurt?" the calm voice on the other end asks.

"Not yet, but they will be if he finds them."

"How do you know—"

"Look, this is Shailene Campbell, and I know who it is because he already shot me once. Ask Detective Baudoin—he interviewed me afterwards. I'm the one who described him to the police sketch artist, so trust me, all right?" As I'm speaking, I think I see him glance back at me, but it's hard to tell because he's in shadow when he maybe does it. I realize I've been speaking loudly, and lower my voice. "Look, the guy that's been shooting people is walking—" I hesitate a second, getting my bearings. "I guess he's walking south, toward the river, on Frenchmen. Will you please send some police over here to check him out? Question him or something? He's wearing dark pants and a dark windbreaker. He has a beard and moustache now, and combs his hair straight back instead of parting it, but it's the guy." I see him turn down a side street and I start walking quickly again to catch up.

"You say he's walking south on Frenchmen?"

"Well, he *was*, but now he's just turned down a side street I don't know the name of—Chartres, I think, and he's headed for the Quarter now. Just send someone over here, and I'll call back when I find him again, OK?" I take the phone from my ear, stop to find the hang up button, and press it. I pocket the phone and start walking fast again. I think about taking the Glock out, but decide it wouldn't be a good idea to be running around with a drawn weapon, especially if the cops are on their way. *They are on their way, right?* Plus, now if I do shoot him, they're gonna know *I* did it, since I just told them my name and that I'm following him. *Shit.*

Forty-Four

Is that...? James wonders, feeling alarmed, for a moment finding himself in the strange and unhappy position of thinking like the others and doubting his sanity. The paper said the woman he shot, the bitch queen who'd been following him around that night, was from out of town. *Well, she could have revisited*, he tells himself. He watches her turn into the doorway of an apartment building and it looks like she presses one of the buttons by the intercom mounted next to the front door. He glares and stares at the back of her as he passes by. There's a light on over the door, and he sees clearly the short blonde hair, the small frame. He can't be sure, seeing her from across the street and having not gotten a good look at her face before she turned away from him, but this person could in all possibility be her. At least the brief glimpse of her face *seemed* to correspond with his memory of her.

If she did return, then she's back for me. It does seem a pretty bizarre and improbable coincidence, assuming this is the same woman, that he would encounter her again, in a different neighborhood, more than a month and a half later, at night, on a residential street otherwise devoid of people. *Of course she's back for me. She's the queen of all the cunts, returned for revenge.*

He sees one good way of determining if it is her. He continues walking and takes a left on Frenchmen. That other night nearly two months ago, she'd followed him tenaciously, unrelentingly. He wasn't sure how much time had transpired all together, but it was at least half an hour after he'd noticed her, and he remembered passing her, or someone strongly resembling her, some time preceding that. Then, when he'd thought he'd exhausted her, she appeared again at exactly the worst time, surprising him just as he was drawing down on the bitch in the car. He hated that, being affronted by her in person. *Obviously she has no idea with whom she's dealing, no inkling of the magnitude of my wrath.* It occurs to him that possibly she enjoyed being pierced by him, and wants to be penetrated again by his steel. *Isn't that what all her kind want? A good reaming?*

But the thought of shooting her face to face makes him feel queasy. He imagines shooting her from behind and likes that better. He shot her in the back before. He feels the memory move in his groin. As imperiled as he'd been that night, it had also been a sensation like no previous experience. During the time after that incident when he'd been staying covert and inert, but after he'd been growing the beard for a couple weeks, he returned to the corner of Fulton and Girod and reenacted it in his mind: the bitch in the car adjacent to her john, and the bitch on the street—two at once. When he relived and re-imagined it, both vaginas were cut down dead, but now he's confronted with the truth that the bitch queen escaped.

It occurs to him to turn around and go back to the apartment building she'd pressed the door button on, theorizing he'd be able to spot her through a window and reach her with his fire from the street below—reach out and puncture her through, completely without warning, make her experience his pain, drill her through... His stomach clenches with the excitement, and he stops and turns, looking back down Frenchmen.

The cunt is on the corner *talking on a cell phone. Talking about me, no doubt, calling out the police.* Then the plan comes to him and he smiles, turns quickly away, and resumes walking, making a right at the next corner, on to Chartres Street.

Forty-Five

I turn down Chartres and follow it to a fork. Chartres doglegs here, and another residential street branches off to the right. *Which way?* As I cross the intersection, I slow and look down the sidewalks and street to the right, but see no one. I turn my head left, and see a lone figure walking just on the other side of a divided avenue. Guessing that's him, I continue down Chartres to the street with a median of trees and grass separating the two directions: "Esplanade Avenue" I see from the sign. Glancing left and right, I cross. The itching of my scar has been basically constant, but as I reach the other side of Esplanade the itching intensifies into a painful scratch. *Closer.* This block is pretty well-lit by a combination of gas and electric lamps, the light reflecting off the parked cars along the opposite side of the street, but otherwise revealing the street to be empty. I follow a series of brick walls down, mostly passing under balconies, while the pain mounts steadily. I slow my pace. Halfway down the block my scar is on fire, and before I reach the corner the pain has gone deeper and harder, the sharp cramps twisting inside me, burrowing in the direction of my heart.

I stop just before I reach the cross street, the pain stabbing away at near maximum intensity just below my heart. I figure he's got to be only a few feet away now, but where? I put my back against the brick wall and look around anxiously, fighting the urge to run away from him and the pain, back the way I just came. Across the street I see a couple old but well-maintained creole-style cottages with ornate detailing along the eaves of their roofs, their doors and tall windows covered by wooden shutters. There's no parking on my side of the street, but two cars and an SUV are parked in front of the cottages. I study the vehicles, suddenly feeling like a target pinned to a wall, but I don't see him. The pain tells me he's close—very close.

Are you sure? You don't even understand what this sense is, and you're going to bet your life on it? You don't know how close he is.

He's got to be within a few feet of me—got to be. It hurts now almost as bad as it did when I was sitting at the table with the couple in Florida. He has to be around the corner—the corner *right next to me.*

Oh shit, no! I think with horror at the dawning realization. *He's found a target—where the fuck are the cops?* I put my hand inside the heavy shirt, silently draw the Glock, and hold it at shoulder level, muzzle pointed up, the damp pad of my index finger resting lightly against the trigger. I'm really glad there's no safety to fuck with. I slide the remaining two feet up to the corner of the building at my back, then rotate my body and turn my head to peek around the edge.

Forty-Six

Penis pressing against the inside of his pants, he waits in a recessed doorway a few feet from the corner of Chartres and Barracks. He mentally plays out how he will rape the Bitch Queen to death with his seed: She'll pass him, continuing down Chartres in her pursuit. His gun is already out, and when she passes by he'll bring the gun up, aim into the center of her back and *drill drill drill* her. His stomach tightens and he feels lightheaded for a second. His seeds will open her up, penetrate her body, and claim her for him.

What if she doesn't continue down Chartres? James doesn't understand how, but that night when he shot her he'd been unable to evade her for perhaps an hour. Somehow, even after he did lose her for several minutes, she discovered his location again. So what if she, instead of continuing down Chartres, turns down this street instead? He presses his back harder into the iron bars covering the window on the recessed door, and looks to his right, considering moving away from the corner to the next alcove down, but sees no advantage in that, especially if she stays on Chartres like she's supposed to. *I'll just have to gun her right here if she comes for me.* Up close. He shuts his eyes tightly. *I can do it. I can fuck her right here.*

Forty-Seven

As I look down the cross street I remember the killer standing next to the parked car and pulling out his weapon. There is a line of parked cars along the nearer curb now, but I don't see anyone by them. I tilt my head a little further out so I can see more of the street: still no one in sight. My gun arm is pretty much trapped between the building and me, but I don't switch it to my left hand, which has never fired a gun. Something in my peripheral vision causes me to tip my head a few more inches out beyond the edge of the building so I can shift my gaze closer in, to the wall, which is broken up by a series of four tall, slightly recessed arched doorways. The doors are white, but my eyes flick to a dark shape in front of the nearest one and I see him just a few feet away. He is standing with his back pressed against the white door and his eyes are closed.

The eyes pop open, and there's a stunned moment when we just stare at each other. He looks startled and makes a small noise of surprise, and then his gun arm is coming up toward my face. I pull my head back a moment before the gun fires and, like a sprinter out of the blocks, I run diagonally across and back down Chartres toward the only cover available—the line of parked cars across the street. The street only has room for one traffic lane, but the thirty feet or so I have to cover is a really long way considering I only have about ten feet and a couple seconds head start on a maniac with a gun. As my feet leave the sidewalk, I stretch my gun arm back and, glancing over my shoulder, fire in his direction.

Forty-Eight

Did I hit her? James thinks not, but there's a glimmer of hope. He hesitates just a second, the gunshot still ringing in his ears, then steps off the threshold he's been standing on and strides to the corner. Even if he missed, she'll soon be his. He'll run her down like a cheetah taking a gazelle. He'll drill her through and watch her blood run out onto the pavement. Fairly vibrating with power and excitement, he reaches the corner and sees her running across the street. He stops, raises his weapon to fire, and sees her, still running, look back and raise something in her hand to him. There's a flash and a loud crack.

Shit! James falls back behind the shelter of the building and presses his back to the brick wall. His heart is pounding in his ears, and after a couple seconds he realizes he is holding his breath and exhales. *Shit, the fucking bitch.* He takes a couple deep breaths, his mind racing in place. Still pressed against the wall he turns his head and looks toward the edge of the building, and a bead of sweat rolls down his cheek. *Shit, fuck, shit.* He swallows, then, keeping his eyes on the edge, he shakes his head. *This, no, this shit cannot stand. Who the fuck does she think she is? Fucking little cunt. This shit cannot stand; I'm taking her down. I'm finishing this* right now. Another drip of sweat rolls down his cheek; he swallows, then pushes off from the wall and peers out at the street and the line of parked cars he saw her running toward. He studies the scene, looking for where she might have gone. The only hiding places are behind the cars. She was headed away from the cross street, so she has to be back up Chartres somewhere—has to be concealed by the cars.

He hears a woman's voice speaking anxiously from across the street. He can't make out the words, but remembers the cell phone the bitch used earlier. He shifts his gaze, trying to pinpoint where in the line of cars she's hiding, but can't be sure. He looks at the nearest car, the first car in the line, a reddish convertible. *I'll start there, go down the line.* The female voice keeps chattering away. *Got to shut her up.* Now that he knows she's armed, he's ready for her. The gun just surprised him before, that's all. He's not afraid; she's just a cunt. And he's going to shut her up for good *right now*.

He raises his weapon in his right hand and pushes off the edge of the building with his left, sprinting for the first car in the line and firing repeatedly at the gap between that car and the next one, where she had been headed before, and where he thinks he heard her voice. A tail light shatters, a car alarm begins blaring. Four or five shots, and he's behind the first car, license plate JAG ONE.

Forty-Nine

"Yes, he shot at me!" I try to convey the urgency while still keeping my voice down, hoping, if he is still around, he won't be able to hear me.

"OK, where are you now?" The calmness of the voice sounds patronizing, and it's making me crazy, but I have to make sure he understands, so I tell him again.

"I'm on Chartres—Charter," I try an Anglicized pronunciation to try to make clear the spelling. For all I know, that's how they say it here. "Charter Street, in the French Quarter, between Esplanade and whatever street is next. Inside the Quar—oh shit!"

I see him come out from behind the building at a run, gun raised. I pull my head in from the back bumper I'd been peering around. BLAM-BLAM-BLAM. Rounds slam into the car I'm hiding behind and a car alarm starts up right next to me. The noise is deafening. "Shit!" Phone still clutched in my left hand, I push off from the metal flank of the car and run crouchingly up the sidewalk toward Esplanade. The next vehicle is a big hulking SUV, which for once I'm glad to see, and after that there's a break in the line of cars for a driveway. Taking the opportunity, I get in front of the SUV and pause a second, gun up and ready, trying to figure out where he went, which way I should go. Over the car alarm I manage to hear running footsteps approaching up the sidewalk side, so I bolt into the street.

There are three more cars in the next group, and as I pull even with the back window on the first one there's another gunshot and a *thwack* sound from the glass next to me. I crouch lower and, hugging the flanks of the vehicles, try to move my legs faster. I make the middle of the second car and glance back past my right shoulder in time to see him emerging into the street. I throw my right arm back and, holding the weapon sideways, I fire. He jumps back behind the cars, I make the front of the third car and duck behind it.

I squat by the front fender of the lead parked car and try to quiet my breathing enough to hear what he's doing. Feet slap the pavement, running up the street side of the line of cars. I spin and launch myself toward the corner of the last building on this side of the street—about twenty feet away. *Where the fuck are the cops?!* I fire once more to cover my retreat, but without really looking long enough to see where he is, and then I'm at the corner of the building and past it, sprinting down Esplanade, then ducking between a flatbed truck and a little compact car.

Tires squeal behind me. There's a blast from a siren and an amplified voice: "Freeze—police! Drop the weapon and put your hands up!" *Finally!* I stop between the truck and the car and cautiously peek back down the sidewalk. I don't see the shooter, but the police cruiser is turning and heading up Chartres, siren wailing.

I stand up, my chest heaving for air, sweat running down my face, and consider simply walking back to my room. The police are on it now, they'll catch him, put him in jail, mission accomplished. My work is done here. *Right?* I would kind of like to see them take the bastard down, though, just to be sure. I step out from between the car and the truck and, still breathing hard, begin walking down the sidewalk back to the corner on wobbly legs. I realize I'm still holding the cell phone in one hand and the Glock in the other. I holster the gun and look at the cell phone. It's still on, connected to the emergency dispatcher. I press the End button and put the phone in my pocket.

As I approach the corner, the pain below my heart is ramping up fast. I stop, a couple feet from the edge of the building, and despite the siren and car alarm in the background, I notice the sound of running feet hitting the pavement is getting louder. *Shit!* The pain tells me he's almost even with me. I crouch low and put up my left elbow, angling for what I hope is the level of his gut while bracing my left fist in my right hand. I launch myself forward and to the left, around the edge of the building. My elbow connects with his ribs instead of his stomach, but I still trip both of us up, and we hit the concrete side by side. The gun goes off again, but the round goes zipping across Esplanade. I manage to jump on him, and see the weapon still in his hand, outstretched in front of him on the sidewalk. I launch myself toward it just as his gun arm starts to curl up and back toward me. My hands are on his wrist and I slam his hand back to the ground. I slam it into the concrete again, dimly aware of the pain in the knuckles of my right hand as they meet the pavement.

"Drop it! Drop the weapon!" a male voice behind and above us shouts.

The shoes and legs of a cop appear in my field of vision. The killer drops the gun and I stop pounding his fist into the ground. The cop kicks the gun out of reach. Before I can start to get up, I feel hands grip my shoulders. Instinctively, I try to break free and scramble away, but the grip tightens.

"Easy! Take it easy!"

I hear the words and know they're from a police officer, but even more I feel hands on me and keep struggling.

"Just let her stand up," the cop in front of me says.

The hands release me and I get away from the killer and on my feet. I put my hands in the air on either side of my head and turn to face the officers. One of them, the one who had been pulling me off, takes a step toward me, then stops.

"Hey—Shailene?"

"What?" the other cop, who is still pointing his gun at the prone killer, looks up at me and asks, "You came back?"

We're right next to a street lamp, so there's enough light to see it's Remi and Paul. I nod. "Hey guys," I gasp still fighting for air.

"I'm surprised you came back," Remi says, studying my face as if he can't quite believe what he's seeing.

"Officer Menard," Paul says.

"Hunh? Oh!" Remi turns from me and pulls a pair of handcuffs from his belt. He kneels and cuffs the guy on the ground.

"I didn't think the description I gave your sketch artist was good enough to catch him."

"How's your shoulder?" Remi asks, standing up and turning toward me again.

"Hey! Can I get up now?"

We all look down at the killer, who is straining to keep his face off the sidewalk while on his belly with his hands shackled behind his back.

"No," Paul and Remi say together.

Remi looks back at me. "So, your shoulder?"

"Better—a lot better," I say. "Although it's starting to ache now. Would it be all right—" I motion with my raised hands.

Paul waves at me a couple times. "Oh! Sorry, yeah, put 'em down."

"Hey, she's armed too!" the prisoner yells from the ground.

Remi and Paul look at him, then at me. "That true?" Paul asks.

Oh shit. There's no point in hesitating; I just nod.

Remi and Paul look at each other. "Cover him," Paul says, then looks at me. "Step over to the car."

Oh shit. I walk over to the police cruiser, Paul a couple steps behind me. When I'm close he tells me to stop and turn around. I do as I'm told.

He stands a couple feet in front of me and asks in a low voice, "Are you carrying a gun?"

I nod.

"I don't suppose you're licensed to carry in Louisiana?"

I shake my head.

"OK, where is it?"

I undo the single button holding closed the oversized shirt I'm wearing as a sort of jacket, and hold it open to reveal the Glock.

"Don't be nervous: I'm just taking the gun, all right?"

I nod and swallow.

Paul reaches in and takes the Glock out of its holster. "Any other weapons?"

"Pepper spray in my pocket."

"Better give me that too."

I take the small canister out of my hip pocket and hand it to him.

"That it?"

"Yeah."

"OK, take off the harness." Another cruiser comes down Esplanade, its roof lights flashing, and stops at the end of the street. Paul looks over at them, then back at me. "Come around the other side, then hurry up and give me the harness."

We both move to put the vehicle between us and the other cops, who are now out of their car and walking over to Remi and the prisoner. I take the big shirt off, then manage to get out of the harness and hand it to Paul.

"OK, that's everything, right? No other weapons?"

"That's it."

Paul opens the front passenger side door and throws my stuff in. "When you give your statement, don't say anything about this gun, or about what we just did, clear?" He fixes my eyes with his.

"Absolutely," I say, nodding.

He looks at me a few more seconds, then says, "You're gonna have to go over to the station and give a statement. We'd take you ourselves, but we gotta take this guy in, and probably you don't want to ride over with him."

"OK," I say, nodding and thinking about the $800 in weapons and accessories I just lost. We walk back to where the other cops are.

"Actually," Remi is saying to the other officers, "*she* got him—tackled the son of a bitch."

Fifty

The door to the small, bare room opens, and I look up from the top of the steel table to see Detective Baudoin coming in. Despite it being about two in the morning, he is freshly shaven and looks neat and professional. The dark ovals under his eyes tell me he's tired, but there's a brightness in his eyes that I interpret as excitement over having the so-called Grandson of Sam in custody.

"We meet again, Ms. Campbell," he says as he pulls out the metal chair across from me and sits down. I can't tell if he's making a joke or if that's the way he normally speaks. He lays on the table copies of the statement I gave Remi about an hour ago after we arrived here at the French Quarter police station. Baudoin then takes out a gold pen and twists the barrel to prepare it for use. Suddenly he becomes very still and looks up at me, catching and holding my eyes with his. "You really have it in for this guy, don't you?"

I'm not sure what he wants me to say; he's smiling, but his eyes look intense and questioning now. Not sure what else to do, and feeling a little paranoid, I shrug, but continue to hold his gaze. "I thought I could help, so I thought I *should* help. That's all." I shrug again.

He has me tell my story again, occasionally interrupting with questions about details, like street names and times. I tell him most of it, but I leave out the part about my sense, saying only that when I first saw him there was something familiar about him, and I was able to recognize him despite the changes in his appearance. I also leave out having a gun and shooting back.

"So level with me—how'd you find him?"

I look across the table at him, meeting his gray eyes. He looks genuinely interested, and I think this might be my chance. If he's truly curious, maybe he'll be open to the truth; maybe he'll believe me. If he does, then I can really work *with* the police, and I *will* be able to avoid confronting the violence directly. I look down, doubting my ability to convince him, then look up again. "This might sound a little—" I stop short of the word crazy, then continue, "*strange*, but I can tell when I'm near people like this guy. I, uh," I hesitate, not wanting to talk about what happened to me, about the Bad. "I was hurt…by someone like him when I was a kid. Now, when I'm near people like that, I feel the same pain I felt when I was hurt." I look at Baudoin's eyes again, trying to connect, but I see his eyes have narrowed, and I realize I'm losing him. "Look, the closer I am to him, the more of this pain I feel. Even now, with him somewhere else in this building, I can sense his presence—there's this scratchiness…" I meet the detective's eyes again, and now there's irritation mixed in with the skepticism and disbelief. "Well you asked how I found him. That's how."

"You, uh, you can *sense* his presence. It makes you itchy."

Even I think it sounds bizarre when *I* say it. When *he* says it I feel like a complete lunatic. But at this point I have to persist. "Yes. I mean, I have to be kind of close—maybe within a block, or a little less—I don't know, something like a hundred yards or so. It starts as an itch, but as I get closer it becomes pain—more and more painful."

"You feel pain."

"Yes," I respond simply, deciding further elaboration won't help my case. There's a patronizing tone in his voice now, and I want to shout something like "I'm not crazy!" but I also realize the more I proclaim my sanity, the more insane I'll sound. "All right, Detective, you tell me—how did I find this guy? Twice. As a newcomer to *your* city, when you and the rest of your police force couldn't. You tell me. I might also point out he looks quite a bit different now than when I first saw him, with the beard and the different hairstyle. I wouldn't have recognized him if I hadn't sensed him first."

"I don't know." He looks down, sighs, and makes a wide-eyed, raised eyebrows face at the table that says *whatever—it's late, so let's just get through this*. When he looks back up at me and resumes speaking his facial expression and tone of voice are back to neutral, dispassionate, no-nonsense cop. "Fortunately, I don't think you're going to have to testify. He's already signed a confession and said he intends to plead guilty. I think he realizes he doesn't stand a chance now, what with a witness, and with his gun being tied to all the rounds in those cars and bodies by ballistic signature. I think he figures he might as well embrace his celebrity and make the most of it. I guess there's a chance you'd be called to testify during sentencing, but I doubt it. Everybody knows what he did, so I don't think you'll have to appear in court. But if you do, Ms. Campbell," he locks eyes with me, "if you *do* have to testify, do us all a favor and keep this bit about you sensing his presence to yourself, all right? No judge or jury's going to buy that. Let's just say you had a gut feeling about him the first time, because he was behaving suspiciously, and you managed to recognize him this time, and we'll leave it at that. You and I both want this guy put away where he can't hurt anyone anymore, so don't do anything to jeopardize that."

"Fine," I say. I knew it probably wouldn't fly, but it's still hard being told I have no credibility.

And I'm still on my own with the sense and the responsibility it entails.

Fifty-One

After Baudoin finishes questioning me, he says, "Ms. Campbell, as you might have noticed, I'm not a real personable guy when I'm at work, but I want you to know the department and the City of New Orleans appreciate your help. If you'd like, we have a couple officers available to give you a ride back to your hotel. It'll help you evade the press contingent that's gathered out front waiting for you."

My first impulse is to say no thanks—at this point I really just want to be alone as soon as I can, get back to the guest house and get some sleep. But the little place I'm staying in is several blocks away, back in the Marigny neighborhood, and the prospect of having to run a media gauntlet like I did when I checked out of the hospital a month and a half ago is pretty daunting. "Actually, that'd be great," I say. "Thanks."

I step out into the corridor and find Remi and Paul sitting on a wooden bench drinking coffees in green and white paper cups from the Café du Monde. Remi notices me and elbows Paul, and they both stand up.

"Hey Shailene, we're ready to take you home," Paul says.

"Want some coffee? Beignets?" Remi asks, holding up a paper bag. "The coffee's almost warm."

"The coffee will keep me awake, and I really need to sleep, but a beignet sounds good." Remi holds the bag open and I reach in and take out one of the deep-fried rectangular pastries covered in powdered sugar. As I do, I notice how well the sugar shows up against the dark blue of Remi's uniform. "Uh, Remi," I say quietly as I step back with my beignet, and gesture with my free hand at the front of my shirt while looking at his.

He looks confused for a moment, then looks down at his shirt. "Oh sshh—crap," he says in surprise and starts brushing at the white specs.

"Sorry—just didn't think you'd want to be reinforcing any negative cop stereotypes."

Paul smiles.   "He hasn't quite mastered the technique yet," he says, sticking his chest out and gesturing at his own uniform.   "Needs a few more years of practice."   He starts walking down the corridor and we follow, Remi still brushing at his shirt.

The beignet is soft, sweet, and delicious. It'd be even better with some of that strong New Orleans coffee, but, even as tired as I am, I'm afraid it'd keep me from sleeping. I finish the pastry; mostly it makes me realize how hungry I am. "Hey, Remi?"

"You can have the rest, Shailene—Paul and I already had three each."   He hands me the paper bag, and I take out another treat.

We go down a flight of stairs to the side, police-only entrance of the building. "Wait here, Shailene," Paul says. "We had to park down the street; we'll pull the car around so the press don't notice you walking by."

They leave and I wait by the door, chewing the last beignet and gazing blankly out the window. A local TV news van drives by, then a police cruiser. A couple minutes later another cruiser pulls up and an officer gets out, pushes through the iron fence, and approaches the door. When I see it's Remi, I push through.

"Hey," he says and smiles before turning and heading back to the car. He holds the back door open for me.

"Thank you sir," I say as I give a little bow before getting in. Maybe it's the sudden influx of sugar into my exhausted system, but I'm suddenly feeling a little giddy.

Remi smiles and gives a little bow back, then closes the door and gets in the front.

"You'll want to scrunch down, just in case we pass any reporters on Conti Street. We don't want anyone following you back to where you're staying," Paul says, looking over his shoulder at me.

I shift to the middle of the seat and slide down until my knees touch the back of the front bench seat, the Café du Monde bag cradled in my lap. As we drive away the scratchiness across my scar fades out, and I feel safe, calm, and pain-free for the first time in hours. Safer and happier, actually, than I've felt in weeks, since that day in the library when I first read about the shootings in New Orleans.

"Hey Shailene." The voice is calm but insistent. I open my eyes and see the clear barrier separating the back seat from the front, but no one is in the front seat. I look to my right and see Remi looking in at me through the open door. "We're here, Shailene—the place you're staying at."

"Sorry guys, guess I dozed off." I feel embarrassed. I slide across the back seat and get out of the police car.

"You definitely earned the right," Paul says. He holds out a brown paper grocery bag to me. "This is your stuff."

I take the bag; the weight and feel confirm that the Glock, and presumably the holster and pepper spray, are inside. "Thanks."

"Don't mention it. Seriously." He holds my eyes for a second, serious.

I nod.

"So, Shailene," Remi begins a little uncertainly. "I'm having a cookout Sunday afternoon at my place over in Metairie—we'll be boiling up some crawfish and shrimp. Paul's coming and we thought you might like to get some real home cooking before you leave. My grandmere's going to be making something too."

It sounds appealing and intimidating at the same time. These guys seem kind and friendly, and it'd probably be good for me to have some normal, non-work-related human interaction. But there would be all those new people to meet and talk to. Anyway, the question is moot. "Thanks guys—that's really sweet of you to invite me, but I have to drive home tomorrow—I have to be at work Monday morning."

Remi looks disappointed, then brightens again. "How 'bout later today—maybe I could—um—take you out to dinner?"

This surprises me, and I wonder if this is what it sounds like it is—if he's asking me out on a date. At some level I know I should feel complimented, but my gut reaction is the opposite of that. I wonder if I did something to make myself seem attractive, if somehow I flirted with him at some point. I start to play back every interaction with him I can remember, but stop myself. "Uh, actually, I think I might go home later today—I just really want to sleep in my own bed, be at *home*, you know?" I see the mixture of hurt and disappointment on his face, but all I can manage is "thanks anyway." He seems like a good guy...under different circumstances, in a different life, maybe...

"Well, we should get going," Paul interjects. "We've got to finish out our shift, and you clearly are due for some rest. It's been nice meeting you, Shailene." He puts out his hand and I shake it.

"Yeah, absolutely," Remi says, smiling again, though not as brightly as before. I shake hands with him too, and they turn to go back to their car.

I turn and start to walk down the short path from the sidewalk to the iron spiral staircase that leads up to the garret room I've been staying in.

"Hey, Shailene."

I turn and see Remi jogging toward me. When he gets near he slows to a walk and hands me his business card.

"If you ever come back to New Orleans, give me a call, all right? Give me a couple days advance notice and I'll put together another cookout."

I take the card and smile a little. "Thanks, Remi. I'll do that."

He starts walking backward, and puts his hand up in a quick wave. "OK, drive safe now, when you go back to Alabama, I mean." Still walking backward, he trips over where the path meets the sidewalk, but recovers before falling.

"OK, you too!" I say, smiling more now. A little voice inside says maybe I should take him up on his offer of dinner, but then I turn and continue up to my room. Less than a minute after locking the door, I'm partially undressed and completely unconscious in the bed.

Fifty-Two

Later that day, Saturday, I roll out of bed feeling better than I have in weeks, so much lighter now that my work here is done. I have lunch at my sanctuary, the courtyard of the Royal Blend coffee house, then head back to my room, pack my bags, and check out. Because of the late notice, I obviously still have to pay for Saturday night. I consider staying, but I really do want to get home, so I put Stacey on I-10, headed east.

It's an overcast day, although the cloud cover is thin enough to permit watered-down amber-tinted sunlight that has a surreal quality to it. It's just bright enough to make me squint a little, so I put my sunglasses on. I push in the tape I made of the Radiators CD's I bought after my last trip to New Orleans.

Maybe it's one of the the songs I hear, but I find myself thinking of Remi, standing there on the walk next to the house last night—early this morning, really. I see again the mix of emotions on his face as he handed me his business card, and then him doing a Buster Keaton as he backed away from me. He seemed like a nice guy, I guess. I try to figure out if I think he's good-looking, but I'm not sure how to tell. Thinking about this makes me feel uneasy and a little dirty. My mind flashes to me posing for those pictures back in high school with my teammates on the field hockey team—the pictures where we "vamped it up" and tried to look sexy, the pictures that got my parents killed, the pictures that got me—

OK, so...going home. I swallow hard and ignore the wave of nausea that's swept over me. I think of my apartment waiting for me, and mentally see the picture of The Tower taped to the cupboard in the kitchenette. I remember the smell of autumn in the northeast—that certain crispness in the air that foreshadows winter, but is still comfortable and invigorating, and filled with the dry, happy smells of fallen leaves, smoke from the first wood fires of the season, and apple cider.

While I'm going home to Alabama now, I think about going home to New England. Of course, given my present employment, the Army tells me where home is, but I've been hearing through the alumni grapevine that a lot of my West Point classmates have already left the military. These days, with the Soviet Union and the Gulf War fading into the past, there's a push to reduce the Army's population, especially the number of officers since we cost more. Coming out of West Point, my classmates and I owed the government five years of service, but now Uncle Sam is more interested in saving money by cutting the payroll. So why not me?

I joined the Army because I wanted to be strong and learn how to protect myself. I think I accomplished that, and I'd do the same if I had to live that part of my life over again. But I don't fit in well with the Army culture—the emphasis on socializing for one thing, the conservative politics for another. If the Army is looking for people to leave, maybe I should be one of them.

And then there's this sense—that's another reason to get out. After my tour of duty at Fort Rucker ends, I'll probably be sent overseas again—maybe to that mess in what used to be Yugoslavia. It's hard enough tracking down bad guys in this country, where I speak the language and know how things work. It'd be really difficult to hunt serial murderers in a foreign country. Seems to me my primary responsibility now is to use my sense to protect people.

Damn, is this for real? Is this ability to find bad guys— sociopathic killers or whatever—is this going to dictate my life from now on? I sit quietly, driving automatically down the mostly straight freeway, trying the idea on. Even if it won't be my whole life, it's definitely part of my life from now on. There's no escaping that.

And I have to plan on dealing with the bad guys myself. When I counted on the police to do the heavy lifting, people ended up dead because I wasn't ready to do what had to be done. Even when I got the cops to listen to me, I still ended up taking the fucker down myself—*literally* taking him down. "Oh shit," I sigh. But better—and safer—to recognize the reality of my situation and prepare for it.

I think about the Glock handgun resting a few inches below my butt, under the driver's seat. I've killed three...*humans* I think, not sure what word would be appropriate for them—*monsters* maybe...but the three times I killed, I was fighting for my life. Sure, in Florida I went chasing after them, but when the killing happened, it was them or me, and they were clearly doing bad things to people. That's different from me coldly stalking and executing someone only because he triggers the sense in me, isn't it?

What would Harold say? I think wryly. For years, since the Bad, I've been convinced there is no God and, lacking moral laws handed down from divine authority, I've had to figure out my own ethical answers. But since that evening in the hospital six weeks ago, I haven't been so sure. *An atheist's crisis of faith: maybe God* does *exist.* I feel the corners of my mouth tip down. *Well,* if *he exists, he has a lot to answer for.*

I look out the side window at the mass of trees, occasionally interrupted by breaks for farms or other human settlements.

But there's a lot of order for the universe to be completely arbitrary; a lot of universe to account for—where it came from, what it's purpose is, if it has a purpose.

None of this helps me with my present situation. I think again of the Glock under my seat, and the scar near my heart.

Acknowledgements

This book is a work of fiction. It should be understood that, except for the occasional passing reference to a public figure, the names in this book are made up and the characters are fictional and not intended to represent anyone real, living or dead. One exception to this is The New Orleans Radiators, who have been a very real and very talented band since 1978. Tipitina's is also real, and it is The Rads' home club. There is a Tipitina's in New Orleans' French Quarter on South Peters Street, but The Radiators play at Tipitina's larger uptown venue; I put them in the Quarter for the sake of the story. I want to personally thank The Radiators for all the great music I've enjoyed over the years since 1988, when I first heard them on Armed Forces Radio in, of all places, Athens, Greece. Thanks to them also for permission to use the lyrics from "Untouched by Human Hands", lyrics and music by Ed Volker, Fish Head Music (BMI), copyright 2001.

There are factual inaccuracies in this novel, some of them deliberate, and undoubtedly some unintentional ones as well. All are my responsibility. I already mentioned the bit about The Rads playing on South Peters Street, and about the particular song she hears, which wasn't copyrighted until six years later. Another place where I bent history is with Shailene's weapon, the Glock 26, which actually wasn't available for sale to the public until 1996. I feel it is the perfect weapon for her, and I only had to fudge the timeline by several months, so I went with it. Likewise with the laser sight.

I'd like to thank Henri Chouinard and the American Firearms School for hands-on experience with Glock handguns, Chuck Hawks and his website gunsandshootingonline.com for advice on personal firearms, and Travis Noteboom of Crimson Trace Corporation for information about laser sights.

For valuable insight into the technical details of police work and the lives of police officers, thanks to the Cumberland, Rhode Island, Police Department for their Citizens Police Academy, and especially to Officer Paul Gagnon, who worked late one Sunday morning after completing his night shift to spend time with me.

I first came up with the idea for Shailene while I was listening to an audio edition of Dean Koontz' novel *Intensity*. That story, with its compelling characters and almost unbearable suspense, was a mental catalyst for me, and a lot of fun to listen to. Thanks to Mr. Koontz, and also to actress Kate Burton, who did such a great job bringing the characters to life.

Finally, a special thanks to Lisa for giving me the aforementioned audio book, for help in shaping the structure of this story, and for the countless other things she does to make my life happier than it's ever been.

About The Author

Like Shailene, Max Salt is a graduate of the U.S. Military Academy and a former helicopter pilot. Now employed as a computer geek and living in Rhode Island, he is hard at work on preparing two more novels about Shailene's adventures for publication. You can learn more at www.maxsalt.com.